Angels Three Five

Don Candy

DON CANDY

Angels Three Five

Second Edition

This novel is a work of fiction. Names, characters, places and incidents are either the product of the author's imagination or are used fictitiously. Any resemblance to actual events or locales or persons, living or dead is entirely coincidental.

No part of this material may be reproduced in any form without express written permission from the author and/or publisher.

No representation is expressed or implied, with regard to accuracy of the information contained in this work of fiction and no legal responsibility can be accepted for omissions and/or errors.

Copyright © 2014 by Donald W Candy

All Rights Reserved.

ISBN: 978-0996440905

ANGELS THREE FIVE

This work is dedicated to my grandchildren; Austin and Ashleigh Candy, and Payton and Kaylie Furtick.

Acknowledgements

There are some people I'd like to thank for their support in this effort: First, my wife Karan for her encouragement. Captain John Tuthill, a Marine F-4 pilot in Vietnam; Bob McLendon, a TI Supervisor and friend; Norm Lofgren, Captain, USN Retired; Former Marine Captain and retired FBI agent, Don Ramsey; Lieutenant Colonel Walt Capps, retired Army pilot; Jim Vineyard, retired Air Force Colonel; Lieutenant Guy Hackman, Aerial Artillery Forward Observer in Vietnam and Stuart Brown of *Skipper Press* for the use of one of his beautiful paintings for the cover.

Angels Three Five

Prologue

Twenty miles southeast of Hanoi, Vietnam
Tuesday, July, 8, 1967

"Hawk's Nest, this is Redtail one, feet dry at 0317, strangling the parrot."

"Roger that Redtail, happy huntin' brother."

Lieutenant Commander Bo Jameson, leader of Redtail Flight, a two plane mission over Vietnam, winked at his Bombardier-Navigator (BN), Commander Joe Garcia as he peeked out from behind his hood in front of the right seat of their Grumman A6B Intruder aircraft. Barely perceiving the wink in the dim red illumination of the cockpit, Garcia gave Jameson a 'thumbs-up', meaning that all his complex systems designed to hunt and kill soviet built SA-2 Surface to Air Missile (SAM) installations were working properly. Redtail flight was now over land (feet dry) southeast of Hanoi with all lights and identifying electronics off. Strangling the parrot meant turning off the transponder used to transmit ("squawk") the aircraft's identity, location and altitude. They were now just a shadow in the night sky headed for a SAM site northwest of Hanoi via the northern route.

Bo Jameson stood six foot two, about 190 pounds, muscular, closely cropped sandy hair, and sky blue eyes with a perpetual look of determination. He was an accomplished pilot who left his civilian aviation career to fight in Vietnam simply because he loved his country. Joe Garcia, on the other hand, was about five foot eight, also weighed around 190 pounds without an ounce of fat. He had dark eyes, a wry grin and a fireplug build. When he (seldom) got angry even a Sumo Wrestler would back away. Unknown to Bo, and almost everyone else actually, Joe was an accomplished, though undecorated, Navy SEAL – he belonged to a unit that didn't exist.

Depending on the purpose of the mission these "Iron Hand" or "Wild Weasel" missions, as they were called respectively by the Navy and Air Force at that time, were typically a prelude to a bombing run by two or more Navy A6As (each carrying up to five 500 lb bombs) or Air Force F105 Thunderchief fighter/bombers, headed for a high value target protected by SA-2 SAMs. Or, the mission could be just a hunt and kill mission to eliminate SA-2 sites that were deemed strategic to the enemy. This flight was of the latter type – there would be no other friendlies in the area tonight - just Jameson and his wingman, Andy Jones. Tonight the cuffs were off, meaning that the normal political rules of engagement that disallowed the U.S. from destroying the enemy's SAM sites (due to potential collateral damage) unless done as part of a larger operation, were ignored.

The A6 Intruder was a sub-sonic attack aircraft whose purpose was to destroy enemy targets on the ground. It wasn't a fighter, it carried no defensive weapons and had no afterburner. Its primary weapons were intended to destroy SAM sites or other strategic enemy installations. The Shrike AGM-45 Anti-Radiation Missile was the weapon of choice for SAM site hunting during this period. And it worked pretty well – most of the time.

The basic attack strategy was a team effort. Two A6Bs would approach the site. One approaching the known or suspected location of the SA-2 site at medium altitude, daring the SAM site to "lock him up" (turn on the SA-2 guidance radar and lock onto the A6B), the other executing a low altitude approach. When the ground based guidance radar started sending signals to the SA-2 and the A6B launch warning sounded the lower Intruder would dive to the deck making a hard S turn to approach from a different direction while flying very low altitude "nap-of-the-earth" with his radar altimeter driven navigation system. The final approach to the target would be below the site's radar capability, allowing the lower Intruder to pop up and lob-launch a Shrike at an upward angle of between 15 and 35 degrees depending on the range to target while the other A6B remained aloft as 'bait'. The risk in this game of aerial chicken was, of course, the enemy's anti-aircraft guns protecting the site for the low aircraft and the possibility of being blown out of the sky by one or more of the SAMs for the high aircraft.

The night was not ideal - but not the worst case for a hunt and kill mission either. A thick layer of clouds blanketed the area from a base around a thousand feet above ground level to tops at ten to fourteen thousand feet. They were in the soup shortly after flying north to a point east of Hanoi where they turned northwest. Everything was done on instruments, but then the A6B had one of the most sophisticated sets of instruments of any vehicle on earth.

Joe Garcia growled, "About time to start evasive action. We've got three searchers (search radars) lookin' at us," over the intercom. The North Vietnam Army (NVA) ground-based radar-guided Anti Aircraft Artillery (AAA) wasn't very good at tracking and hitting anything that was unpredictable in its path of flight at higher altitudes so if a pilot at mid to high altitude made random course changes and varied his altitude randomly at the same time they didn't even bother shooting. There was an area, however, between about 1,500 feet up to around 5,000 feet where it worked pretty well in spite of evasive action on the part of the Intruder.

They stayed well north of Hanoi on a route that would eventually hook back to the west of Hanoi and bring them within range of their target; a brand spankin' new SAM site guarding one of the supply depots feeding supplies to the Ho Chi Minh Trail.

"Dropping tanks," Jameson announced on the intercom.

"Hey man," yelled Garcia, "I don't like what I'm seeing here. I've got a searcher in a valley one ridge over, northwest of our target, definitely undocumented. He just lit us up and he's close enough to screw with us big time. Better hit the deck before… DAMMIT! We're locked! – I've got a launch indication waiting for guidance."

The SA-2 (Soviet designation: S-75) was a two stage missile. The first stage was solid fuel and unguided. It burns for approximately six seconds. The NVA recently learned to hold the guidance radar (called 'Fan Song') in standby until the second stage lit off, giving them a six to eight second advantage on the Shrikes.

"I've got guidance, come to two niner zero, punch aft chaff, break hard to port (left) and down - on my mark . . . NOW!," Garcia said in his stern command voice.

Chaff is made up of small metal particles designed to explode into a cloud of metal that resembles an aircraft to a radar system. The guidance radar for the SA-2, the Fan Song, is located on the ground and sends guidance signals to the in-flight missile. Fortunately, this builds a small delay into the control loop for the missile which usually works to the advantage of the prey, in this case Jameson and Garcia.

As he almost simultaneously fired the chaff canister, hit full throttle and pulled a six g diving turn to 290 degrees, Bo Jameson realized that Garcia had turned him directly toward the SA-2. This was risky in the clouds. They were at 15,000 feet – about the altitude that the SA-2 reaches its maximum velocity of mach 3.5. At that closure speed Bo would have very little time to avoid a direct hit. Just as the A6B g meter hit 6.1 g's the cloud lit up like a roman candle. The missile plume, clearly visible through the water vapor appeared like a ring of fire, meaning the missile was headed straight for them. Gradually, in what seemed like several seconds but was actually less than a second, the ring was broken and was taking on the shape of a missile plume seen from the side as it passed not 30 yards off the starboard (right) wing. The Soviets had never gotten the SA-2 proximity igniters (designed to detonate the missile warhead when it got close to the target) to work very well due to the high velocity of the missile – another break for the A6B crew because the missile exploded in the chaff cloud about a hundred yards above the plane. Unfortunately the SA-2 warhead was a fragmentary design, much like a giant hand grenade, and the plane took several hits. One big hit at the starboard wing root – just outside Joe Garcia's side of the cockpit.

"Redtail two, this is one. We got a non-lethal hit from that SAM. What's your situation?" called Bo, checking on his wing man, Andy Jones.

Andy replied, "we dove to starboard (right), we're on the deck below the searcher. If you can draw another SAM from above the clouds, we can pop up a couple of Shrikes, take out his guidance radar before he gets you, and then go in for the kill. There doesn't appear to be any AAA – strange; maybe a technical problem or it's not operational yet? It's got to be a new site since we don't have it in our data base yet. Anyway if you're ok with this and it works, we'll go in VFR (Visual Flight Rules – below the clouds), locate the bastards, blow out both radars and then take out the site with two of our 500 pounders. The ceiling's up to about two thousand down here – looks like the weather's getting better!"

"Two, this is one, we got surprised by this site – he wasn't supposed to be there and we weren't ready. I was going to let you stay high and we'd do the dirty work down below but since you're already set up, let's do it! When I report breaking out on top you start a twenty mile run toward the ridge. When we hear the Fan Song and guidance alerts I'll let you know and you can let 'em have it," Bo said as he looked over at Joe to get his input – a thumbs up. They had used this 'split strategy' on their last four or five missions and it had worked well. Usually the roles are reversed, wingman high and leader low. On this mission when Andy heard Bo taking evasive action he headed straight for the ground to take on the ambush role.

That's one thing Jameson liked about having Andy Jones as his wingman – more often than not Andy correctly assessed a situation like this one and took the appropriate action before Bo even gave the command. Jones was the best wingman he'd ever known.

"Joe, we've got a little problem here; it appears we've got a leak in the starboard wing tank. I'm initiating fuel transfer to port. Looks like we lost close to a thousand pounds," Bo groaned through the intercom, "we'll have to go light on the throttle or we'll go bingo before we get the real mission done. I'll tell our Buddy to rendezvous at point Charlie and hold 'til we get there." 'Bingo' means just enough fuel to return to base with minimum reserve. In this case the base was the USS *Ranger*, sitting about ten miles off the Vietnam coast just southeast of Hanoi. 'Buddy' is the KA6-D tanker version of the A6 family capable of re-fueling another A6 with up to ten thousand pounds of fuel.

As they rose out of the overcast at 13,500 feet and Bo reported "we're clear" to Andy, the whole world took on a new perspective. Visual reference brings on a feeling of mild elation after flying on instruments for forty five minutes. The elation didn't last long. The Fan Song radar lit up and locked on to them as they passed through 15,000 feet.

"Two, we've got lock, waiting for launch. Commence your run," called Jameson. For some reason the gooks didn't launch right away. But after about five seconds the launch indicator started its little routine designed to awaken any sleeping pilot with a message of death - unless he got his shit together.

"Two, we've got launch – go get the fuckers."

"Roger, One, we're lobbing one on guide and one on search." This action would disable both of the SA-2 operational radars, leaving the site disabled for a few days, typically.

Five seconds later Bo saw the SA-2 break through the clouds and harmlessly veer away crossing their path at a point approximately where they had been five seconds prior.

"Good shootin' Two, we lost both search and guide radars at exactly the same time."

"We can see the base on fire – I think we took out at least one SAM on the ground. We're gonna finish them off with two of our 500 pounders. Two out." The destruction caused by the bombs would likely disable the site for a couple of weeks to a month.

"When you're done," said Bo, "form up with us at the mission target's IP (Initial Position) at angels fifteen. Confirm."

"Roger One, fifteen thousand at primary IP. We'll be about a minute or so behind you. Two out."

On this run to the original mission SAM site Andy and his BN would play the high altitude target role, so as they left the IP they headed away from the site and climbed to twenty thousand feet to become the target.

The good news for Redtail Flight was that at two thousand feet Redtail One would have visual contact with the ground. The weather was improving. Bo would fly on a vector ninety degrees away from the IP before turning back toward the target when Andy got the Fan Song signal. The flight path had been carefully planned to give them the best avoidance of AAA which was their biggest problem simply because of the shear volume of it. The AAA started about twenty miles out and increased, with a few really close calls, until Andy got locked up at twenty thousand feet and they began their turn back to the target, still on the deck.

Then Andy reported: "We've got launch," and a few seconds later, "and guidance."

"Hey Bo, take it easy on that wing," Garcia yelled as Bo was pulling up to lob the Shrikes. "I'm not sure how much damage that SAM flack did – could be some of it's structural."

At twelve miles out they lobbed their Shrikes, four in all. Two on search and two on guide. Then it happened. When they popped up and the radar guided AAA guns re-acquired them, things got crazy. Bo's A6B took several thirty seven mm (millimeter) rounds – a couple in the starboard wing, close to the leading edge. A third explosive round, probably a fifty three mm, caught the starboard wing just in front of the previous damage. The explosion shook the aircraft so violently that Bo's helmet hit the instrument panel causing him to momentarily black out. As he got his senses back he heard Joe yelling:

"EJECT! EJECT! EJECT! We lost the wing!" Before the hit Jameson had started his nose-over at about five thousand feet after launching the Shrikes - this probably saved their lives. The wing failure occurred at almost zero g, so they had a split second to eject before the falling plane started its violent spin (which airplanes are prone to do when they lose a wing) from which ejection can be very dangerous, if not impossible.

After a successful ejection when he broke into the clear under the clouds Bo looked around but couldn't find Joe. He could see a glow off to the southeast, hopefully a SAM site on fire after having its radars destroyed. As he drifted down the glow disappeared behind the ridge they had popped up over and all he could see was the remaining flames of their plane. The five hundred pound bombs had not yet been armed for the bombing run back to the site so the wreckage was just burning beneath the jungle canopy below him about a half mile away. Everything else was black. He couldn't see a thing and had no idea where the bottom was or what was down there waiting for him. He wanted to yell out for Joe but knew he couldn't. He needed all the stealth he could muster to keep the NVA at bay. "My God!" he remembered, "we're northwest of Hanoi." As he finished that thought he saw something below – could it be the ground? Not to be; he was descending into a large tree. Suddenly he felt a searing pain in his right forearm. A limb his lower body had broken off sliced through his right arm which was holding on to the chute's shrouds. The jagged edge of the break in the limb tore through his flight suit and ripped open his arm from an inch above his elbow to two inches below his wrist. He continued downward, slowing as his ripping parachute tangled itself in the upper branches. Then he stopped – but where? He couldn't see a damned thing, even after raising the visor on his helmet. He had a knife in a flight suit pocket below his right knee, but if he cut himself loose, how far would he fall? No, he would have to hang there until twilight at dawn to figure out what to do and then do it quickly.

He heard a jet engine approaching from the north. That would be

Andy headed for the SAM site to finish it off since they couldn't. He heard the explosions and saw the flash over the ridge, then nothing.

He felt his arm, which was now growing numb, to try to assess the damage and found he was bleeding pretty badly. He was going to have to apply a tourniquet or he might bleed out before dawn. He retrieved his knife with his left hand and discovered he couldn't hold his right arm up without using his left. When he lowered his injured arm it throbbed with pain and the bleeding increased significantly. He found the small emergency medical kit in the side pocket of his flight suit, retrieved the rubber tube tourniquet, and with great difficulty got it tied around his injured arm just above the elbow using his good arm and his teeth. But he needed to tighten it more than he could with only one hand. He inserted a ball point pen between the tubing and his arm and twisted it. With his knife he poked a hole in the remaining material of the arm of his flight suit into which he inserted end of the pen after he had what he thought was the right amount of pressure on the tourniquet. After a few minutes of holding his injured arm up to reduce the pain and bleeding he tied a small loop of cord around the nylon strap that connected to the shrouds and forced three fingers into the loop to keep his arm elevated. He had a radio but his survival training told him not to use it until he was sure he was in the clear – which he knew he was not. There were probably Viet Cong or NVA crawling around right below him.

He thought more about the tourniquet – he didn't want to lose his arm but he didn't want to bleed to death either.

Then he passed out . . .

Chapter One

Thirty miles southwest of Manhattan, Kansas
Tuesday, July, 5, 1976

The big old radial engine up front fell silent as the plane rolled over on its back and headed straight for the ground. I had no idea what was happening and I was scared shitless. I tried to pray but my mind was paralyzed and the ground kept getting closer. I was going to die on this beautiful Tuesday morning. Then, just as I closed my eyes certain that we were going to bore a hole into the rapidly approaching corn field below, I felt pushed down into my seat like I must have weighed five hundred pounds. "He's going to try to pull out of this dive – but it's too late – he's gonna pull the friggin wings off," I thought to myself. Then we leveled off about a foot above the four foot tall corn stalks and all was well. As I regained my senses, I looked back and saw a flat cloud of insecticide dust settling slowly into the corn and the wings were still attached to the plane. "Thank you Lord – you saved my sorry ass again" I said as my adrenalin rush began to subside.

I'd flown many times with Bo, but never on a crop dusting job in his old Stearman. If my mom knew where I was right now she'd be waiting for us at the hangar with dad's old double barreled twelve gauge shotgun; and she'd be gunning for her brother Bo, not me.

We sprayed three sixty acre fields that day, refilling and refueling back at Uncle Bo's airstrip after each job. When we were finished we checked our stories to be sure my mother wouldn't be suspicious.

My dad, Scott McKensie, died during a night Wild Weasel mission in Vietnam nine years ago. He was flying an Air Force F-105G Thunderchief (fondly known as the "Thud" by its pilots, because of the noise it made when landing). My mom hates airplanes; her husband died in one and she had convinced herself that her brother would also meet his demise in one. I, of course, was totally absorbed in aviation. At fifteen I had already logged the forty legal hours allowed as a student pilot and another one hundred and fourteen un-loggable hours flying with Bo, most of which my mother was unaware of. In two months I would turn sixteen and take my private pilot's check ride. Then, two years later on my eighteenth birthday and out of high school I would go for my commercial ticket followed by instrument, multi-engine and instructor ratings. Uncle Bo had pretty much assured me of a position on his staff of pilots. I would be the fifth and most junior pilot working for him.

Bo's real name is Humphrey Bogart Jameson. If he knew that I knew that, I think my life would be in danger. He had it legally changed to Bo H. Jameson just before he joined the Navy. Bo had a couple of years at Kansas State in aeronautical engineering before being accepted to the Navy OCS to become a pilot. He was an accomplished pilot at twenty having flown over eight hundred hours crop dusting and another six hundred hours flying charters, instructing and towing banners (aerial advertising) with a little fun flying mixed in. My mother's name was Lauren Bacall Jameson until she married dad and it changed to McKensie. My grandparents were a little weird with the name thing, but they were really just kind and generous plains people enamored with Hollywood. Mom liked Lauren a hell of a lot more than Bo liked Humphrey, but only a few people know her middle name. My name is Sam; Samuel A. McKensie.

My parents both graduated from K-State; Dad was in the Air Force ROTC program and wanted to be a pilot. The FBO (airport management company known at every small airport as the Fixed Base Operator) at the local airport was certified to give K-State ROTC cadets a government designed and approved flight instruction program to see if they had what it takes to become an Air Force, Navy or Marine pilot. These programs were actually designed to wash out those cadets that couldn't hack flying, thereby saving the government tons of money. Bo was an instructor there while attending school. My dad was his ROTC student and Bo introduced his student to his sister – and after a while there was me.

According to Bo the Air Force and Navy pilots in Vietnam didn't have much contact during the first part of the war, but they were both in Vietnam at the same time so they communicated when they had the chance. Dad knew Bo was flying the Grumman A6 Intruder and Bo knew Dad was flying the Republic F105 Thunderchief or Thud and they both knew where the other was; Bo was based on the USS Ranger, somewhere at sea near Vietnam. Dad was based at the Korat Air Base in Thailand. In mid-summer of 1965 Dad set up a "social" visit for the two of them at the R&R facility at Subic Bay Naval Air Station (NAS), the Philippines. Bo thought it strange that Dad wanted to meet at a Navy facility but he was over due on his required R&R and was able to make the trip. As it turned out, Dad was one of four squadron leaders assigned to a new joint defense suppression mission development program called 'Iron Hand'. The Air Force pilots who flew the missions were known as 'Wild Weasels'. This program was implemented in response to the loss of U.S air supremacy over Vietnam in mid 1965 due to the deployment of Soviet made, ground radar guided, SA-2 Surface-to-Air-Missiles by the North Vietnamese Army (NVA). Dad was there to recruit Bo as the fifth member of the team and to meet with the other Navy team member, Lt. Cmdr. Jason Cameron who just happened to be stationed at Subic Bay. The Air Force had deployed an earlier version of this defense suppression system using F-100F Super Sabers, but it had little success (about 50% attrition) due to the speed limitations of the F-100s, the immaturity of the attack strategies and the limitations of their electronic systems.

Each service had aircraft, missiles and radars that could be modified to meet the SAM suppression mission requirements. The heart of the system would be the AGM-45 Shrike anti-radar missile developed in 1963 by replacing the heat-seeking guidance system on the front end of the existing Sparrow missile with a radar-seeking guidance system. The Navy had the side-by-side A6 Intruder, pilot on the left, Bombardier-Navigator (BN) on the right and the Air Force had the Thud trainer - the only two man (tandem) version of the F-105 – the F105-F. Both aircraft had radars and navigation systems that could be quickly (but expensively) modified to meet the mission requirements of the first version of the new system. The Navy called their mission "Iron Hand" and called the modified A6 the A6B. The Air Force called its mission "Wild Weasel" and their aircraft the F105-G. Both aircraft required Electronic Warfare Officers (EWOs or BNs) to handle the radars and navigation systems and to give both targeting and evasive commands to the pilot. Hence, the two man requirement; a pilot and an EWO in the Air Force or a pilot and a BN in the Navy.

Basically, the mission was a deadly, split second game of aerial electronic chicken. During a bombing mission the Intruder or Thud would fly ahead of the bombers toward NVA SAM sites in 'hunt mode' (all emitters on) daring the enemy site to launch a SAM at them. When launched, the SAM relied on the ground based guidance radar to guide it to the target, so elimination of that radar meant loss of guidance for the missile. When the aircraft detected a SAM launch it would then launch one or more Shrikes to home on the site guidance radar and destroy it before the SAM got them. Often the aircraft would have to evade the first SAM using chaff grenades and proven evasive maneuvers – but this didn't always work. My Dad flew twenty seven of these missions before he lost the game.

The subsystem and initial systems testing of the new system were done at Subic Bay. The Navy completed the training of the first five crews of fourteen at Subic Bay and then finished the training program in carrier based operational squadrons. The Air Force trained at Eglin Air Force Base, Florida.

* * * *

After attending Dad's funeral service in Arlington, Bo made visits to several suppliers having problems delivering critical updated systems for the A6B and then returned to Vietnam as an A6B squadron leader completing fifty six Iron Hand missions. He then returned to the Naval Air Station at El Centro, California to participate in a new development program before leaving the Navy in December of 1973. I was almost seven years old when I lost my father. I was too young to understand much of what had happened. But Bo came back when I was twelve and as time passed he slowly became my second father. My mother resented Bo because he taught dad how to fly and led him into the war. He came home and my dad didn't. Also, I think, because I had so easily accepted Bo as a substitute for my dad. She didn't want me anywhere near airplanes.

About a month after he came home I overheard an argument between Bo and my mother about him taking me around the traffic pattern in his new Cessna 182. As he walked away she said to me, "Your Uncle might as well have taken your father out behind the barn and shot him dead!" She was crying uncontrollably and ran into her bedroom slamming the door. It was then that I began to understand the depth of her pain in losing my father. My mission in my young life then became the destruction of the wall built by my mother between her and her brother Bo. Much easier said than done.

Jameson Flight Service was on an old family farm southwest of Manhattan Kansas about a half mile south of highway US-40. My grandfather died in a highway accident when Bo was eighteen and my mother was sixteen. The farm was already part crops and part private airport. In two years Bo turned it into one hundred percent airport by selling off land and investing in a large hangar with a shop in the rear that would hold ten medium sized airplanes plus three in the shop, a separate office and two runways; the old east-west 2,200 foot grass strip and a new northeast-southwest 3,500 foot paved runway which favored the prevailing winds better than the older one. His chief pilot, Jim Harrison, was a middle-aged ex-Navy pilot with a pretty good head for business. Jim ran the business while Bo headed off to college and taught ROTC cadets how to fly. When Bo joined the Navy Jim took over as general manager and grew the business considerably during Bo's six year tour of duty. He had eight aircraft when Bo left and fourteen when he returned. According to their agreement when Jim took over as Chief Pilot and Manager he had earned just over 23% ownership of the business, including aircraft, land and facilities.

Bo and Jim were both FAA Designated Flight Examiners, meaning they could administer both written and flight tests to students seeking a private or commercial pilots license and upon passing both tests, issue the student a temporary license valid until replaced by an official FAA license.

Chapter Two

Jameson Flight Service
North Central Kansas
Saturday, September 1, 1979

The next two years went by in a flash. I got my private license and started logging time toward my commercial rating. I wasn't on the flight crew payroll – I was more like the hangar grunt. My jobs were fueling aircraft, washing airplanes, cutting grass, office crew (Jim, Bo & I shared this job) and mechanic's assistant. But in my spare time I flew errands picking up parts, equipment, training material and office supplies, usually in Manhattan (that's Kansas), Kansas City, Wichita or Tulsa, with a few longer trips to places like Milwaukee, St. Louis and Denver. Bo was careful to be sure I wasn't flying "on the clock" – I couldn't get paid to fly until I got my commercial license.

I got that license on my eighteenth birthday, but not with Bo. Earlier that summer I walked into the office one morning bright eyed and bushy tailed, ready to do what ever was needed. Bo was sipping his morning cup of coffee and studying a sheet of paper.

He looked at me and said, "They want me back, Sammy."

I never let anyone else call me that, but with Bo it was ok – sort of.

"Who wants you back, where?" I asked, pretty much dreading the answer.

"They want me to run a test program at the El Centro Naval Air Station. Comes with a bump in rank and a chance at several new opportunities," Bo replied with his head lowered, frowning at the paper.

Bo drank his coffee, keeping his focus on the paper and gradually his expression lightened.

"I never told you much about what I was doing during my last two years in the Navy, mainly because most of it was classified. When I was flying Iron Hand missions in the A6B, my BN was a guy named Joe

Garcia. He was a Commander, out ranking me. His prior duty was in special ops. On one of our night SAM suppression missions I zigged when he told me to zag and we got hit by some AAA. Lost the whole starboard wing. Just as the plane went into a spin we ejected. We were northwest of Hanoi, well into North Viet Nam territory. During flight school I had gotten a healthy dose of survival training, but I gotta tell you Sam, if it weren't for Joe I'd be either dead or a prisoner in the Hanoi Hilton right now. It took us three and a half months to get back to a clear area in the south where we could call for a Jolly Green to come pick us up. Joe did two things that were critical to our survival: We headed northwest, the direction least likely to be searched by the NVA. They knew we were out there somewhere but thanks to Joe's Special Forces skills they never found us. The second thing was radio silence. Joe insisted that we stay off the radio until we were totally in the clear.

"That's where I got this scar on my arm. He found me unconscious hanging thirty feet up in a tree, almost dead; cut me down without killing me. He saved my life Sam. We flew a dozen or so missions after that one and then Joe's rotation date came up. He asked me to do one more tour with him in a Special Forces unit. He was being re-assigned to El Centro to work the kinks out of automatic HALO missions and add some modern technology to the equipment. HALO is a stealth ingress method allowing special ops troops to jump from a very high altitude and open their chutes at a very low altitude; High Altitude Low Opening – HALO. There are several very hi-tech subsystems needed to automate this type of mission, the most important of which are the automatic low opening capability and the night vision system. Anyway, our job was to manage the automation program and develop system test procedures as well as operational procedures. During this program I did 183 HALO jumps, all but six at night, testing the system we were developing. I guess you'd call me the Program Test Jumper. Bottom line is I now have more night HALO experience than anyone else in the US Military – so they want me back."

"They're gonna drop you into some jungle somewhere and I'm never gonna see you again," I was beginning to get the picture. "You can't go 'til after my check ride, damn-it," all my plans were evaporating right before my eyes.

"Here's my proposition Sam; first of all, I don't know what they want me for and even if I did, I probably couldn't tell you. Jim has this place running like a sewing machine – I couldn't ask for a better manager. I'm not needed here. I'm gonna talk to him about something your mother and I have been discussing. We both want to see you get a college education. I'm gonna give him the reins on this place and up his ownership to 35%, fixed. He keeps the income he needs and reinvests the rest back into the company minus your college expenses. You can help out with part time instructing at K-State. I'll talk to Bubba up there, he'll be happy to have you. If I accept this, they want me down there next week, two weeks max. Jim is an FAA Designee. You can get your commercial check ride from him. Neither he nor I can give you your Instructor's ride. You'll need to go down to the FAA office in Tulsa. You've met Tim Reed down there; he'll treat you fairly and Tim will make sure you're ready."

I'd never seen Bo so serious, but suddenly his expression changed to one of pleading.

"Sam, you know how your mother feels about me; but as time goes by her feelings are softening. She sees a lot of your dad in you. She had her dreams shattered by what happened that night in Nam but she knows you've got flying in your blood. You're following in his footsteps in many other ways also and she wants whatever's best for you. We both want you to get a college degree. You don't know this, neither does she; I promised Scott if anything happened to him I'd see to it that you got a college education. I don't want you to buck me on this. This is the best direction to go at this point in time for all of us. Think about it: You get a college degree, which is far more important than you might think right now. Your mother and I will have a chance at reconciliation, which we all want. Jim gets the opportunity to secure his retirement for his family. You get a chance to teach others and stay plugged into aviation while you get your degree and accomplish something important to your dad, your mother and me. And I get to go somewhere where I'm needed and dabble in something I'm interested in."

"Damn-it, Bo, you should have been a used car salesman," was all I could say. He shot down every counter argument I could think of. What could I say? I'd thought about college and didn't really object to my family's desire for me to go, I just didn't want to rock the boat on the plans I had – most of all, I didn't want Bo to go off on some special ops fupah. I couldn't handle losing another father.

ANGELS THREE FIVE

* * * *

Commander Bo Jameson – He got the well deserved orders in the mail yesterday dropping the Lt. From his Lieutenant Commander rank and giving him some additional unclassified information about his new job. Bo had studied the problem as much as he could during the short notice he'd gotten from his new boss, now *Captain* Joe Garcia. The program looked like a huge opportunity - to fail. He hoped Joe could convince him otherwise.

* * * *

And so it came to pass: Bo left on his escapade; Jim passed me on my commercial check ride and signed me off for my Instructor's check ride.

I Called Bo and told him I got my commercial, no sweat, and was set to go on my instructor's check ride in October. School was going ok but I bitched about all the pretty girls and me with no spare time.

Bo responded, "Too bad Sam, that's the way we planned it! We all knew you would do ok -- you're a carbon copy of your father."

* * * *

I was enrolled at K-State in Aeronautical Engineering, had a cheap room off campus and had set a date with Tim Reed, the FAA examiner in Tulsa, for my Instructor's check ride. I was five weeks into my first semester taking calculus, physics, chemistry and English (the only foreign language I'd ever planned to take). Then bright and early on a Saturday morning I was off to Tulsa to see what Mr. Reed thought of my teaching skills. The FAA Single Engine Land Instructor's rating is more about teaching than flying – I wasn't worried about the flying thing. I had close to five hundred hours, most of them under the careful scrutiny of Bo Jameson, the best damned pilot in Kansas -- if not the world. But the teaching thing was a little new to me, although it was fairly easy to convert what and how I had learned from Bo into a role reversal. It must have worked. As we taxied back to the FAA ramp, Mr. Reed said;

"I like your air work Sam. Being Bo's nephew, that's not surprising. I hear you're going to work for Bubba up at K-State. You passed your written and your flight tests, but you will need to study *their* manual before you do too much instructing up there. They're on a government approved program so they have their own manual written by the military services. Study that manual, then come down here over your Christmas break and get your Advanced Ground Instructor's ticket. Bubba's program needs work in the ground instruction area – his test scores are below the average level the government expects and if he doesn't improve his average scores he could lose the program. Don't tell him I told you that, but believe me, he knows."

How in hell did he know I was working for Bubba? Bo, of course, always looking out for me. So here I am, a hotshot flight instructor getting ready to teach a flock of students, the youngest of which will be two years older than me. Bo had put me at ease about that before he left. He'd said I could pass for twenty two easily and after the first flight with me I'd have the student's ultimate respect. This was the nature of all serious students, military or not; always respect those from whom you can learn. These were ROTC flight candidates, seniors who wanted badly to fly; they would listen and show respect.

When I got back from Tulsa I called and chewed on Bo a little because he told Tim Reed about me working for Bubba. I told him Reed had failed me because he didn't think I was ready to teach in a military approved program. "How did he know that, huh Bo?" After a long silence I laughed and told Bo I was just kidding and thanked him for looking out for me. Bo told me about Bubba's ground school needs and explained that I could make more money in less time teaching ground school. If I played my cards right I could make three hundred dollars a week for five or six hours effort just teaching ground school and I could still fly students during the week and charters on weekends. I wanted to know where the girls fit into this schedule. Bo said, "They're letting girls into ROTC now, maybe you'll meet one," and hung up.

Chapter Three

HALO & HAHO

The history of jumping out of airplanes is as difficult to follow as much of its technology is to understand. General Billy Mitchell proposed using combat parachutists as early as 1917; only fourteen years after Wilbur and Orville made their first flight. Things have advanced considerably since then. The Germans, Russians and Italians were among the first to develop the technique for mass combat troop insertion via parachutes. The Germans made the first mass troop drop in World War II over Holland in 1940. This was a major part of Hitler's Western European 'Blitz Krieg' leading to the fall of six countries in less than a hundred days and the eventual extraction of over 300,000 British and French troops from Dunkirk in early June of 1940. From this point forward most countries with air combat forces began advancing the art of dumping soldiers out of airplanes. The largest air drop ever made was also over Holland, but during the joint American and British Operation Market Garden, two and a half months after D-Day - June 6, 1944.

During the Korean conflict improvements were mostly limited to reliability and fine tuning of the chute designs. It was after the Korean War and during the Vietnam conflict that the military thinking turned toward covert insertion of Special Forces (SF) via parachute systems. In a nutshell, covert insertion means getting one or more Special-Forces soldiers into the bad guy's back yard without his knowledge.

Over the years, technology and mission profiles have not necessarily matured in concert. In the beginning of this thought process parachutes were round and therefore difficult if not impossible to guide toward a target while falling in variable winds with the chute open. Any wind (and there was always wind) would cause moderate to large amounts of drift. However, to be covert it was necessary to fly high enough to be un-noticed from the ground, jump and then open the chute as low as possible. Hence the HALO (High Altitude Low Opening) moniker. The paratroop would free-fall from high altitude, directly over the landing target with some capability of maneuvering his flight path by varying his body position. Then at a very low altitude deploy his chute close to the target to minimize drift after the chute opened.

There were two major problems with this scenario; enemy radar and noise. Obviously, detecting an aircraft at high altitude with radar was possible even during the latter part of World War II. But in many mission profiles there is a very small probability of radar presence, so while the vulnerability of the HALO system to radar detection in the particular mission must be considered, it was usually not a mission killer. The other problem with HALO is the noise the chute makes when it opens. The early round chutes made a loud 'pop' when the canopy deployed that could easily be heard and identified, even at an altitude of several thousand feet. Once again, this was a problem that must be considered when designing the particular mission.

With the advent of the ram-air, inflated cell, rectangular airfoil parachute, a new mission profile began to emerge; HAHO, High Altitude, High Opening. The airfoil chutes became more and more like gliders as their development evolved; to the point that from thirty five thousand feet a modern airfoil chute bearing a two hundred fifty pound load can approach a horizontal range of forty kilometers, more or less, depending on the wind and weight of the load. Fitted with the appropriate pressurization and oxygen equipment a Special Forces operator can jump at current airline altitudes up to 42,000 feet with a range of up to sixty kilometers when using separate cargo packs for equipment. This is far enough away from the target to avoid detection and still maneuver to the target with relative ease using GPS.

Throw in night missions in bad weather and the ability for a single automated system to support both HALO and HAHO capabilities and you have a very complex set of requirements depending heavily on technology not yet fully developed and in some cases not yet even invented.

Chapter Four

El Centro Naval Air Station
El Centro, CA
Monday, September 17, 1979

"Commander Jameson reporting as ordered, sir."

"Sit down Bo. Nobody's here but us chickens," Joe said as he gave Bo a warm handshake.

"Captain Garcia! Jesus Joe, you could have your own ship."

"Commander Jameson! Jesus Bo, you could be CAG (Commander, Air Group) of your own Air Group."

"Touché brother," Bo mumbled as he collapsed into the over stuffed leather chair that faced Joe's desk. Joe spent some time getting him up to speed.

"I've been here a month and already we're six months behind schedule. This new system is a little more complex than the conceivers thought. The specs call for it to support HALO/HAHO jumps from thirty five thousand feet with an immediate or delayed opening. That's *angels three five* Bo, colder than a well digger's ass with nothing to breathe; and then descend through clouds with a minimum ceiling of 200 feet AGL at night into a landing area of less than 20 feet in diameter. With the highly maneuverable ram-air chutes and a pressure suit this is doable in daylight CAVU (Clear And Visibility Unlimited) conditions. But as we both know from our little party in Nam, night jumps through clouds in bad weather are fraught with potential disaster. We were lucky, even though I had to cut your bony ass out of that tree.

"Let me start by describing what we need and then digress to what we can do right now. We need an integrated helmet system that provides peer-to-peer communication among a falling task force of up to thirty men with programmable sub-nets for squad isolation. The network should be voice activated, secure, with multi-channel data/voice exchange, and a satellite link. Also integrated into this helmet should be a HUD (Heads-Up-Display) capable visor with IR (Infra Red), starlight and clear vision modes. This helmet and visor should also be an integral part of a pressurized jump suit. Information on the display should include a grid showing the wearer's relative position to the center of the drop zone as well as that of up to five additional team members, color coded. To one side of the visor, certain information should be displayed in real time like AGL (Above Ground Level) altitude relative to the landing zone, the preset automatic opening AGL altitude and a preset local or ZULU time (ZULU stands for Greenwich Mean Time - nobody knows why). This system cries for GPS but we won't see that technology in a single chip form factor for another 3 to 4 years. So we have to design it using a ground locator beam and homing receiver until GPS gets here. The challenge here is to make the system such that we can raise the hood, pull out the homing receiver and slide in the GPS receiver - not as easy as it sounds. I want you to make your first daylight HALO jump using the new prototype equipment tomorrow. We're using the new chutes, guaranteed to deploy quietly in 130 feet from a spread eagle position. You can imagine what that means to the low end of HALO. It's classified. I'll give you the specs when your clearance papers get here tomorrow. Right now I've got you set up in a one bedroom O-6 suite at the VOQ (Visiting Officers Quarters)."

"Joe, I'm not an O-6."

"Don't sweat it Bo, I am. That'll probably work ok for you unless you can find something better off base."

At 0700 the next morning Bo reported for familiarity training with the newest HALO/HAHO equipment. Although he had 183 HALO jumps behind him this was his first using the more advanced equipment required for the concept validation phase of the new system. At 1000 hrs (10:00 a.m.) as he walked out to the C-23 Sherpa transport plane they were using for testing, he saw another guy dressed like himself coming out of the Base Operations Office, headed for the same plane. It was Joe.

"Didn't know I was going to have company," Bo said with a smile.

"Well, if there's a tree within a mile of the target, I'm sure you'll find it and I'll be there to cut you out," he said grinning like a Cheshire cat. "Actually this is forty something jumps for me with these rigs; we've still got a few kinks to work out of the plain vanilla system, then we'll get you plugged into the prototype test program."

At fourteen thousand feet the crew chief lowered the tailgate of the

C-23 Sherpa and they took their tumble. When doing practice jumps from high altitude it's good to tumble on exit now and then to test your ability to stabilize. Three rotations or less is good. Once stabilized, it's amazing how much you can do with just small movements of your body and how much lateral range you can cover even without a wing suit.

They played for the first eight thousand feet and then got down to business. Bo got his stop watch out of his left sleeve pocket without losing control and got ready for the jolt. These chutes don't have a drogue chute; they're loaded with a pyro-spring system, similar to the air bags currently being developed for cars. The chute is packed to be blown out of the backpack and when it does it deploys very quickly. The 'pop' you expect to hear from the rapid deployment is surprisingly absent compared to the older 'dragged-out', round chutes. And the jolt is more gradual.

Bo nearly lost his stop watch. He looked at it but couldn't read the numbers through the visor. Later, he checked the 1.1 second expired time from deployment to full chute on his stopwatch against the table in the manual and found that his chute had fully deployed in only 123 feet. The system was set to trigger at 1200 feet which means he fell to 1077 feet before he was safely floating toward the ten foot red circle on the field below – impressive! But also scary; this means when necessary HALO jumpers will be able to get even closer to the ground before their chutes open. Bo hadn't seen the specs yet but he was praying that Joe didn't expect him to do a 300 foot opening on a test jump. They spent the next three days with the Advanced HALO/HAHO design personnel and their primary contractors going over the detailed specs and making final decisions on which capabilities would appear in the first version. It looked like they needed to add quite a bit to the prototype that had already been designed and tested before it made sense to go into production with the first version. No decision was made on whether there would be two or three versions before they got to where they needed to be. The biggest problem facing version one was the altimeter. Using a barometric altimeter in a precision system like this just wouldn't work. The barometric system works for aircraft sky-diving and current HALO systems, but it wasn't good enough for very low openings from freefall in abnormal weather conditions. So the only options left were a secondary laser or radar altimeter. Radar altimeters were too large, heavy and complex to be applied to this problem at this time. Laser technology, however, looked promising. The barometric altimeter would feed the system altitude until the secondary laser became effective after breaking out of the clouds. The problem here is, of course, interference. Multiple jumpers requires multiple channels for the laser signal, otherwise you don't know whose laser ground reflection you're receiving. The contractor said they had a six channel prototype working, but the spec calls for up to thirty man teams. So the six channel unit will be in version one and the contractor(s) will have to figure out how to meet the spec in version two, or maybe three, or maybe eliminate the requirement altogether. There were other capabilities that had been tested in the lab and not yet integrated into the prototype, like the IR night site and the mode controls to be integrated into the jumper's gloves.

Bo was feeling better about his new job. Over the next month he made seventeen more jumps, two from a classified altitude, collecting data and writing test reports as well as test plans for the phase one prototype. He had one malfunction and had to deploy manually. He waited a little longer than he should have and was under seven hundred feet when he pulled the plug – still plenty high for the new chute but not high enough if it malfunctioned. Emergency chutes take too much time at five hundred feet for full deployment. Got his ass chewed by Joe,

"I didn't cut you out of that fuckin' tree and drag your bony ass through the Vietnam jungle for three and a half months to have to clean your smelly guts off my tarmac"…and on, and on…

He raised the test floor from twelve hundred feet to fifteen hundred feet, which doesn't really affect the tests; it just makes everything safer. Truth to tell, Bo was pretty impressed with the current system. But then it had evolved for almost four years since he did his last HALO jump. The new one, if the damned thing ever worked, would be fantastic.

Chapter Five

Jameson Flight Service
North Central Kansas
Friday, December 14, 1979

I got home late on Friday the 14th of December and got my Ground Instructor's rating on the 15th. But when I got home from Tulsa Jim was pulling out what little hair he had left. Dale Rand, an old crotchety flight instructor and banner pilot, had walked away from Jameson Air the afternoon before because he "didn't want to pull those damned banners any more." Jim thought he could get a quick replacement. He had several qualified pilots, but the rest were all out of town or otherwise unavailable. He waited 'til I got back from Tulsa to let me know that he had a five hour tow the next morning. Bo had checked me out on the banner towing procedures early last summer in anticipation of my becoming a commercial pilot. I picked up a banner, climbed to altitude, circled over the field and switched fuel tanks, then came in low, dropped the banner and landed. I did this three times.

Manhattan Kansas was a fairly typical mid-western college town, population about 33,000 excluding non-resident students and growing. The city government was very particular about the demeanor of the city with plenty of parks, public landscaping, attractive public buildings and city facilities. It also had several shopping centers. Jim had just landed a contract with the largest of these to tow an advertisement over the city every day from December 16th until January 2nd. It was a fourteen thousand dollar contract and I got Christmas day off but he'd pay me anyway. Such a deal! There went two thirds of the time I had planned for getting ready for finals which start three days after Christmas break. On about my fifth or sixth day over the city I began to understand why Rand had quit. This was the most boring job I'd ever had; you're flying low and slow with no where to go. I also found out it's pretty important to limit myself to one cup of coffee before 8:00 a.m. and hit the head just before take off. For me five hours is a long time doing nothing and wishing I could figure out how to pee in this little cramped airplane. When Bo started the towing business (we also tow gliders) he bought a PA-11 Piper Cub with a run out 65 hp engine, replaced it with a freshly overhauled 90 hp engine and added a second 17 gallon gas tank in the left wing and a larger oil tank. With 34 gallons of gas a banner pilot could tow up to eight hours. Since then Bo had converted two more identical Cubs for towing banners and gliders.

Just as I landed on Christmas Eve it began raining cats & dogs. It rained the rest of the day with a sharp drop in temperature that night. Christmas morning when I woke it was snowing like a banshee. We took the day off and Jim invited my mother and me over for Christmas dinner. After dinner Jim and I retreated to his den to watch football and have a little nog without the egg. It was then that Jim dropped the bombshell on me. The shopping center PR guy called before it started raining yesterday and wanted to extend the next three tows to eight hours each – after Christmas sales or something like that. There was a thousand dollar bonus involved that Jim said he would split with me. He had Eddie, the gofer that replaced me when I left for school, put the banner together last night and told him to be on duty at 5:30 to plow the hard strip. The weather was supposed to be clear and cold in the morning with 20 knot winds from the west-northwest and warming somewhat during the day.

This was not good. Taking off to the southwest in a 20 knot 60 degree crosswind on ice was going to be a little hairy but it was the landing that had me worried. They always used the grass strip for towing operations. You could come in low & slow with a little bit of power, count to four after crossing the end of the hard runway and drop the banner and then just cut the power, flare and land. On the hard strip you had to drop the banner in the grass between the runways then maneuver to which ever end of the hard strip you needed to land on. In this weather I would probably have wind due north at 25 knots gusting to 35 by the time I landed eight hours later. Landing to the northeast, that's a 30 knot 45 degree crosswind on ice.

I expressed my concerns to Jim, "Jeeze Jim, I just started flying for you and you're already trying to kill me!"

"Relax Sam, you're a good pilot, the take off and pick up should be no sweat. I'll have Eddie back-plow and roll a 200 foot section of the field with a taxi trail to the hard strip." Back plowing meant dragging the plow blade backwards and packing the snow. This was the only way to plow a grass strip into a snow covered field without tearing it up. "We'll put you straight into the wind for landing; drop the banner in the snow wherever's best for you."

My only remaining concern was the take off. "Have Eddie throw all the snow to the south side of the hard strip when he plows it. He'll need to make at least three passes and I want 300 feet of grit on the hard strip's ice. Also, I want the red & white plane. It's got the best cabin heater."

"Done deal Sam – you'll be fine," Jim said with a big grin.

I showed up at 7:00 the next morning, semi-dehydrated with a single bottle of water and a ham & cheese sandwich. I also brought a jury rigged in-flight toilet using a 2 liter plastic soda bottle, some tubing and some other interesting parts. I hoped it would work and hoped even more that I wouldn't need to test it. Eddie showed up late and was only on his second pass on the hard strip. I was supposed to be banner-up at 8:00.

Jim smiled and said, "Don't worry Sam, he's moving pretty fast. He'll get the grit down by a quarter 'til and we'll have you banner-up by eight." As we were talking an old weather-worn pickup truck rolled up and an even older, more weather-worn Butch Cassidy stepped out.

Jim said, "I called Cassidy & asked him to come out and help this morning just in case." Butch (Beckum) Cassidy was Bo's line man for three or more years before Jim became the manager and Cassidy quit.

"He can gas up your left tank while you do your pre-flight and get settled in and he can watch the office while I supervise Eddie on getting this place operational after all this snow. I had Eddie plow the middle six hundred feet. That ok with you."

"I'll be off in less than four," I said, thinking about how I was going to perform this miracle.

They pulled the plane out onto the ramp which Jim had plowed with the small plow that fits on the front of his pickup. I did my pre-flight inspection while Cassidy went up to the office to get the key to the gas pump. As Cassidy lumbered up to the plane with the ramp ladder and began climbing up to top off the left tank, I used the little glass jar Jim kept in all the planes to drain about two ounces of gas from the left wing tank to look for water or other contaminants in the gas. I noticed a small amount of water in the bottom of the jar. This wasn't the plane I had been using and I had no idea how long it had been since the left tank had been topped off. I completed my preflight by checking the gas in the right tank sump. No water in this tank, which was not surprising.

By this time Eddie had finished plowing and was hooking the grit spreader to the tractor. I climbed aboard the plane and asked Cassidy to give me a prop (pulling the propeller to start the engine – these planes had no starter, they didn't even have a battery). The engine caught on the fourth pull. I let it idle for about five minutes to get everything warmed up a little before I added rpm to taxi. When I got to the runway everything looked good. I taxied down the runway about three hundred feet just to look everything over, after all this was my butt on the line. All the plowed snow had been blown and pushed to the south side of the runway. My concern in this situation was that I needed to keep the right wing low in the crosswind takeoff while staying as close to the right (north) side of the runway as possible to be as far as I could be from the five foot snow bank on the other side of the runway. This morning I had 25 knot winds gusting to 30 and the wind was close to 50 degrees off the nose so I had to keep the plane on the runway until I was more than 5 mph above flying speed and then yank it off the ground to gain enough altitude quickly to miss the snow bank in case of a gust.

I taxied back to the northeast end of the plowed area and did my run-up to check the engine. I got into position and pushed the throttle all the way forward. The instant I fire-walled the throttle I got a blast of cabin heat. The take-off was a little hairy, but I did ok. "This is going to be a piece of cake," I mumbled to myself.

The banner pick-up was no problem; wind actually makes it easier to make a good pick-up. I released my tow-line (cable) which is connected to the tow hitch just above the tail wheel on one end and on the other end it is coiled and attached to a grapple hook resting just inside the left window. Releasing it involves simply throwing it out the window after which this morning, thank God, I could slide the window shut.

A quick pass over the two guys holding the loop in the banner line at about 20 feet to check for a fowled tow hitch then a wide turn with a fairly long run dead into the wind leveling off at about 12 feet; full throttle when about 10 feet from the loop then count to three and pull the stick back to a near vertical climb. At the top of the climb (about 200 feet) push the stick forward to lower the nose and pay careful attention to the rudder to avoid dropping a wing into a spin. I entered a gentle climbing turn up to 500 feet, and then turned to cross the hard strip at the mid point heading northwest. The standard procedure is to level off, then switch tanks right as the plane crosses the field. The theory being: if anything's wrong with the other tank, better to find that out over the field than over the city. So I switched tanks and was on my merry way.

Then the engine quit. . .

Chapter Six

Wednesday, December 26, 1979

Over Jamison Field

North Central Kansas

Almost 600 hours and I'd never had a single problem. Now I'm towing a banner dead stick (no engine), it's 24 degrees outside and my cabin heater just quit. Can I think through this? Our procedure says to begin a gentle glide straight ahead until you're clear of the runway, then release the banner, turn downwind to the runway you intend to land on and make a dead stick landing. I knew what I was supposed to do – but in these conditions?

I thought to myself, "I had done several dead stick landings with Bo when training for my Commercial flight test – so I can do this! Well, maybe these conditions were a little different, but hey, here I am, and I've *got* to do this."

Gliding into this wind while pulling this load the plane seemed like it was barely moving. And, I was losing altitude fast. I had to release the banner soon if I was going to hit my preferred landing spot at the beginning of the grit on the runway. It quickly became obvious that I had to release the banner *now* or miss the grit, so I released it. The plane immediately gained a little airspeed and assumed a normal power-off glide. I turned right to enter a downwind approach to the hard strip. I was down to 250 feet so I made an immediate turn onto the base leg and looked at my relationship to where I wanted to land. I had two problems; first, I was too low to make the grit covered area and worse than that, the banner had settled across the runway right at the close end of the grit covered area and was blowing near vertical to the runway, both ends caught in the snow. I was going to have to land short of the grit and immediately run into the four foot high banner. I had two choices. I could lengthen my base leg and slip the plane to lose additional altitude and then try to land on the ice - or maintain as much altitude as I could to get as close to the grit as I could and hit the banner. I decided on the latter because if I landed on the ice I would surely be blown into the snow bank. I had Eddie put all the snow on the left side of the runway so I could make a fairly safe right wing low take-off, but I hadn't planned to land on this runway. Now the five foot high snow bank on the south side of the runway posed a real threat to this cross wind landing on ice. I'd rather land close to the grit and take my chances with the banner. Flipping the plane would take out the prop, damage the vertical stabilizer and rudder and probably do light damage to the wings. Sliding into the snow bank would likely cause a cartwheel and total the plane.

As I approached the landing my right wing was almost touching the snow on that side of the runway and the crosswind was still causing me to slide left toward the snow bank. Then as my right wheel touched the runway I hit the banner! I pulled the stick all the way back and leveled the wings. The banner wrapped itself around the wheels and the plane's nose started down. Fortunately two thirds of the banner was on the right side so the drag form that side was enough to offset the fact that the left side was draped over Eddie's snow bank. The net result was that the plane travelled relatively straight down the runway with its tail at least ten feet in the air – I almost nosed over but the plane stopped quickly and the tail came down with a loud 'whap'. It sounded like something back there broke.

Jim, Cassidy and Eddie had seen the whole thing and were standing about ten feet behind the snow bank watching. By the time the tail came down they were running to help. The banner was pretty much destroyed in the area affected. It was rolled around both wheels; the nylon fabric of six or seven letters was torn beyond repair and some of the straps were broken. Some of the other letters that were dragged through the snow were torn, but Jim said his wife could fix them.

"I'm going to sit here in the cockpit for a few minutes and try to settle down." I told Cassidy and Eddie. Jim was in the back inspecting the tail wheel.

Approaching the cockpit he said, "One of the spring sheaves is broken, so I'll have to replace the whole unit. Couldn't trust that wheel, bearing or the rest of the spring after smacking the ground like that."

"Jim, I'm sorry man, I probably should have lengthened my downwind and tried to land on the ice"

"No way Sam, we were at the hangar when we heard the engine quit. I watched you all the way down. If anybody's at fault it's me. If we had started running right away we might have been able to clear the banner from the runway before you landed. But we stood there dumbfounded, wondering why the hell the engine quit. On the other hand if we had tried to clear the banner we might have made things worse. You followed the procedure exactly as we wrote it and practiced it – but I'm going to make two changes: We're going to climb to pattern altitude (600 feet) before switching tanks and we're going to switch fuel tanks 200 yards before crossing the runway so an immediate release can be made if there's a problem. You did exactly what I would have done, no one got hurt and there is only minor damage to the plane; it could have been a lot worse."

"Thanks for the kind words," I said, "but I still feel bad about this. How are we going to get this tow done now?"

"Well, you're gonna have to get out of the airplane and we're gonna have to cut the banner away and push this plane back to the hangar," Jim's business demeanor had returned. "If you're still up to it, the yellow and red plane is only a few gallons short of full. I'm pretty sure you could get seven hours in, but the cabin heater isn't as good. I'm assuming we had a fuel contamination problem here, so I don't want to use gas from the pump until we know what's going on."

"I'm good to go," I said, still feeling bad about the whole thing.

Jim got Cassidy and Eddie working on getting the airplane untangled and back to the hangar. He and I headed to the hanger to get the yellow plane out on the ramp and checked over. Then Jim went to the back of the hangar to get the six new letters that he knew we needed to splice into the banner to repair it while I ran back out to the runway to inspect the rest of the damage so we could splice new letters into those locations. While we were working on this Jim asked, "What do you think caused the engine to croak?"

"I think it was something mechanical – the prop froze." When you shut an engine down on the ramp, at idle, the prop still turns over several times as the engine shuts down. In the air it will windmill for a while even hauling a load. This prop turned over a maximum of two times and then froze.

"Sam, that sounds like it could be water contamination. If you get a significant amount of water in a fuel line, that's exactly how an engine with a barometric carburetor will shut down. Barometric carbs hold much less fuel than gravity fed carbs so water in the gas runs right into the engine very quickly and the engine loads up very quickly. It's not like you're running out of gas, it's like you're running into water. When we get this banner fixed let's look at the gas in that left tank."

Jim filled a drinking glass from the left tank, smelled it, and then tasted it. "Here Sam, want a drink – it's pure water."

"But when I tested it, it was gas with just a small bit of water. What happened?"

"Was that before or after Eddie topped off the tank?" Jim asked.

"Actually, it was during. I took the sample just as he started filling the tank."

Jim thought for a minute, and then said, "I've got five gallons of 100 octane avgas in a jerry can in the back of the hangar. Let's top off this plane and get you in the air. I'll figure this out while you're gone."

"You de boss, let's do it.," I said handing the glass back.

So, repeating my first take off and climbing to 600 feet before switching tanks well before I crossed the runway, I was off on an eight hour tow over the beautiful snow covered city of Manhattan Kansas.

I spent the first hour beating myself up over the morning's events. The first lesson I learned was to be sure to check the gas *after* topping off the tank. The second mistake I'd made was following a procedure that didn't comprehend the conditions. On a typical day with no howling wind, snow banks and ice on the runway, I could have turned down wind immediately, not caring where the banner landed because I could adjust my approach to land short or long to miss it. As it was I had tried to get the banner as far away from the runway as I could before releasing, but I had to release before I wanted to because of the wind and loss of altitude. In hind-sight, I should have released the banner immediately; the wind would have taken it well to the south of the runway – live and learn!

When I got back everything worked as planned. I taxied up to the gas pump only to notice that it was locked, so I taxied on over to the hangar, shut down, jumped out and tailed the cub into the spot the guys had left for it in the hangar. When I got back to the office and some warmth for my frozen feet Jim handed me a hot cup of coffee saying:

"Somebody ran over the standpipe. It had to be that good for nothing mechanic I hired to rebuild those three run-out 65 horse engines."

The standpipe was a three inch iron pipe through which the fifteen hundred gallon fuel tank buried under the ramp was filled. The cap on the pipe had a built in filter and served as the breather for the tank. It stood about a foot above the ramp and about three feet behind the gas pump – out of the way of airplanes.

"Whoever it was, broke the pipe clean off, then stood it back up and pushed gravel around it. That and the snow is why we didn't see the problem. He parks his truck on that side of the hangar and when he backed out, day before yesterday, dollars to donuts he broke that sucker off and then tried to hide it. Then came the big rain. I've seen water on the ramp at least an inch deep in that area before. I'm positive that's what happened," Jim said disgustedly.

Pouring myself another cup of coffee I asked, "how're you gonna get it out."

"I called Tom Johnson, our fuel dealer – he'll bring his service truck out in the morning and suck all the water out and replace the standpipe. Be interesting to see how much water is in there. Tom said the pipe to the pump is set six inches above the bottom of the tank and over the years with a tank that isn't filled often the water from condensation will eventually reach the delivery pipe and it'll start sucking water. Tom checks our tank once a year and has never had to pump it out. Last year it had less than an inch."

The mechanic showed up the next morning and simply turned around and left when Jim asked him about the standpipe.

The rest of my Christmas break flights were uneventful, but I had precious little time to study for finals. Oh well, I had three days after I got back to school before they started – but still I was worried about school.

Chapter Seven

Yuma Proving Ground

Near Yuma Arizona

Thursday, January 7, 1982

It was a cool windy day at Yuma Proving Ground, Arizona. YPG is actually an Army facility used for testing various Army ordinance, combat vehicles and equipment. The Space and Missile Systems Organization (SAMSO), was a tri-service organization tasked with development and testing of military satellite and missile systems. They were using YPG to test the full up Global Positioning System (GPS). GPS required a user to receive signals from a minimum constellation of four satellites to provide an accurate position in three dimensions and time. SAMSO had placed four satellite transceivers on the ground at high points around YPG. Initial testing with these four 'satellites' proved the concept but provided very sub-marginal accuracy. When they got the first GPS satellite properly placed in orbit, accuracy was greatly improved but still not to specification. Now they had two satellites up and accuracy looked better. But Captain Garcia and his team weren't satisfied that the ultimate accuracy was going to be good enough for some of the HALO/HAHO scenarios they had been tasked with. An old friend of Bo's at Texas Instruments in Dallas, where three of the early GPS User Equipment systems were being developed, hinted that a new Differential GPS would soon be tested at YPG and they expected outstanding accuracy. When Bo told Joe about this he immediately got on the phone and got Bo invited to the first test flight of the new system.

Bo was delighted to see his old friend there on the ramp that morning. He brought Bo up to date on what he'd been doing for the last eight years and on the basic operational concept of GPS.

"Bo, you don't look a day older than you did last time I saw you on the Ranger boat. Must be the Navy life agrees with you," said his friend Don Campbell, a former Navy A-6 pilot.

"Hey Don, how's civilian life treating you? Looks like you're doing some stuff that will revolutionize the way we navigate - You learn anything useful career-wise from your Navy tour in Nam?"

"Yeah Bo, I learned some stuff in Nam. I learned that to fight effectively we need to integrate our electronic warfare systems across our military services by using today's technology and systems integration capabilities. No more of this separate air, land and sea crap – one fighting force with integrated air, land, sea, intel, planning and battlefield strategy systems that rely on the technology we use so effectively in our private sector. GPS will provide a key part of that capability but that's just the tip of the iceberg. There's a new name-of-the-game in warfare, Bo; 'integrated systems'."

Bo was tempted to respond with a comment on the DEVGRU strategy to do exactly that at the Special Forces level, but decided there was too much opportunity in a conversation like that to divulge TS information.

Don looked older, hair thinning and graying a little, added a little weight and he was a year younger than Bo. "Maybe all this conditioning for the test program is keeping me in shape," thought Bo.

"Let me bend your ear on something real quick before this show gets on the road," said Bo with a quizzical grin. "Why do I need to look at four satellites to find my three dimensional position?"

"Because your receiver needs to adjust its clock to GPS system time. The user's time must be identical to GPS time and that makes his solution dependent on very near perfect knowledge of system time. If the user's time were one second off, the error in the position would be about two miles. And that means you have four unknowns; three position coordinates and time."

"I could never figure out why the *user* needed to know the time to within a few nanoseconds and I guess the answer is he doesn't; but his GPS system does – dumb-ass me," Said Bo smiling at his friend.

"What can Differential GPS do to make such an accurate system even more accurate?" Bo asked.

"Well, as you know, no system is ever perfect. There are little errors in the system that each degrade its performance somewhat. The primary systemic error in GPS is what we call ionospheric refraction. The signal path gets 'bent' by the ionosphere like light bends passing through a prism. We lump that error in with all the other errors into what we call our "system error correction factor".

"Last summer, when we concluded the formal ground tests here at YPG the Colonel authorized a pig roast celebration – I was one of the contractors invited and, of course, I had to pay my own way. But I wouldn't have missed it for anything. Anyway, the co-program manager of the SAMSO User Segment development programs, Major Jim Abbott, and I had been tossing around ideas to significantly reduce all errors in the system. After the pig roast, in a bar just down the road from the YPG main gate somewhere past midnight Jim and I literally designed the system we called Differential GPS on some paper we borrowed from the bartender. We left the bar when it closed at 2:00 am; Jim with the original and me with a copy, both annotated with our go-do's. He had to find out what had to be done to upgrade the YPG laser tracking system and how much it would cost. I had to flesh out the design and do a cost estimate of the software modifications and the new software necessary. Turn's out the software was fairly easy; the biggest cost was the mods to the YPG laser tracking system to triple its accuracy and the cost of the Huey UH-1 helicopter we chose as the test vehicle.

"DGPS is also a simple system. It's intended to be a 'local' system for airports, aircraft carriers, local combat arenas, etc. So we 'surveyed in' a modified Ground Segment transceiver that constantly monitors the visible constellation of satellites. The DGPS transceiver knows exactly where it is and exactly where each of the satellites should be at any given point in time. So all the local ground unit has to do is take the difference in the transmitted range and the actual range of each visible satellite and upload that difference as a correction factor to that satellite on a continuous basis. Then each satellite can broadcast its own error correction factor on its data stream. So a user system in the same general area can apply those correction factors to the range of each satellite it is tracking and get extremely accurate results. Our calculations show that a hundred miles away from the local transceiver a user should still get better than ninety percent of the correction impact. Today's test will confirm all that."

As they spoke a gray government sedan drove up to the ramp and a well dressed gentleman got out.

"That looks like Jeff Sperry, Under Secretary of Defense

(USECDEF) – this could mean trouble for me," Said Don.

"Why?" Bo asked, wondering what the hell was going on.

"I'll tell you later," he said as Sperry approached us.

"Good morning, gentlemen, I'm Jeff Sperry, Under-Secretary of Defense. I'm here to ride along on your DGPS test flight," said Sperry as he flashed his ID.

Bo introduced himself and Don and asked, "Does Colonel Bryan know you're here?" Bryan was the base commander and Bo wondered to himself why he wasn't here.

"Yes Commander, he does," Sperry replied, "we'll all get together after the test. Now if one of you gentlemen will be so kind as to explain what I need to look at during the test, we'll be on our way."

The call came and Sperry, the UH-1 pilot, Daryl Furgussen and Stan Southgate, the TI engineer who rode on all test flights in case of equipment problems, climbed aboard, took off and headed for the range. Forty eight minutes later they were back. Sperry walked up to Campbell and said:

"I'm sorry Mr. Campbell; I'm going to have to classify this mission. The system, the data and the fact that the test even occurred will be classified SECRET. I will need everyone, including Mr. Southgate and Lt. Furgussen to accompany me back to Base Headquarters to meet with Colonel Bryan and verify your clearances. Then we'll all sign some standard Non Disclosure Agreements (NDAs) pertaining to this test."

Bo whispered to Don, "I'll probably have to get Captain Garcia to provide 'need-to-know' for us before we can even look at the data."

Campbell replied, "Even though I'm the TI program manager on this gig, I may never get to see the data 'cause I will not have a need-to-know until we get a new development contract – but the fact that Sperry flew the mission and then classified the data tells me it must have worked as well as we thought it would, or better. Tell the good Captain Garcia that we at TI are happy to provide him with the accuracy he needs for his new system – whatever accuracy that might be."

As Bo drove back to El Centro he tried to estimate in his own mind how long it would take a contractor like TI to integrate and miniaturize a system like GPS such that it would be useful to a system like the Advanced HALO/HAHO. He was aware that we were working well into the future on several of the system's major components. While the display system had come a long way and parts of it were being used in the current test program, those parts had yet to be integrated into a single display light enough and rugged enough for deployment. They needed that visor display 'now' but it appeared to be at least two years away. The laser altimeter was coming along nicely and they'd probably have an operational version in a year or so.

They were past the concept definition phase of development and into the concept validation phase and Bo wondered if they'd ever get out of it. How can our program influence technology development such that all the needed parts come together at the same time? Obviously, money was a key factor. But leverage through other programs was also important. Bo learned from Don today that the system development he saw tested was actually funded by the Federal Aviation Agency (FAA) and the HALO/HAHO power's that be knew absolutely nothing about it until two weeks ago.

When Bo got back to his office, Joe asked, "How'd it go."

"You don't want to know," Bo replied looking frustrated, which he clearly was.

"That bad eh?"

"Nope, the test flight was great! Too good, actually." Then Bo told him the USECDEF story.

Garcia smiled and said, "Actually, Bo, it's probably better for us that it is classified. I knew it might be. Got a short message from the Admiral a couple of days ago saying just that, but it didn't say anything about Sperry showing up. This tells us that there's a lot more military and civilian interest in GPS with this new capability. More interest means more funding and faster development. The GPS timeline might just coincide more closely with ours now – we'll see."

Chapter Eight

Mountain Villa
Southeast of Mazatlan Mexico
Monday, March 15, 1982, 8:30 a.m. MDT

Maximillion Horte (or-tay) settled into his soft leather upholstered dining chair for breakfast, joining six of his most valuable and trusted employees and Jaimie (hi-mee) Sanchez, whose first anniversary with the team they were celebrating.

Horte's villa was located on the western side of a three thousand foot mountain range thirty five kilometers from Mazatlan Mexico as the crow flies - but more than twice that by road – the last twenty five kilometers of which could hardly be called a road. Horte was in the transportation business and over the last four years he had become very successful. His transportation services covered air, land and sea routes and his team had developed a very diverse capability for getting drugs from Mexico and countries south to several locations in the U.S. His focal point in Mexico was Mazatlan, a city not currently in the cross hairs of the U.S. Border Patrol, FBI, DEA or the Mexican Federales for drug trafficking. And then from Mazatlan on to a variety of U.S. cities via ship or air freight. This was becoming the preferred alternate drug route as the scrutiny at the Texas, Arizona and California border crossings began causing major problems for the Central and South American drug lords.

Max Horte's team had developed a relatively sophisticated system for moving large shipments of drugs from Mazatlan to key points in the United States and the drug kingpins were willing to pay huge sums for his service because it had greatly reduced their losses and the system required significant support on the U.S. side of the border that would take the drug industry years to implement. To stay ahead of the game Max had to constantly devise new schemes and routes causing him to reinvent his methods and move his in-country (U.S.) personnel fairly often.

To run an organization of this sort required absolute loyalty from his team and ruthless response to any sign of disloyalty. Horte had a list of nine unbreakable rules enforced by certain death if broken. Among these were; his employees were absolutely forbidden from ingesting any form of illegal drug, from stealing product from his clients or from him and from displaying anything short of complete honesty in his duties to the organization.

So Jaimie Sanchez was a little worried when first invited to the villa for his anniversary celebration, as well he should have been, because he'd been skimming coke from a valued client, using a little and selling the rest.

He was seated by a servant at the end of the table opposite Max Horte with the six other men, three each on the left and right sides of the table. The table was of rough hewn mahogany or teak and he noticed many lighter spots to the left of his place setting and many more to the right – maybe defects in the wood? He also noticed a small cup with no handle in the center of his place setting.

"Jaimie, tell us how you've progressed over the past year. Have you learned the trade? Are you happy with your compensation? Are you being treated well by your comrades?" asked Max Horte.

Jaimie steadied himself thinking this really is a meeting to honor him for his first faithful year of service to the organization. After all he was a hard worker and had covered his tracks well on his little scam.

He replied, "Yes sir, no problems, I love this job and I'm very happy with my pay."

"Jaimie, every month I invite several employees to breakfast for a little test. It's really very simple and it only takes a few minutes," Horte said as he stood and began clipping a few strands of hair, close to the root, from each man on Jaimie's left. He put each man's hair into the small cup.

Jaimie's face began to pale as he realized what was happening. By the time Max Horte approached Jaimie he was quite pale and had lowered his gaze to the table to avoid revealing the terror building in his mind.

The servant, a large muscular Hispanic man, followed Horte collecting each cup and depositing a small piece of paper in each. When the process was complete the servant left the room with the tray of cups and then returned with a pot of coffee, pouring coffee for each guest and providing sugar and cream as requested. Then he and a second servant brought out two plates at a time brimming with eggs, sausage, bacon, fried plantains and an English muffin buttered and spread with orange marmalade. Max and the other six men engaged in a lively conversation concerning an up-coming soccer tournament. Jaimie sat silently eating what he could to appear unconcerned.

After breakfast and another round of coffee the servant returned with the tray of cups. Each cup had a name taped to the side. The servant placed a cup in front of each man. Jaimie's cup contained his hair clippings floating in a light purple liquid. Glancing to the left, he could see that his neighbor's cup contained hair in a clear liquid.

Max Horte rose from his chair and began walking around the table stopping behind each man and commenting on the result of his test.

When he got to Jaimie he said, "Jaimie, you've taken coke within the last week. Can you explain this?"

"Yes sir; a friend had a party last Saturday night. I was there and there were drugs and booze. I guess I drank too much and somehow took some drugs. I don't remember doing it." Jaimie was shaking and his voice was cracking.

Behind him Horte picked up a nail gun from beneath a cloth napkin on a small table by the wall and with a swift motion grabbed Jaimie's left forearm and drove a nail through his hand deep into the table. Meanwhile, the servant who was positioned behind Jamie on his right side grabbed his right forearm and Horte nailed that hand to the table also.

"Gentlemen," he said over Jaimie's rather loud screams and moaning, "please excuse us. Mr. Sanchez and I must have a little talk as soon as he calms down. Wait outside; we'll continue our meeting shortly."

After his comrades had left the room, Max said softly, "Now Jaimie, tell me where you got the coke and be very careful not to lie to me."

Jaimie had already lied; he didn't know what to do now. Either way, he was doomed. He had heard the stories of what happened to employees who lied to Max. He had stolen and used Horte's cocaine and he had lied. He was in a situation from which he could not escape.

As sweat trickled slowly down his face he pleaded, "Please Mr. Horte, I lied and I stole a small amount of coke from the last delivery, but I swear it won't happen again. Please don't hurt me."

"Jaimie, how can I be absolutely sure you won't ever lie to me or steal from me again?" Jaimie's head was wavering, his eyes rolling and saliva was dripping from his mouth.

He gurgled, "Because I swear it won't happen again."

"Jaimie, there's only one way I can be *absolutely* sure," Horte whispered as he pressed the nail gun against the back of Jaimie's neck just below his skull and fired a nail through his brain. The point of the nail came out of Jaimie's skull about an inch above and right between his eyes. His head fell to the table, eyes wide with terror.

Max Horte calmly walked to the door and called the others back to the table for their Monday morning meeting while the servants removed Jaimie's body and cleaned up that end of the table. He demanded absolute loyalty from his employees and this was his primary method of achieving it.

Chapter Nine

Kansas State University

Manhattan, Kansas

Saturday, May 26, 1984

I was jubilant. After four years of blood, sweat and tears I'd finally come to that day where college would be forever behind me. My mother and Uncle Bo were dutifully present as if they needed to be personally assured that I'd really made it to graduation.

Actually I was graduating with honors from the College of Aeronautical Engineering at K-State and I had done so completely on my own, while teaching the art of basic flight to ROTC candidates both in the air and on the ground. I never asked for a penny from Jameson Flight Service and Jim Harrison, the manager/chief pilot of JFS, was able to invest all of the money Bo had set aside for my college education right back into the company. In return for this 'above & beyond the call of duty' effort on my part, Bo, with Jim's concurrence, made me a 10% owner in JFS.

I had accumulated 3,959 hours over my nearly seven years of flying, mostly as a commercial pilot. I was ready now to go do something I wanted to do – but what?

At the after-the-ceremony celebration Bo asked me, "So Sammy, how did you like college life?"

I replied, "It wasn't as bad as I thought it might be . . . *Humphrey*." The scowl on Bo's face told me that I would never be called Sammy again.

After a long silence Bo's scowl changed to a smile and he said, "touché, my smart ass nephew. What are you gonna do now? Graduate school?"

"No way. I'm tired of school and instructing. I got my instrument and multi-engine ratings along the way and I also picked up a limited

ATR (Airline Transport Rating) with a Convair 440 type rating. That ought to be good for something."

Bo's eyebrows rose in a seldom expressed look of surprise, "Wow, you *have* been busy. Tell you what; the Navy is looking for test pilots at the San Diego Naval Air Station. Mostly testing avionics and missile systems, but it could get you into jets pretty quickly. I know the chief pilot over there – want me to talk to him? Your degree would be a big plus because the systems they're testing are pretty complicated. Can't guarantee anything but it might be worth a try."

"How come the Navy is using civilian test pilots? Don't they have enough pilots of their own?" I asked.

"Well, some of the systems we're testing these days are more technical than the average pilot can handle. The Navy saves time and money testing these systems with pilots that can understand the systems they're testing."

"I'd be really stupid to turn down an offer like that – given that somebody made me an offer like that – you think it's possible?"

"Don't know but I'll find out early next week," Bo said with that signature shit-eatin' grin on his face.

The following Tuesday my phone rang, "Get your butt down here Friday if you want that job," Bo said with no particular excitement in his voice. "The Test Wing Commander is interested – don't blow it, you won't get another chance."

"I don't know what to say," I said. "I'll be there, but I need to know where there is"

"Get a flight into San Diego Thursday afternoon. Let me know when and I'll pick you up at the airport."

Chapter Ten

San Diego Naval Air Station

San Diego, California

Friday, June 1, 1984, 10:15 a.m. PDT

"Captain Johnson, I'm Sam McKensie, pleasure meeting you sir," I said, trying to not sound overly militaryish. "Commander Bo Jameson at El Centro said we should talk."

"Glad you could get down here as quickly as you did Mr. McKensie. Truth is, we need test pilots yesterday. I read your resume - pretty impressive for a young civilian pilot-engineer. Let's take a ride in my T-38. I know you don't have any jet time – doesn't matter, jets are much easier to fly. We can talk up there. Since you're not in the military, please call me Ben and if you don't mind, I'll call you Sam."

This was about as unexpected as an engine failure on take-off. While we were in the locker room suiting up (he found a nearly new flight suit that fit me like a glove – actually, a little tight) he gave me the run-up procedure and take-off numbers and went over the T-38 / F-5 flight characteristics on our way out to the plane.

The flight was great – I think he was hands-off all the way. The T-38 is a sweet little airplane – we didn't go supersonic but we could have. I immediately felt at ease with Ben. He asked me to go through the basic flight maneuvers and then, while I was showing him I could fly, he started telling me about his latest woes. He'd just lost one of his best technical test pilots in a skiing accident, of all things.

"Eric caught a ski tip in the eye last weekend that will likely end his flying career. He was wrapping up the final phase one of the integration flight tests of the HARM (High speed Anti Radiation Missile) AGM-88B system," the Captain said with his head bowed and eyes closed. It was obvious that Eric was a friend and he was worried about his future.

This system was the latest in the radar hunter/killer missile systems, successor to the AGM-45 Shrike. Most of the data on the system was classified, but he needed me to complete the last two flights and he needed to figure out how to get me a secret clearance as soon as possible. He was already two pilots short when he lost Eric and while he could "borrow" pilots from operational units, that wouldn't solve his long term problem – he needed experienced pilots with engineering degrees, preferably aeronautical and/or electrical. His problem was compounded by the on-going product improvement test flights of the operational AGM-88B missile, executed using the Naval Weapons Center (NWC) A-7 test vehicle; and the ever expanding list of integration test flights on new versions of the F4 Phantom sold to NATO and other allies by McDonnell Douglas.

I guess he thought I was his man 'cause he said, "Let's get back to the base and get started on the paper work, assuming you want the job. To get you on board immediately we'd have to bring you in as a civilian contractor. If things work out we can get you through OCS and commissioned as an O-3 (Lieutenant) later, provided you like the job. The fact that you have an engineering degree, taught ROTC for four years, and have excellent flight experience will allow that to happen.

I'd landed here at a little after 9:00 a.m. It wasn't even noon yet and I already had the job! While we were headed back to base he interleaved traffic pattern information and calls to the tower with questions about my background, obviously interested in finding out how quick my security clearance would come through. I accepted his offer.

"I noticed in your flight resume you've got some time in the old Grumman Hellcat" Ben quipped between tower calls. "Compared to a Hellcat this plane's a pussycat; approach at 130, 110 over the threshold and begin your flare at 95. Welcome aboard! We'll get you checked out in an A-7 tomorrow - take a ride up to Edwards Air Force Base where the testing is done and introduce you to Jim Rankin, the range officer at Echo Range, then we'll make a run by the Naval Weapons Center which is home base for HARM development and testing. I need your security papers filled out before quitting time today. You got a passport?"

Chapter Eleven

San Diego Naval Air Station
Officer's Club
Friday June 1, 1984, 7:15 p.m. PDT

"And then I landed the damned thing – I love that airplane. Guess I've entered the jet age at last," I said to Bo as I cut into my steak – his treat.

"Yeah, we've got several at El Centro. They're the most economical way to get around – that airplane and its F-5 sister have the lowest cost per mile factor of all military jet aircraft. I use ours to stay flight current. Fun little airplane."

"So, fill me in on the HALO stuff you're doing."

"Well it's coming together – slower than we had hoped - but keep in mind when this whole idea was conceived there was not a single new component available off-the-shelf. We were pushing technology from the git-go; and still are. When it became obvious that things weren't going to come together until the late eighties, the powers that be made the decision to freeze the operational system specification where it was (spring of '83) and concentrate on one subsystem at a time. This is working pretty well because we're doing more day jumps with this strategy. I didn't mention this at your graduation because your mother was always around; we lost a jumper about a year ago. Best we could tell from telemetry and high-speed photography, the chute never got a deploy command from the computer due to a laser altimeter or interface malfunction and the jumper was trying to fiddle with the altimeter when he realized he was too late on the manual pull. I was the first on the scene and he was a good friend. You don't want to ever witness something like that.

"That slowed things down a lot. We had to try to figure out what went wrong with a subsystem that'd been working beautifully for almost two years. Never did figure it out – just one of those things. Joe moved the pull altitude up to 1800 feet and we all did a reset on our reliance on proven equipment.

"As of now we've got a multi-mission rapid deploying, ram air cell inflated, gliding chute, with a laser altimeter and oxygen system for the HALO/HAHO missions. The primary computer is chest mounted with laser transmitter and receiver hard mounted to the motherboard. What we're working on is the integrated helmet. This helmet will have an integrated oxygen system, projected display on the visor, a GPS receiver and a communications transceiver. Problem is; the projector lens or the visor surface keeps fogging up and the image goes south. Our contractors are finding it very difficult to design a HUD (Heads Up Display) like system that works at the altitudes, pressures, humidities and temperatures in which this system has to work.

"GPS is coming along nicely. We'll have an eight channel differential GPS chip in less than three years. That will allow us to put the GPS receiver in the top of the helmet, where it belongs, with optimal antenna orientation for both HALO and HAHO missions.

"So you're going to be a Navy test pilot – albeit civilian. Your dad would be damned proud of you Sam, once he got over the Navy thing. You'll do a damned good job too – welcome aboard."

Bo had to get back to El Centro that night – big meeting with Joe & the Admiral the next morning. But it was great to see him again since the older I got the more he became the only father I could remember. I started to worry about his job.

Chapter Twelve

Max Horte's Mountain Villa
Southeast of Mazatlan Mexico
Tuesday, November 20 1984

Max Horte's servant, Valentin Hillo (he-yo) was busy disposing of another vehicle and body. It had been almost a year since Max had needed to invoke the service of his nail gun. This poor bastard had nearly pulled the nail heads through his hands before Max was able to inject an additional nail into each. Then he let him sit there for over an hour before he finished the deed.

The villa sat on a mountainside plateau which was about half way up the mountain, about eight hundred feet above the valley below and about twenty miles from the western coast of Mexico as the crow flies. The private road approaching the villa was crushed rock with several switchbacks and many washouts due to a lack of proper drainage. To the southwest of the villa was a gorge cut by the river that eventually came through the valley leading to Horte's villa. A hundred yards to the southwestern side of the villa the woods at that end of the plateau ended suddenly at the edge of the gorge and there was about a five hundred foot nearly vertical cliff where the river made a sharp bend far below. Max had a path cleared just wide enough to drive a vehicle through the woods to a point just above the cliff. This is where Max dumped his dead (or sometimes almost dead) enemies and former employees. Valentin figured this was number nineteen, but he wasn't absolutely sure. Somewhere around twelve he thought he might have lost count – what did it matter anyway?

The approach to the villa was heavily guarded although it would be hard to detect any of the defenses Horte had set up. After turning off the two lane dirt road, just a hundred yards up the poorly maintained access drive and sitting about fifty feet up the hillside to the left was a well camouflaged observation post with a clear view of the first 200 feet of the driveway. This post was always manned, although both visible light and infrared cameras kept constant visage over the road. A friend, enemy, intruder or sightseer would never be stopped at this point but the observer would alert the villa, re-run the video tape for digital copy at the villa and await instructions. About two thirds of the way up to the villa the road turned straight up the mountain for about 200 feet. This section was crudely paved to allow enough traction for most vehicles to climb the steep slope. This was Max's killing zone. He had two bunkers, again well camouflaged, one on each side of the road at the top of the zone with a manned thirty caliber machine gun in each. If he gave the command, the vehicle and its occupants would be obliterated.

Max's business was thriving. The Americans were developing a prosperity induced lust for drugs and Max had become the go-to man for many of the South Central and South American drug lords. He no longer took a cut of the value of the drugs he transported to the U.S.; he had moved from an outsourced transport function to a partnership – of sorts.

Max Horte had eight major transportation fronts to "legally" move tons of "illegal" drugs into the United States. One each in Honolulu Hawaii, Juno Alaska, Portland Maine, Chula Vista California, Charlotte North Carolina, Memphis Tennessee, Evansville Indiana and Denver Colorado. His technical staff, two PhD chemists whose names were Alberto and John, engineered a method for chemically "hiding" cocaine in a raw naphthalene product during its manufacturing process. Naphthalene is a coal tar derivative and the primary ingredient in mothballs. Max manufactured a version of Naphthalene that contained 21.5% cocaine by weight yet retained all the same physical and most of the chemical characteristics of naphthalene. This product was shipped to his processing plants in the U.S. where it was chemically processed to yield a variety of products for dozens of downstream manufacturers including three types of insecticide, gasoline additives, five varieties of cosmetic product additives, eleven polymer components, mothballs and of course cocaine, which itself was then processed into five varieties of street drugs by the distribution labs in the U.S.. The process itself was pretty foolproof. It would take a very sharp chemist who knew exactly what he was looking for to find the cocaine in the naphthalene and no dog would ever risk his olfactory assets on the raw material. Even humans couldn't stand the smell.

Max now bought the drugs directly from the cartels at 38% of the 'off-the-dock' price he sold them for in the states. The drug lords were happy because Max eliminated most of their 30% attrition rate at the border and the additional cost of implementing their own, usually not so successful, transportation strategies. And why shouldn't he get this kind of margin? He was the one with the operations in the U.S.; operating right under the noses of the DEA and other government organizations like the FBI, Coast Guard and ATF. His primary risk was internal betrayal, hence the nail gun.

Chapter Thirteen

San Diego Naval Air Station
Officer's Club
Monday, June 24, 1985, 9:05 p.m. PDT

After completing four AGM-88 (HARM) integration test suites at China Lake and Ben having brought on another pilot so he could spare me the time, I spent twelve grueling weeks, starting in January, at the Naval Aviation Officers Candidate School, Pensacola Naval Air Station, Florida. Then I was commissioned as a Lieutenant (O-3).

****

"When I started this gig I thought a 'test flight' meant up at 6 a.m., climb in my A-7, fly up to China Lake (NWC), stick the missile on the bird and be on the Edwards range by 9, make some runs on some classified radar sets and be home by 5 – no later than 6," I complained to my new friend and fellow test pilot, Lieutenant Jimmy Clayton. "Nobody told me I'd be spending so much time at China Lake, and all the crap involved in one lousy test flight. I'm lucky if I don't have to spend the whole week up there. The VOQ stinks compared to the one down here and I just got my new apartment near the beach in La Jolla (la-hoy-ya) – something's got to change!"

"Cool it man, things'll get better. Lieutenant Commander Dickerson and his crew report to Captain Johnson. You're still the newbie and they don't want you to fuck up – looks bad for them. That's why they want a lot of your work done up there, like pre & post test flight reports. You didn't grow up in the Navy and they want to see standard Navy crap going to the Group Commander. Don't fight it – get it right. Then they'll loosen the reigns and you'll get your freedom."

"Yeah, I guess you're right. I hadn't thought of it like that," I said as

I held up two fingers to the waitress as her eyes passed us on her bar room scan. "One more beer and I've got to go. Who's the looker with the geek at the table behind us?"

Jimmy got up for a trip to the head. When he came back he informed me, "That's Ashleigh Garrison. She's a lieutenant, flight instructor, basic jet, T-38. Nice gal, good lookin', fun lovin', serious Navy, but I guess I'm not her type. We had a couple of dates but nothing came of it – want me to introduce you?"

"Yes, but not now – I've really got to scram. I'll put the beers on my tab – you can buy next time."

****

China Lake Naval Weapons Center is located smack dab in the middle of the Mojave Desert. Right across the street was the sometimes sleepy little town of Ridgecrest California. A few decent places to eat, some seedy motels and some of the nicest, most down-to-earth people you'd ever want to meet. Many of them worked for Texas Instruments, the only major contractor (that I knew of) in town. Last summer, on my first trip to Edwards AFB, we landed at China Lake & met the crew there. Ben wanted me to get some technical understanding of the HARM (AGM-88) system so he arranged a two hour tour of the nearby TI facility which lasted almost four hours. One of the TI experts, Jason Robins, gave me a one hour presentation on the system, its successes, which were many, and its problems, which were few. I had no idea our smart missiles were smarter than me, or any human for that matter. The amount and accuracy of the information passing between the seeker computer in the missile and the avionics computer in the aircraft was amazing. And the guidance and decision making power of the post-launch missile gave me goose bumps. That was when I began to understand why my engineering background was going to be important to the program and also when I had made the decision to do the OCS thing and join the Navy.

****

Over the past year I found the TI crew to be great folks who were absolutely dedicated to the Harm program. More than once it had crossed my mind that that was partially because there wasn't much else to do in

ANGELS THREE FIVE

Ridgecrest California. I was accepted as one of the team right away and over time became tightly integrated into the TI HARM team – even got invited to a Fourth of July pig roast at Travis James' house. Travis was a single engineer with a house meant for partying. I told him I'd try to make it and asked if I could bring a date.

Chapter Fourteen

Greater Downtown Inyokern Airport
FBO Flight Office
Thursday, July 4, 1985, 11:00 a.m. PDT

Jimmy did introduce me to Ashleigh several nights later when we all happened to be having our end-of-the-day ritual beer at the O Club. She was with her geek friend again who happened to be the other basic jet instructor on base. It took me about five seconds to determine that there was no romantic involvement between them. So I invited Ashleigh to the pig roast at Travis' house. During our conversation she referred to me as a 'sailor' and I admitted that I'd spent very little time near the water and most of that was at the beach.

"But," I told her, "I do have a hundred or so hours in gliders, so I guess you're not too far off base calling me a sailor."

With a sparkle in her eyes she said, "I've always wanted to fly a glider, but never had the chance."

That's how we ended up at Inyokern Airport (IYK – the jewel of the Mohave Desert) on the morning of the fourth. A couple of the TI guys belonged to a glider club at IYK, about fifteen miles northwest of Ridgecrest, and I arranged a rental with tow for noon on the fourth. I asked Ben if there was any way I could use one of the T-38s to make the trip since I had to be up there on the 5th anyway and I was using the China Lake A-7 for the flight tests.

He looked at me as if I'd just lost my mind and said, "You can't take a civilian in a Navy aircraft without paperwork!"

"Don't need paperwork; she's a flight instructor here at the base."

"Ashleigh Garrison? You're taking Ashleigh Garrison to a contractor's pig roast?

"Sure, go ahead, she can bring my plane back and you can hitch a ride home," Johnson replied with a fading look of surprise. "Be sure you pay for whatever you eat and drink – both you and Lt. Garrison and get a receipt."

We climbed into a brand new two seat, retractable engine, sail plane built in Austria. I had never flown a glider with an engine. The guy that ran the club said the small two-stroke engine with two gallons of gas weighed less than 40 pounds and though it cost more to rent you saved the price of a tow and didn't have to get an additional tow if you wanted to fly longer. The price for this aircraft for two hours was just a little more than a conventional glider for two hours with two tows. I was an easy sell.

"Ready to go up there?" I said in a voice slightly louder than normal – we didn't rent the intercom which came separately.

"Why don't you take it up, then I'll give it a try – remember, I've never flown one of these things."

Both cockpits had a small convex mirror on the left side of the instrument panel and I could see the smile on her face expand as we headed down the runway and into the air. When we got to twenty five hundred feet I said, "Want to do a loop?"

She said, "Go ahead."

The engine was extremely easy to operate. There was a throttle looking thing that was there just to make a pilot feel at home. If you pushed it forward the engine popped out right behind the aft cockpit and started up at half speed. About 20 seconds later, after warming up, it went to full throttle and stayed there until you pulled the throttle back at which time the engine throttled back to half speed for about 20 seconds, then stopped and retracted – a simple switch would have worked just as well.

So I pulled the throttle back, waited for the engine to shut down and retract, lowered the nose and then began my loop. A good loop in a sail plane is about one and a quarter g when vertical, about three quarters g on top and about one and a half g on the bottom. Mine was pretty decent but not perfect. I traded some speed for altitude and asked, "Want to try one?"

"Sure."

She lowered her nose and entered the loop about twenty miles per hour faster than I did. We came out of the loop at about 2 g, after one of the best loops I'd experienced in a glider. I could tell; this lady was going to be tough on my aeronautical ego. "Not to worry," I thought, "I don't have much of an aeronautical ego."

"Your stick - let's go find some thermals," I said as I watched her smile in the mirror.

In the Mojave Desert, thermals are not hard to find. We climbed to five thousand feet outside the cylindrical controlled airspace around the airport and then headed directly over the control area ceiling where the hot air rising from all the airport's concrete and cleared desert land provides excellent thermals. At ten thousand feet we just started having fun.

Ashleigh turned out to be one hell of a pilot. If I ever had an aeronautical ego it was now shot to hell. It was obvious she was having the time of her life and I was just happy to watch her be happy. We overran our two hours so I called the club to see if we could do a little overtime. When we (she) landed we were thirty minutes late. We pulled the glider up to the hangar, I paid for the extra time and we headed to Travis' house for an evening of food and fun.

When we got there the party was in full swing. Fourth of July in the desert. People milling around; some playing golf on Travis' five hole, par two course. Others settled into conversation around myriad tables, or stood in line for the variety of craft beers being drawn from six pony kegs or for a variety of California wines poured from three liter bottles.

At 5:15 p.m. two fire trucks pulled up in front of the house and about six guys and girls bailed out of each. Travis' uncle was the Ridgecrest Fire Chief and, of course, a permit was required for fireworks in the desert and a manned fire truck with adequate brush fire equipment had to be present. Obviously, two trucks were better than one and Travis let the firefighters in free. Travis told me there would be more trucks and firemen/women if there were any more – we were looking at the entire fire department. I asked him about the cost of the evening and he told me it was twenty five dollars a head. I gave him a fifty and he said he'd get me a receipt – he was aware of our 'pay your own way' policy and reporting requirement.

I met Dick Granger, the TI Facility Manager. It didn't take me long to see why his people worked so hard and accomplished so much. His people skills fit the environment like a glove. The TI Ridgecrest organization had a long line of on-budget and on-schedule very successful programs – mostly through the Navy at the Naval Weapons

Center, China Lake. They called themselves the "desert rats."

The pulled pork and southwestern cuisine was as good as it gets and then there was the fireworks – what a night! Of course it didn't hurt that I had the most beautiful lady at the shindig on my arm for most of the evening. My attitude had definitely adjusted itself for the better and I was evidently beginning to fall for Ashleigh Garrison. But then I warned myself; "that'll probably wear off, as usual. . . "

Chapter Fifteen

Drug Enforcement Administration Office
Washington, D.C.
Friday, July 5, 1985, 11:00 a.m. EDT

The Washington D.C. office of the DEA was pretty much like all the other regional offices spread over the United States, but it was not a national headquarters. The Special Agents at this office, however, were closely tied to the political objectives of the administration. A small group of analysts at this office had been gathering data over the past eight years trying to show the improvement in drug interdiction since the implementation of the administration in 1973. Their problem was that there had been no improvement. In fact, the problem had gotten much worse and seemed to be accelerating out of control. Where were the drugs coming from?

The senior analyst, Bob McFadden, got funding in the 1983 DEA budget to look for 'undiscovered methods for the transport of illegal chemical substances into the United States'. To date the drug interdiction focus of the Administration had been on the southern border and the entire coastline of the U.S. from Main to Washington State with primary emphasis on the southeastern and southwestern areas. They knew they couldn't find and confiscate all the drugs coming across the border but with the knowledge they had gained about the operation of the cartels, their ability to successfully find and confiscate a significant portion of the drugs coming into the country and with their continued injection of technology and upgraded operational strategies and tactics, the DEA thought they were stopping at least 20% of the illicit trade and that number was rising. In other words, it appeared that they were slowly winning the war on drugs.

The first phase of this study was to accurately define the quantity of drugs being consumed in the continental U.S. At a little over a year into this first phase they began to realize the magnitude of their error. The numbers were telling them that the consumption was actually at least five times their previous estimates. This meant that if their latest interdiction data were correct they were stopping only 4% of the national consumption. But this wasn't the only surprise. As they began the second phase of the program; tracing the drugs from the consumer back to the out-of-country supplier they found a large number of routes that didn't match up with their previous data. The obvious conclusion was that there were huge drug routes that they new nothing about. They weren't winning the war on drugs – they were losing it, big time.

"My God, someone is pumping drugs into this country through a pretty big pipe, or network of pipes," said McFadden to two of his senior agents, Ivan Brankovich and Charlie Stormer.

"We need to firm up this data, make sure of our findings and go get some more funding and people. We've got to find this pipeline and shut it off! I'll call a meeting of the director and all district directors and set up a secure video conference," said McFadden, as he tossed a chewed-up cigar into the trash. "Charlie, we need better commitment from the districts. We need serious focus on this job right *now*, damn-it! We can't wait for more money and people; we need a better corporate understanding of this mess ASAP. There's got to be some sort of scheme that hides the drugs in some commodity that is routinely shipped into this country without much oversight. We caught 'em shipping porcelain figurines full of coke and a dozen other similar schemes over the last two years, but this has to be much bigger than that."

"Ivan, crunch the data, tweak the models and do whatever it takes for us to understand more about how this stuff's getting in here and where it's coming from. We're losing it folks! We've got to get our own people refocused on the larger problem. Don't worry about making waves or ruffling feathers, when the man upstairs understands what we're about to tell him, he'll be pissed, but he'll pull out the stops on getting the resources we need. Damn-it, we will prevail in this effort and we will catch those slimy bastards and string 'em up by their nuts!"

Chapter Sixteen

Officer's Club, Naval Air Station
San Diego, California
Saturday, July 6, 1985, 7:23 p.m. PDT

Well, this thing with Ashleigh definitely wasn't wearing off. We had a quick breakfast at the O Club the morning after Travis' pig roast and made a date for tonight at 7:30 for dinner here at the O Club and then a little night clubbing afterward.

I had ordered our drinks and the waitress was just bringing them when Ashleigh slid into the booth next to me, smiling that smile that was keeping me awake nights.

She said, "Hello sailor."

"Hello to you gorgeous," I smiled back. "Did you like the sailing?"

"I thought I loved flying jets but flying with no power trumps it all. I had a great time, let's do it again sometime."

"I have an uncle that's in Special Forces Weapons Development at El Centro. He belongs to a glider club there on base. It's closer than China Lake and we could go weekend after next if you're free." I didn't want to take anything for granted.

Her baby blue eyes flashed through her killer smile, "I'd love to – can I meet your uncle too?"

"Actually he owns his own single-seater and if he's not busy I'm sure he'll want to go play with us. I'll call him tomorrow and let you know."

This little lady was really getting under my skin. About five foot four, perfect figure, closely cropped and lightly streaked blonde hair and that smile that amplified her beauty by 10X. Just looking at her raised my heartbeat from my normal 60 to about 90. Sitting next to her was like running the first mile of a marathon. Second date and I was hooked. My problem now was keeping cool until I earned her respect.

"I'm go for the flight," she said, still smiling, as I realized another thing I liked about her – we both spoke the same crazy pilot lingo. This girl was way too easy to fall in love with.

"Great, I'll make some calls and see if I can get everything set up. You mind staying at the VOQ? It's better than the one at China Lake."

"It's good by me. How's the gliding over there?"

"Don't know, never flown there. But it's at the bottom of Death Valley and sailing on desert thermals is almost always good."

We decided to order only appetizers and another drink here, and then have dinner at Harry's downtown, great food, great bar and live entertainment. One-stop-fun.

The dinner at Harry's was fabulous, and the country band was prone to my kind of music, slow and romantic. The female singer was comfortable all the way from *Blue Eyes Crying in the Rain* to *Cotton Eyed Joe.* We danced and had a few more drinks and then decided to drive up to the beach near La Jolla to a stretch we both liked but had never been to together, and take a moonlight stroll along the beach so we could talk and actually hear each other.

It was a beautiful southern California evening. If you get far enough from L.A. the skies are really clear. The sea was calm except for the occasional set of rollers coming from some distant boat. A few puffy clouds drifting along, dying in the cool evening breeze and the moon was just peeking over the mountains to the east. We talked about almost everything; the Navy, flying, her family, my family, future plans, travels, places we wanted to go. The more we talked the more I felt a building attachment to this pint sized bombshell of a woman who could fly better than me and was probably smarter than me; whose eyes and smile put me into some kind of trance. This was getting serious – for me at least.

She told me she had an older brother who was a senior agent and southwestern area director for the DEA and although he lived in Escondido, just a few miles north of Miramar Naval Air Station, she hardly ever saw him. Her parents lived in Pasadena. Her father, a retired Navy Captain (go figure), her mother, a semi-retired pediatric cardiologist. But, she said that although her whole family conveniently lived in southern California, they rarely got together as a family.

We walked about a mile up to the rocks at the mid point of the beach which were navigable on the water side at low tide but impossible without great effort at high tide. We sat on an outcropping about eight feet above the beach and continued our conversation. Ashleigh told me she had been married before – right out of high school.

"Bad decision," she said, looking wistfully at the sea. "We were just kids full of dumb ideas. I thought I was in love – I thought he was too. I don't know what he really thought but it didn't take long to figure out we weren't operating in the same universe. We were separated before our first anniversary and divorced before a year and a half. I joined the Navy, did a tour as crew on a P3-Orion, went to school, got an engineering degree, OCS, flight school, T-38 instructor, yada, yada, yada.

"I wanted you to know this for two reasons; first, I'm beginning to think about you a lot more than I probably should - and I don't want to pretend to be someone I'm not. I've done a few stupid things in my life and that was the biggest. Second, the stupid things I've done have taught me to try hard to not make the same mistake twice, so I tend to be maybe a little too suspicious of men that I like. That's why the Navy's a good place to be – most of the men want the same thing and it has nothing to do with commitment. You might be different, I don't know yet."

"Yeah, I'm different. We've known each other, what, a little over two weeks now? It's been the most remarkable and perplexing two weeks of my life. I don't know what effect you're having on me, but I don't want it to stop. You're the first woman I've known that makes me want to behave like a gentleman, not like an animal and that's probably a good thing - but I'm not sure, 'cause I've never been here before."

It was my turn to reveal my past, which didn't take very long. I told her all about Bo and my mother, dad and Jameson Flight Service and how I got to be a Navy test pilot. What I didn't tell her was that I was falling head over heels in love with her.

As we reached the beach after climbing down from our perch she grabbed my other hand and we kissed after which she smiled that smile, her eyes twinkling in the light of a full moon that was now almost directly overhead. As we walked back to my car at the other end of the beach we vowed that we'd take this thing slowly – then kissed again, long and wet. This was our first show of affection for each other. My thoughts turned to how two Navy pilots could survive life together. There were a lot of obstacles.

Chapter Seventeen

Drug Enforcement Administration Office
Washington, D.C.
Friday, July 19, 1985, 08:07 a.m. EDT

Bob McFadden had been a busy man. He held secure video conferences with the national and district DEA Directors on the 8th and 15th of July. After he filled them in on the validity of the data and the magnitude of problem he asked for ideas from the directors. The first meeting didn't yield any likely answers but it motivated a team of the country's most experienced drug interdiction experts to begin a very serious search for the answer that would ultimately eliminate this national threat.

Bob was certain now, after searching for two weeks for the most likely methods of bringing ten metric tons of cocaine into the United States every week, that they were looking for some sort of scheme that 'hid' the drugs in a common product routinely imported into the U.S. The DEA had spent large sums of the US taxpayer's money using x-ray and other non-intrusive technology to look 'through' various suspected products imported from certain countries and had found and disabled several fairly sophisticated schemes to get drugs into the U.S. So he was reasonably certain that they were looking for some bona fide manufacturing business that imported raw materials with cocaine somehow hidden in it to be processed into a product or products within the U.S. Then after the cocaine was separated during the process it could be shipped by normal methods throughout the country. And, he feared that the ten ton number was understated by a factor of two, maybe three.

This meant that the drug use in the US was at least three times the amount the DEA had postulated during its studies performed over the past three years - prior to their current consumption study. These older studies were based on trafficking, not actual use. If this were true it meant serious trouble for the country, the DEA and of course that included McFadden and his team.

During the second meeting on the 15th McFadden proposed developing a list of likely operations to investigate and then devising a stealth method to perform an 'inspection' of the operation. When he got agreement from the directors, he informed them that his team had already developed such a list that he would forward it to them with a request to review, comment and add to the list. He also suggested that each regional team find a method suitable for infiltration of each suspect operation with the intent of discovering illegal drug activity. He also suggested that where an operation involved food, food ingredients or legal drugs, the 'inspector' take on the identity of a Food and Drug Administration (FDA) agent making a routine inspection. And, if food or legal drugs were not involved, then the use of an Occupational Safety and Health Administration (OSHA) identity should be used. In both cases samples of product at various process stages could be obtained for lab analysis.

McFadden's list contained ninety three facilities involved in processing raw materials which his team suspected might be used to 'hide' cocaine. And the list was growing daily.

Chapter Eighteen

El Centro Naval Air Station
El Centro, California
Saturday, July 20, 1985 PDT

I picked Ashleigh up at 8:00 at her place and we headed for El Centro, stopping only to grab a quick breakfast at the Denny's just off IH-8 in El Cajon. We met Bo at the El Centro O Club for coffee and a briefing on what to expect on the afternoon flight we were looking forward to.

As we exchanged pleasantries, I could see that Bo was affected by Ashleigh's charm and beauty much as I was. Hell, who wouldn't be? She was the most amazing woman I had ever met. I gave Bo the hands off evil eye and got a smile in return. As Ashleigh headed for the rest room Bo said, "Uh-oh Sam, she looks like a keeper – I'm thinkin' you're in way over your head bud, and you might even be a little out-classed."

"Yeah, I think I've already swallowed the hook. We're both pretty realistic about the future though – we're not rushing into anything, just having fun.

"What's the agenda for the weekend?" I asked wanting to change the subject.

"Thought we'd tour the ridges this afternoon. We don't have any of those fancy powered gliders here so we'll have to get a tow. Usually, you can go all afternoon on a two thousand foot tow. I reserved a two seater for you two, I'll fly my own. We'll get airborne right after lunch. Did she get any stick time on your last flight?"

"She flew the whole two and a half hours minus take-off, climb out and one loop – maybe fifteen minutes. She's a damned good pilot – maybe better'n me," I said, not wanting to openly admit that I thought she was.

"On a different note, I just got Jim's monthly report for June. He's hired two new pilots, one young instructor/banner pilot and a full time charter pilot with a resume as long as your arm. The charter pilot lives in Manhattan and Jim has the Cherokee Arrow hangared up there for his use since most of our charters are originating from Manhattan. June broke the record for revenue for the third month in a row. He wants to buy a used Cessna 310, hangar it in Manhattan and bring the Arrow home – what do you think?"

"I'd say go for it, he's got everything paid for and 200K plus in the bank. I can't think of a bad business decision he's ever made – can you?"

"Nope, that's what I thought you'd say. I'll call him and tell him to get on with it."

Ashleigh came back and we settled in for some coffee and chit-chat before we ordered lunch.

We got our tows up to 2000 feet and began looking for thermals. We followed Bo since I figured he knew where they were and sure enough before we had lost 400 feet we began spiraling upward at 250 feet per minute. At 7000 feet our rate of climb was down to about 75 feet per minute when Bo called on the radio.

"See those ridges over there to the east? When we get to 7500 feet we'll make a nice and easy run over there. Sometimes you can find an elevator up to 12,000 along those ridges. If everything works out we can play over there all afternoon and get back on a single run."

And play we did. I hadn't ever had this much fun in a glider. We looped and rolled, did chandelles, lazy-8s, spins and even a few hammer-head stalls. Ashleigh did something I'd never done – she called it a topside loop. Actually it was a split- S into a loop followed by an Immelmann at the top to get right side up again. In non-fly-talk; roll the plane over on its back and enter a loop from the topside, complete the loop and roll right-side-up when you get back where you started from. We made two trips up that thermal and then moved over to another one that was a little closer to the airport. Two more trips up this elevator and we were done for the day – time to head back to the barn.

Bo had made reservations at Al's, a steakhouse on the outskirts of El Centro proper. During dinner we talked about the airport business, the Cessna 310 and new charter pilot Jim hired. Jameson Flight Service was on a steady revenue incline with no debt not counting the $60,000 loan Jim needed to buy the $300,000 C-310, and about Bo's job – at least as much as he could talk about.

Ashleigh talked a little about her older brother, Mark. She was becoming concerned about his job. He was the Director of the Southwest District of the U.S. Drug Enforcement Administration and his elevated stress level was noticeable even over the phone. She said she was sure something was going on in the DEA and that Mark probably couldn't talk about it.

Desert nights are cool and beautiful. Stars you've never seen before fill the sky. After dinner Ashleigh and I walked around the base and talked for about an hour. I think we both knew what lay ahead for the two of us – the love we shared for one another, the difficulties we might encounter due to our jobs and the lack of control we ultimately had over our future. But we both had a positive outlook on whatever happened in the future so there was no discussion about any of our problems being insurmountable or even stressful.

As I lay in bed that night thinking about Ashleigh there was a light knock on the door to my room. . . I said a little prayer of thanks that my O-3 rating warranted a double bed at the El Centro VOQ.

Chapter Nineteen

Albright Chemical Company
Chula Vista, California
Monday, July 22, 1985, 9:04 a.m. PDT

Tony Fescola brought the meeting to order after asking everyone to be seated. This was the Albright Chemical Company's monthly review of operations during which the various departments reported on production volumes, shortages, sales, scrap, gross revenue, expenses, profit margins and operational issues.

The company produced six primary products and eight secondary products. The six major products were asphalt, fertilizer, solvents, insecticide, plasticizers (all profitable byproducts of naphthalene) and what the company called process slag. The latter product was actually 99.9% pure cocaine which had been chemically combined with pure naphthalene at a petroleum distillery near Mazatlan Mexico. The secondary products were moth balls, skin products, dyes, wetting agents and a variety of polymer byproducts.

The "process slag" was removed in the first step of the production process and comprised 21.5% by weight of the gross. This "slag" was immediately packaged and stored for shipment to "other companies for further processing." Only three people at Albright Chemical knew what the "slag" was; Tony Fescola, the president and CEO, Frederico Alverez, the decomposition process manager and Miguel Guerrero, who was responsible for packing and shipping the 'slag' to distribution points all over the U.S. The slag recovery process consisted of a software modification to the automated vacuum distilling tower originally used for the decomposition of naphthalene into the five 'useful' byproducts. This modification added a new and separate process step at the very beginning to remove the "slag" (cocaine). The tower was about the size of two 55 gallon drums stacked on top of each other with a six inch pipe housing a condensing system attached near the top. Each of the six serial process steps was performed quickly and accurately by computer control of vacuum, heat, and other process parameters resulting in a close to 100% recovery of each of the six components. The cocaine was then packed into small 15.5 gallon steel pony kegs similar to those used for beer with an air tight sealing lid. Once sealed the containers were thoroughly washed in a mild acid solution to remove any trace of cocaine and a standard Albright Chemical Company label was added listing the contents as "Naphthalene Byproducts." The shipments were made through normal carriers to chemical distribution warehouses throughout the country where the 'customer' could order delivery of the product only by pre-payment directly to an off-the-Albright-books shadow company.

There were seven other similar naphthalene processing plants strategically located throughout the U.S. to enable the distribution of product and to provide the necessary low profile operation and avoid scrutiny from any potential threat. Each of the eight plants were separate businesses, competing with each other, with from twenty seven to thirty four employees each. Each had only three members who were aware of the drug extraction end of the business. The eight CEOs reported directly to Max Horte. The other employees reported to a process manager who reported to their respective CEO. And, of course each company was owned by Max Horte. Each CEO participated in quarterly meetings at Horte's villa, each was acutely aware of the loyalty requirement and each was paid very well. If any of the CEO's suspected disloyalty of one of the first step process workers or knowledge of the first step process by any of the other workers, that person was invited to join the CEO at the next meeting at the villa. If that proved untimely an immediate meeting at the villa was arranged. There were at least eight of his former factory employees at the bottom of the gorge at the rear of his villa, Max recalled, but he couldn't remember – there might have been more - he'd have to check his records.

As the meeting proceeded each of the product managers presented an overview of his particular product responsibility from raw material acquisition to receipt of payment, with a profit analysis for the period. This was a real business selling real products and making real profits. The naphthalene based products provided a typical profit margin of eight to ten percent above all operating expenses. And, of course, the books reflected exactly that. The first step of the process typically reported two to three percent profit since their product was that part of the raw material that they deemed not profitable enough to process and was therefore sold off to others who could make use of it. In reality, the first step always generated nearly twelve thousand percent profit margin on Max's 'other set of books'. . .

Maximillion Horte started this business with the then existing Chula Vista plant in 1975. Fescola and Alverez had been "recruited" into Max's organization because they had the necessary process, business and market knowledge to not only continue the business successfully but also to train other of Max's leaders to take over the future acquisitions he planned to make. He bought four of his competitors in the 1978-81 time frame and built the last three plants over the last four years. He maintained separation by "giving" the individual businesses to his most trusted comrades. Only the CEOs and the front end process managers knew of the tie at the top.

* * * *

Fescola gathered the data from his monthly operations review and summarized it into the quarterly presentation he would make at Horte's villa the following week.

When Tony returned from that meeting he was approached by Frederico Alverez asking for a private meeting.

"Hey boss, we might have a problem," Freddy said as Tony closed the door. "We got a notice from the Food and Drug Administration asking us to schedule a 'routine' process inspection. You were in Mexico so Anna gave it to me – three days ago. What do we do that the FDA should be interested in?"

"Relax Freddy. We make some compounds that go into skin products and some polymers that are used in drug and food products. Schedule it out at least two weeks – we'll have to clean up the front end, remove the slag process step from the controller and move the packaging machine off-site. Then we'll just run the process using pure naphthalene. That's why we keep ten barrels of the pure stuff in the back. I've got the label serial numbers in my safe. This'll cost us three days of production; one to clean up, one for the inspection and one to get back into normal operation. I'll let Max know about the situation."

"Ok Boss, when I get the inspection scheduled I want to walk through all the steps with you so we don't have any screw-ups. Man, I don't like the idea of Feds snooping around here."

"The important thing, Freddy, is to go over the downstream process with a fine tooth comb so they don't find any process problems we need to fix and then have re-inspected. Every inspection costs us three days in production which is a little over a million bucks to Max."

Chapter Twenty

Home of Frederico Alverez

South Chula Vista, California

Sunday, August, 18, 1985 PDT

"Daddy, that's not fair! All my friends are going and they all have dates. It's just a pool party and Janie's parents will be there. You've met Tim – he's a nice boy. I'm almost thirteen – I'm not a baby any more."

"We'll talk to your Mother when she gets back," Alverez scoffed at his too beautiful, too free spirited, too mature, twelve year old daughter, "You're too young to date. Supervised pool parties are ok, dating's not."

"Daddy, you're too old fashioned, Mom'll understand," whined Sylvia Alverez, Freddy's oldest child.

Frederico Alverez wasn't in the mood to argue with his daughter. He had other things on his mind. Back in 1976 when he'd agreed to the offer made to him by Tony Fescola, who had already aligned himself with Max Horte, he was the plant foreman at Albright Chemical earning almost twenty thousand dollars a year. The offer for sixty thousand a year plus bonuses was overwhelming. He couldn't turn it down. But Freddy was a very smart man. He knew there would be a very real possibility that at some time in the future the system would be compromised. He devised a scheme to protect himself and his family. His salary was now one hundred and thirty two thousand a year, thirty two thousand on the Albright books and the rest on Max's books. Over the last nine years he had amassed 1.3 million dollars in off shore accounts and managed to live on his Albright income and his wife's part time nursing income. They owned a nice home in a nice area of Chula Vista.

Freddy had made careful notes and obtained several samples of the raw and finished 'product' of the cocaine operation which he kept in a lockbox at a bank at which he did not have an account. He planned to use this detailed knowledge of the operation only if he began to suspect its demise. Although the FDA inspection had gone fairly well, Freddy had become even more suspicions about why a federal agency, strapped for funds, would waste its time on an upstream chemical company that produced only a few bi-products that had anything to do with food or legal drugs. The inspector had, what appeared to Freddy, valid credentials, although he had never before seen the ID of an FDA inspector. Freddy's primary concern stemmed more from the fact that the inspector was more interested in the process than the cleanliness and sanitation procedures of the facility. Also, he took samples from each stage of the chemical process and checked the paperwork on the raw material and processing chemicals. When the inspector left, apparently satisfied with the inspection, Freddy was much more suspicious than when he had arrived.

Freddy's plan had always been predicated on an exit strategy that would insure the safety and well being of himself and his family – perhaps it was time to pull the trigger. He thought about his wife, his twelve year old daughter and his nine year old son. What would be the impact on each of them if he deployed his exit plan? After rethinking his plan carefully he once again concluded that if executed properly, the net impact on his family would be positive. He had to move quickly, carefully and with fearless determination. And, he had to do it now!

Chapter Twenty One

El Centro Naval Air Station
El Centro, California
Monday, August, 19, 1985 PDT

Bo Jameson slammed the phone down against its cradle. He was pissed. Another delay in delivery of the redesigned visor system. This was going to push out the delivery of version one of the Advanced Integrated HALO/HAHO System by six months. Even by shortening the final integration tests of the visor system three months by testing all other subsystems before final integration they would now be looking at mid-86 for deployment. "This program," Bo thought to himself, "is really snake-bit."

He reached for the phone, dreading the call to Captain Joe Garcia – he didn't want to actually see the look on Garcia's face even though his office was just next door. But the phone rang just before he got to it. He answered.

"Bo, got some possible good news for you."

He recognized Don Campbell's voice immediately.

"I could use some good news for a change, whatcha got?"

"I just got permission to talk to you about this – it's friggin' unbelievable how uncooperative the different government organizations are with each other, and it's not just the military.

"Anyway, we just successfully tested the first integrated GPS system. It's a six channel set with damned good, but classified accuracy and it can be easily ruggedized to greater than thirty g's static and 200 g's for a 3 milliseconds peak. Fits on four square inches with a one dimension minimum of one inch. Uses a 2.4 inch antenna encased in a quarter inch fiberglass tube. This set will far exceed all of your specs that I've been given. And it works with the new differential system.

"The owner is a classified spook organization. I finally talked them into opening this up to some Special Forces programs to offset some of their deployment costs. Bo, their specs are almost identical to, but tighter than yours. I can get you read-in to the program if you still hold your TSEB (Top Secret Extended Background) clearance. What-say?

"Hold on a second Don, I'm just gathering my body parts off the floor. What's the price and when can I get it?"

"What's your GPS budget?"

"200K"

"That's the price. I can deliver five units in three months if you don't change the 1 by 4 inch layout very much."

"What's the output format?"

"ASCII latitude-longitude every thirty milliseconds in UTM (Universal Transverse Mercator) or Spherical – your choice, which I'd bet is spherical for your application."

"What's the power draw?"

"Sixty two milliamps at five volts."

"Sign me up for five units in three months. When can I come to Dallas to have a look-see?"

"Soon as I get your clearance – you'll have to get read-in at the Pentagon – these spooks are super paranoid. I'll have our security guys send you the read-in meeting details on a secure line. We're back in business, Bo."

"You just made my day, brother. I'll be at your place as soon as I'm legal."

Chapter Twenty Two

DEA Southwestern Division Headquarters
San Diego, California
Wednesday, August, 21, 1985

Mark Garrison, the senior agent in charge of the DEA's Southwestern Division was meeting with the four agents he had assigned to inspect manufacturing facilities form Bob McFadden's list of suspects in his area. The agents had made two inspections each using DEA IDs that had been modified to emulate FDA IDs. Mark Garrison had been told by McFadden that what they were doing was normally illegal, but that a court order had been issued at "the highest level" allowing us to proceed.

Four of the facilities had been over-the-counter drug manufacturing companies, two had been prescription drug manufacturing companies and two had been chemical companies manufacturing products that were used in the food industry. All of the inspections had produced "unremarkable results" and Garrison held in his hand the report on the seventy three samples taken from each process step of each product manufactured by the eight companies.

"Nada, a big fat zero. We got nothing from all this work," grumbled Garrison. "And we've got nineteen more facilities on our list and McFadden says the list is growing. I sure as hell hope this isn't a wild goose chase."

"You know boss, I've been thinkin' a lot about what we're doin' here and it makes sense to me. We've suspected for several years now that there's some kinda underground river of coke comin' into this country that we didn't know about and this could be it," drawled Bud Nichols, one of Garrison's best 'old tough guys'.

"Oh, it makes sense alright, but we need the ability to pull surprise inspections to keep the bad guys from cleaning up their act temporarily.

The court order won't allow that. I'd like to put more agents on this but we're strapped for manpower as it is.

"So here's what we're going to do. Tighten up your inspection schedules. Let the plant manager know at noon that you'll be there at 8:00 the next morning or if they work shifts tell 'em you'll be there at the start of second shift. Don't give them time to change the process. Then watch the shipping docks for unusual behavior. We'll follow up with letters to the eight companies we've already inspected stating that one of the process samples we collected contained foreign material and that we will return at an unspecified date and time to collect another sample from that process to eliminate contamination in our lab as the source. Then we'll watch 'em again. I've been authorized overtime for this so don't hesitate to do whatever's required to find these guys. We are the second most likely region, after southern Florida to find the river Bud mentioned.

"Remember, we're talking ten, maybe twelve tons a week or more. Make a note of the capacity of each plant you visit. This is either one huge single operation or a number of smaller ones, probably owned by a parent company - but that link, if real, will probably be very well disguised.

"Let's get this done, guys – pull out all the stops!"

Chapter Twenty Three

La Jolla beach
La Jolla, California
Friday, August, 23, 1985, 8:30 p.m. PDT

After dinner and drinks at Harry's in downtown San Diego, Ashleigh and I decided to retreat to our favorite strip of beach to be alone. Things had progressed to the point that we both felt another heart to heart talk was in order. We'd known each other barely two months but to me it seemed like a year. Neither of us wanted to rush into anything. Our current situation seemed perfect, but we both wanted to know a little more about the other's expectations – no better place to talk than our favorite rock on our favorite beach on a clear night under the moon and stars.

"Bo pinged me yesterday about maybe coming over to El Centro to help them with their Special Forces project. He's got a major schedule glitch because one critical contractor is late and another one's early. The Harm testing is winding down and Captain Johnson won't really need me for several months. The good news is it's close to here and we'll still have weekends. But we need to realize that this is a potential problem that we'll probably have to face again at some time in the future. You want to move on to Hornets and will likely be deployed to an aircraft carrier. I'm just a techie test pilot. Ben gave me an eval last week. He's recommending me for a fast-track program to Lt. Commander. He said with continued outstanding performance, another year in-grade and an additional two year commitment, I could make Lieutenant Commander. He said that this is a rare opportunity and he'd have to get it approved by the selection board which includes Admiral Bennington. I think I'm gonna give it a shot – what do you think?"

"Sam, that's a great opportunity. I think you ought to go for it. I just got recommended for Lt. Commander last week, pending a new assignment – haven't gotten a chance to tell you 'til now. There are two openings coming up in the Top Gun school at Miramar late this year. Two of the senior pursuit pilot/instructors are retiring. Wouldn't it be great if we could both land a cushy job like that?"

"You know Ash, I'd love nothing more than being where you are and doing what you do, but we're both really good at different things. I am absolutely sure that you'll be selected for the job at Miramar – you're more than qualified for it. I, on the other hand, am more qualified for developing advanced SF systems and Bo really needs me. Everything will work itself out – it always does," I said, hoping I was right. . .

Chapter Twenty Four

East Lincoln Avenue
Anaheim, California
Sunday, August, 25, 1985, 2:45 p.m. PDT

Frederico Alverez parked his car two blocks south of an Amoco gas station on Lincoln Avenue in Anaheim and walked to the pay phone on the corner outside the station. He dialed a number and got a voice recorder, which he expected because it was Sunday and even the DEA didn't work on Sunday, at least not in their offices.

He left a message explaining that he had information about a drug operation that was importing "tons" of cocaine into the U.S. every day. He explained that he was very concerned about the welfare of himself and his family as well as several hundred innocent people who were involved without their knowledge. He said he would call the following Sunday at the same time to talk to the person in charge of the southern California area of the DEA to discuss ideas about how to safely eliminate this organization. And, we could call him Daniel.

Chapter Twenty Five

El Centro Naval Air Station
El Centro, California
Monday, August, 26, 1985, 7:30 a.m. PDT

I pulled into the small parking lot next to the Special Projects building at El Centro NAS and parked my new Corvette in the corner of the lot farthest from the few cars there. I told Bo I'd be there at eight and I was half an hour early. But I saw Bo's truck in the lot so I decided to head on in.

"Sam you're early. I thought the Navy would make a sluggard out of you – such an easy job and all."

"How's my favorite (and only) uncle? If you've got time I'd like to see what's going on over here, let you know how complicated my life's becoming and skedaddle on back to my real job."

"Anything, anytime for my favorite nephew, sit down – let's talk."

"What's going on over here and why would you need me?"

"We just got a shuffle in our delivery schedule. GPS is coming in almost a year ahead of when we expected it. So it looks like we'll only need to develop two successive models instead of three. That means a potential savings of about 1.8 million dollars in development costs plus whatever savings they get in logistics and training by eliminating a version deployment and upgrade costs. Could top 10 million. But we're going to need additional people to make that happen. Right now it looks like there would be a spot for you on the team until next April, June at the latest.

"This program is becoming more and more important to the Special Forces in all services. The CIA and the Joint Chiefs are pushing a two million dollar budget increase through Congress as we speak – spend two to save ten, not a bad deal."

Bo opened his mouth to continue but I cut him off; "Captain

Johnson is recommending me for a fast track program for promotion to Lt. Commander with an additional three year commitment. I didn't even know that anything like that was possible. Ashleigh wants me to go for it and I'm inclined to do so – what's your take?"

Bo's eyebrows shot up, "Lt. Commander? It took me nine years to get there – you've just barely been here one year."

"Yeah, but it'll be a year and a half more in-grade and including my civilian time, I'm close to seven thousand hours; that's more than most combat pilots. Experience counts for something, right? And besides, I've been working my butt off on the test job up at China Lake. We qualified the new HARM 88B on eleven aircraft, including two new U.S and three new NATO planes. Ben had me handling the technical reports as well as the flight reports. The TI site manager put two of his best engineers on site and we were solving problems over night. In my eval he told me he'd never had such a successful test program. If I don't fuck up, we'll be done in three weeks – that's three and a half months ahead of a schedule that was almost five months behind. He's happy with my work and I think he wants to give me a break and I damn well believe I deserve it!"

"Hey man, don't get defensive," Bo said under his signature grin, "I'm happy for you. I hope you take him up on it. Does this mean you won't be joining our little fun & games show here in the desert?"

"Not at all, that's why I'm here. I'll be finished up at China Lake in three weeks if my luck holds out on the last twelve flights. Ashleigh is going to audition for a pursuit pilot billet up at Miramar next week and she'll probably get the job – first ever female Top Gun pursuit pilot. So the good Lord willing and the creek don't rise I can be here in a little less than a month. Ben won't need me back 'til April maybe May. Is that enough time to be helpful to you?"

"I'll take whatever I can get. But I reserve the right to fight to keep you past April, May, June or whenever and I'll bet you a case of beer if it comes to that, Captain Joe Garcia will win that battle."

"I love it when people fight over me," I gloated as I shook Bo's hand. "It's a deal. My only problem is gonna be the distance between Ashleigh and I."

"As the crow flies, it's probably less than 150 miles from here to Miramar. I didn't mention this when you and Ashleigh came over last month, 'because I wasn't sure I was really gonna do it. I just bought a

Mooney M20J. Cruises at 200 mph – less than an hour to Miramar. You can use it – just pay for the gas."

As I walked out to my new car I couldn't help thinking, "Actually joining the real Navy was never even entertained as a possibility in my neatly, well organized life's plan. What the hell am I doing here? Seems like I've lost control of my destiny . . . . again!"

Chapter Twenty Six

Reno, Nevada
Eldorado Hotel Casino
Sunday, September 1, 1985, 2:45 p.m. PDT

Freddy Alverez selected a telephone on the hotel side of the Eldorado Casino complex in Reno and dialed the number that he had left a message on the Sunday before.

When the phone was answered with no greeting Freddy said, "This is Daniel"

"Hello Daniel, my name is Mark Garrison. I'm the Director of the Southwest District of the DEA. I understand you have some information for me."

"Well Mr. Garrison, yes I do. But before we get to the details, I must receive a guarantee from you that you will listen to what I have to say, analyze and verify it completely and determine a plan to totally eliminate this operation with primary regard to the safety of myself, my family and the hundreds of innocent people involved in this operation without their knowledge or intent."

"Yes Daniel, if what you are telling me is true, I can grant that guarantee."

"Good, I would prefer to meet face to face and have our meeting video recorded twice. One copy for you and one for me. And I would also suggest that we meet in a rented office somewhere in southern California – the location of which you may choose. I will call you Thursday evening at your office at 7:00 p.m. for directions to the meeting place. I will be un-armed; you may bring your side-arm if you wish.

"This is likely the largest drug import operation our country has ever encountered. I warn you of this because I believe the only way to kill this devil is through a well designed multi-national strike. It will not be easy and people will die executing it.

"I work six days a week. The only day I have to meet is Sunday. If I am absent any other day suspicions will be raised, people will expend significant effort verifying the reason for my absence and my help in this issue will be compromised. Do you understand?"

"Yes Daniel, we have become aware that there is a very large quantity of drugs coming into the U.S. that we can't account for. Your coming to us with this information is indeed timely. I agree that careful planning is imperative and I'm willing to listen to any ideas you have. What do you suggest we do to meet?"

"When I call you at your office Thursday night it will be from a remote phone. You will tell me where we will meet and we will agree on a time. There should be just you and I. You should bring two video cameras with tripods and enough tape to last four hours. I will bring coffee and donuts. Is this acceptable?"

"Absolutely Daniel, and I give you my word; I will do everything within my power to protect you, your family and the other innocent people involved in this operation."

"I need to tell you Mr. Garrison; I am not innocent, but I plan to negotiate my freedom based on the information I give you."

"I understand. Let me assure you that I will do everything in my power to preserve your freedom through your cooperation. Without your knowledge it would be very unlikely that we could be complete in eliminating this threat to our country. I thank you for coming to me with this opportunity to plan a complete elimination."

"Until Thursday at 7:00, goodbye Mr. Garrison."

"Until Thursday, Daniel."

Chapter Twenty Seven

DEA Southwestern Division Headquarters
San Diego, California
Monday, September 2, 1985, 10:00 a.m. PDT

Mark Garrison called his top four agents the minute he got off the phone with Daniel (Frederico Alverez) and summoned them to a meeting in his office at 10:00 the next morning.

"OK guys, we've gotten a break on our big job. A whistle blower, an inside man, has contacted me and wants to talk. I will meet with him next Sunday at an undisclosed location. This operation is huge. It's going to take a lot of planning and coordination between agencies to be successful. So for now I want this to be eyes only among us five. I will let the Director know what we're doing but no details for now. We don't discuss any of this anywhere but here in this office – no phone or any other external comunication. I'll call meetings here when I get information you need to know. Beyond that keep working on your current assignments."

Chapter Twenty Eight

San Diego NAS Officer's Club
San Diego, California
Wednesday, September, 4, 1985, 5:30 p.m. PDT

"Hey beautiful, how'd it go at Miramar?" I asked as Ashleigh Garrison slid into a booth next to me. My attraction to Ashleigh seemed to grow each time we met. "She's got to be the right one," I thought to myself as I gave her a quick kiss and held her eyes with mine for a moment.

"I flew the aggressor role against Commander Erickson in one of their Soviet disguised F-5s. I think he was impressed – I got three hits and he got two. I don't have the job yet but he said he'd be back to me soon. There are six people (five guys and me – all Lieutenants) applying for two positions. I'm not sure whether the female thing is a plus or a minus. But I should know something early next week. I still wish you'd consider trying out for one of the spots."

"Hey Babe, like I said, you're a better pilot than me and Bo really needs me at El Centro. He's up to his neck in alligators – contractors late, technical problems, system failures, you name it. Part of what he needs from me is my engineering skills but I'm sure he'll want me to do a bunch of testing, which means jump school at the Army's 82nd airborne school at Fort Bragg, North Carolina. Bo said they have a HAHO class starting in October for three weeks."

"Have you ever jumped out of a plane?"

"We had a jump club at Bo's airport when I was working there. I've got a hundred plus jumps and probably two or three hundred hours of dumping club members out of the club's Cessna 182. I never belonged to the club. I just traded hauling jumpers for jumps. Bo doesn't think I need the school but he doesn't have the time to devote to getting me up to speed on the newer gear. Getting me HAHO qualified is the all around best solution. Bo's going to have Captain Garcia call Captain Johnson and see if I can get released at the end of next week to Bo's unit. I'll be attached to a Special Forces outfit.

"We'll be a couple of hundred miles apart for a while but Bo has a new plane – Mooney M20J - I can use on weekends. Right now I have no idea what I'm doing – but hey, that's nothing new. . . ."

Chapter Twenty Nine

DEA Southwestern Division Headquarters

San Diego, California

Thursday, September 5, 1985, 7:00 p.m. PDT

Mark Garrison answered his office phone at exactly 7:00 p.m., "Hello, this is Special Agent Mark Garrison, can I help you?"

"Mr. Garrison, this is Daniel. Do you have a meeting place and time in mind?"

"How about meeting at El Toro's in down town San Diego for dinner tonight. Then we can talk about several options for our meeting on the following Sunday, the 15th. I have three possible locations in mind but I want to be sure we're both ok with the site and time."

"That will work for me, what time tonight?"

"Is 8:30 ok? I'm buying."

"That will be fine, I'll see you at eight thirty; I'll be wearing a yellow golf shirt. Good bye Mr. Garrison"

Chapter Thirty

El Toro's Gourmet Español Cuzine Restaurante
San Diego, California
Thursday, September 5, 1985, 8:00 p.m. PDT

The unseasonably warm weather hinted at the possible early arrival of the Santa Anna winds off the desert. These winds are caused by the typical early autumn northeastern movement of the Pacific high pressure system from its normal semi-stationary position in the central Pacific Ocean. Mark Garrison decided to leave his jacket in his car and loosen his tie as he arrived at the valet parking area of the restaurant. He was half an hour early, his normal practice when meeting someone discretely for the first time. He had made reservations for two at 8:30 and asked for a secluded table if available. He found a stool at the bar that gave him a good view of arriving guests as well as most of the seating area. He ordered a draft Coors Light and settled in to watch for Daniel.

At 8:20 a trim, muscular, medium height man wearing a yellow golf shirt arrived alone. Garrison downed the last swallow of his beer and approached the man.

"Daniel?"

"Yes, Mr. Garrison?"

"I asked the Maitre' D for a table in the back. Let's see what she's got."

After being led to a suitably remote area the two men exchanged pleasantries and Garrison said, "Daniel, I would prefer to not discuss detailed business tonight. Let's just get to know each other and agree on a meeting place that I can have scrubbed and properly prepared for an interchange between us. I want to be able to guarantee it to be secure. We'll need to make it Sunday the 15th. Is that OK with you?"

"Whatever you think, Mr. Garrison. The work we have to do will take months to accomplish. A week will not be detrimental. It's better to be safe."

The waitress appeared and they ordered drinks and accepted the menus.

"Daniel, I want to be sure you understand; I am committed to your security and safety, as well as that of your family and the innocent people at your company and the others. I want to establish a high level of trust between you and me before we proceed."

"Mr. Garrison, at this point, I don't have a choice – I must trust you."

"My real name is Frederico Alverez. I prefer to be called Fred, although many of my co-workers call me Freddy. I have a wife and two beautiful children. I entered into this business with only partial knowledge of the process or the business itself. None-the-less, I am not an innocent man. I appreciate your offer of safety and security for my family and I will cooperate fully with your requests. I hope I can help you understand the breadth and complexity of the issues we face. I wish I had never become a part of this. I am guilty but I pray you will judge me on my willingness to help you destroy this terrible machine."

The waitress reappeared with their drinks and took their order.

"I'll call you Fred and please call me Mark. From this point forward we should consider ourselves partners in this venture.

"As I mentioned, I have located three potential meeting places in Southern California. One is in Long Beach, one in Oceanside and one in San Diego. These are all locations we have used for discrete secure meetings before. We know the owners and management – there should be no problems.

"Your request for filming the meeting is a good one. If we are successful in this project I intend to use my copy to help me secure your freedom and protection. Which location is most suitable to you?"

"I live on the outskirts of Chula Vista; tell me about the San Diego location."

"It's in Logan Heights just off IH-5, near the piers. It's a small office complex renting to small companies. It has a section dedicated to temporary offices nicely furnished with a receptionist, phone, copy and cleaning services. It's called the Brandon Office Complex and the suite number is 118. My only concern with this location is its proximity to your home."

"That shouldn't be a problem, Mark. I've carefully covered my absence from home on Sundays and my family is unaware of any of this.

Actually, I would prefer this location from a timing standpoint. I've missed church with my family for the last two weeks and they will surely want to know what is so important that I would have to miss another service. This way we can go to church and then I can leave for a few hours for an important business meeting."

"If you're sure no one is suspicious we'll use that one – it'll be best for me also. 1:00 ok?"

"1:00 will work well. I have nothing written down, but it will still take several hours to tell the whole story. Please excuse my wariness. I am very concerned that everything we do be done with maximum forethought regarding safety and security."

"I certainly understand, Fred. We'll get through this together – I am also very concerned. If you need to contact me for any reason, call my office and ask for Luke. My secretary will contact me as quickly as possible and I will return your call at five and forty minutes past the hour until you answer.

"I will also order a watch on your number. The watch is undetectable and will notify me immediately if anyone attempts to tap or otherwise tamper with your phone. If this happens, I will call you from a pay phone as Luke asking if you could possibly pay me the fifty dollars you owe me by next Tuesday – I'm running a little low on cash and need to make a payment on my credit card. Then you do nothing other than your routine activities until you hear from Luke again.

"Here comes our food. Do you follow the Padres? Looks like we've got a shot at the Series based on this season's performance."

Chapter Thirty One

DEA National Director's Office
Washington DC
Friday, September 6, 1985, 8:00 a.m. EDT

James Doddington, DEA Director, set aside the briefing he was studying and answered his secure phone which he kept in his upper left desk drawer, "DEA, Jim Doddington here."

"Director, this is Mark Garrison, southwest."

"Yeah Mark, why are we secure today?"

"I've got something you need to know about and I think we need to act on," said Garrison.

Jim Doddington was a man of few words, "Shoot," he said.

"I've been contacted by a planner; spoke face to face last night."

A 'planner' is a whistle-blower who has participated in an illicit activity for some time, planning all along to take the operation down, if necessary – usually a very intelligent person.

"This looks like a big chunk, and possibly all, of our current problem. I've got him set up for a Sunday, the 15th, disclosure. He suggested recording. My initial investigation has him as the number two man at Albright Chemical in Chula Vista. They process Naphthalene. He asked for protection, which I granted. This guy is intelligent and sincere – I would recommend TS (top secret) for the time being. Albright was one of the companies we inspected as FDA routine. We must have scared him into action. He already has samples and docs secured in a safe deposit box. Your take?"

"I'll set up a meeting next Monday; say 3:00 which should give you time to get here. We'll have FBI and CIA Directors and CJCS (Chairman, Joint Chiefs of Staff) present. Ok by you?"

"Yes, I would recommend keeping it to no more than that at this time. Also, I'll have a video of the meeting."

"Good work Mark, see you at 3:00 a week from Monday" Doddington added as he signed off.

Chapter Thirty Two

Officer's Club, San Diego NAS
San Diego, California
Monday, September 9, 1985, 5:30 p.m. PDT

"Hey, hot shot," Ashleigh Garrison grinned as she slid into 'their' booth at the O Club bar, "I not only got the job, I've already got the damned orders – hot off the telex, haven't even read them yet. First female pursuit pilot/instructor in the Navy Top Gun School. Are you happy for me?"

"Couldn't be happier. Couldn't think of a better qualified or more deserving pilot for the job," I said grinning. "This is way better than getting an operational billet on a carrier even though I know how much you want that."

"I'll tell you what Sam; I've been re-thinking my priorities. First of all, I never really, deep down, believed I'd get this job. And second of all, I've put you, and by that I mean 'us', above the Navy in my list of priorities. We're now just below God, in whom I have a deep faith even though right now I'm not what you'd call a church goer.

"A tour on a carrier in a Hornet squadron would have been fun but this will be just as much fun and we'll be seeing a lot more of each other which is more fun than either of those.

"How'd your day go?" she said smiling.

"Well, I got a call from Ben confirming a 'temporary' transfer to Bo's unit at El Centro and I guess I'm excited about it, even though I don't yet really understand what 'it' is. I guess we're relegated to weekends for a while, but then again, we don't have much more than that right now, time wise. I'll have to do three weeks at jump school starting October 2nd. I doubt I can commute from North Carolina but I will if I can."

"Sam, I know this is like the pot calling the kettle black, but I'm starting to worry about you and this jumping thing. I'm not one to worry about anything, but then I've never cared so much about anyone as I care about you."

"Hey blue-eyes that's a two way street you know; I'm going to be in a carefully controlled test program with at least two levels of back-up. You're going to be playing the *aggressor,* flying against some of the craziest pilots in the Navy. Who should be worried about whom?"

"Yeah, you're right; we need to have respect for each other's job. It's just that my love for you is telling me we should be on an isolated island somewhere with everything we need or want and not a worry in the world."

"I hate to pull you back to reality. What we need to do is promise each other we won't take any unnecessary risks and get on with life in the military," I said as I gently kissed her on her forehead.

"Dinner here or somewhere else, then go to the rock?" I asked.

"You got it flyboy!" she replied, eyes twinkling.

Dinner was quick and romantic at a little seafood place just south of 'their' beach that features fresh shrimp and scallops. Now they were perched eight feet up on 'their' rock.

"I love you Sam McKensie," whispered Ashleigh as they parted from their ritual kiss once situated on the rock.

"And I love you Ash, more than I ever thought possible. We've known each other just a little over two months and I feel like I could marry you tomorrow."

"And if you ever asked me I *would* marry you tomorrow"

"I just did!"

"Then I will!"

I smiled and kissed her again, while pulling something out of my pocket. "Try this on."

"Oh Sam, it's beautiful," she said, her voice breaking up as she began to cry.

"Hey flygirl, don't cry."

"I can't help it – I've never been this happy."

Then she smiled that smile and I damn near cried, because when I thought about it I realized I'd never been this happy either.

"You'll have to meet my mom, dad and brother. And I want us to tell your mother and Bo at the same time."

"Married life will not be easy for us but I think it'll be one hell of a lot better than not being together. You agree?"

"I wouldn't have said yes if I didn't agree. We need to think about when."

"I think we ought to wait until we have a chance to meet and get to know our respective families – and until we get settled into our new assignments – your thoughts?"

"I agree. Tomorrow would be great but a little discretion and planning is certainly in order," said Ashleigh, clearly ecstatic.

Sam jumped down to the beach and Ash jumped into his waiting arms. After a long wet embrace I asked, "Your place or mine?"

"Mine's closer!"

"Yours it is!"

Chapter Thirty Three

DEA National Director's Office
Washington DC
Tuesday, September 10, 1985, 8:15 a.m. EDT

Jim Doddington had called the directors of the CIA and FBI and the Chairman of the Joint Chiefs on his secure phone to set up the meeting at three o'clock, Monday, September 16, with an alternate time of five o'clock the same day. Two of the three had other commitments on their calendars but agreed to re-schedule them when Doddington explained the subject and urgency of the meeting.

He was considering informing the President and asking him to attend if he could. His decision was to do just that and if the President couldn't attend he would arrange a dinner meeting with himself and Mark Garrison to give him a heads up on what was going on. Doddington was concerned about getting too many people involved. He believed as did Garrison that this lead could potentially eliminate twenty to forty percent of the current flow of cocaine into the U.S. But the action had to be carefully planned by a small, carefully selected team committed to the elimination of this newly discovered threat to national security – and that is exactly what it was, a threat to national security. The President would likely want to get the Secretary of Defense and his National Security Advisor and maybe even the Director of the NSA involved. That would be a problem he would have to deal with – it was imperative that they keep the team to an absolute minimum need-to-know group and add to it only those resources absolutely necessary for ultimate success.

Doddington pressed the POTUS button on his secure phone. President Stevens answered almost immediately, "Stevens here."

"Mr. President, Jim Doddington here. We've gotten a break on the issue we briefed you on last week. A whistle blower who's a planner. He claims he can help us take down an organization bringing tons of coke into the U.S. daily. Our Southwest Director will hold his initial debriefing with the gentleman Sunday afternoon. He'll be here for a Monday 3:00 p.m. briefing. Because the solution will require simultaneous national and international action, I've limited the team to only need-to-know leaders and classified it TS-NTK. (Need To Know). Sir, you certainly need to know, but I'd like to keep it to as small a group as possible. Can your schedule handle a 3:00 meeting Monday?"

"I've got some things I can move around – how long will it last?"

"He's bringing a video of the briefing. Could be an hour and a half or so."

"Hold it in the secure briefing room downstairs. I'll be there. I agree – keep the NTK list as short as possible. Good news, Jim. Keep it coming; Stevens out."

Doddington caught the military termination of the call, reminding himself that as the former Navy Seal and JSOC (Joint Special Operations Command) Commander, President Bradley Stevens was about as good as it ever got, Commander-and-Chief-wise. Including him now was a wise choice.

Doddington dialed Garrison's cell phone. "Keep the briefing as to the point as possible, the boss will be there. Call me on your secure line when you get back to your office."

Chapter Thirty Four

El Centro Naval Air Station
El Centro, California
Thursday, September 12, 1985, 11:35 a.m. CDT

Don Campbell, Texas Instruments' Program Manager for Special GPS Projects, signed in as a guest at the Station Security Office, El Centro NAS and called his Navy buddy Bo Jameson on the office phone.

"Better late than never – my puddle jumper out of Phoenix had some kind of mechanical problem and it took them two hours to decide they couldn't fix it and another half hour to clean up and fuel a plane that had arrived from somewhere else. Any way I'm here."

"Did you bring it with you?"

"I knew that'd be the first thing you'd ask. Of course I did. What good would I be without the prototype?"

"Let's go back to the lab," Bo said grinning like a kid on Christmas morning.

Campbell turned the prototype over to Leroy Schmidt, Bo's civilian engineer and then he and Bo went to Bo's office to talk about the state of the firmware in the current design of both the GPS unit and the MCS (Master Control System) in the HALO/HAHO system.

"I think we've got everything nailed down. That new 1553 bus specification sure helps," Bo said.

"How's your Spherical coordinate to Polar coordinate (POL) conversion software working?" asked Campbell.

"Actually we stole, well borrowed, that code from a project in work at NWC. Captain Ben Johnson asked Dick Granger at TI to give us the code and show us how it worked. Leroy and I took Joe's T-38 up there, got the code and a demo and were back here before noon – saved us a couple of months development time."

They talked a little about past missions in Vietnam but were interrupted by an excited Leroy Schmidt – this was the first time Bo had ever seen him this way. Now *he* looked like a kid in a candy store.

"Everything works, far as I can tell from the bench test. Come on back and I'll show you."

"This is the setup. We're looking at what the jumper will see on his EOVS (Eyes On Visor Screen) on this monitor. I'm running a simulated HAHO jump on the production version of the MCS. The GPS sends the MCS spherical position coordinates every 30 milliseconds. The MCS converts that to POL using a plug in digital map of the area. We're using the HSD (Horizontal Situation Display) mapping software also developed at China Lake and in use in most attack aircraft used by the Navy. The digital map is created from satellite data using classified technology.

"So what you're going to see here is the last three minutes of a HAHO precision landing – at night!"

"This is the un-cooled infrared system you're looking at. You can see the land ahead – we're aiming for that clearing up ahead with the small building to the right. See the small green X on the ground?

"OK, I'm going to pause the simulation here because Commander Jameson, my boss, didn't ask a question I expected, and that would be: 'Where are the GPS signals coming from'?"

"Well, I expected you had also simulated the output of the GPS," said Bo

"Ah yes, but that wouldn't *test* the GPS, a critical part of the total system, which is what we're trying to do here – *an end-to-end system test.* A couple of weeks ago I called our TI friend here and asked him if we could borrow a GPS simulator. Two days later it showed up – one of only three existing NAVSTAR GPS Satellite simulators capable of simulating an extremely accurate eight satellite constellation for any local mission scenario necessary, including Minute Man 3 staging. This mission should look familiar to you Bo. It's one of your night jumps at the Yuma Proving Ground last month. What you may not have known is that you were jumping in the middle of the YPG laser tracking system. You were being accurately tracked, with your position recorded every 30 milliseconds. We took that data, fed it into the GPS simulator modeling software and created a data set that very accurately drives the simulator to output GPS radio signals exactly like the real system – a GPS receiver can't tell the difference. Notice; there are no wires from the NAVSTAR simulator to our system and therefore the only input to our system is via the signals received from the simulator by our GPS antenna. So what you're looking at here is truly an end-to-end test of our system."

Leroy pushed the resume button. Bo was completely flabbergasted. He knew the folks he was working with were the best in the business but he didn't expect to see this kind of progress. He watched as the Jumper (actually Bo himself) S-turned to adjust his altitude. As he turned his head the visual field moved accordingly but the X stayed glued to the target spot. He remembered the jump and that he had overshot the target by about ten feet – pretty good for a night jump. Then, in the simulation, as he approached the target the X began to move to the bottom of his visual field and then disappeared just as he landed. He turned around to see how far he had missed the target and there it was, the green X right on top of the black & white bull's eye he was aiming for about ten feet behind him.

Bo didn't know what to say. He had allowed what he thought was an aggressive three weeks for the progress he just witnessed in ten minutes.

"I have to admit, I hadn't thought about doing a complete end-to-end test in the lab – didn't even know it was possible. Leroy, how did you know to ask about the GPS simulator?"

"Actually, I didn't. Don called me soon after your agreement to take five prototypes, told me about the simulator and that we could use it, but that I had to get you up to the YPG laser tracking range for a night jump. I 'forgot' to tell you why we changed ranges. You were up at China Lake the next day so I got Captain Joe up to speed on the project. He told me to keep you out of the loop on the simulator and the laser tracking range because that capability would take a month or more out of your schedule and you needed to take a little surprise vacation."

"Leroy, go get Joe. He's got to see this and I've got to figure out how to get even."

Captain Joe Garcia was anticipating the call and hurried back to the lab to see the expression on his friend's face. And of course he wanted to see the simulated test.

"Joe, I don't know what to do about you – there's no way I can ever repay you for saving my ass every time I get in trouble"

"Hey man, I didn't save your ass this time. I just arranged a little surprise for you, schedule-wise, so I could order your sorry ass to take a couple of weeks leave. You're working way too hard and I think I just helped prove you've got a very capable team here to cover your sorry ass while you take a little time off."

"Ok Joe, I'll go. Right after I make a night jump with GPS integrated into the system."

Captain Garcia turned to Campbell and asked, "Don, I wondered how you guys jumped out in front of your two competitors in the original GPS development program. It was the simulator wasn't it?"

"Yep, we got a contract to build a GPS set to ride in a Minute Man III ICBM. SAMSO had tracking data on both staging events and we knew we'd have to build a pretty sophisticated simulator to be successful. It's expensive to shoot a missile every time you want to test your software. So, first flight success became our mandate.

"I led a team of three engineers and two technicians to build a simulator that could handle the extreme dynamics of staging – that's where you see extreme changes in velocity, acceleration and jerk (rate of change of acceleration). We focused on modeling jerk since that represented the huge staging dynamics best. I designed the digital electronics, another engineer did the modeling software, another the run-time software and the technicians used the radio frequency modules of the production GPS receiver to convert the digital position signals to GPS range signals. It's really simpler than it sounds. Anyway, when we were able to test and tweak our systems in the lab we began to have consistent first time success in the field which by the way was Yuma Proving Ground. And, we had a first time success with the Minute Man III, saving SAMSO the cost of a second launch they had budgeted. You just witnessed what has become routine for us; a first time success – at least it will be when Bo field tests the full up system tomorrow night."

The next day Leroy Schmidt integrated the small GPS unit into the HALO/HAHO helmet. Then he ran tests on the data transfer and power consumption successfully. And finally he ran the simulated jump scenario with the fully integrated system while wearing the helmet. Everything worked perfectly.

That night Bo climbed aboard YPG's C-130E for a jump from 35,000 feet. The service ceiling of that aircraft is 33,000 feet, but with a light load 35,000 is no problem – it just takes a while.

Bo was testing the complete HALO/HAHO system minus the laser altimeter which is only used in the HALO mode. So if tonight's test was successful the HAHO system specification would be certified. And the HALO spec would await a later test for certification with the multi-channel laser altimeter.

"Johnny, take us to *Angels Three Five*," Bo barked into the intercom as the big transport began its takeoff roll.

Angels three five is military pilot-speak for 35,000 feet and it would take the big plane fifty five minutes to get up there. This is the altitude at which commercial jets cruise and even above the desert it would be well below zero degrees. This would actually be the first test from the specification altitude of thirty five thousand feet.

At angels one two, Bo donned an aircraft oxygen mask and at angels two four he discarded the aircraft oxygen mask, pulled on his HAHO helmet and transferred his communications, oxygen supply and pressure system to the HAHO suit and plugged in a charging cable from the aircraft power. After a brief system check, he relaxed for the last thirty minute haul up to thirty five thousand feet.

"Commander, we're eighteen miles southwest at *Angels Three Five*," said Johnny Sullivan, the pilot, "you've got the ramp, jump at will."

Bo disconnected his system charging cord, activated the button that equalized the ramp pressure, lowered the ramp at the rear of the aircraft and stepped carefully down to its edge. After a brief hesitation he stepped into the void. He counted off five seconds and pulled the ripcord. Suddenly everything was quiet. Bo turned the chute to the northeast and found his green X on the landing target. Forty five minutes later he landed on the green X after traversing eighteen miles to the target. Time for a vacation!

Chapter Thirty Five

Naval Weapons Center
China Lake, California
Friday, September 13, 1985, 4:20 p.m. PDT

I climbed down from the Royal Air Force F4-K after the last successful integration test with the AGM-88B Harm missile. This finished up the test program that Jimmy Clayton and I had conducted over the past four months. Now I was free to join Bo and Captain Garcia at El Centro.

"Hey Sam," called the flight desk orderly as I entered the building, "you got a call from a Commander Jameson, said it was important, left this number."

I walked over to his desk and dialed the number. "Sam, we just finished the GPS integration tests and Joe is making me take a week off. How'd your flight go today?"

"Same thing – I'm done here," I said. "All I've got to do is write the Test Report and I'm all yours."

"How about taking a week off with me and going up to surprise Jim?"

"Gonna take your Mooney? If so, do we have room for Ash?"

"Of Course."

"I'll call her and see if she can get away."

"Let me know where to pick you guys up."

"Will do."

I dialed Ashleigh's number, expecting to get the answering machine but she answered.

"What are you doing home so early?"

"They want me at Miramar in two weeks. The guy I'm replacing is retiring at the end of the year but he has a month of leave he has to take before then. He decided to take November off so they want me up there on the 1st of October. I'm thinking about taking a week's leave between now and the first. Why don't you take off too? We could spend some quality time together before we get plugged into our new jobs."

"You won't believe why I called. Bo and I both finished up our test programs today and we're thinking about running up to his airport to check on things. I wouldn't go without you – that's why I'm calling. We could spend a little time there, you could meet my mother and Jim, we could make our little announcement and then we could fly wherever we want to for a few days alone. What do you think?"

"I can be packed in twenty minutes. When do we leave?"

"Let me get back to Bo and I'll let you know."

Chapter Thirty Six

Jameson Flight Service Airfield
North-central Kansas
Saturday, September 14, 1985, 5:15 p.m. CDT

"JFS Unicom this is Mooney November 7095 Poppa, inbound, ten miles southeast at thirty five hundred feet, over."

"Mooney 95 Poppa we're landing runway 225, wind 245 at 8 knots, altimeter 29.93. You've got a Cessna 172 doing touch & goes. Student, I think."

"Roger JFS, we'll spot the Cessna and report down wind, 95 Poppa out."

"Strange voice," thought Bo – "must be one of the new pilots."

We three weary Navy pilots were ready for some food and a good night's sleep. Bo left this morning at 7:30, picked up Ashleigh at around 9:00 at San Diego NAS and me at China Lake at 10:05. They didn't have anything but jet fuel at China Lake so we jumped over to IYK, grabbed some lunch and some gas and headed for Denver. We landed at Denver, had a coke while the line boy toped off the tanks and then took off for Jameson Field. It was a little after five thirty when we touched down.

We met Jason Siebert, the new instructor and the voice on the Unicom.

"Where's Jim," asked Bo. "We were hoping to take him and Janie out to Jake's for a few beers and dinner – you're invited too"

"He went to Kansas City to get some magneto parts for one of the Cubs – he should be back already, he -" the Unicom squawked to life. It was Jim. We walked outside to watch him land. As usual he made a feather-bed landing. He was surprised to see us because Bo didn't call him.

Bo asked, "You guys want to go down to Jakes for some beer and Barbeque? – I'm buying."

"Hang on a minute. I'll call over to the house and see if Janie's game," Jim said.

I chimed in, "Hey Bo, Mom would probably like to see us too, should I call her?"

"Sure, we'll stop at the store and get a bottle of her favorite wine." Lauren McKensie didn't drink beer and Jake didn't serve wine.

A half an hour later we were all gathered around the big round table in the back of Jake's, ordering our drinks and food. When all that was completed I stood up, re-introduced Ashleigh and announced:

"Well folks, we couldn't find any better time to announce to the world that Ash and I are getting married, we're just not exactly sure when or where. I'm going to work for Bo down in El Centro and she's transferring up to Miramar to become the first ever female pursuit pilot instructor at the Top Gun school. Somewhere along the way we'll tie the knot. We know being married in the service isn't a bed of roses but hey, neither is *not* being married in the service. We're very much in love and when the time comes we'll bail out, settle down in a little house on a beach somewhere, have kids and grow old together."

Bo stood and toasted us with a spiel that finally got cut short when the food arrived. Mom was crying.

Chapter Thirty Seven

Brandon Office Complex, Suite 118
San Diego, California
Sunday, September 15, 1985, 1:00 p.m. PDT

"Come in Fred, I'm Mark Garrison," said Garrison opening the door after Alverez' knock at exactly 1:00. "This guy is disciplined," he thought, "almost like ex military – a stickler for details. That should work to our advantage."

Alverez entered and placed the coffee and doughnuts on the small conference table in the center of the room, then shook hands with Garrison, "Mr. Garrison, good to see you again. Let's get started."

After they got the cameras set up and turned on and were situated facing them at 45 degree angles Frederico Alverez started by explaining from the beginning how the original company was started and grew, how the products and processes had been developed and refined and how the business had become a growing, profitable concern. Then he relayed the events that led to the 'partnership' between the company and Maximillion Horte. Freddy gave Mark everything he knew about the operation from A to Z. And, Freddy knew a lot since he had planned this exit strategy from day one.

Within weeks of the "merger" Freddy had copied the key to the new lock that Tony Fesco, his boss and CEO of Albright Chemical, had installed on his office door. When Tony was out of town Freddy had plenty of after hour access to all sorts of information about the "slag" business beyond his local Albright knowledge. He knew how many plants were involved and where they were, how much "slag" each produced, where Max's Villa and the naphthalene plant near Mazatlan were, and how Max got the Cocaine out of Mexico and into the U.S. This was all valuable information for the elimination strategy yet to be devised by the DEA and other U.S. agencies.

As the story unfolded, Mark began to realize how difficult that plan would be to conceive and execute. But he knew it was a 'must do' and they'd find the resources and strategy to make it happen – somehow.

Chapter Thirty Eight

Jameson Flight Service
North Central Kansas
Sunday, September 16, 1985, 12:50 p.m. CDT

After sleeping in and having an old fashioned country brunch at Mom's new condo we spent Sunday getting caught up with all the Jameson Air business. Jim was doing quite a good job at growing JFS. All indicators were positive; new pilots were busy and happy with their jobs and. Jim had a little over sixty thousand dollars in the bank – life was good at JFS. Bo (and I) couldn't be happier. Mom was in good health and she and Bo seemed to be loving brother and sister again. I guess time heals most wounds.

Ash and I wanted to get away for a few days so we started planning to disappear as soon as we figured out where to go. I was thinking south, she was thinking north – was this a sign of things to come?

Then she suggested South Dakota – the Bad Lands, Black Hills and Mount Rushmore. All places I'd always wanted to go. A little hiking, a little camping out, for sure some camping in, not too far, not too expensive – done deal!

Around 6:30 we all headed back to Jake's. Jake was born and raised in Pflugerville, Texas and his family owned and operated one of the best barbeque restaurants in that great state. He and his brother and sister inherited the place when his parents died in a hotel fire in Pennsylvania in 1972. Long story short, he ended up here in an old saloon on a corner of my grandfather's land right on Highway 40, started cooking his famous barbeque and now folks come from many miles away just to eat here.

So that's what we did. Ash and I switched entrées. She had the 'fall off the bone' baby-back ribs and I had the mouth-watering brisket. Both were pecan smoked with Jake's famous Texas sauce.

"Ash and I are going to take a few days off and go up to the Black Hills," I announced after we were finished eating and another round of beer was on its way while Bo was filling Mom's wine glass.

"Oh, Sam, you've got to go to Custer. That's where Scott and I went shortly after we were married. You'll love the area and it's close to everything you want to see – lots of history too," Mom chimed in.

"Well that's one of the things we were going to ask about – and now we know. I'll check out nearby airports in my directory and we'll file a flight plan tomorrow and be back Saturday. Is that schedule ok by you Bo?"

"Just right, we need to head back Sunday morning."

Chapter Thirty Nine

DEA Headquarters
Washington, DC
Monday, September 16, 1985, 1:22 p.m. EDT

Jim Doddington, U.S. DEA Director, pulled away from the curb at the General Aviation building in an un-marked forest green sedan with a bleary-eyed Mark Garrison in the passenger seat. The DEA Lear 55 "bus" was an unmarked, plain white jet that that the agency kept in one of the General Aviation hangars at Washington National Airport – just down the river from the Pentagon and not far from the White House. Doddington sent the plane to San Diego Sunday afternoon to fetch Mark Garrison at 0500 the next morning. It's a 4 hour and 10 minute flight with nominal winds plus three time zone changes. The jet-stream had been kind this day and Jim and Mark would have an hour or so to discuss the upcoming meeting at his office before leaving for the White House. Mark made a condensed 45 minute video from his debriefing of Alverez containing the information needed for the meeting.

When they arrived at Doddington's office, Jim got Mark a large cup of coffee asked him to summarize his team's activities leading up to Alverez' appearance and then add the details of Freddy's involvement and approach to the DEA.

During his presentation, Jim asked several pertinent questions and seemed satisfied with Garrison's responses. When Mark was done Jim asked to see the video.

"OK, that's exactly what I want you to give the audience at our 3:00 meeting. President Stevens will be there – I think you met him at our awards ceremony a year or so ago, correct?"

"Yes," Garrison replied.

"Don't expect him to remember. He will ask most of the questions I just asked – maybe a few more. How many people at your end know about this? He'll want that up front, but let him ask. When the intro is over, show the video. We'll be in the President's secure briefing room in the basement of the White House. The briefing system there will have cables that will fit your laptop's audio and video outputs. Don't change a thing. What you've got is damned compelling. This is the biggest break this agency's ever had. Damned good work Mark!

Chapter Forty

Presidential Briefing Room
White House, Washington, DC
Monday, September 16, 1985, 2:55 p.m. EDT

"Gentlemen, please be seated. President Stevens will be here soon. He has asked that this meeting be limited to himself and those present. Coffee, juice and light snacks are available at the rear of the room. Please make yourselves comfortable. The restroom is also located at the rear of the room – the door to the right," said Robert Sanders, the President's Chief of Staff. He spoke rather robotically, obviously miffed at the purpose of a secret meeting that he wasn't invited to. Sanders was a true friend of Stevens as well as his primary political advisor. There were very few meetings he wasn't involved in.

"The only communications in or out of this room is the Presidents secure phone. If you need anything, he can use it to call upstairs," he said as he turned and left closing the door behind him. Thirty seconds later the door was opened and President Bradley Stevens entered.

"Greetings gentlemen. I want to thank each of you for the schedule changes you had to make to attend this meeting. You've each received a short secure briefing by me – At this point you know as much as I. Jim Doddington and Mark Garrison, Director, Southwest DEA will fill us in. My take is that we're on to something big, thus the need-to-know limits I've put on this subject. It will be classified TS NTK and regarded as a National Security Threat. At the end of this briefing we will decide who else needs to be involved. Since this is a closed, secure meeting I prefer first names – any objections? Good, let's get started. Jim –"

Jim Doddington got up, walked to the back end of the conference table to address the group.

"In addition to what the President, er, Brad, briefed you on, we have a significant amount of detailed information from a three and a half hour interrogation executed in San Diego yesterday by Mark Garrison. Mark will get us up to speed then show a forty five minute highlight of the yesterday's interrogation. This will give you an idea of the quality of our informant. Mark, if you please."

Mark Garrison was a little nervous but was able to maintain his composure in spite of his audience: the Chairman of the Joint Chiefs, the Directors of The CIA, FBI, DEA and the President.

"Gentlemen, I'm Mark Garrison, Southwest DEA. Let me give you a little background on how we got to where we are now.

"A little over three years ago we asked for and were given funding to do a study on drug consumption to see if it matched our estimates of the inflow of illicit drugs into the country. This study, performed by Bob McFadden's group right here in D.C. concluded that we, as a nation, were consuming at least 2.4 times our then current best estimate of border traffic. We further concluded that there must be one or more large inbound pipelines of illicit drugs that we were totally unaware of.

"We began looking across the country, paying special attention to the borders, but aware that the drugs could be so well disguised that the destinations could well be anywhere in the interior as well. We developed and prioritized a list of likely schemes to bring large quantities of drugs in to the country. We were focused specifically on cocaine because our consumption analysis indicated that's where the problem was. We started with a list of ninety three suspects, twenty seven in the southwest district alone. With the cooperation of the FDA we ran inspections of prescription drug and chemical food ingredient companies first.

"After the first twenty or so of these inspections we found nothing suspicious, but we got lucky. A planner, which is a whistle blower who has planned for some time to illuminate an illicit operation, came forward, exposed himself to us and gave us information on what is possibly a single pipeline that covers the entire discrepancy between the study and our estimates. It turns out that our inspection of his company, one of the first eight on our list, triggered his action.

"The company is Albright Chemical Company in Chula Vista, just south of San Diego. They import raw naphthalene, a coal tar derivative that is a white crystalline substance that smells like moth balls on steroids. They process it into about a dozen different products ranging from polymers and cosmetic components to mothballs. Ten years ago a

Mexican National based near Guadalajara hired a German PhD chemist to develop a process for combining cocaine and naphthalene into a product that was, in look, feel and smell, identical to naphthalene. And, it was easy to decompose back into naphthalene and cocaine using a precision vacuum still, a piece of equipment commonly used to decompose naphthalene into its various components. The raw material is processed in a plant located south of Mazatlan and shipped directly to eight plants in the U.S.

"The yield of the first step in the process of each of these companies is 21.5% cocaine by weight. The average daily throughput of all eight plants is 3.8 metric tons of naphthalene each which yields 6.5 metric tons of cocaine *per day* total. That means each of these plants ships almost a ton of cocaine off their back dock each day.

"The cocaine leaves the plant in sealed and acid washed steel pony barrel containers labeled as "Naphthalene By-products." Shipments at the Chula Vista plant are made on Tuesdays, Thursdays and Saturdays. The ship to address on the paperwork is blank. We don't know who applies the address label. Probably the plant manager, our planner's boss.

"The operation started eight years ago with just the plant in Chula Vista and expanded to the eight current plants a little over three years ago. Gentlemen, *this quantity exceeds our consumption study by more than 2X.*

"I am speculating here, but I believe they're storing up to half of the stuff to control the street price and provide a hedge on discovery. There could be over two hundred tons of cocaine stored in warehouses throughout the U.S. Our problem is we have no information on what warehouses and how to locate the drugs inside once we find the warehouses.

"Our planner has no knowledge of what happens to the cocaine after it leaves the plant. Obviously, we don't know everything about this operation yet. We need a team of integrated agencies to get the information needed to obliterate this organization.

"Please allow me to show you a forty five minute excerpt of the interview I conducted with the planner yesterday. When finished, I will try to answer any questions. Thank you for your attention."

Garrison struck a key on his laptop and the 4.5 X 8 foot high definition screen at the front of the room came alive showing the video of the interview between himself and Freddy Alverez. The interchange contained many details that would obviously help in the job that lay ahead of the team, but at the same time it galvanized in their minds the enormity of the task at hand.

As the video concluded Garrison shut down his laptop and asked, "Questions?"

The entire audience looked dumbfounded – there were none.

Brad Stevens summarized his ideas on what needed to happen, "Looks like we'll need at least ten teams to take the operation down, as we understand it today. Our biggest unknowns are; are they storing the stuff and if so how much and where? The where is what bothers me. It could be in ten, twenty, or hundreds of locations. We've got to get a lot more details about this thing before we move. Give me your thoughts; Jerry first."

Admiral Gerald Sterett, Chairman of the Joint Chiefs of Staff of the Armed Forces cleared his throat and proceeded.

"As I see it, from what we've heard today we've got exactly the right people involved in this project and that credit probably goes to you and Jim. We need a lot more information on what's going on in Mexico and how deep we need to go to get that part of the operation shut down. CIA Operatives and Special Forces can perform the shut down as soon as we figure out what we need to do and how we need to do it. I would suggest a covert operation. I honestly don't know who we can trust in Mexico. What say you Bill?"

William Conroy, Director of the CIA stifled a smile shaking his head in agreement.

"There *is no one* we can trust in Mexico. I agree Jerry; our only hope of succeeding at this is a quick coordinated covert strike. We need a lot more intelligence before we can even begin to plan a strike."

Brad Stevens interrupted: "You guys are right on. Put your best two experts working together on this and have them report directly to you. Bob, what about the domestic strategy?"

Robert Gilmore, FBI Director, responded, "Same thing here, Brad, we've got a much larger footprint though. It's going to take several of my top agents to run this thing to the ground. Jim and I will have to work together closely. Jim?"

Jim Doddington said, "Yeah, our problems are spread all over the country. The thing that worries me most and the thing we know least about is the probability that they've got this stuff hidden in many areas no where near the plants we know about. That implies domestic operatives our planner knows nothing about – a shadow network. This isn't going to come together overnight."

"I hear your frustration," said the president, "the good news is we do have quite a bit of information. We all need to keep a low profile while we un-ravel this mess. Use a small number of senior agents on a short leash. Compartmentalize the operation as best you can – nobody outside of this room needs to know anything more than is required to successfully complete his/her assignment. We can't screw this operation up. It *is* a grave matter of national security. Let's, the six of us, set up weekly secure video conferences to be sure we're all on the same page all of the time. Any comments?"

There were none.

"We'll get together at 8:00 pm eastern time, every Tuesday – that ok?"

Blank faces.

"Good," said the President, "Mark mentioned that the work done by Bob McFadden and his team in the Washington DEA office led to this discovery. Keep those three guys closely plugged into this thing. They and Mark have done one hell of good a job, Jim"

Chapter Forty One

6,500 Feet Above Northwestern Nebraska
Monday, September 17, 1985, 10:30 a.m. CDT

"Mooney 95 Poppa this is Kansas City Center. You're leaving our airspace. Contact Minneapolis Center on 126.50."

"Roger Kansas City, Minneapolis on 126.5. Have a good day," Ashleigh responded. She had insisted on handling the radios and navigation to keep from dying of boredom. With her and the autopilot doing all the work it was I who was dying of boredom.

"You too ma'am. KC out."

"Minneapolis Center this is Mooney November 7095 Poppa, IFR at six thousand five hundred in route to Custer County South Dakota."

"Mooney 95 Poppa, squawk ident please."

"Thank you 95 Poppa, radar contact. Be advised, there is no IFR (Instrument Flight Rules) approach to KCUT" (Custer County Airport).

"Minneapolis, we're VFR (Visual Flight Rules) now; would like to request VFR to KCUT."

"7095 Poppa, proceed VFR, weather clear to KCUT, no current traffic, have a good day ma'am."

"Roger, Minneapolis, proceeding VFR. Thank you sir – you have a good day also, 95 Poppa out."

We had taken off a little more than an hour earlier in the clutches of the first cold front of the fall and climbed to our cleared altitude of eight thousand feet where we were on top of the scud and could clearly see the scattered cells along the front which we easily avoided. When the front cleared and we were able to request and receive VFR clearance to KCUT the flying got a lot easier and the boredom increased.

This was a five day vacation that we really needed. The last couple of months had been hectic for both of us. Time alone was going to be great and we had a lot to talk about – like planning the rest of our lives.

Ash found a quaint lodge in a wooded area on a lake with five individual cabins. She picked the only one available – the one farthest from the main lodge – perfect! We rented a car at the airport and planned to hike the lake today, visit Mount Rushmore tomorrow, see the other sites near Custer on Thursday and Friday, sleep in on Saturday and rest up in Custer before heading back to JFS that afternoon..

We landed in beautiful clear, crisp weather with a little crosswind on runway two six at a little after noon. The wind was out of the northwest and the autumn chill was setting in – perfect hiking weather. The elderly gentleman at the desk in the lodge informed us that although check-in was at three o'clock, he felt certain they'd have us in at around two. I gave him my cell number and we headed to greater downtown Custer, South Dakota to find something to eat.

The lake hike was great. We found a small garden area about half way through the five mile trail with a bench near the water line facing the lodge on the other side of the lake.

"Kinda reminds me of our rock on La Jolla beach," Ash opined as we looked out over the lake. "I miss our time together alone. We've got a lot to talk about and some pretty important decisions to make. At least we've got one family informed. Now we need to set something up in California that can lure my clan together. That's easier said than done."

"Hey doll, you're the worlds only lady Top Gun pilot, you'll figure something out. I've been thinking, we could probably take a week off between Christmas and New Year, get married and either go skiing at Tahoe or go sailing in the British Virgin Islands, What do you think?"

"Let's do both. We could get married at a little church I know near Vail, kinda half way for both families, ski three days, fly to the BVI and sail for a week. After Christmas we don't have a TG class scheduled until mid January. Can you get away from Bo for that long?"

"Well I've got more than two weeks of leave piled up. I'm pretty sure he'll go along with the plan if I work real hard to get us a little ahead of schedule – we'll ask him when we see him Saturday. Maybe at dinner Saturday night with everyone there - how could he say no?"

Chapter Forty Two

Max Horte's Mountain Villa
Southeast of Mazatlan Mexico
Wednesday, September 18, 1985, 9:00 a.m. MDT

"Welcome gentlemen, I'm happy to report that we've had a record fourth quarter this year – if your estimates for the remainder of September are correct – as I suspect they are." Maximillion Horte ran his business on the same quarterly calendar as the U.S. government. It just made things easier to understand from a cash flow standpoint. "Your bonus checks are beneath your plates. As always please remove them and open them in private after the meeting. I'm happy to say these checks are also setting a record – well done my friends!

"Now let us have a wonderful breakfast, and then we'll discuss business." As Max placed his hands palm down on the table the four waiters sprang into action, bringing the first course of four along with coffee and fresh chilled orange juice to each guest.

When all were finished the conversation migrated to business.

"I am also happy to announce that we will have an additional plant coming on line soon in Puerto Rico. This operation should completely satisfy the insatiable appetite of the entire Caribbean from Puerto Rico down to Argentina plus the Bahamas. It will provide some real competition for eastern South America. Of course the margins will not be as high as in the U.S., but we can make up for much of that with volume.

"Joining us today is the CEO of our new venture. Julio, please stand for a salute."

Julio Mars stood straight and tall, unusually tall for this group at six foot two, and proposed a toast to the continued success of the entire enterprise with an added commitment to do his part. The others rose and downed their shot of tequila that had been quickly poured by the four waiters into the sterling shot glasses included in each place setting.

"I have read your reports with much interest and satisfaction. And I accept each with my deepest gratitude. We have indeed gelled into a magnificent organization. I have but a few questions before we adjourn to our morning skeet competition: Tomas, You met your forecast for revenue but you produced ten percent more than your production forecast. Was it not feasible to increase your sales as opposed to adding to the inventory?"

"Senor Maximillion," Tomas Cortez began…

"Tomas, Tomas, Tomas, we are all on a first name basis here – I am Max, nothing more."

"Sorry Max, I must work harder at being less formal. We received twelve additional barrels of raw product during the last week of August. I held my people over for two Saturdays to process the over-shipment. I have temporarily stored the excess at an approved location and plan to increase the sales forecast for November and December to generate the increased revenue."

"Tomas, that is exactly what I hoped you'd say. I knew Geraldo had received more product than he had requested and that he had processed it. I just didn't know what he did with it. Tomas, you did well – your next quarter bonus will include an amount for the increased revenue and a little something extra for thinking on your feet.

"Geraldo, if this happens again, please let me know what you do with the excess, why there is a shortage and who it affects, understood?"

"Yes Boss, I'm not used to looking at the big picture like you do – It won't happen again."

"Geraldo, you and your crew are among the longest term employees in this enterprise. Your operation supplies all of our plants. You all work very hard and everyone here appreciates that. I didn't mean that as a scolding. Knowing where product is and where it's going is what I do and you can make it a little easier for me if you do this, ok?"

Geraldo, smiling at this praise, assured Max that his reports would include every gram of product, pure and hybrid, that entered and left his plant – where it came from and where it went.

"One last question; Tony, why do you suppose the U.S. Food and Drug Administration requested an inspection of your facility?" And before you answer that I need to let you know that you and Freddy handled this issue in exactly the right way. There's nothing I would have done differently and I appreciate your immediate notification and continuing information as it became available.

"I'm just curious why an overworked and understaffed agency of the U.S. Government would bother looking at the manufacture of naphthalene byproducts."

"I understand, Max. At first I chalked it up to the fact that we create polymers and other byproducts that are used downstream in both food and drug products. That's when I sent the query that I copied you on out to the other CEOs asking if they had been contacted by any U.S. Government agency. The negative reply got me wondering why our plant was targeted. As you know I received a second notice indicating that one of their lab technicians contaminated one of the samples and that they *may* have to return and collect another sample. That was the last I heard from them. I have no theory that makes sense. I don't know what they're up to. I do know that there was not a trace of product in that plant the day the inspector came and Freddy stuck to him like glue."

"Could we have a snitch?" Max asked.

"I don't see how. Freddie, Miguel and I are the only three that are aware of the process. As you are fully aware, we were your first stateside plant. These people all worked for me at least three years before we became part of your operation and that's going on nine years now – so for twelve years, no new employees. We've never had even the smallest security issue at our plant. I know each employee. I know their families. I trust them and they trust me. They are treated well and love their work. That's why they stay. I thought about this also, Max. But I crossed it off my list of weird things that could cause the FDA to go nuts. And I don't have anything else on that list except one possibility.

"What if the DEA is getting spooked about the shear amount of product that is coming into the market? Might they be looking for some new avenue across the border? That's the only other thing I can think of."

"Interesting thought Tony. Let's you and me do some exploring into this later. Good work, my friend.

"Now we will each take a few minutes to review our individual operations status and field questions and comments from each other. Then we will shoot some skeet, enjoy a wonderful luncheon prepared by Jose and his staff and adjourn for an afternoon of leisure and games.

"Tony, since you're up, let's start with you. . ."

Chapter Forty Three

Secure Video Conference
Washington DC and San Diego DEA Offices
Tuesday, November 19, 1985 8:00 p.m. EST

"Gentlemen, it appears we've gotten some additional information from our planner at Albright Chemical," remarked President Brad Stevens after his opening pleasantries. "Mark, why don't you fill us in?"

"Certainly Mr. President: Frederico Alverez, our planner who we continue to refer to as 'Daniel', contacted me Saturday evening using our agreed to signal for contact. We met Sunday afternoon. Daniel was visibly concerned. After meeting with Max Horte, the master mind and leader of our cocaine problem, his boss, the CEO of Albright, filled Freddy in on a potential problem discussed at the recent quarterly meeting. It seems that our visit to Albright Chemical using the FDA cover has caused some concern by Horte. He advised Fesco to enlist Freddy to generate a plan to discretely look into the possibility that the DEA was behind the FDA inspection they underwent last July but not to proceed with the plan until reviewed by Horte himself and to involve no one else. The good news is that our guy is a trusted participant in the plan. The bad news is that they suspect that we are looking and are developing counter-measures to figure out who and how. Freddie is, of course caught in the middle and wants us to give him direction. I told him to proceed as if our contact had never happened. The more loyal he is and the better his performance the higher our probability of succeeding in bringing down the operation.

"Of course if we decide otherwise, I can easily change his direction."

President Stevens responded, "My feeling here is that we go with Mark's call with the option of changing direction if needed. We have a lot of information already, but we're facing two very difficult problems: how to take the entire operation down in a very short period – I would think a few hours if possible, twenty four hours max. And, of at least equal importance to that; where is the missing cocaine?"

"One other significant tidbit," continued Garrison, "They're bringing on another plant – in Puerto Rico. Freddy will get us more info on this new development as soon as he can. I warned him to be careful."

"This will cause significant additional planning and complicate the plan," commented Stevens. "We'll have to get a couple of other people involved. We have DEA, CIA and FBI people in Puerto Rico. Jim, if you had to pick one from these three agencies which would you go with?"

"I would also consider the Governor," responded Doddington.

"The Governor is a given – which agency would you pick?"

"I would pick the FBI," responded Jim Doddington.

"I would too – anyone have objection to the FBI?"

No one objected. After spending another twenty minutes discussing the plan, President Stevens named it *Operation Clean Slate.*

Chapter Forty Four

El Centro Naval Air Station
El Centro, California
Friday, December 20, 1986, 3:45 p.m. PST

Testing of the new HALO/HAHO system was now almost four weeks ahead of the original schedule and one and a half weeks ahead of the revised schedule Joe had imposed on the program when the GPS subsystem became available early. The phase one prototype was meeting most of the phase two requirements and Captain Garcia had officially requested the elimination of phase three by moving its requirements down to phase two; effectively eliminating a complete phase of development and saving millions of dollars. The Admiral was pleased, to say the least.

Bo convinced Joe Garcia that I could learn what I needed to know about HAHO jumping from him quicker and better right there at El Centro. I was making night jumps after only three days and had been instrumental in the schedule advancement. My engineering background and ability to interact technically with Leroy and the development techs had resolved the hardware issues quickly and the remainder of the 'system tuning' was primarily software, Leroy's forte.

The GPS integration with the rest of the subsystems gave us additional capability that we had not even contemplated in the original specification. For example: accurate computation of wind speed and direction, which I 'stole' from the autopilot software used in the A6 Intruder aircraft. This capability led to an automatic landing system capability that literally put the jumper on the target when engaged at an altitude of 300 feet or more above the target. This was the system I was currently testing, and we were close to nailing it.

In order for the system to control the chute we had to "invent" a compact, light weight, gas operated, shroud puller. Each chute required four of these. Our techs were master (almost magic) small system designers. In less than a week they had converted a small gas operated cylinder (designed to hold up the hood of an all terrain vehicle while servicing the vehicle) into a computer controlled shroud puller which could be productized into a compact, seven ounce, five by one inch cylinder, located at the base of the shrouds where they wouldn't interfere with the deployment of the chute. The prototype was a mechanical kludge, causing me to have to jump with the chute partially deployed, but the results were better with each jump.

Bo and I were discussing last nights test results when he got a call from Captain Garcia, two offices down the hall, requesting we both report to him ASAP.

"At ease you two, nothing formal about this meeting. Bo, why don't you brief Sam on the matter we've been discussing?"

I sat at ease and Bo started with: "Sam, the HALO/HAHO system we've been working on has, as you know, been pretty damned successful. In short, we've given the Special Forces of all the services a whole new set of operational opportunities and they're beginning to rethink many of their operational strategies based on these new capabilities. We need to recognize that this system has several important features that were added to the original specification and greatly enhance the utility and reduce the operational expense of the system – thanks largely to the people in this room – especially you Sam.

"That being said, Joe & I approached the Admiral with a request concerning you that we need to make you aware of. But before I get to that there's some information that the Admiral has deemed as "need-to-know" for you. This is Top Secret, Compartmental information, and for your part, is not to be discussed outside the present company. Understood?"

"Yes Sir"

"Joe heads up a Special Forces unit that except for the Joint Chiefs and the President, doesn't exist. Officially chartered as SEAL Team VI, it is now known as the Naval Special Warfare Development Group or DEVGRU for short. You'll learn more about that later. Everyone associated with the HAHO/HALO program knows Joe is a Special Forces guy but no one except me is aware of his operational status or the details of his unit. When he convinced me to re-up, I also became a member of this elite group. So what I'm saying here is that this unit that Joe commands and I belong to is an operational team, not just a development unit. Any questions, so far?"

"No, Sir."

"We want to give you the opportunity to become the fifteenth member of this unit. This requires Special Forces training; eight weeks of basic conditioning and nine weeks of land training; four and a half weeks in Panama and four and a half weeks in Alaska – this training makes your OCS training look like a cake walk, but we are pretty sure you can handle it physically and mentally. This is the Basic Underwater Demolition / SEAL (BUD/S) training minus eight weeks of diving training which will be delayed for you and three weeks of parachute training which will be waived for you. But if you don't want in, we don't want you. Is that clear?"

"Yes Sir. What about Ash and I?"

"Seven of the current members of this team are happily married. We're not asking for your life, just your body and soul. Most of what we want is continued advanced Special Forces system development – something you've turned out to be very good at. Your skill set matches our needs to the extent that we have secured permission to offer you a promotion and a position in an elite organization that would otherwise be impossible. There could be some field work in this job – you would be, after all, a Navy SEAL and among the youngest Lt. Commanders in the Navy I might add. Talk to Ash. Think about your career – either here with us or somewhere else. With your flight experience you could land a cushy job with an airline or any of a number of other pilot related jobs, probably making more money. But the question is; what do you and your wife to be want to do?"

"I think we all know what she'll say, but we'll talk. Thanks for giving me this opportunity. You guys have taught me a lot and I want you to know I appreciate it."

"One more little item", interjected Captain Garcia. "There's a BUD/S survival course in Panama starting January tenth."

Chapter Forty Five

White Bay Beach
Jost Van Dyke, British Virgin Islands
Thursday, December 26, 1985

The wedding was a simple though fairly expensive affair. Ash and I had spent a weekend with her parents in Pasadena at their beautiful estate the week before Thanksgiving. Her brother Mark managed to break away from whatever was over-stressing him to join us for Saturday evening.

I guess I got the family nod. We all got along well – no one fainted or even frowned when we announced our plans. And Mark and I hit it off great; his personality was remarkably similar to Ashleigh's – good eye contact, straight forward communicator, jovial in spite of clearly being on edge about something.

Her father was a retired Navy Captain, so we developed what I hoped to be a good rapport. We talked shop a little. I asked his opinion on my Special Forces opportunity and he responded favorably, which I expected. Her mother was pleasant and bubbly and I could see where Ash got her eyes. Ashleigh looked like her mother and Mark looked like his father.

We told them we were going to get married between Christmas and New Years Day and queried their plans during that period – they had none as important as this.

We'd already decided when and where we wanted the wedding; we rented the Sand Castle Hotel at White Bay on Jost Van Dyke in the BVI for three nights. It was just the right size and it had a killer bar, the *Soggy Dollar*, right on one of the world's most beautiful beaches. So our Christmas present to our families was the trip, the wedding and a nice vacation in the BVI. We got airline tickets for Ash's family and my mother. Jim and his wife Janie, Bo, Joe, Ash and I flew the Cessna 310 down.

The wedding, right on the beach in front of the hotel, went off without a hitch. Beautiful bride, beautiful weather, beautiful wedding. Our mothers both cried, her father and brother smiled. Everyone else looked a little bored. Then the bar was opened, everyone changed into swim wear and the fun started.

It was good to relax after all the pressure most of us had been under recently due to our various occupations. Mark and I talked for over an hour shoulder deep in the clear blue-green water, taking occasional breaks to refill our 'Pain Killer' drinks (an island favorite). He was obviously interested in checking out his new brother-in-law and I wanted to find out what was bugging him. He let me know that the DEA was working a big international problem, pretty much 24/7 but that's all he could say. A few more PKs and he loosened up. I could tell we were going to be good friends.

Bo chartered a forty six foot Leopard catamaran that slept all ten of us for a four day, four night mini cruise around the islands starting the morning after the ceremony.

When the week was over Ash and I said goodbye to everyone else and set sail in a smaller boat for Anagada, a small coral atoll at the north end of the BVI. We spent two beautiful days alone at Loblolly Bay, snorkeling and lying in the sun on the other most beautiful beach in the BVI. On the third morning we sailed back to White Bay on Jost Van Dyke and picked up a mooring for two more nights. On both evenings we dinghied over to Great Bay for dinner, the first night at Tommy Dorsey's *Paradise Island* and the second night at *Foxy's* for his famous barbeque feast.

Then we had to head back. We sailed past Soper's hole at the southern tip of Tortola and motored up the channel, into the wind, back to Road Town to turn in the boat and catch a taxi to the Beef Island airport.

It was tough going back. We'd had the best wedding I could imagine. Ash was positively glowing, eyes sparkling, perpetual smile – yep, I made the right choice!

Chapter Forty Six

Secure Video Conference

Washington DC and San Diego DEA Offices

Tuesday, February 18, 1986 8:00 p.m. EST

CIA Director Bill Conroy led off the conference:

"We've been successful in getting our #3 polar bird (spy satellite) positioned over Horte's villa. Its period is ninety four minutes with an eleven minute window at wide angle. The Ruskies and Chinese will notice the change and probably spend considerable effort trying to figure out what we're doing. Looking at Mexico will *not* be one of their considerations. I hope it drives them nuts.

"We're getting good visual and IR intel on the villa and the Mazatlan plant, the best of which I will show you here and then send the detailed package to the execution team at the center."

The "execution planning center" was a secure multi-force facility at Fort Knox Kentucky used for joint covert operations planning by the CIA and NSA and multi-force Special Ops. There were usually several teams operating in the facility and security had been implemented to afford maximum isolation and security to each team.

"Keep us aware of Horte's status, Bill. We'll need every bit of intel we can get to pull something this complex off. Bob, what's the story on our friends in Puerto Rico?" said Brad Stevens in his friendly but focused no nonsense manner.

The FBI Director responded; "We've completed our preliminary investigation on the plant in question. We put one of our guys inside as a delivery driver. It appears that the capacity of this plant is in the range of 1.5 to almost two times that of Horte's continental plants. There's evidence of construction to isolate the front end of the process. We've got intel on every employee, the company history and public financial data. We'll dig deeper than that and expect to have details on which employees will be involved in Horte's organization before next week."

"Good work, Bob – keep us posted on your findings. Jim, Bob, how's the domestic plan coming – Bob first," the President asked.

"We've identified agents in each domestic area to form the nine take down teams. The teams will consist of FBI and DEA agents with a local police representative to be brought in at the last minute. These operations are not expected to cause a large scene and in all cases can probably occur with minimal exposure to the other employees or to neighboring businesses. Jim, can you continue from here?" asked Bob Gilmore.

Jim Doddington replied, "Sure. As Bob implied, our plan is to keep the take down as a low profile operation. We've scouted the plants and all have fairly low apparent security. There are video cameras on each loading/receiving dock. Each plant makes several shipments a week of all products including the cocaine. Once the cocaine leaves the isolated extraction/packing area it is treated just like all other shipments – no special treatment. In fact it is picked up by a shipping company along with several other naphthalene byproducts. Some plants use different shippers and several use multiple shippers.

"In all cases there are three employees who have knowledge of the cocaine byproduct: the CEO, who is located in an office just outside or fairly near the front-end area, and the extraction and packing employees inside the area. One of our agents will pose as an interested customer with ID showing him as a buyer for a large respected user of products the plant produces. A tour of the part of the plant that generates the product or products of interest will be scheduled for the morning of the day of the execution. After the tour the buyer and the CEO will retire to his office to discuss pricing, quantity, etc."

"The agent will then inform the CEO that he is under arrest and that his plant is surrounded by federal agents and request that they quietly enter the front end area to inform the other employees there.

"We don't expect any armed resistance. But we'll be ready for that if it occurs. We're also making plans to inform the company's board of directors (only two have a board of directors) of the situation later that day so they can address the continuation of business as usual. Where the plant is owned by Horte, which is the case in all the rest, the primary financial person will be identified as a probable candidate to run the company until a suitable CEO can be found. It is our desire to affect the unknowledgeable employees as little as possible by impeding the continued operation of the business as little as possible. We have a good bit of additional work to be done in this area.

"Obviously, we'll plan the Puerto Rico take down in a similar fashion. It will just be coming on-line in that time frame and the plan will accommodate its status accordingly."

"The President responded, "Sounds like you've been working well together. It's good to hear the concern for the innocents in this plan. I want to caution you guys though: Be damned sure we don't put our people in harms way – I don't want any dead agents or innocents! This has got to be a clean operation. What about the in-plant and en-route naphthalene/cocaine mixture?"

"We plan to leave a two man team with each plant to supervise the extraction of the coke from the raw material until the supply line is dried up. We'll deliver the coke to our secure destruction facility and hand over the plant operation to the new management as soon as a new source of raw naphthalene is secured. This plan gets us all the in-process coke, but lets the plant operate as normal as possible during the transition."

Stevens said, "I like that. No sense screwing up the lives of all the non-participants. Do you have any dates yet?"

FBI Director Robert Gilmore responded, "We could be ready in as little as three weeks. Puerto Rico is our long pole in the tent since we've had less time to integrate it into the plan. I think, however, the domestic plan is a piece of cake compared to the foreign plan – that's where we'll see the armed resistance."

"What say you Bill?" asked the President.

"Bob's right, replied CIA Director William Conroy, "we've got quite a bit of additional intel to gather before we can go in with high confidence of success. At a high level here's what we've got: We need to hit the villa and the plant at exactly the same time at night. We need to be sure Horte is in his villa. The weapon of choice could be a Cruise Missile for each. This would keep us outside the twelve mile limit. But this choice would give us uncontrolled collateral damage, loss of the potential cartel infighting alibi and possible destruction of location related intel if we don't already have it going in."

There was a pregnant pause while the President pondered the situation, then asked, "Admiral, do we have any new fangled capabilities that might enable a more covert interdiction in this operation? We need intel from the villa site that might shed light on where the hidden coke is."

"Admiral Gerald Sterett answered, "Well, Mr. President, um, Brad, I've spoken at length with Admiral Bennington about this and it appears that we are on the cusp of having such capability. As you know, his people are working on a highly covert, automated, HALO/HAHO system. The HAHO mode is working quite well with more than a dozen rather astonishing and successful full-up tests. Our problem with this is there are only three test jumpers, two are SEALs, who are totally familiar with the system and of those only one has any combat experience.

"At this moment they are adding an automatic landing capability to the system that would greatly reduce the amount of training necessary to bring combat experienced operators into the picture. Initial tests are good – check that, damned near perfect, but it will take some time to get the final package finished and replicated. We have four pre-production units. All have been used in the test program with remarkable reliability.

"This is the covert approach I would recommend if the timing's right. I suggest we add George to our team and bring him into our next meeting with more specific information."

"Would you use the same approach on the plant?" asked the President.

"Probably not. The plant is located just off the coast slightly south of Mazatlan. The refineries in the area supply most of the raw coal tar. Best we can tell the plant has gone from a pure naphthalene producing plant, prior to the coke business, to shipping 100% hybrid product. That sort of gives us a look at the size of our problem here.

"We're looking at a classic covert SEAL Team approach on the plant. We don't have to blow it up, just light it – it'll blow itself up, nicely. Do it successfully at night – nobody knows what happened and no innocents get hurt."

"Admiral, I like what I'm hearing. If we get caught diddling in Mexico's affairs without their knowledge it'll be a political nightmare almost as bad as the Bay of Pigs. This way it just looks like drug lords trying to eliminate each other. We can dis-inform a few folks to help that notion blossom. Let's keep pushing this plan. If it costs us a few weeks, so be it. We need a foolproof plan that gets us in and out with no casualties and the Mexican government scratching their heads. That'll also give us more time to get intel on the hidden coke."

"Mr. President, I'll personally get with Admiral Bennington and his people and come back with a realistic, achievable plan next week." Rear Admiral George Bennington, commanding officer of the United States Naval Special Warfare Development Group (NSWDG), the Navy element of the Joint Special Operations Command (JSOC) responsible for satisfying the technical and operational needs of Special Forces covert operations. DEVGRU was originally known as SEAL Team VI.

"OK, let's recap. FBI & DEA: Fine tune your plans and get Puerto Rico caught up with the rest. Our must-do here is simultaneous take-down of all domestic operations with no casualties on either side and as little impact on normal plant operation as possible. Plan on an early morning domestic operation. This will be the same morning just after the foreign operation, before the druggies or the Mexican government can figure out what has happened, if they ever do.

"CIA, work with Admiral Sterett's Special Ops and provide the necessary intel to meet operational requirements. Consider pulling another bird over the target area to increase the window and come back with a window table showing strike opportunity.

"Gentlemen, this has been a very productive meeting. I think we have a pretty good idea of what we need to do and how we might do it. Let's pull out all the stops to get this done. Once again, this *is* a national security threat. Use priority one if obstacles present themselves but only if absolutely necessary. Next week we'll meet at 7:00 EST – plan on two hours. Then we'll go two more weeks on that schedule. God Bless you all! POTUS out."

Bradley Stevens was not new to these sorts of operations. He began his career as a Navy Pilot, joined the SEALs early in his career, rose to become Commander of JSOC as a Rear Admiral at the age of forty four, retired at forty eight, ran for Congress, became a Representative from the state of Texas, then a Senator. In 1976 he was appointed Director of the CIA and performed exceptionally through two terms before running for and becoming President of the United States. He never micro-managed his people, but he had an innate ability to lead good men and women to the right decisions and exceptional execution of plans. His presidency was a glowing example of this ability.

Chapter Forty Seven

Home of Frederico Alverez
East Chula Vista, California
Sunday, February 23, 1986 11:30 a.m. PST

"Daddy, Momma said it's ok with her if I go over to Maria's house this afternoon to work on our science project if it's ok with you, is it?," asked Freddy Alverez' thirteen year old daughter Sylvia as the family entered their home after church and their usual Sunday morning breakfast at the Denny's just three blocks away and around the corner.

"Sure, you can go, but first call Maria and be sure it's ok with her parents. And, be sure you two actually get something done on your project. So far I've seen a lot of talk with very little progress – understand, young lady?"

"Ok Daddy, we will."

Before Sylvia could get to the phone a man dressed in black stepped out of the hallway connecting the living/dining area to the bedrooms. He had a gun!

Chapter Forty Eight

Chris Steakhouse

Miramar, California

Sunday, February 23, 1986 6:30 p.m. PST

The Maitre 'D found us a table for two toward the rear of the restaurant. Ash ordered the petite fillet mignon and I got the nine-ouncer. I had just returned from my four week SEAL training in Panama and was still trying to replace the eight pounds I lost. While I was gone Leroy started work on six new prototypes of the Automated HALO/HAHO system – this would bring us up to ten operational units. Ash and I had flown up to her parents Saturday for the day, after getting caught up on some mighty good sex Friday night. Then today, we visited with her brother Mark for a couple of hours after church.

This was our first chance all weekend to really talk and we had a lot to talk about.

"Just as I was about to leave Friday evening to jump into Bo's Mooney and fly to Miramar, Bo, who had just returned from a meeting with Joe Garcia said to me in a low voice, "we might go operational with our prototypes – soon."

"I asked him if he could tell me about it.

He said, no.

So I said, "See you Monday."

"So what do you think it's all about?" queried Ashleigh.

"Don't know, but depending on the operation, I could be involved. I'm the only one who knows the detailed design of the system and also knows how to use it – in fact, I now have quite a bit more test experience than Bo does."

"Did Mark seem a little up tight to you this afternoon," asked Ash, "and what's your take on his sudden interest in what you're doing?"

"You noticed that too. Could be a connection here – a drug bust somewhere? I asked him about his interest – he changed the subject."

"Are you still scheduled for your Alaska survival training next month?"

"Yeah, it's the last group of the season – only five of us. Doing that program after mid April doesn't make sense. That's why they only do three groups a year.

"We have two weeks to get me out of my place and into yours. Do it next weekend? I don't have much stuff," I said, grinning at Ash.

"Sam McKensie, you have less 'stuff' than anyone I know. We can do it on Saturday and have Sunday to get 'our' place straightened out." What time do you need to be back at El Centro tomorrow?"

"I told Bo I'd try to be there by ten. I shouldn't have a problem with that unless you keep me up all night – again."

Chapter Forty Nine

Southwestern DEA Headquarters
San Diego, California
Monday, February 24, 1986 7:30 a.m. PST

Mark Garrison approached his office engrossed in thought about the Horte take-down plans. As he looked up he noticed a cube shaped package, about a foot on each side, parked dead center in front of his office door. He unlocked and opened the door, careful to not disturb the package. He examined the package without touching it. It had just a shipping label on it with no return address, wrapped in brown paper.

"Hey boss, what's up?" drawled Bud Nichols as he walked down the hall toward Garrison.

"Don't know. This wasn't here at ten Saturday night when I left. Whoever left it got into the building somehow. I'm going to go examine the entrances – you go downstairs to the weapons locker and get our portable x-ray unit – this could be rigged to explode. Bring the explosive sniffer too."

"Aye, aye, boss," Nichols said as he turned for the stair well.

Garrison carefully stepped around the package and retrieved his fingerprint kit from his bottom left desk drawer. A quick dusting revealed no prints on the box. He then carefully examined the second floor entrance for any sign of forced entry – none. Not surprised, he took out his cell phone to call his friend Rob Tomlin, a Lieutenant on the San Diego police force. Then thought he'd better wait for Nichols to return with the x-ray unit and get a peek inside before bringing in the locals.

Nichols came huffing and puffing down the hall yelling, "That damned elevator never goes to the basement when it's busy. Here boss, let's take a look."

He unpacked the unit which consisted of two square panels about 15" on each side. One was a flash x-ray emitter and the other a solid-state fluoroscopic imager. The unit emitted x-rays about 10 times weaker than a chest x-ray unit so they weren't concerned about the exposure.

Nichols held the imager while Garrison triggered the emitter. "Oh my God," Nichols mumbled as he looked at the image. "It's a head Mark. It's some poor bastards head."

Garrison pulled on his latex gloves and carefully lifted the box and carried it into his office. He carefully cut the tape on the top and opened the package. Inside was the head of Freddy Alverez, eyes wide open, and pupils dilated, skin pasty gray, a look of horror on his face.

"This is not good, Bud. This is our snitch."

Tucked in next to one of the three cold packs surrounding the top and both sides of Freddy's head was a folded sheet of copy paper. Garrison carefully removed, unfolded and read the message: "Don't fuck with me or I'll fuck you better," signed Max.

"Bud, grab Gary – he just came in – and get over to this address," barked Garrison pulling a card out of his wallet. "I'm concerned about Freddy's family. He's got a wife and two kids, a girl thirteen and a boy ten. Treat the house like a crime scene. Look for any indication of a struggle, blood, hair, weapons, shell casings, whatever. Get there quick and call me on my cell when you're inside – knock first but break in discretely from the rear if you have to. Be careful. There's no reason to believe that asshole would still be there, but he's crazy enough to wait there for me. Check your weapons and take a few extra clips. Talk to no one but me!"

Garrison carefully closed the package and placed two small strips of scotch tape on the flaps to keep them down. He took the package to the break room at the rear of the office area and after rearranging the contents of the refrigerator and removing one shelf he placed the package inside, turned the thermostat to max cold and closed the door. He sealed the door with crime scene tape and taped a note with his signature on the front: "OPEN THIS DOOR – LOSE YOUR JOB."

Chapter Fifty

DEA Headquarters, Washington DC
James Doddington's Office
Monday, February 24, 1986 11:13 a.m. EST

"James Doddington's office," said Mary Pierce, the petite middle aged, but still pretty Executive Assistant.

"Mary this is Mark, is Jim in?"

"I'm sorry Mark, he's in a meeting."

"Mary, this is an emergency, possibly life or death – can you get him out?"

"Wait a moment," she said and then put him on hold.

"What's up Mark," said Jim Doddington after picking up the phone in the conference room.

"I found Freddy Alverez' head in a box in front of my office door this morning. I sent two of my guys to his house to see if the family was involved. I thought about calling the local FBI boys but thought it better to get them involved through you so we don't screw up our security."

"Yeah Mark, that was the right thing to do – so happens I'm in a meeting with Bill Conroy and Bob Gilmore right now, hold one," Doddington said as he pressed the hold button. A minute later he came back on line: "I got Bill and Bob up to speed on what we're talking about, I'm going to put you on the speaker – ok?"

"Sure."

"Mark, we know where Horte is right now and we've had him under surveillance for two days. He's in the States but hasn't been near California since he arrived on a flight from Bogota, Columbia to Chicago. He's traveling under a false passport. Sounds like this is the work of a hired hand. Was there any claim attached?"

Mark read him the note and said, "It's signed 'Max'."

"This guy's been doing business under the radar for at least eight maybe ten years now. Suddenly he's gone public with us in what sounds like a declaration of war – not uncommon with these drug lord assholes. Problem is, when they go public, heads start to roll, literally."

"Jim, I'm worried about my family, can you handle getting the FBI, CIA and whoever else we need plugged in while I make a couple of phone calls?" Garrison said, his voice showing deep concern.

"Yeah Mark. Take a complete inventory of family for your whole team and any others you feel the need to. Warn them without divulging what's going on. This could change our plans somewhat."

"Oh, by the way, I've got Freddy's head in our fridge. It's secure for now but I'll need to know what to do with it sooner or later. I'll have my mobile phone with me at all times. Let me know what you guys decide to do. I'm signing off for now," Garrison said as he hung up the phone.

Chapter Fifty One

SW DEA Headquarters, San Diego, California
Mark Garrison's Office
Monday, February 24, 1986 8:20 a.m. PST

"Mom, I'm really glad you answered, where's Dad?" Mark Garrison queried with a sigh of relief.

"He's down at Starbucks getting our coffee. What's wrong son you sound upset?"

"Ok, Mother dear, it's time for you to listen to me and do exactly as I say. We've got a nut-case on our hands and there's reason to believe he might try to harm some of our loved ones. So here's what I want you to do. Go get two suitcases out of the storage closet. Pack one for yourself and one for Dad. Pack casual clothes and some clothes suitable for hiking and maybe one nice outfit for dining. When Dad gets back, get in the car and drive toward Tahoe. Call me as soon as you're in the car driving and I'll tell you where you're going. Do you understand everything I just said?"

"I may be old but I'm not senile – yes, I understand. We've been talking about getting away for a while. Looks like you just gave us the reason. We worry about you all the time Mark. We've noticed that you seem pre-occupied much of the time we're with you lately, which, by the way, isn't nearly enough. We'll be ok – just let us know when to come back home. This will be an adventure for us – a forced vacation – never had one of those. Is Ash ok? We worry about her too. I don't know what ever got into your sister's head to start fooling around with those damned airplanes! Doesn't she know it's dangerous?"

"Mom, don't worry about Ash. I'm calling her as soon as I get done talking to you. You need to promise me you'll do exactly what I told you to."

"I promise, call me when you know where we're going. Bye dear."

"That was easier than I thought it would be," thought Mark Garrison as he dialed his sister's number in La Jolla. She didn't have a cell phone.

No one answered. He dialed again and left a message for her to call back as soon as she got it. He called Sam on his cell phone. No one answered. This was not good. Then he called Sam's uncle Bo at El Centro.

"This is Commander Jamison, can I help you?"

"Bo this is Mark. I'm trying to find Ashleigh. She's not at her condo and Sam doesn't answer his cell."

"Well, I know where Sam is. He's on his way back here in my airplane."

"Damn!" Mark said, "I forgot all about that. I saw them at my place yesterday afternoon. Sam mentioned that he had to be at work in El Centro by ten o'clock this morning, so he'd have to leave around seven thirty and Ash said she didn't have to check in until noon so she was going to return some wedding presents for stuff they really needed, then go to the base. I'll call the base around eleven and leave a message for her. Thanks Bo, sorry to bother you."

"Not a problem, Mark. When you get hold of her tell her thanks for getting that good for nothing nephew of mine out of bed and in the air on time!"

"Will do Bo, see ya."

Chapter Fifty Two

Frederico Alverez' House
East Chula Vista, California
Monday, February 24, 1986 8:55 a.m. PST

Bud Nichols and Gary Parker had finished their preliminary examination of the Alverez home and Nichols dialed Mark Garrison's cell phone.

"Hey Mark, this doesn't look good. We've got three dead bodies – they're Freddy's family. Our hasty reconstruction looks like this: Someone was in the house, probably when they got home from church. Probably a single perp. Freddy was quick-cuffed (plastic zip-tie hand cuffs) to a chair and forced to watch his family tortured and murdered. His wife and daughter were naked and missing fingers which we couldn't find. Cuts all over their bodies and throats slit. The boy was shot through the head. This is the most gruesome thing I've seen in my twenty six years with the DEA. Freddy's body is not here.

"We can't call the local cops. What do you want us to do?"

"This sounds like what they do to each other down in Mexico. I'll get Jim to contact the FBI and get back to us on how they plan to handle it. Can you secure the house?"

"Yeah I picked the lock on the back door. It'll relock it from the inside and it will remain locked when closed. This is probably how the perp got in. I was real careful not to contaminate the door knob or anything else in the house – the crime scene is un-compromised."

"Good work, Bud. Can any of the bodies be seen through the windows?"

"Yeah, but I can drop one set of blinds and fix that."

"Is Freddy's car visible from the street?"

"No, it's in the garage."

"Where did you park?"

"About two hundred yards away and around a corner."

"Before you secure the house, put on a fresh pair of gloves each and look for a safe deposit drawer key without disturbing anything or compromising the scene. I have no idea where to tell you to look, but that key is very important, so do the best you can."

"Don't spend more than an hour looking for the key – if you guys haven't found it by then it's either hidden somewhere else or, God forbid, Horte's got it. Then secure the house, leave one at a time through the rear door. Approach your car from different directions."

"Exactly as I had planned it. Gee boss you're pretty good!" Bud Nichols was one of the DEA's most experienced agents. His feathers occasionally got ruffled when Mark gave him instructions on how to do his job.

"Don't go there Bud!"

Chapter Fifty Three

DEA Headquarters, Washington DC

Jim Doddington's Office

Monday, February 24, 1986 11:55 a.m. EST

Jim Doddington, Bill Conroy and Bob Gilmore were in his office awaiting the arrival of Admirals Gerald Sterett and George Bennington and Captain Jeffrey Stallings, Joe Garcia's counter-part in DC, responsible for the operational section of the NSWDG. Admiral Bennington had arrived in DC last night and had been conferring with several military tactical advisors all morning. Doddington had arranged a working luncheon in his conference room which was just barely large enough for the six of them and the carts of food and drinks necessary for a working lunch.

Doddington's assistant announced over the phone/intercom that his guests had arrived and he asked her to show them in.

"I've asked Mary to delay lunch until 1:00; we've gotten some new developments we need to discuss first. Everyone ok with that?" Doddington asked.

"No problem for me," said George Bennington, "They had a big spread at the hotel – I ate too much. I'm glad to see water on the table – I'm coffeed out."

"Ok gentlemen; please have a seat while I get you up to speed on the recent developments. I got a call from Mark Garrison at 11:13 this morning – that's 8:13 his time. It seems that he had a gift left at his office door placed there some time during the night before. It was Frederico Alverez' head all neatly packaged with cold packs which were still partially frozen. A note telling us not to fuck with him signed by 'Max'. Looks like we've lost our primary source of intel. His family was brutally murdered. When we take this operation down Max Horte needs to meet the devil!

"I've told Mark to secure his family. Two of his agents who've been read in to the mission and are working on this project examined and secured the crime scene. They're standing by about a block away waiting for instructions. Bob, can you have a stealth clean-up crew visit the scene & remove the bodies? I suppose we'll need to get the locals involved to the lowest extent possible so we can use the city morgue."

Robert Gilmore cut in, "I'll get on it right away Jim. Our guys do a really good job of keeping the locals at bay when we occasionally get into a mess like this. We'll keep the lid on the project. I'll need the address of the scene."

Jim handed Bob the address and Gilmore retired to the back of the room to make a few calls. When he returned he asked; "As I understand it we've got all the body parts except for six fingers and the rest of Freddy. Any ideas on that?"

Doddington replied, "Bud Nichols speculated that his intact body was taken to a place where it could be properly decapitated and the head packed for delivery. He had no ideas on where that could be or whether the rest of the body was intact after the head-chop. Bud is one of our best."

Chapter Fifty Four

NWDC Lab, El Centro NAS, California

Leroy Schmidt's Office

Monday, February 24, 1986 9:00 a.m. PST

Commander Bo Jameson knocked twice on Leroy Schmidt's office door which was normally open.

Leroy Schmidt responded, "Yeah, come on in."

"What's our status on parts?", asked Bo.

"It looks like we have enough parts to complete the other six units you asked for including enough for one unassembled spare – except for the laser altimeters. The contractor can't get the sensor to meet spec since his number one supplier went out of business. We've got five of them, four in units and one spare," Replied Schmidt.

"Build the six units with barometric altimeters. Keep the spare laser sensor as a spare and jump on the contractor to solve the problem."

Schmidt gave a curt, "Aye, aye, sir," as he brushed past Commander Jameson on the way to the lab.

"Hey hot-shot, how long 'til I have the ten working units?" yelled Jameson.

"Five and a half days - plus any of my time you waste asking questions."

"Smart ass," thought Bo.

Chapter Fifty Five

El Centro Naval Air Station, NWDC Lab
El Centro, California
Monday, February 24, 1986 10:10 a.m. PST

"Hey Bo, I gassed up your plane and tied it down. When can we do a full squad test?" I asked, wondering when we could make a six man test jump. I didn't expect any major problems. The six channel laser altimeter worked in the lab and two channels had been tested by two jumpers but we'd never done the full up test because we hadn't been able to get our hands on the parts we needed for six units – we only had four working systems.

"We're going to test without laser altimeters for now. Barometric altimeters will work fine for the HAHO scenario. Leroy will have the units ready by the end of the week and the techs will write a dummy routine to stub off the software interface. We'll test next week."

"You saw Ash this morning didn't you?"

"Yeah, I left our place at 7:30, why?"

"Mark called looking for her at about 8:30."

"She was getting ready to go into town to do some shopping – didn't have to be at the base until noon."

"Yeah, he remembered that after I told him you were on your way back this morning. Wouldn't hurt giving Ash a call to let her know he's looking for her."

"I'll do that a little after noon, before she's suiting up for her one o'clock flight. I'm going to buy her a cell phone this week – she's too damned hard to get in touch with. I think she likes it that way."

Chapter Fifty Six

DEA Headquarters, San Diego CA

Mark Garrison's Office

Monday, February 24, 1986 10:30 a.m. PST

"Hi Mom, this is Mark. Is Dad driving?"

"Yes he is – I don't think he trusts me any more since I hit that parking meter with my car. Will you talk to him, He just can't drive forever – he'll fall asleep at the wheel."

"Yes I will Mother Dear – now I've got some important information for you and Dad. I want you to go to that place we spent two weeks at six years ago in June – all four of us. I've made reservations there for you both for a week. Don't say the name of the place on the phone – just let me know that you understand which place I'm talking about. It's important that you stay there and not make any phone calls on your cell phones." Mark always called his Mom 'Mother Dear' when he needed her to know something important was about to be said.

"Yes, Mark – I understand which place and we'll be able to get there from here easily. Don't worry about us – but we're worried about you. Are you in danger?"

"No Mom, this is just a precautionary thing. And don't worry about Ash. I've got a call into her at the air base. She should call back in about an hour," he lied.

"I'll call you in a couple of days. By then this should all be over," he lied again. "But I've already paid for the week and I want you and Dad to have a great mini vacation – they had a special weekly rate," he lied yet again.

Chapter Fifty Seven

DEA Headquarters, Washington DC
Jim Doddington's Office
Monday, February 24, 1986 1:50 p.m. EST

Jim Doddington's assistant, Mary Pierce, buzzed him again on the intercom interrupting a conversation that had begun during lunch but was still far from forming any conclusions on what to do next.

"Mr. Doddington, you just received a secure telex from Mr. Bob McFadden. You might want to look at this. It could have a bearing on your meeting."

"Thanks Mary, I'll be right out."

"Gentlemen, excuse me for a moment. We might have just gotten some information that's relevant to our meeting – I'll be right back."

He left the room, walked down the hall to Mary's desk, read the message and hurried back to the meeting.

"Ok, listen up, this telex is from Bob McFadden, our Senior Analyst. He and his crew have been studying the consumption and distribution of drugs in the U.S for close to four years now. They developed some interesting data that led to uncovering the network we're working on here today.

"His team has analyzed the Horte operation. This analysis is based on data obtained from Frederico Alverez and verified by close, covert observation of four of Horte's naphthalene plants not including Chula Vista where Freddy worked. The data for the other plants are practically identical with the Chula Vista plant. Running the numbers tells us that Horte has imported three times as much cocaine over the last eight years as the US has consumed. That means these guys are definitely planning for the future. As we have speculated, there is a Horte sub-network out there somewhere that we know nothing about, ready to distribute a huge cache of cocaine should the naphthalene source be compromised. Using the current consumption and growth rates of the market, that's a twenty two year supply of cocaine.

"The problem is, this coke is distributed using U.S. shippers under U.S. laws. It appears that the labeling and packaging practices do not violate any US regulations for the products that are supposed to be in the containers. These shipments are made through distribution centers to warehouses and other unknown locations all over the country. Without the origin documents we have no way to locate the storage facilities or the location within each facility. McFadden believes they might then be shipped to a smaller number of locations controlled by Horte. Truth is: we don't know.

"One thing for damned sure: There is a list somewhere that contains the location of every sealed 15.5 gallon pony drum of cocaine being hidden in the U.S. We knew they were shipping the drugs all over the country and strongly suspected that they were storing some of the shipments for later use – we just didn't realize the magnitude of the problem. The location and destruction of this drug cache is mandatory. If we don't accomplish that we will have failed."

Doddington continued, "I'm going to try to get on the President's schedule for tomorrow to get him up to speed on our latest progress. When and if do, I will let you know where and when and request your attendance if at all possible."

Chapter Fifty Eight

Miramar Naval Air Station, Miramar CA
NWFS Top Gun Training Command
Monday, February 24, 1986 11:00 a.m. PST

"Good morning, NWFS Top Gun Training Command, Petty Officer Renner speaking. Can I help you Sir?" said the young lady at the Top Gun flight desk.

"Yes Ma'am. I'm Mark Garrison, Ashleigh McKensie's brother. I realize she's probably not there yet, but I need to leave her an important message. Please tell her to call me on my cell immediately. I have some very important information for her."

"Yes sir, does she have your number?"

"Yes she does. Please be sure she gets this message."

"Yes sir, I will be sure she gets it the moment she checks in – she's due to be here at 12:00 noon."

"Thank you very much Petty Officer Renner."

"You're welcome Mr. Garrison, good bye."

Chapter Fifty Nine

DEA Headquarters, San Diego CA

Mark Garrison's Office

Monday, February 24, 1986 12:05 p.m. PST

"DEA, Mark Garrison speaking," Garrison spoke quietly into the phone, praying his sister was on the other end.

"Hi. Is this the Mark Garrison who has a sister named Ashleigh but never calls her? What the hell's going on Mark?"

"Ok, I guess I deserved that, but I've got a situation here that's as serious as I've ever had in my life. We've got a drug lord whose operation has been compromised by a snitch I cultivated. Somehow he discovered the snitch and tortured and killed him and his family. Our problem is we don't know how much he knows about what we know and what he's going to do about it."

Ashleigh broke in, "What about Mom and Dad?"

"They're ok. I called them this morning. They're on their way to parts unknown for a little R&R. They were worried about you so I told them I'd call them as soon as we talked.

"Can you stay on the base for the next few days until we get a better handle on this mess?"

"Sure. I'll need to go home and pack some clothes."

"Do you have a service weapon?"

"Yeah Mark, but this is peace time – it stays locked up at the range. I qualify with it four times a year. I have a Glock 40 at home, and a license to carry but I can't carry it or even leave it in my car on base."

"I'll work on that problem. Right now I need to know what time I can pick you up at the base. I'm going to drive you up to your condo to pack and then back to the base. If there are no suitable officers quarters available, get a room at the VOQ temporarily. I need you to stay on base until we can unscramble exactly what's happening here. You ok with that?"

"I am, but I'll bet Sam won't be"

"I'll talk to Sam – as soon as we hang up. Now go fly and teach some cowboy how it's done. I love you Sis - and Mom and Dad. If anything happened to any of you guys I'd go nuts. I feel responsible for getting us into this mess, so please let me get us out."

"Now I can see what's been bugging you. Don't worry about me or Mom and Dad, we'll do what ever you say and we'll be very careful. If there's anything I can do to help, let me know. How much of this can I tell Sam?"

"After I talk to him he'll know as much as you do – for now that's all I can say.

"I've got to run now. When can I pick you up?"

"How about 6:30 at the flight ops desk?"

"See you then Ash – love ya!"

"Love you too, Mark, bye."

"Lieutenant Sam McKensie, please," Mark said into the phone.

"Who should I say is calling?" replied the young female voice.

"Mark Garrison, his brother-in-law."

"One moment please."

After about eleven moments I said, "Hey Mark, what's up?"

"Listen up Sam, I need your help." Mark explained the situation to me and I replied;

"What about the weekends? I could take Bo's plane to Miramar and we could disappear to places unknown – that might even be safer."

"Well, I guess that would work, I just want to emphasize to you the danger we're facing here. This nutcase has a network of killers inside the U.S. When you fly, go VFR with no flight plan. But call me first on a land line and let me know your plans. Do you have a hand gun?"

"I've got two, a Glock .40 and a 9mm Sig Sauer ."

"Take your best handgun with you at all times. Please fill Bo in on this situation and let him know he could be a target also. Ashleigh has permission to take her Glock on base," he lied.

"Will do Mark. How're you gonna catch this guy?"

"It's going to be a huge operation. I'll try to get you and Bo read in to the mission next week."

Chapter Sixty

Miramar NAS, Miramar CA
Base Headquarters, Base Commander's office
Monday, February 24, 1986 4:55 p.m. PST

"I'm Mark Garrison with the DEA to see Captain Baker – he's expecting me."

"Just a moment, I'll buzz him," said the attractive civilian receptionist.

A shorter than expected Base Commander, Captain Reginald Baker appeared at his office door and said in a lower than expected voice, "Come in Mr. Garrison," followed by, "what can I do for you," as he shut the door behind them.

"I need a favor. My sister is Ashleigh Garrison – I mean McKensie - you may know her."

"You mean the First Lady of Top Gun? I know her well – I've flown with her. She's one hell of a good pilot."

"We have reason to believe that her well being might be in danger through no fault of her own. Actually, it's due to a highly classified program that I'm currently involved in. I've asked her to remain resident on base for an indefinite period of time due to security issues."

"We can certainly arrange that with ease. Is that what your visit is about?" queried Baker.

"Actually no. She will have reason to leave the base from time to time. My request is for a waiver to the base fire arms regulations to allow her to bring her civilian permitted hand weapon, a Glock .40, on base under the condition that while on base the weapon will remain locked in her vehicle."

"I'm actually not authorized to grant that waiver."

"Admiral Bennington or Admiral Sterett?"

"Either will do, preferably Bennington."

"Do you have a form for that?"

"The Navy probably has a form for everything but that."

"Do you have a problem with me approaching Admiral Bennington with this request?"

"Not at all, he may need to know the reason."

"Actually, he already does. I felt it important to make the request to you first, after all it is your base."

"And I thank you for doing that. I hope this won't affect your sister's performance."

"That's the other reason I wanted to talk to you first. I wanted you to rest assured that Ashleigh will not be affected by this in any way. She, her husband and her father are all career Navy. Ashleigh has always been able to focus on her job no matter what the outside influences. She'll be fine – by the way, check her record. She's shot expert with her service weapon four of the last five re-qualifications. She'll be ok," he said, as he thought – "God, I'm praying that I'm right."

Chapter Sixty One

Miramar NAS, Miramar CA
Top Gun Flight Operations Desk
Monday, February 24, 1986 6:25 p.m. PST

"Hey big brother. You found the Flight Ops Desk. I'm impressed!"

"I might be a lowly DEA gofer but I can find my way around – especially when I'm looking for the 'First Lady of Top Gun'."

"Where did you hear that?"

"I stopped in to let Captain Baker know that I was going to get you a waiver to bring your personal weapon on base as long as it remains locked in your car. I can't expect you to be totally cooped up on the base for ever. Sam wouldn't like that. But I want to re-emphasize that the danger here is very real. A drug nut has brutally murdered a family of four and he might try to get even with me through my family."

"You're going to get me a waiver? How?"

"I know the Admiral."

"Oh. Ok. Let's go."

"After you, First Lady. We'll take my car if that's ok."

"Sure."

As they drove through the automatic gate at the exit of the base Mark noticed a late model Toyota, dark, maybe blue, parked on the side of the road facing in the same direction they were driving. When the road curved a quarter mile ahead he glanced back to see if the car was behind them. No, it was still parked, lights out – probably nothing.

"You want to load your stuff, then eat or vice versa?"

"Let's eat on the way back – it's not that far. Did you get Mom and Dad settled in."

"Yeah, they're already making plans for the week – They're in one of the cabins up at Mono Lake, the place we stayed back in '79 - they're fine."

Mark glanced once again in his rearview mirror. There was a car, hanging back. Same car? Don't know.

"I need to get some gas soon, may as well be now," he said as he pulled off the road at a Texaco. He chose a pump closest to the road so he could observe the car. A dark blue late model Toyota, hmm. Well, take your time and see if he shows up again.

On their way again, Mark gave Ashleigh as much information as he could on the Max Horte saga – which wasn't much. Although he kept a lookout for the blue Toyota for the remaining thirty miles to Ashleigh's condo in La Jolla he saw nothing of it. They got three suitcases of 'girl stuff' which included clothes, make-up, shoes, meds, books and the most important item, her Glock .40 model G22 Gen4 semi-automatic pistol and six, fifteen round clips.

On the return trip to Miramar NAS Mark looked for the Toyota but saw nothing.

Chapter Sixty Two

Secure Video Conference
Washington DC and San Diego DEA Offices
Tuesday, February 25, 1986 7:00 p.m. EST

President Stevens led off: "The first item I'd like to cover tonight is the demise of Frederico Alverez and family. Mark, your people were first on the scene. Tell me about it from the very beginning."

"Yes Sir," replied Garrison who proceeded to give a detailed account of the murder of Freddy Alverez and his family. He ended his response with, "That's about all I have at this point."

The President stared at the opposite wall, eyes unfocused, for about thirty seconds before asking; "Jim, what do you think Horte will do to protect his enterprise?"

"Hard to tell Brad, as you know, we've seen all sorts of reactions from illicit drug operations after discovering a leak in their security. The action on Alverez was business as usual, not a reaction of revenge. I would give a reasonably high probability to the fact that Horte has the key to the safe deposit box and will shortly have found the location and obtained its contents. We know that Alverez kept all of the information he had collected and undoubtedly his video copy of his interview with Mark in that box.

"Bill and I have a tag team watching him while he's in the U.S. Right now he's in Memphis Tennessee meeting with the CEO of his plant there. This is the fourth plant visit he's made. He's obviously shoring up his security and giving his people an update on recent events. This guy is globally clean – no wants or warrants anywhere. And, we were surprised to find out that he holds dual citizenship, Mexico and the U.S. But he doesn't travel under a U.S. or Mexican passport. He travels under a Columbian passport with papers identifying him as a Columbian Coffee Broker. We believe his Mexican passport is fake.

"We are certain he has a network in the U.S. that handles the coke after shipment, actually controls the street price on drugs made from cocaine but we have yet to uncover this network. This group is obviously responsible for distribution, security and storage of the product. And, we're reasonably sure that the two groups are totally unknown to each other – only Horte knows both. This guy is smart. Smarter than any drug king we've encountered to date. His communication link with this network is currently unknown to us and we're pulling out all stops to find it. We've *got* to find it before we can execute *Clean Slate*. Leaving that network in place with a huge supply of coke hidden in-country would give us anything *but* a clean slate. Our job here has become an order of magnitude more difficult than we originally thought.

"Our only leads right now are the Alverez crime scene and watching Horte like a hawk where ever he goes. Let me defer to the FBI and CIA on recent actions to obtain the information necessary to go forward."

"Thanks Jim," said the President frowning at the depth of complexity that this operation had taken on in just the last week, "Bill, where do we stand on the surveillance of Horte's Mexican facilities?"

"We've added another bird and placed both in tandem in a ninety minute orbit over both sites of interest and we've enabled focal scan on both. As you know the focal scan mode uses a significant amount of energy so we've dedicated these two birds to *Clean Slate*. The ninety minute orbit will give us a stationary window of eighteen minutes in IR mode. We're gathering significant intel at both sites. There's no indication that either site has altered their operations to avoid surveillance. We've also got three agents in the area. We're planning a small joint reconnaissance operation with a couple of Jerry's Special Forces guys and one of our former SEALs. We'll take a look-see at both facilities. Our intel shows us the exact layout of the top floor of the villa and the plant and to a lesser extent the bottom floor of the villa. The plant is one hundred and twenty three thousand square feet mostly single story about twenty feet high. There is an office area of nine hundred seventy square feet in a second floor area that spans the front of the facility about ten feet high. Both targets employ guard dogs. The plant runs two overlapping shifts: six a.m. to four p.m. and three p.m. to midnight, five days a week. This suggests a preferable execution early on a Sunday morning. We've initially set the window on the birds to give us an eighteen minute view from 1:13 to 1:31 in the morning – easily adjustable.

"George and I have been planning the take down. He's better equipped to talk about that. Any other questions for me?" asked Bill Conroy.

"Not right now, thanks Bill. Admiral?"

George Bennington continued, "The plant will be by far the easier of the two targets. A four man SEAL team with a seaward approach to the beach about a half mile south. The security right now is pathetic – of course that will likely change given recent developments. The dogs will have to take a nap so we'll have to use two dart guns to get them both at the same time. We know from the satellites exactly where the naphthalene and coal tar are stored. We'll use cardboard thermite flares to light it up. The flares will be remotely ignited after the team is well clear of the site. The explosion following the involvement of the volatiles will be huge. Coal tar comes to the plant in fifty five gallon steel drums and leaves as naphthalene combined with cocaine in the same drums. We don't know which is which but either will do – they're both highly flammable as are the petroleum by-products. The thermite will burn through the steel lids, vaporize the naphthalene, and then things will go in a hurry.

"The villa, on the other hand, will be somewhat more difficult. Please look at the satellite photos Bill sent us all. Horte's villa is located on a plateau on the side of a mountain ridge about five hundred feet above a river valley. It's on the west side of the second mountain ridge over from the Pacific. Very difficult access. If you'll look at the infra-red photos, numbers four through six, you'll see that the only access road is heavily guarded. The human figures you see circled in these IR photos are in well concealed bunkers – not visible in daylight photos. Referring to daylight photo number three, the bunker locations along the access road have been circled. As you can see from this photo the plateau has been almost completely cleared except for ornamental palms close to the house. On the southern end and western side the land slopes downward toward a nearly vertical cliff. Here the jungle vegetation has not been cleared. There is a path wide enough for vehicles that winds through this vegetation to the south and terminates at the top of the cliff. At the bottom of the cliff near the river are a number of vehicles that have been dumped there from above – probably Horte's graveyard. The plateau is twelve hundred feet north-south and three hundred fifty feet east-west at its widest spot. We have to assume the bunkers are all equipped with infrared cameras and machine guns, and that there is a fairly sophisticated electronic perimeter surveillance system. There are two large dogs on the property. They are always outside the house and at night they sleep in positions on either side of the gate to the access road about a hundred feet from the edge of the clearing. We think these are the locations where their food and water are placed. We could detect no form of restraint.

"On the fairly high probability that we won't find the locations of the cocaine caches in the U.S. before we initiate the action, we've assumed that this operation must depend heavily on stealth due to the importance of taking Horte alive and his villa intact.

"As you know, I have a small team working on the new automated HALO/HAHO system. Captain Joe Garcia and Commander Bo Jameson, both Navy SEALs are the key officers on the program. I would highly recommend reading this team into the mission. In your information packet you will find the specification for this system. Note the classification level.

"These guys have developed a stealth ingress system that exceeds specification in almost every dimension. They are making jumps from thirty five thousand feet and landing, not close to, but exactly on the target. From that altitude the range with no opposing wind and a separate equipment pack is sixty kilometers. It uses Differential GPS, a satellite navigation system that has the classified accuracy you see on the spec sheet. To get this level of accuracy it's necessary to plant a portable DGPS transceiver within three miles of the target. That will not be a problem. Two of Bill's in-country Special Ops agents can plant the unit at the very top of the mountain, just above Horte's villa, approaching the location from the other side. We looked at the 'over-the-mountain' ingress option but rejected it because of the 600 foot shear cliff above Horte's villa. This guy found himself a true jungle fortress with as many natural barriers as I've ever seen to keep people out.

"Our biggest problem right now is availability of systems and operatives. We currently have four systems and four trained SEALs. Garcia says training is not really a problem for jump trained SEALs and since two of Bill's in-country agents are former SEALs, we should have no problem fielding a six man team. Problem is, as we gathered intel on Horte's fortress we've already gone from a three man team to six. We might need seven or eight. We should have this firmed up by next week. Garcia's people are frantically acquiring parts, assembling and testing six new units. He says he can be ready in a week. This may be so, but experience tells me we're still three maybe four weeks out from execution. Once again, by next week we should have a better handle on that. Any questions?"

"How do you plan to handle the dogs at Horte's villa?" asked President Stevens.

"We're using the Navy H&K MP5-N with the 'not yet available' SD suppressors. This assault rifle has single shot, two or three round burst and fully automatic modes. Two SEALs will approach the dogs on descent from opposite directions. As you can see from the spec. the HAHO helmet visor has an infrared display mode – the dogs will be clearly visible. The latest feature added to the system is not in the specification yet. It can be programmed for automatic flight and landing. That feature can place both SEALs on an opposing forty five degree angle at fifty feet off the ground at the same time. Their MP5s will have two of our classified non-lethal 9 mm dart rounds, one in the chamber and the other at the top of the magazine. At fifty feet, on auto-pilot, this will be a simple pot shot."

"How do you design an auto-pilot for a parachute?" asked Stevens.

"Ingenious. It uses GPS, the chest-pack computer and four computer controlled, gas operated cylinders to pull on the shroud controls. This is what gives us stand-up landings exactly on target. In wind up to fifteen miles an hour, by the way."

"Impressive, can you get Captain Garcia and his team patched into our video conference next week? I'd like to meet them and I'm sure they will have valuable insight into whatever problems we come across before execution," Stevens added.

"Yes Sir, the best way to do that is have them jump in their Sherpa and fly over to the NAS to join Mark and his team in a secure conference facility. Meanwhile, I'll have to get the rest read into the mission. Garcia is the only one aboard so far."

"Do it George, and give these guys some kudos – they're magicians in my book.

"What about egress?" Stevens asked.

Admiral Bennington replied; "We'll have two MH-6 Little Bird helicopters on a coast guard ship at the twelve mile international waters line directly off the west coast. This is the same ship from which the plant team will operate. A call from the villa team will initiate the egress operation."

"Anything else we need to discuss tonight?" queried the President.

No one spoke up and the President adjourned the meeting.

Mark Garrison, Bud Nichols, Gary Parker, and Admiral Bennington comprised the members of the team who met on Tuesday evenings in the Admiral's secure video Conference room at San Diego NAS. Mark dismissed his two agents and then said to the Admiral:

"Because of my relationship to Alverez and the demise of him and his family, I have taken action to protect my family. My parents are secure in a remote location known only to me, but my sister is a Lt. Commander in the Navy. I need a waiver from you to allow her to bring her personal handgun onto Miramar NAS with the condition that she leaves it locked in her car while she is on base. Can you do that for me?"

"Does she have a California carry permit?"

"Yes sir, she does"

"Would she be more comfortable with her service weapon?"

"She qualifies expert with her Colt .45 but she is more comfortable with her Glock .40."

"Excellent weapon," responded the Admiral, "I'll fax a letter to Captain Baker tomorrow morning."

"Thank you sir – have a good evening," said Garrison as he turned to leave.

"Garrison," the Admiral quipped, "are we talking about Ashleigh Garrison, the Top Gun pilot?"

"That would be her. Her last name is McKensie now – she got married last December."

"Keep her safe, Director."

"I plan to, Admiral."

Chapter Sixty Three

SEAL Team Four Ready Room
San Diego NAS, San Diego California
Friday, February 28, 1986 9:00 a.m. PST

Master Chief Petty Officer Manny Hernandez had been a Navy SEAL for sixteen years. He joined the elite unit in 1970 after serving as a Navy Underwater Demolition Specialist for two years in Vietnam, only eight years after President John F. Kennedy formally created the SEALs in 1962. Many of the functions performed by the SEALs were being carried out as early as World War II and Kennedy realized the need for such a unit during his tour in the Navy as a PT Boat Commander.

Hernandez was born in British Belize in 1945. His family immigrated to the United States in 1952. His father was a master welder and had secured a job with Norfolk Navy Shipyard, Portsmouth Virginia. Manny joined the Navy in 1965 and began an exemplary career, advancing at time in grade intervals on a regular basis. He was promoted to Master Chief Petty Officer in October following a classified two man special operation at the direction of the President, during which he performed "well above the call of duty," and for which he was awarded the Navy's Distinguished Service Medal.

He called his team together to give them a tentative ready alert. "Ok guys, listen up! We've got a tentative alert for down range action at least three weeks out but maybe as much as five. I have zero information at this time. All leave is cancelled beginning Tuesday. When I get the orders we'll start readiness training. Take this weekend plus Monday off to get squared away and then be ready for a ten day readiness training followed by mission planning and training."

Hernandez was the leader of SEAL Team IV; the SEAL Team responsible for action in Central and South America.

Chapter Sixty Four

El Centro Naval Air Station
NWDC Commander's Office, El Centro, California
Monday, March 10, 1986 10:30 a.m. PST

"Morning Joe, what's up," asked Bo before he finished the last swallow of his Starbucks and tossed the empty cup in the corner trash can.

"Read this." Joe handed him a message from his secure telex.

"Well, you guessed right – won't be the first time."

"It'll be at least two weeks before we're ready. I'm not taking unproven gear into the field on an op like this," growled Joe.

Bo asked, "We can be ready in two weeks?"

"No, we need two weeks to get our systems ready and train two new SEALs on the new gear and then another week or two to train for the mission."

"Yeah, I guess you're right. With two new guys – that means you, me, Rob and Sam for a six man team." Rob Matthews, a member of SEAL Team Four was brought aboard the HAHO test team two weeks earlier to help Bo and Sam get the system operational.

"You think Sam's ready?" asked Joe

"He can do the job and he knows more about this system than anyone else – why don't you ask him?"

"I intend to."

Chapter Sixty Five

Secure Video Conference
White House and San Diego DEA Office
Tuesday, March 11, 1986 7:00 p.m. EST

Admiral George Bennington introduced Captain Joe Garcia, Commander Bo Jameson and I to the President, the Chairman of the Joint Chiefs and the FBI, CIA and DEA Directors. Joe had given Bo & me a thirty thousand foot briefing on what was going on in the world of illicit drugs but I had no idea that the President was involved.

The President began, "Welcome aboard gentlemen. First things first. This is a highly classified operation. Everyone in this meeting holds a Top Secret EB (Extended Background) or better clearance. The information we share here is need-to-know only. And we are the only persons with need to know at this point in time. We must keep it that way. Divulgence of this classified information will be considered an act of treason to the United States of America, and we all know what that means. Is that understood? Captain Garcia?"

"Yes Sir."

"Commander Jameson?"

"Yes Sir."

"Lieutenant McKensie?"

"Yes Sir."

"Good then we'll proceed. First, I'd like to welcome the three of you to our little group. With the help of Admiral Sterett, I've put together a Top Secret document describing the situation, the possible solutions and the four preferred options to execute the solution most beneficial to our country. This document will be distributed to a set of TS containers (safes) at each of your locations that will provide everyone on this team with access to what has transpired to date. This will help us bring others aboard without using excessive time to get them up to speed. The execution plan that this team develops will be compartmentalized. In other words some support folks involved in the plan will not have complete knowledge of the plan. Read this document, then re-read it. It is vital that each of us is fully aware of the situation and the details of the plan we are developing. Do not remove this document more than twenty feet from its secure container. The container owner will need to be present while you have access to the document – he or she as well as you will be responsible for its security.

"All that said, I'd like to ask Captain Garcia to give us an overview of the Automated HAHO System. Captain Garcia, if you please."

"Yes Sir. May I assume that everyone on this team has a fundamental understanding of HAHO and HALO systems?"

Joe Garcia paused for a response – there was none. He continued, "First let me say that this system has been designed to handle both the High and Low Altitude Opening mission. It is fully operational at this time in the HAHO mode only, primarily due to a lack of a critical component for the HALO mode – that being the laser altimeter sensor. The HAHO mode, however, can use a barometric altimeter with absolutely no degradation in performance.

"The system consists of a high altitude helmet with integral oxygen, pressure, high definition view screen, intra-team and satellite communications and a DGPS navigation system. Integrated with the helmet is a pressure assisted jump suit with a detachable integrated chest-pack computer used for precision three dimensional navigation. The system is updated by the integrated GPS with position information every 30 milliseconds. It has an auto-pilot capability enabled by four gas operated shroud pullers. This system can be programmed to take a soldier from thirty five thousand feet to a target sixty kilometers away and land him on a two foot target in winds less than fifteen miles per hour – hands off!

"The visor system has three selectable modes: clear-view, enhanced night and infrared. All three modes have altitude, position, mode, and communication channel information projected at the edge of the visor screen's viewable area. Also projected on the forward area of the screen is the relative position of up to five team members, in different colors, when in the field of view. The system has been designed to support the user during gliding and/or freefall operation from up to forty two thousand feet and then allow him to quickly shed the pressure suit and all systems that were necessary for HAHO but keep the helmet ,chest-pack computer and battery pack for ground operations – all vision, location and communication capabilities are retained. This system can provide a major advantage to the operator by allowing quick conversion to ground operations, day or night.

"We have twelve of these systems assembled. Four have been tested with remarkable performance in all areas including reliability. The system exceeds all of its current specifications. The other eight systems have just recently been assembled and lab tested. Two will have their first test jump tonight. If our luck holds we'll have eight of these systems operational this week and all twelve by the end of next week.

"I don't know if I need to say this since everything said here tonight is classified: All operational capability, specifications, and performance of this system are classified TOP SECRET."

"Admiral Bennington, I want to congratulate you and your team on completion of this system. As little as a year ago we all thought this might just turn out to be a pipe dream and now we've got it and it works beyond our wildest dreams," said Brad Stevens.

"Mr. President, in my job I push a lot of paper and look for good people to do miracles. These three gentlemen with me tonight along with a few more back at the ranch made this happen – they deserve most of the credit. Especially Lieutenant Sam McKensie, our program technical and test manager. There are others who need recognition and I intend to see that they get it – but Sam has performed well above his pay grade. There's no doubt in my mind, or Captain Garcia's, or Commander Jameson's, that without Sam we'd still be scratching our heads about how to make this thing work."

"Lieutenant McKensie, I understand that Admiral Bennington offered you, as a critical member of his DEVGRU team, an opportunity to advance in rank and participate in your BUD/S training as time allows on a path to become a SEAL. I presume that means your training will be piecemeal and not necessarily in the correct order. The president glanced at the Admiral and received a nod. "And I understand that you've undergone part of your land training and performed quite well," said the President.

I blushed and said nothing.

"Do you think you'd like to be a part of this operational team?"

I didn't know what to say – how do you turn down the President. So

I said, "Yes Sir."

"Captain Garcia have you offered him the promotion?"

"Yes Sir, I asked him to think about it and get back to me. So, Sam, is that your decision?"

"Yes Sir."

"Then why is he still a Lieutenant?" The President sounded a little irritated.

"I wanted to let him understand a little more about this mission before I got his answer," replied Joe Garcia.

"So by our next meeting I will be addressing him as Lieutenant Commander?"

"Yes Sir."

For the next two hours the team planned the details of the three pronged mission: the villa, the hybrid plant and all the domestic extraction plants including Puerto Rico which would, more likely than not be operational by then.

In planning Special Operations missions there are several key factors that must be considered to insure success and seven that are absolutely critical:

1. Intelligence: A special ops team can never have enough intelligence. Knowing more about the enemy than they know about themselves is paramount to mission success.
2. Simplicity: Keep the execution phase of the mission as simple as possible. Probability of mission failure increases exponentially with complexity.
3. Security: Nothing can compromise a mission more completely than a security leak.
4. Repetition: The team must learn, review and practice the details of the mission plan until there is no doubt of its success.
5. Surprise: In order to gain "relative superiority" as quickly as possible during the execution phase of the mission, the mission itself must be a surprise. The element of surprise often relies on technology such as the Advanced HAHO System.

6. Speed: The execution phase must be conducted with maximum speed to keep the enemy off balance and maintain relative superiority.
7. Purpose: The Special Ops Team must focus on the mission objective and not let other conditions or events interfere with meeting that objective.

When the meeting concluded the President asked, "Lieutenant McKensie, now you know as much as I about the operation. Your part would obviously be in the assault on the villa. If you wish, you can change your mind about the mission but still continue your journey to become a SEAL. What say you?" asked Brad Stevens.

Once again, how do you turn down the President of the United States? So I said: "Yes Sir, I want to be part of this."

What the hell have I gotten myself into? I'm going to die in the jungle. . .

Chapter Sixty Six

Miramar NAS, Miramar CA

Top Gun Flight Operations Desk

Friday, March 14, 1986 6:00 p.m. PST

"Hi babe, I brought you a present," I said as Ash and I uncoupled from a passionate embrace after a week away from each other. "It's the latest model of the Motorola flip phone with the large battery pack – you can leave it on in receive mode for four days and talk for three hours without recharging. I've got my cell number programmed into it and yours in mine – just hold down the #1 button for a second to call me.

"I guess it's time I gave in to modern communications technology, but I'm not going to join all the idiots walking down the street talking on their phone totally oblivious to traffic or other pedestrians."

"Good to know you won't be a chit-chatter 'cause these things charge by the minute and they ain't cheap. Mark and I both think you need to carry one just for safety. After we talked we decided that it should be ok for you to go off base with either him or me. So let's go to your quarters and get the rest of your stuff – then we'll stop by your car, pick up your Glock and go to our place and plan the weekend – sound ok? We've got a lot to talk about."

On the way out, I looked for a dark blue late model Toyota sedan that Mark thought might be following them two weeks ago when he brought Ash to the base. And there it was, right where he said he had first seen it. It appeared to be unoccupied, but as I watched in my side mirror the Toyota pulled out off the shoulder onto the road about a quarter mile behind us. I drove directly to our condo in La Jolla Shores. The Toyota followed us – there was only one person visible, the driver.

Chapter Sixty Seven

The McKensie Condo
La Jolla Shores, CA
Friday, March 14, 1986   6:40 p.m. PST

We got out of my car and walked straight to our condo. When inside, I called Mark, "Hey Mark, our friend in the blue Toyota followed us from the base. We're in the condo now. I thought I'd call you and get some ideas on what to do. I've got our two night vision prototypes with me, one is starlight enhanced and the other is infrared. We're both armed. I've gotten up to date on the history of our current problem. I figure this guy is likely the one who took out our planner friend and he won't make a move until he sees me leave."

"Sam, I need you guys to stay put until I get there. It ought to take me about thirty five minutes."

"We parked in our covered area. I didn't see him on our way in so we don't know where he is. I'll darken the front and rear bedrooms and use my infrared unit to locate his car. He should be parked where he can watch the rear entrance we used. I'll call you as soon as I locate him."

"Ok Sam, I'm on my way – you guys stay put."

Ash looked at me quizzically and asked, "What the hell's going on here?"

Smiling, I said, "We haven't had a chance to talk since Tuesday. Bo, Joe & I are now part of the operation Mark has been working on for months now. I can't tell you much about the operation, but I can tell you that the guy in the blue Toyota is probably the one who took down our snitch and his family. So we do need to be careful. Don't leave this room without your gun and a couple of magazines. Put a round in the chamber, safety on, and then replace the round in the magazine. I'm going to fire up my infrared system and see if I can locate his car through the bedroom windows. So don't open any doors while I'm in there – ok?"

I slipped into the rear bedroom without letting in any light, then raised the shade and opened the window. Standing back from the window a couple of feet I cranked up the IR prototype, an un-cooled system using ambient temperature as the image baseline. This was a state of the art system and I was very sure he didn't have one like it. Current Thermal IR vision technology used cryogenic coolers to produce an image baseline temperature much colder than ambient, these were the IR systems used on aircraft, tanks and other military vehicles where size and weight weren't as important. This system uses an indium antimonide focal-plane array that can detect temperature differences of 0.4 degrees in a range from -4 degrees to 300 degrees fahrenheit at one thousand feet and it can be made very small and light weight. It is also very expensive.

I first looked east, the direction from which we approached the condo complex – nothing. Scanning west, there he was. Parked across the street, clearly alone and using binoculars, probably starlight enhanced, to watch our rear entrance. He was waiting for me to leave.

I called Mark, "He's down the street behind our condos at the corner of the crossing street on the northeast side facing our condo. Looks like he has a set of starlight binoculars. Why don't you park a block further down the street around the corner? When you're in place I'll leave and drive by him, turn left, park and come back to where he's in view. When he gets out of the car, if he has his weapon drawn I can warn you and we can approach him from both directions. It's better than approaching an armed killer in a vehicle. "

"That sounds like a good plan except that I need this guy alive or slightly wounded where we can patch him up without a hospital visit. I'll take your position to the front right of the vehicle and you turn right, park and come back to a position to the rear left of the car. I have a pair of starlight goggles. He will likely leave his binoculars in the car. As he gets out of the car and closes the door I'll shoot out his right front tire. You then immediately shoot out his left rear tire. I'll tell him he's surrounded by federal agents, hands up, etc. If he draws a weapon shoot him in the butt, left side. That'll cause him to fall away from the car. I'll have the car as a shield to approach him. You yell to me 'he's down, do you want me to finish him off'. I'll yell back 'yeah kill the bastard'. That ought to cause him to turn toward you and I can take him from his blind side. Hopefully, we won't have to do any more shooting at that point.

We'll wait twenty minutes. If he doesn't leave the car by then, I'll approach from his right side, weapon drawn when I get his attention you shoot his left front tire and we'll proceed with plan A."

"Sounds good Mark. Let me know when you're in position."

"Make sure Ash is locked in the condo with her weapon in her hand."

"Will do, see you soon."

Chapter Sixty Eight

The McKensie Condo Neighborhood

La Jolla Shores, CA

Friday, March 14, 1986 7:15 p.m. PST

Mark called and said he was in position behind a wing wall on a home that had been converted to a dentist's office. He could see the guy in his car pretty clearly with his goggles. He wasn't using his binoculars. He said, "remember, go east a block beyond his car, turn south and park near, but out of sight of his car. I think it's best to approach from behind. There's a large tree with some bushes around it about twenty yards from his rear tire. Can you hit it from there?"

I replied, "I've got a laser sight on my Sig Sauer. It's zeroed to twenty five yards – I can hit a nickel from there."

"Good, call me when you get into position, turn your receive volume down and put your phone on vibrate."

"I'm here, did you see me coming?"

"As clear as these things would let me. Now we wait," said Garrison

It was about ten minutes. The man got out of his car, stood for thirty seconds or so with both of his hands in his jacket pocket looking in the direction of the condos. Then he looked left and right, turned around 180 degrees, looked left and right again. As he was turning back toward the condos Mark shot his front right tire. Within a second I shot his rear left rear tire. He drew his gun.

Mark yelled "Federal Agents. You're surrounded; drop the gun, hands in the air, NOW!"

The man held his ground, looking in the direction of Mark's voice and crouching near the front of the car for protection. I didn't have a clean shot at his butt, but I did have a good shot at his left front tire about four inches from his left shoulder, so I took it and immediately yelled, "Hey dumb-shit, we've got six guns on you. You've got exactly three seconds to drop that gun and get your hands in the air or I'll blow your fuckin' head off and save the government a lot of money! DO IT NOW!"

And that's what he did. Mark approached from the front and I approached from the back. Mark kicked away his weapon and turned him around to cuff him and I waved my laser dot in his face and then put it on his chest to keep him from trying anything. Mark used quick cuffs which have a third loop to go through a rear belt loop and around the belt.

He turned the guy around and asked him where his ID was.

"Don't carry ID. I want a lawyer."

"That's ok. We'll classify you as a foreign national and ship your ass to a little Island we rent from some friends where you'll either tell us what we want to know or you'll die in the process. You understand me asshole – you have no rights, you'll get no lawyer." Mark threw him into the back seat of his own car and pressed number five on his speed dial.

The phone answered, "Bill Conroy."

"Hi Bill, Mark Garrison here, we've got the guy who probably took out Freddy and his family. Think your guys can make him talk?"

"I'd bet on it. Where are you now?"

"I'm at my sister's condo in La Jolla. Specifically, Sam and I are at the corner of Lancaster and Ocean View. Can you call the locals off, we had to fire a few shots – nobody's hurt but I'd bet the locals are on their way."

"I'll make the call to the locals and have one of our guys there in, say, twenty minutes."

"That'll work, thanks Bill."

Mark had no sooner hung up than the La Jolla Police arrived. Mark took his Wallet out with his ID and badge showing, held it high in his right hand and walked slowly to the door of the police car.

He said to the driver:

"You haven't gotten a call regarding disposition of this non-incident yet, have you?"

"Not yet," replied the officer

It took only about five minutes before the police radio beeped. The officer took his receiver off the hook to silence the speaker.

"Yes Sir, we're here with them now. Yes Sir, here he is." The officer handed Mark the phone and said, "It's for you."

Mark said, "Yes, this is Mark Garrison Southwest Director, DEA. Yes, we had to take out the tires of the vehicle. Three shots were fired at three tires. We have the spent bullets and casings. That's right, no collateral damage. Thank you Captain."

The officer said, "It's all yours – we don't even want to know what *really* happened," as they drove away.

"Smart ass," Thought Garrison.

About thirty five minutes later a guy - who bore the closest resemblance to a gorilla that I'd ever seen, stepped out of his car, showed us his CIA ID, opened the back door of the perp's car, pulled him out with one hand, dragged him across the street, threw him into the back seat of his car and took off – never said a word.

Chapter Sixty Nine

The McKensie Condo
La Jolla Shores, CA
Friday, March 14, 1986 8:05 p.m. PST

"Ok, now, one more time, what the hell's going on here?" Ashleigh McKensie asked in a terse voice I had never heard before.

"Like I said, Tuesday night Bo and I got drug into the thing Mark's been working on for months – It's finally gotten to the point where action is required. It's highly classified, so there's some stuff I can't talk about. Let's both calm down. Let me gather my thoughts and I'll tell you as much as I can."

"I heard three shots fired out there. Make sure you get to that part!"

"Ok, ok, I will.

"You have a TS clearance - let me start with the stuff I can tell you that's not classified TS Need-To-Know: You're aware of a lot of what Joe, Bo and I are doing with the HAHO system. Well, the capability of the system has exceeded all expectations and it's coming on-line to handle the HAHO requirements which might be the only configuration needed since it fills more than ninety percent of the stealth ingress mission requirements: Stealthy ingression from high altitudes and long distances.

"The spec calls for a well trained operator to be able to jump from thirty five thousand feet, travel twenty nautical miles and land within ten feet of the target. In our test program we routinely jump from thirty thousand feet, travel up to twenty nautical miles and land within one foot of the target in up to fifteen mile per hour winds. The flight suit with integral helmet has been tested to fifty thousand feet in the altitude chamber at Edwards but our modified C-23 test vehicle with a light load can only get us to thirty thousand, so that's where we're testing it. We added a capability, not called for in the spec. – an automatic landing system that can be enabled anywhere between the airplane and three hundred feet AGL. That's where we get all the accuracy – it uses Differential GPS. Ever heard of that?"

"Yeah, we were briefed on it a few weeks back. Several Navy aircraft are being modified to use it. What you're telling me is that it really works."

"Yes it does.

"We brought another SEAL aboard the test team a couple of weeks ago. He'd been to jump school a few years ago, had about thirty jumps including three night jumps. He now has nineteen night jumps with our system from between twenty and thirty thousand feet – all right on target. So what I'm saying here; is that anyone with basic jump training can use this system effectively with a simple one hour briefing – way beyond spec.

"You know that Mark has been mega-focused on his job for the last year or so. The DEA has uncovered a major source of drugs coming into the U.S. Here's what I think I can say about that: This could be, probably is, the largest drug trafficking operation ever uncovered and it might account for half, or more, of the cocaine currently coming into the U.S. The operation has a large number of operatives both outside and inside the U.S. It will require interdiction forces on land, sea and air – you can imagine my part in this.

"I met the President and the Chairman of the Joint Chiefs in a secure video conference Tuesday night. Thursday I officially became a Navy Lt. Commander – but you still out rank me by time-in-grade. I told you about what happened to our whistle-blower and his family before it got classified TS-NTK. So forget about that, but be aware that you and your parents are prime targets for this drug nut in Mexico.

"The guy Mark and I just took down – the three gun shots you heard took his tires out – is very likely the one who took out our snitch and his family. And, I'm pretty damned certain he was after you. And you can bet he's got buddies out there who will take his place in that endeavor.

"Mark and I are going to insist that Admiral Bennington put Miramar on high security status until we get this thing cleared up. And we're going to insist that you remain on base until then. We've already got your parents plugged into the witness protection program. They have a group that handles short term protection routinely and with 100 percent success.

"Don't blame your brother for me getting tied up in this thing. It's what I'm working on that did the trick."

"When will I get to see you?" Ash was as close to tears as I've seen her since I proposed to her.

"I'll fly Bo's Mooney into Miramar every Friday night. We'll get you into married housing – we'll just spend our weekends on base. It won't be long."

Chapter Seventy

Miramar NAS, Miramar CA

Ashleigh McKensie's VOQ room

Sunday, March 16, 1986 6:30 p.m. PST

"Be sure to go by the housing office tomorrow and find a small house on base. There's sure to be several available – nobody lives on base any more," I said to Ash as I was getting my stuff together to fly back to El Centro, immediately regretting the 'nobody lives on base part.

"Nobody except us," Ash griped. "Now I've got my husband *and* my brother to worry about. And, probably my parents too."

"Look at me Ashleigh, Your parents are safe. They're with the best in the business. Mark gets a daily security report on them – they're fine. Don't worry about me. The only bad guy who knows who I am is on his way to an island somewhere in the pacific to be interrogated by a gorilla. I don't want you to worry about anything. You're job requires a clear head. We'll have this whole thing cleared up in a couple of weeks. Go fly and be happy. Remember, I love you, beautiful blue eyes."

She smiled and we kissed goodbye. Truth to tell, I was worried sick about her. Her job was too demanding to have anything like this on her mind.

Chapter Seventy One

Miramar NAS, Miramar CA
Base Housing Office
Monday, March 17, 1986 11:30 a.m. PST

Ashleigh had finished her morning flight by eleven o'clock. The lessons were typically three hours each; an hour of planning and maneuver review before the flight an hour and a half of dog-fighting where the student tried his hardest to get Ashleigh 'locked up' for two seconds – the length of time it took for an AIM-9 Sidewinder missile to be successfully launched. But that was almost always not to be. A thirty minute "lessons learned" session completed the lesson. The point of the lesson was for the student to learn to execute the maneuvers Ashleigh was teaching him and using during the training flight to avoid being shot out of the sky and then to turn the tables on him by using a complement of maneuvers to get behind her student and lock him up. Her better students were able to accomplish this once or twice during the last couple of lessons toward the end of their three week program while Ashleigh was able to get out of trouble and turn the tables on her student almost every time. She had two advantages; first, she was flying an F-5, the single seat fighter version of the two seat T-38 super-sonic trainer which she had flown for two years as a basic jet instructor and she knew the aircraft inside-out. The F-5, disguised as a MiG 23 Flogger, was the smallest, lightest and one of the most maneuverable jet aircraft in the U.S. inventory; second, it was her job – she knew how to out-maneuver some of the Top Gun instructors before she ever took the job.

* * * *

She had found a small on-base house for a reasonable price, set up a tour of the house for that evening at 4:30 and headed out the door to grab a sandwich at the O-Club before her 1:00 student. As she started to cross the street to walk to the O-Club, a block and a half away, a young Petty Officer, approached her.

"Are you Commander McKensie?" he asked.

"Yes," Ashleigh replied, slowing her pace slightly.

"Captain Baker would like a short meeting with you. He sent me to drive you to his office and then back to flight operations. Hs said it wouldn't take very long."

"Actually I'm headed to the O-Club for a quick lunch," said Ashleigh, wondering what this was all about. Had Mark or Sam said something to the Base Commander? "Well, I guess Captain Baker trumps lunch."

"After your meeting I can probably get you back to the O-Club and then wait while you eat and then drive you over to Flight Operations," said the young Petty Officer.

"Ok, let's go."

"I'll park around back while you see the Captain. Is that ok Commander?"

"Sure, I'll go in the back way."

Ashleigh grabbed the door handle as the Petty Officer pulled into a parking slot in the rear of the Base Headquarters building. "This door's locked," she said as she tried to open it.

"Hold on, It locks automatically, I'll unlock it.."

Ashleigh heard a click and felt a sharp pain high in her left shoulder as she fumbled with the door handle. "Oh myyy Gaawwd!" she moaned as she lost control of her body and blacked out.

She woke up somewhere over the pacific ocean in a business jet, her hands handcuffed through a strap holding her tightly in her seat. Her young Petty Officer was wearing dark slacks and a blue golf shirt.

"Don't be alarmed Commander, we don't intend to harm you. We just want your company while we negotiate with your brother."

Chapter Seventy Two

Maximillion Horte's Private Airstrip
Eighty Miles North of Managua, Nicaragua
Monday, March 17, 1986 3:45 p.m. PST

As they approached land Ashleigh was blindfolded. They touched down in Horte's 25G Learjet at his private airstrip in Nicaragua. The strip was used by local rancheros and businesses to ship and receive goods form Managua on the west coast and Bilwi and Bluefields on the east coast. The fees charged for use of the airstrip were low enough to ensure fairly heavy use. Horte arranged to have a single customs/immigration agent located in a modest (for Nicaragua) home near the airstrip to allow the filing of flight plans, immigration and customs duties, and the handling of export/import documents both domestically and internationally. This agent also had a part time job, working for Max. That job paid a little more than three times what his full time government job did. Max traveled abroad as Roberto Gonzales, a coffee broker from Columbia. Only in Mexico and the U.S. was his true identity known and then only by a few people who worked for him. This was his carefully guarded "gateway" from his world into the real world, through which he could take whatever he wanted, whenever he wanted - including hostages like Ashleigh.

They refueled at the strip, filed a flight plan to Mazatlan, which included Ashleigh McKensie, identified as Sara Johnson, and took off for Mazatlan. When they landed they processed through the other end of Horte's gateway. They taxied the jet into Horte's private hangar on the south end of the Mazatlan Airport. The "Petty Officer" left for the customs/immigration office with the paperwork. After he returned with the clearance papers, allowing them to drive through the inner security gate into the airport proper, two of Horte's men loaded Ashleigh into a van and then drove her to Horte's villa..

Ashleigh had decided shortly after she awoke tightly restrained in the airplane that it was useless to resist and that she should say as little as possible and not reveal that she was fluent in Spanish.

Chapter Seventy Three

Maximillion Horte's Villa

35 Miles Southeast of Mazatlan, Mexico

Monday, March 17, 1986 6:15 p.m. PST

"Commander McKensie, welcome to my humble abode," said Maximillion Horte with just a slight hint of an accent.

Ashleigh said nothing.

"Allow me to show you my guest suite up stairs. It contains all the amenities you will require during your hopefully short stay. Follow me, please."

Horte led Ashleigh to a suite that occupied a good portion of the second floor of the villa. "You should feel free to make yourself comfortable and relax. There are comfortable lounging clothes in the closet as well as under-garments and cosmetics. There is a large Jacuzzi-bath for relaxation, a large screen TV, a small well stocked kitchen with dining area and a very comfortable bed. There is a wonderful partly covered deck through that door with a beautiful view of the valley, but beware of our two security dogs that are trained to attack strangers. There are stairs from the deck to the ground below. Please don't open the gate at the top of the stairs. My dogs are really not nice. Juan Carlo, your travel host will be available twenty four/seven to assist you with any need. Please feel free to contact him by dialing zero on this house phone. I will contact your brother tomorrow evening. I'm sure you will want to speak with him. So for now, please relax and make yourself comfortable," Horte said smiling as he turned and left the room.

Ashleigh heard the door lock, but tried it anyway. Yep, it was locked – she was a prisoner in a guest suite of the most well appointed villa she had ever seen.

Chapter Seventy Four

NSFWDC Lab Complex, Sam McKensie's Office
El Centro NAS, El Centro California
Tuesday, March 18, 1986 8:05 a.m. PST

"Mark, this is Sam. Ashleigh and I set up a contact routine just to stay in touch during our little drug drama. I called her Sunday night to let her know I was home safe and she called me yesterday around noon to tell me she'd found a nice little house on base and had an appointment to see it at 4:30 yesterday. She didn't call last night so I called her five minutes ago – the phone went straight to voice mail. Her phone has been turned off! Something's wrong! Can you call the base commander and get someone to locate her?"

"Ok Sam, stay put. I'll make the call and call you back."

Twenty five long minutes later my phone rang. "Sam the news is not good; Ash didn't show for her one o'clock student. A Petty Officer First Class was found bound, gagged and tied to a chair in his off-base apartment late last night. Captain Baker had been notified at five this morning and had been in his office since a little past six this morning trying to figure out what was happening. When I called he immediately called the housing office and sent the duty clerk to Ashleigh's room with a master key. It appears that she had not been there at all last night. The Petty Officer who works the second shift at the Base Exchange said he'd been drugged by someone at the diner where he ate breakfast at around ten o'clock and woke up around seven or eight last night. He tried to make enough noise to alert his neighbors down stairs but they evidently didn't get in until around eleven. The local police came when the neighbors got suspicious and called them. They took him to the hospital to be checked out. Since they found his base ID card, his wallet, car and a uniform were all missing they called base security. The BX reported his absence but no one connected the dots until the police called. Sam, it looks like Ashleigh's been kidnapped by an imposter."

My heart sank down below my knees. A wave of panic came over me like a dark cloak. I couldn't think of anything but the pictures I'd seen of Freddy Alverez' dismembered head. My hands started shaking and I broke out into a cold sweat. The woman I loved more than life itself was likely in the hands of Maximillion Horte!

Chapter Seventy Five

Oval Office, White House

Washington D.C.

Tuesday, March 18, 1986 10:30 a.m. EST

There was a long low frequency beep from the large phone on the President's desk as a red light began flashing at its lower right corner. President Stevens' phone had sixty four direct-dial buttons as well as the normal number pad and intercom buttons – it was intimidating just to look at.

"Excuse me gentlemen," he was discussing a domestic tax-cut proposition with several members of his cabinet, and rose to take the call in his adjoining private office. "I shouldn't be long."

"Mr. President, this is Jim Doddington. I believe our problem has taken a nasty twist. Mark Garrison's sister, Lt. Commander Ashleigh McKensie, has disappeared. Recall that she is also Lt. Commander Sam McKensie's wife and a Top Gun instructor. We're 95% certain it was a kidnapping sanctioned by Horte. I need your permission to get Adam Kivel and a few of his NSA assets involved. I've talked to the rest of the team already; our consensus is that we should act sooner than planned, and that we need to double our intel efforts immediately. Admiral Sterett and Director Conroy say they will be ready by this Sunday morning. Same for Director Gilmore and myself. I didn't want to bother you until we felt confident in our plan being pulled up."

"Ok Jim, here's what I want you to do. Call Adam on a secure line. You read him into the program, security-wise. Brief him on what's at stake here. He has a small team of bird drivers who have a computer that can optimize all U.S satellite assets to support covert ops such as this. As you know, it's damned expensive to move those birds and then move them back. Tell Adam that I concur with this plan and we didn't get him involved at the beginning because of the expense. But now things have changed and we've got to move fast. Tell him I'm tied up until noon – I'll call him then.

"Also, Jim, we'd better postpone tonight's meeting until tomorrow night – after we've gotten Adam on board and have a little better understanding of what's going on."

Chapter Seventy Six

Mark Garrison's Office

San Diego, California

Wednesday, March 19, 1986 7:35 a.m. PST

As Mark Garrison approached his office he noticed an envelope taped to his door. He entered his office, donned a pair of latex gloves and carefully removed the envelope taking it to the break area for examination. As he expected there were no prints and nothing unique about the printer or paper on which the note was written. It read: "I have your sister. She is safe and comfortable and will remain so unless you decide to do something that I deem stupid. If that happens, she will join Mr. Alverez, or what is left of Mr. Alverez in a place you'd rather not think about. But, Mr. Garrison, I would encourage you to think about it a lot!" It was signed, "Your New Best Friend."

Mark carefully faxed the note on a secure line to Jim Doddington with the following note: "I do not want Sam McKensie or Bo Jameson to see this. I'll handle breaking the news to them. These guys need a clear head Sunday morning. I don't think Horte will expect action that soon and I believe we will still have some element of surprise. I also believe that he already has all of his operations on high alert. It's likely that he'll have extra guards posted at the villa even at two o'clock in the morning. Our advantage will be the IR intel from several satellites and the HAHO ingress and IR visual capability. If you have received any new intel on the villa please share it with me." Signed MG.

Chapter Seventy Seven

Secure Video Conference

San Diego, California and Washington D.C.

Wednesday, March 19, 1986 7:00 p.m. EST

"Gentlemen, we've got SECDEF, CJCS, CIA, FBI, NSA and DEA present here. Who's there?" asked President Stevens.

Admiral George Bennington faced the camera and replied, "myself, DEA Director Garrison, Captain Garcia, Commander Jameson, Lt. Commander McKensie and Master Chief Manny Hernandez, leader of Team Four, sir."

"Hello Master Chief," said Brad Stevens; "haven't had the pleasure of working with you since last October. You doing ok?"

"Yes sir, six months older and deeper in debt." Hernandez replied grinning.

"I understand you and your team will handle disposition of the plant near Mazatlan and recovery of the airborne team."

"Yes sir, we've put together a workable plan. The Coasties will help us out with their new super cutter carrying two of our Little Birds on her flight deck."

"Good to have you guys aboard, Master Chief," said the President. "Lets get this show on the road – we've got a lot to cover tonight.

"We've found it necessary to add SECDEF and the NSA to our little band of brothers here. Adam Kivel runs what I call Space Intelligence. His folks control all U.S. space borne assets and the analysis and disposition of the associated intelligence. As you know we already had two CIA birds in tandem polar orbits with a ninety minute period giving us an eighteen minute stationary window over the naphthalene plant and villa area. I asked Adam to use his 'magic machine', a super computer constellation analyzer/controller, to give us a larger stationary window, and I believe he's already accomplished that minor miracle.

Adam?"

"Here's what we've been able to accomplish, Mr. President: First we feed the requirements into our Constellation Management Analyzer System. We call it CMAS. Then CMAS looks at all U.S. assets and responds with the most efficient set of orbital changes. These are reviewed by a multi-service team of senior analysts who have at their fingertips the current mission profile of each satellite. If the individual mission of each selected bird is not critically compromised, the change set can be implemented. In this case we wanted all birds in the lower ninety minute orbit to give us exactly sixteen revolutions a day yielding a stationary window. Director Conroy already had an eighteen minute window set up with two of his birds in tandem so all we had to do was move four of our closest birds into ninety minute tandem orbits resulting in a fifty four minute window over the target exactly sixteen times a day. The window will open for fifty four minutes each morning at 0110 hours (1:10 a.m.) Pacific Standard Time and re-open every ninety minute period thereafter. You can adjust your missions plus or minus a few minutes either way as you please."

"What do you think gentlemen – will that work?" asked the President.

"That's better than I had hoped for," said Bill Conroy. "Captain Garcia, Master Chief Hernandez, what do you guys think?"

"That's fourteen and a half hours of observation a day, right at sixty percent coverage," Joe Garcia said smiling, "that's great! When does it start?"

"The last bird will be on station before this meeting is over," Adam Kivel said confidently.

"Can we get a secure feed down here?" asked Garcia.

"We have a small secure area over at the Naval Base and I can arrange access for your teams. We can feed you real-time IR as well as the best quality structural shots so you can get the layout of the facilities pretty well understood. We can also get you a hot-line to our analysts working the intel for this mission," said Kivel, "and you can use this facility as the operation center when the action starts. We'll all be watching real time."

"I've spent many hours in that place and I think my access is still valid – could you check on that please?" asked the Master Chief.

"I'll have yours and Admiral Bennington's confirmed," replied

Kivel, "and Mr. Garrison, Captain Garcia and Commanders Jameson and McKensie added by tomorrow morning."

Brad Stevens re-took charge of the meeting, "I'm assuming we'll strike both facilities at the same time and that we'll try to take Horte alive. Remember we're pretty certain there is a twenty year plus stash of coke spread around the U.S. in unknown places. We've got to find it. So Horte and his people, computers, PDAs, ledgers, everything we can grab will be very important.

"Adam's guys will track Horte and give you real-time info on exactly where he is when you arrive. We think we have already located Lt. Commander McKensie – Sam's wife. It appears she's been confined to an upstairs guest suite. She's been there since Monday night but with only eighteen minutes out of every ninety, it was hard to be sure."

The President closed the meeting with, "Executing this operation two weeks earlier than planned is going to put a lot of stress on a lot of people, so let's think this thing through. Gather as much intel as you can and use it well. Captain Garcia, Master Chief Hernandez, as team leaders you know the importance of study, plan and practice. I know you're well into this process, but you're time has been cut to three days remaining. Make the best possible use of that time and be sure all members of your teams are involved. We'll meet again Friday afternoon at 4:00 p.m. for a final review. We've got to get this right."

Chapter Seventy Eight

Coast Guard Cutter Jamestown
Pacific Ocean, southwest of Mazatlan, Mexico
Sunday, March 23, 1986 0005 hrs PST

The Coast Guard Super Cutter *Jamestown* lay fifteen miles off the west coast of Mexico in nearly calm seas. Master Chief Petty Officer Manny Hernandez was completing the final briefing to his five SEAL Team IV team mates: "We have the training, intel and tools to get this job done without casualties. That's the way I want it done! Any questions?"

"Yeah Chief," commented Petty Officer Third Class Don Wilson, 'we've trained with these new HAHO IR helmets and they work great along with the laser beam sights. But won't the laser spots and beams give away our position?"

"Wilson, where the hell were you when I explained how that system worked? Everybody listen up – this is damned important for us all to understand: The laser beams are in the IR spectrum – not visible to the naked eye. We are absolutely certain the bad guys don't have un-cooled, portable IR night vision capability – hell, we just invented it ourselves. You guys and the HAHO team are the only people in the world with this technology. The bad guys can't see you or your laser spot or beam, even in smoke. You can see them and your laser spot on them. Even if they turn on the lights your systems will still work – you will not be blinded by the light like you would with the starlight systems. If the lights come on, we take 'em out – we own the night, especially with this new IR technology.

"Remember, if you take your helmet off you have to switch your weapons to from IR laser to visible laser, which will also be visible to the enemy – unless the lights are on where you can turn off your visible lasers and revert to your optical or mechanical sights – but you don't need to remove those helmets. Bottom line; keep the damned helmets on unless they fail – and not one has failed to date. They've been very reliable. And once again, if the lights come on, shoot 'em out!

"Does everybody understand this?"

Wilson nodded his head sheepishly with a thumbs up – all other thumbs were up.

"OK swabbies, let's gear up and slide out the ass end of this here water truck."

Chapter Seventy Nine

C-23 Sherpa Cargo Plane
El Centro NAS Tarmac
Sunday, March 23, 1986 0023 hrs PST

Captain Joe Garcia gave the start engines command to the pilots and returned to his seat on the starboard side of the C-23. This was the same aircraft the HAHO Team had used for the past year testing the HAHO system. The pilot's job was simply to stay twelve miles off shore, run down to Mazatlan, dump the six man team and return home. Not a bad night's work.

The team, however, had a daunting task ahead of them. The fact that my wife was being held hostage in the building that we planned to attack complicated things significantly. The plan looked good though and I was given a right of final approval since Ash was involved. We had to make this work. Of the six team members five were SEALs; the two new guys, Danny Labow and Mike Jako were HALO experienced SEALs and adapted quickly to the new HAHO system. Joe, Bo and I had lots of experience with the system. Lieutenant Hal Nicholson, my HAHO system test partner for the last two months knew the system well but, like me, this was his first combat mission. The team had convinced me that I should be the one to land on the villa's twelve by fifteen foot open area on the second floor deck to rescue Ash from the guest suite.

At first we couldn't understand why Ash didn't try to escape. But then we got the high resolution NSA visual spectrum photographs from different angles we could see a tall wire fence topped with concertina wire surrounding the complex right at the tree line and intersecting with the six hundred foot vertical rock cliff at the rear of the cleared area surrounding the house. And we realized she had no where to escape to. And then there were the dogs. In reality, the gate at the top of the stairs leading up to the deck was protecting her from the dogs. During the day the dogs walked the fence in opposite directions. At night they slept in the open in good weather not far from a tin roof structure that was likely their shelter during bad weather. Joe and Bo would take out the dogs with darts which would keep them down for at least four hours. I would then land on the deck, get Ash out of the suite somehow and then get us both around the gate at the top of the stairs and retreat to the right rear of the property where there was a gate leading into the woods. If we could break through the gate we would take up a defensive position just inside the tree line and drop any bad guys headed our way. If we couldn't penetrate the gate our defensive position would be under the deck.

Our biggest advantage, of course, was the IR night vision. Each of our helmets had a small IR emitter on the very top. This was designed into the system to aid in visual contact during descent in a tactical HAHO or HALO mission. As we developed our plan for tonight's raid we realized that this IR light would allow us to easily tell the good guys from the bad guys. Ashleigh, of course had none of this equipment. So my job was to remain stationary in a defensive position protecting her. Our plan called for 'shoot to disable', not to kill. If at all possible we needed every one of these people alive. If the target presents itself the aim point of choice would be the upper right shoulder to greatly degrade his (or her) offensive capability. Our biggest unknown was the likely increase of the alert status of the compound due to Ashleigh's presence. We should get real time updates from the NSA guys five minutes before the first man leaves the plane, which will help.

This was going to be an interesting night.

Chapter Eighty

Zodiac F470 Combat Rubber Raiding Craft
Five miles off the coast of Mexico
Sunday, March 23, 1986 0030 hrs PST

"Ok Jimbo lets take her down to five knots. We've got plenty of time and we need a little less noise," yelled Master Chief Manny Hernandez. Jimbo was the Coxswain, or boat captain. His job was to drive the boat, stay with it at all times and ensure the safety of its passengers while under way..

"Listen up guys; we need to talk a little while we still can. When we get a half mile out we go to hand signals and down to three knots. Remember everything you saw in the reconnaissance photos. Tommy, you and Don have the doggie stoppers. You've got to shoot through the fence and you've got to hit the buggers, preferably in the butt. They guarantee four hours with these darts – we shouldn't be there more than a half hour if everything goes right. When we get through the fence each of you grab a dog and drag him back to the hole in the fence. Hopefully they'll live through this – hopefully we will too. And don't forget, you've got a second dart round in your magazine that you've got to get rid of if your first shot's good.

"We don't expect more than a single guard and he will likely be asleep. But Horte has a hostage now and he might have more armed guards if he expects us to take action this soon. So we all need to be extra cautious. Keep your silencers on your MP5s. Single shot or two round burst – no automatic fire. We've been over this a dozen times – everybody knows what to do. We're shooting to disable – not kill. I don't want to see any dead people or dogs and I for damned sure I don't want any hurt SEALs – That understood? Any Questions?"

There were none. As they headed into the cloud covered darkness on a calm sea they began to pick up the coast line with their HAHO helmets. They were wearing the ground battle subset of the HAHO system which gave them all of that system's capabilities sans the pressure suit and its support subsystem. Both the airborne and ground teams had decided that for this mission they would train with and use only the IR visual capability. Each man was armed with a silenced MP-5 Assault rifle and a nine millimeter Beretta pistol custom built for SEALs.

The SEALs beached their 'RIB' (Rubber Inflatable Boat, the nickname for the Combat Rubber Raiding Craft or CRRC), disembarked and gathered in a covered area inside the tree line. They were waiting on the latest intel from the 0110 hrs window of the first NSA satellite over the target area. Master Chief Hernandez had his com channel tuned to the NSA network and was listening intently. At 0111 hrs he heard, "Gummy Boys this is Plato, sitrep, Site Delta," (code name for the Mazatlan plant), "two guards, one at northeast corner, other at southwest. Two dogs, front center of building twenty yards out. No motion." He then heard the report on the villa: "Site Victor, ten guards, four at the corners, one each center of sides and one at each gate. One man in each machine gun bunker. One man in entrance bunker. Two dogs, north of building, fifteen yards behind main gate. Four occupants. Hostage in normal position. Others, near center of first floor. No motion. Plato out."

"Ok guys, listen-up," Hernandez said in a low voice over the group channel. "We've got two guards to take down. The guards are on the northeast and southwest corners of the building. The two dogs are where we expect them to be. We'll take all four targets at the same time through the fence. I've got a half dozen extra darts. I'm thinkin' we'll use the darts on the guards also, then zip tie them after we get through the fence. We've got to get them back to the boat alive. If they've been darted they won't be screaming and we won't have to gag and blindfold them but we will have to carry them back. Comments?"

There were none.

Chapter Eighty One

C-23 Sherpa Cargo Plane, 15 miles off the Coast of Mexico climbing to 30,000 ft

Sunday, March 23, 1986 0112 hrs PST

"OK guys, listen-up," Joe Garcia said through the group channel, "I just got the NSA sitrep for our site, Horte's got ten armed guards surrounding the villa, three in the bunkers and two more plus Horte inside the villa. So we're gonna be out numbered 16 to 8 when we include our CIA buddies on top of the mountain. He's got one on each corner, one at the center of each side and one at each gate plus the guys in the bunkers and the villa. The dogs are where they're supposed to be. Bo and I will get the dogs as planned. Danny and Mike, you're programmed to come down just inside the gates. Do you think you can take out those two tangos from the air?"

"Sure Boss", "Yeah Cap'n," the two responded.

"Ok Hal, put Danny and Mike in our jump sequence; Bo and I together, wait two seconds, then Danny and Mike together, wait four seconds, then Sam, four more seconds and you go last. That'll give Danny and Mike a chance to take out their targets while the guy on the northeast corner and his buddy at the center of the east wall are trying to figure out what's going on with the dogs. Guys, you're going to have to shoot to kill on these two. After we get these two it'll be a fair fight. If they have lights, they'll likely come on about the time Danny and Mike hit the ground. The lights will be our first and primary targets until they're all out. Even though the lights don't bother us, we have the lights-out advantage – the night belongs to us – that understood?"

Garcia heard five yeses in quick sequence. "If they turn on lights we'll have an advantage: They'll expect us to be blinded and they won't have their starlight night vision on if they even have it. So speed is imperative; we've got to have these targets on the ground, unable to shoot before they can take up defensive positions. We'll get real time updates on movements inside the villa from NSA. Sam, you'll be two seconds behind Mike. You're going to have to ditch your chute, break into the suite, grab your wife and take a defensive position on the deck quickly. Forget going to the gate, too many bad guys. You brought her weapon – right?"

"Yeah Captain, right here in my pocket and six more clips on the other side," I yelled through the noise as the huge cargo ramp lowered at the rear of the plane

"We'll be on the open channel along with Garrison, the NSA, CIA, FBI and God only knows who else – so watch what you say. Helmets on, system check, com check," Garcia yelled.

Chapter Eighty Two

Just inside the tree line on the beach
South of Mazatlan, Mexico
Sunday, March 23, 1986 0112 PST

"Ok Team Four, let's do our thing," said Master Chief Manny Hernandez over the group channel.

Jimbo took a defensive position in a tree about five yards from the RIB as Hernandez led the other four through the trees to a levy on top of which ran the rail tracks that serviced the naphthalene plant. A hundred yard northward trek down the low, landward side of the tracks brought them to the fenced five acre site which housed anywhere from eighty to a hundred and thirty tons of naphthalene and twenty to thirty five tons of cocaine. Tonight they were using thermite flares similar to the grenades used by the military for destruction of classified systems that must be destroyed on the battlefield. The team carried twelve flares, each weighing a little less than two pounds. The flares were to be distributed throughout the area where naphthalene was stored in fifty five gallon drums. Each flare would simply be placed on top of a drum and its remote igniter activated. When ignited the thermite would penetrate the steel drum in about twenty seconds and continue downward into the naphthalene, vaporizing and igniting it, thereby causing a horrific explosion. All of the igniters would be electronically detonated within a millisecond of the remote detonation command transmitted by the SEALs in their RIB as they motored back to the awaiting Coastguard Cutter.

Senior Chief Petty Officer Rob Curtis, Chief Petty Officer Tommy Gilbert, Petty Officer First Class Steve Thompson and Petty Officer Third Class Don Wilson took up positions around the perimeter chain link fence and awaited the execute command from Master Chief Hernandez. As the command was given each SEAL fired a disabling dart from his silenced MP-5 assault rifle at his particular target – the two guards and the two dogs. After a thirty second observation of each target to be sure they were down for the count, Wilson began cutting a sizeable hole in the fence with bolt cutters. Within twenty five minutes they had succeeded in entering the plant, setting and arming the thermite flares, and binding and dragging the guards and dogs back through the hole in the fence. They carried the dogs twenty yards down the tracks and placed them on the seaward side of the levy. Then the four SEALs went back for the two guards. It was a long trip back to the RIB carrying the guards and they were exhausted when they got there. It took all six to get the RIB back down to the water, load the limp guards aboard and get the boat clear of the beach.

"I think we're far enough from the plant to blow it away," Said Manny Hernandez on the group channel, "Are we ready Director Garrison?" It was exactly 0150 hrs

"Go for it," said Mark Garrison over the satellite link. "Maybe we can see it from here," he joked.

When Hernandez hit the ignite button on the remote, nothing happened. This he expected due to the twenty second delay while the thermite burned through the drum lids. First they heard a low pitched whistle, then a rumble followed by a huge explosion and a fireball that looked like an atomic bomb. They were at least a mile from the plant and looking almost straight up at the fire.

"Well, I guess we did it," said Hernandez. "Hope the dogs made it."

Chapter Eighty Three

C-23 Sherpa Cargo Plane

El Centro NAS Tarmac

Sunday, March 23, 1986 0131 hrs PST

The SEALs in the cargo bay checked their HAHO systems and were lined up in jump order ready to go when the red jump light began flashing. Jameson and Garcia jumped together. Two seconds later Danny Labow and Mike Jako jumped. Then four seconds later I jumped, followed four seconds later by Hal Nicholson. We all used a quick two second count for opening to be sure we cleared the plane and that our initial entry onto the glide-slope was identical for each jumper.

Everything looked good. I could clearly see the helmet mounted IR locator lights on the four chutes ahead of me. My autopilot was making minute changes in my flight path by pulling gently on the four primary shrouds of the chute. My barometric altimeter was reading twenty nine thousand four hundred feet. So I was six hundred feet below the airplane and it looked like I was about a hundred feet above Labow and Jako, in front of me. The clouds looked like a fluffy blanket spread out in all directions. There was a waning moon behind me to the west – it was a beautiful night.

I turned to look behind me to see if Nicholson was doing ok. Turning your head with the helmet properly mounted to the pressure suit was difficult and I guess I tried a little too hard – I heard a pop and immediately knew something was wrong. The small window in the lower right corner of my display disappeared. This was the window that gave the jumper nav commands to keep him on his preprogrammed glide path when not using the autopilot. With the autopilot functioning, this window was necessary only as a backup. If the autopilot failed, the jumper simply followed the commands in this little window and he would proceed in manual nav mode – which was all we had before we added the autopilot capability. I had made hundreds of jumps using manual nav. But now I had *no nav!* And, I had four to six thousand feet of clouds to penetrate with mountains and jungle below them. "Why me Lord?" It seemed that every time I put my life on autopilot something got screwed up. My mind flashed back to that cold snowy day when I nearly destroyed one of Bo's banner planes and then to Bo's nightmare mission where he wound up hanging in a tree in enemy territory in North Vietnam. We were both lucky then – would I be lucky now? I was thinking, maybe not.

"Focus, Sam!" I said, not remembering that my com unit was active and that the half of the US military command chain, all of whom outranked me, were probably listening. That thought led me into an analytical mode. What just happened? I either broke or disconnected a connector between the helmet and the chest pack. Which one? There were only three. It couldn't be the power connector (Thank God!). So it had to be one of the nav connectors. I remember Leroy complaining about the fact that there weren't enough pins on the nav connector to accommodate the autopilot function when we added it to the system. So it looks like when he added the third connector he moved the manual nav command signals to the new connector to keep all of the nav signals together. I had, therefore, simply lost my ability to control my chute with any knowledge of where I was going. Wait! Not totally true. I still had location information which was generated in the helmet by the integrated GPS and passed to the chest-pack computer for use by the navigation system which in turn sent the nav commands back to the helmet for manual mode nav and to the shroud pullers for automatic nav mode.

I immediately confirmed that my analysis was correct. Switching to nav mode, through tiny Klixon buttons sewn into the finger tips of the suit's gloves, I could still see the location of the four jumpers ahead of me and just above that string of colored dots I could see a tiny green x – my target. Just below the center of the screen I saw another colored dot – Hal Nicholson. I didn't even have to try to look back at him – just change modes. Stupid dumb-shit me! Just like the banner screw-up, my fault again. If I live through this without being captured or killed I'll for damned sure add a couple of paragraphs to the training manual about this.

I began checking my mode control functions. When I gave the IR mode command I went back to the view of the four helmet mounted IR locator lights of my team mates. I couldn't see Hal because the IR sensor only covers the visual range of the jumper. All the other modes checked out, so I was simply missing nav command, whether manual or automatic. The cloud of fear and uncertainty began to lift, but the real clouds were rapidly approaching and a little fear began creeping back. This was the same situation Bo was in during his Vietnam incident – well maybe not exactly the same. He had absolutely no idea where he was when he broke through the clouds – I, at least, had my five colored dots and my little green x.

Suddenly on the com net I heard the voice of Joe Garcia: "Mama Eagle, this is Eagle one, how read?" Mama Eagle was our in-country CIA agent, Marco Juares and his partner Alberto Salvador, both former Team IV SEALs. They were perched at the top of the six hundred foot cliff behind Horte's villa, not far from the Differential GPS unit Marco had placed there three weeks ago. Marco was using the IR scope on his MP-5 rifle to observe the villa. The Differential GPS unit knew exactly where it was and could generate range errors on all visible satellites and relay the corrections to any DGPS receivers in the area – the six of us.

"Eagle One, this is Mama Eagle, five by, how you."

"Mama, Eagle One, five by. Sitrep?"

"One, Mama, DGPS nominal, no movement visible, ceiling fifteen hundred AGL at target, visibility unlimited.

"Mama, One. Can you take the tangos (targets) at the East Center wall and South East corner on command?"

"One, Mama, roger that, will do."

Mama, One, we are at angels seven, everything nominal, standing by.

"One, this is Mama, standing by"

Well maybe our situation wasn't entirely nominal. Of course, Joe didn't know that. Should I tell him? No, he doesn't understand the system as well as I do. He might make an unnecessary tactical decision that would put us at higher risk based on what I could tell him in the little time we had left. It would certainly occupy his mind with things he didn't need to be worrying about right now. I screwed up, but things were not as bad as I thought. If I can just get through those damned clouds.

As I entered the clouds I was relieved to see Mike's and Danny's IR locators, clearly and Joe's and Bo's faintly. I switched the mode to combine the GPS and IR views. Now I could see the four colored dots ahead of me and one behind me. Mike's and Danny's IR locators and colored dots were co-located. All I had to do was follow the leader. Altitude control wasn't as difficult as I had originally thought. The dots in front of me were separated because we were at different altitudes. As long as I kept the dots at the same separation, I was on the glide slope. Things would change when we approached our respective targets but all I needed to do then was maneuver for my green x using the same approach that I had programmed into the now defunct autopilot system.

Just as I was coming out of the clouds I heard: "Eagle Two, delta tango (dog target), ready?"

"Two ready," replied Bo.

"Execute."

About a second later I heard, "Mama, execute," and then immediately, "Eagle Three and Four, execute."

I couldn't hear the shots but I could see a small muzzle flash from the MP-5 silencers. The dogs jumped up, stumbled around in circles for a few seconds and then laid back down. The guards at the gates took head shots and were out of the game. The east center guard took a shoulder hit from Mama One and was lying on the ground screaming. At the same instant the southeast guard was taken out by Mama Two as he ran toward cover. The northeast guard ran toward him and was taken down by Joe with his second dart right after he landed. Bo used his second dart on the north center guard just as he came around the corner. The two darted guards were trying desperately to raise their weapons and return fire, but soon were fast asleep.

I had my spot in sight and was in a manual s-turn to bleed off my last fifty feet of altitude when the lights came on. I had already watched the southwest guard join the south central guard. They were trying to figure out what was going on and what they should do. I figured I could get one, but not both before I landed, so I fired at the best target and got him in the right shoulder from the rear. The other guard immediately dove toward the building and out of my sight. Three seconds later I landed on the deck. I quick released the chute which, in spite of my efforts to haul it in, partially draped over the railing. I could see Hal landing on the south side with no target in sight. He ditched his chute and headed for the south side of the house.

I called, "Eagle Six, this is Five, be aware, at least one tango under the deck, proceed with caution." I then broke the large picture window with my rifle butt and began to enter the suite where I hoped to find my darling wife. She was in the bathroom with the door locked – good thinking. I was going to have to raise my visor so I could talk to her. When she heard my voice, the door flew open and she was in my arms kissing me, helmet and all, getting camo grease all over her beautiful face. I handed her Glock to her and signaled quiet just as I heard a key in the lock of the door to the suite. This was likely Horte or one of his top goons. There were only three people in the villa other than Ash. I pushed Ash back into the bathroom and took up a position behind one end of an over-stuffed sofa and waited for the door to open. A rifle barrel edged its way through the partially opened doorway. I had my MP-5 on single-shot. As the door slowly opened I saw my shot and got him in the right shoulder. This wasn't Horte but the guy didn't go down and damn-it, it looked like he was left handed. So as he raised the gun with his left hand I shot him in the left shoulder. But he shot at the same time penetrating the back of the sofa and then hitting me in the upper right arm. Now with holes in both shoulders he finally fell to his knees, unable to do anything with his weapon.

Bo and Joe had secured the darted and screaming guards with quick cuffs and were running toward the northwest corner when they heard my caution to Hal. Joe called, "Five and Six, this is One; One and Two at northwest corner. We have deck and stairs covered. Three and Four are outside the fence on the west side and will dispatch the west side tangos.

I closed the suite door and locked it, then quick cuffed the target and turned him over.

"That's definitely not the guy that impersonated a Petty Officer First Class to get me in his car, but he and Horte were here this afternoon and they're probably still here," said Ashleigh.

"Eagle One, this is Five, Eaglet is secure, I've got one tango down and secured up here. Other two likely still in the house. One is likely Horte. The other is likely Petty Officer – both were here this afternoon."

Chapter Eighty Four

Max Horte's Villa
Southeast of Mazatlan, Mexico
Sunday, March 23, 1986 0200 hrs PST

"Shark-tank this is Eagle One. Send over both little birds ASAP," Captain Joe Garcia barked over the group com net. Shark-tank was the Jamestown Cutter now exactly 12.1 miles off the shore of Mexico. The little bird is a six passenger, small, agile helicopter used to get into and out of tight places by the SEALs and other Special Ops Teams. The Jamestown could carry two Little Birds on its aft helicopter deck. "We've got sixteen tangos. Two dead, nine disabled and immobilized, two still in the villa and three still in the bunkers. The Eaglet is secure – Eagle Five is wounded. Send a replacement from Hernandez' team if you can. We're gonna need three trips to finish this up and we've gotta be out by dawn. I need the latest IR sitrep – before our window closes.

"Eagle Two, take Three and Six and secure the villa. Two tangos inside. Sitrep coming. Four, with me," barked Garcia

"Eagle One this is Skyspy, latest intel at 0203 shows five tangos in villa, three in Eaglet suite and two just outside the door. One tango in each bunker." Skyspy was the call sign for the secure NSA room at the Navy Yard, San Diego.

"Skyspy, Eagle One, FYI, two of the three inside the suite are Eagle Five and the Eaglet, both armed and in an oblique defensive position. The tango with them is secure."

"Roger that, good luck Eagles. Skyspy out."

Using his finger buttons, Bo Jameson commanded his com. system to open a private sub-net between Eagles Two, Three, Five and Six – himself, Danny Labow, me and Hal Nicholson. He needed their undivided attention to accomplish the take-down of Max Horte and one of his top body guards – alive.

"Ok, guys, here's what we're going to do and we've gotta do it fast. Danny, you and Hal quietly climb the stairs to the second floor but stay below the floor level. I'm going up the stairs to the deck on the other side of the villa. Sam, unlock the door to the deck then you and Ash take up prone defensive positions. I will let you all know when I'm in place. Use a mirror stick to locate the tangos and report their position to me – whisper, it's imperative that they don't hear or see you. Keep below the floor level on the stairs. I'm going to sweep a 40 round magazine of 7.62 AP (Armor Piercing) through the door at one foot above the floor level. I need an immediate report on their condition. If they're both down and you can advance, do so. Keep your weapons on each tango's right shoulder. Shoot both if either moves to raise a weapon. Quick cuff them and secure their weapons. Hal, you, Sam and Ash might have to slide them down the stairs. Their legs should be hamburger. Danny, you and I need to go assist Joe and Mike with the bunkers when this is over.

"I'm in place" said Bo over their private net.

"Roger Bo," whispered Danny. "We're in place. tangos are just outside the door. One is on a cell phone or walkie-talkie. They have their heads together. Their stance gives you a good shot. Sweep the entire width of the door and you should get them both. I'll yell 'down' when they're both down so you don't kill them. Turn up your volume so you can hear me."

Four seconds later Bo began his forty round sweep. Once across in full automatic mode is all it took. Danny yelled 'down' and the two SEALs advanced down the hallway and kicked their weapons out of reach.

"Open the door – we've got 'em" said Danny, grinning as he quick cuffed the one he assumed to be Horte.

Bo called over the net, "Hal, get Ash, Sam and the tangos down stairs. Danny, we've got three more to go. Joe needs our help. Let's go."

Bo and Danny took the deck stairs down to ground level and then ran along the fence to the main gate. They started down the road until they got to the top of the paved 'killing zone'. The NSA pictures they had studied showed a path on either side of the road that led down to the bunkers. Joe and Mike had already started down the paths and were probably waiting for them just above the bunkers. Each bunker held a machine gun, probably a thirty caliber, and one man. "I'm going to set our com back to the group. Joe, Mike, this is Bo, how you read?"

"5-by," "5-by," were the responses.

"Danny, you read them?"

"5-by on both," whispered Danny

"Ok, everybody's up. We've located the paths up top, where are you guys?"

"We're about fifteen yards down from you," replied Garcia. "Here's the plan. We reconned the bunkers. Each is built into the hill with concrete front and sides and a door on the side farthest from the road. The entrance is probably locked from the inside, but we don't know that. Each bunker has a four by forty inch rectangular gun opening. We've got six SG-3 stun grenades. One man pulls the pin, releases the handle, counts one thousand one, one thousand two and then drops the grenade through the gun hole. The grenades are guaranteed to have a four second fuse plus or minus 150 milliseconds. When the grenade blows the other man breaks through the door. Kicking it in is probably the quickest. If that doesn't work, tape a three inch piece of C-4 next to the keeper and shoot it from ten feet away. We have no idea on weapons inside, so be careful. These guys ought to be totally disabled – probably won't be able to hear for a week."

When Bo and Danny arrived they moved into position using hand signals.

"Ok, grenades ready?" said Garcia softly.

"Ready."

"Ready."

"Execute!"

Both grenades went off within a half second. The noise was muffled somewhat but still almost deafening. The doors were blown open with C4 and both tangos were down, hands over their ears, writhing in pain.

While Mike and Danny were cuffing the two goons Joe said, "You two head on down the hill and get the guy in the surveillance bunker. We don't know how he's armed, so be careful. It's about a kilometer down the road so you need to hurry. Take him unharmed if possible so you don't have to carry him back up the hill. We've still got a lot of work to do up top so we can be clear of the coast by daybreak.

"Bo, as soon as we get these two up top you and I will dump the two dead tangos into Horte's graveyard. We'll use one of Horte's three vehicles to get that done quickly. Then we'll make a final sweep of the villa to see if Hal and the new guy missed anything."

"Mama this is Eagle One. Go ahead and lower the DGPS unit down to us. We'll get it back to its owner."

"Roger that One, will do."

* * * *

The last Little Bird left the site on its final run back to the Cutter Jamestown overloaded with computers, the contents of a three file cabinets, a 250 pound safe that couldn't be opened on-site, two answering machines, a nail gun, five tape recorders, the pilot, Captain Joe Garcia, Commander Bo Jameson and Chief Petty Officer Danny Labow. In all it took three round trips for each of the helicopters to get the fourteen living bad guys, four of the now seven SEALs and Ashleigh back to the boat. This fourth and last trip was hauling the three remaining SEALs, all the remaining intel loot, the HAHO gear and the DGPS unit back. It was 0435 hrs – they should all be safely aboard the Jamestown and headed north by 0500; thirty minutes before sunrise.

Chapter Eighty Five

Coast Guard Super Cutter Jamestown
Twenty Miles off the Mexican Coast Steaming North
Sunday, March 23, 1986 0510 hrs PST

The CIA had boarded three of their best interrogators on the cutter when it left San Diego the afternoon before, believing the number of prisoners would be a maximum of eight. As the prisoners were brought aboard they were segregated and guarded, while the cutter steamed north staying in international waters. The first Little Bird free of egress duty was refueled and sent back to San Diego to pick up three additional CIA Interrogators, two more Navy surgeons and another trauma nurse. There was a lot to be learned and the CIA preferred to stay outside the jurisdiction of the USA while learning.

My arm hurt like hell. The Navy Doc didn't even take the bullet out. He said I'd need a little surgery to remove some bone fragments and they would get the bullet then. I got a sling, a large band-aid and a shot of morphine. The good news; the bone was just slightly fractured – could of been a lot worse. The bad news; I was headed back to San Diego on the second Little Bird and straight into surgery. Ash and I had other plans.

As the morphine kicked in I began to feel much better. Ash and I walked out on the rear deck to wait for the last flight to arrive. Just as we got there, the cutter started slowing and we saw a light come on about two miles behind us.

"That's gotta be the chopper," said Ashleigh pointing toward the light. "I hope the guys got the intel they needed," she added.

As the Little Bird was about to touch down on the aft deck, Chief Petty Officer Mike Jako stepped through the hatch. Looking a little surprised he yelled, "Sir, what the hell are you doing up wandering around," staring at me with a frown.

"It's called morphine," I yelled back over the noise of the Little Bird, "Doc said he'd give me another shot right before I leave for shore – I feel great!"

"Be careful sir, you've lost a lot of blood. First time I got shot, I got on a morphine high and was running around like, no problem man. Two hours later I was in shock. The docs will only give you so much morphine – then they cut you off – make you take aspirin or somethin'."

"Thanks for the heads up Chief. I'll head back to sick bay soon as I say hey to the Captain and Commander. Would you go round up a couple of swabbies to help unload the chopper?" I asked.

"Sure, I'll get four," replied Mike

"You really ought to head back now," chimed Ashleigh.

"You can walk me back as soon as I talk to Bo and Joe," I groused.

The rotors were slowing down but not nearly stopped when the three SEALs jumped out and started grabbing papers, computers and all sorts of other stuff out of the rear of the helicopter. Ash and I walked over so I could get the final scoop on what went down.

"Hey Sam, just a little scratch like I told you right?" Bo said as he climbed out of the Little Bird. Joe headed straight for the bridge.

"Yeah, it's not too bad. Problem is, it went in but didn't come out – messed up the bone a little. Gonna have to go back to the Base Hospital for a little surgery. I'm taking Ash with me.

"So what do we have? Horte? The list of cocaine caches?" I asked, hoping this nightmare was almost over.

"It might be more complicated than we thought. We've got somebody who looks exactly like Max Horte but we've only got two decent pictures with us, both taken on his last visit to the U.S. These pictures show a distinct scar above the right eye slanting down into the eyebrow. This guy doesn't have the scar. Could be Horte had a fake scar. Could be this guy is his twin brother. Could be this is some guy off the street that looks just like him. He hasn't said a word yet. We've got his prints and they'll be matched against prints the FBI obtained while he was under observation during his last visit stateside. The CIA is taking him and the rest of his thugs to site zebra for interrogation as soon as the docs get them patched up. Nothing yet on the list. That might take some time. Joe and I are going back with you and Ash to sit in the situation room while the rest of the operation goes down. Launch for all domestic sites is at 0830 hrs PST. We found a short wave radio set in the villa – brought it with us. We're hoping Horte, or whoever he is, wasn't able to warn his stateside operations. The teams are being beefed up with standby agents just in case. If this guy isn't Horte we're in big trouble. That's all I know. Where's the galley?"

"Down one deck amidships. The doc doesn't want me to eat, but I got some pretty good black coffee down there. I'm headed back to sick bay. Don't want to push my luck."

Chapter Eighty Six

Navy SEAL Little Bird Helicopter
Five Miles Southwest of San Diego NAS
Sunday, March 23, 1986 0540 hrs PST

When I got back to sick bay I couldn't find the doctor, or any doctor or nurse or medical aide for that matter. I found out they were spread all over the ship because the CIA wanted the bad guys to stay separated and get patched up ASAP. Bottom line – I didn't get my second morphine shot. But, I got to sit up front in the Little Bird 'cause my arm was starting to hurt again and it was easier for me to get in and out of the chopper up there.

"Where is the hospital?" I asked the pilot.

"Near Balboa Park," he responded.

That shot my plans all to hell. I'd hoped it would be on North Island near the Multi-Force Situation Room where Joe and Bo were headed to review the observed action at the villa and watch the results of the domestic cocaine-naphthalene extraction factory compromises.

"We're going to drop them off first because it's sort of on the way," added the pilot. Of course, cater to the hot shots while the wounded peon suffers. I didn't really mind though, as long as I had Ash back and she was going with me.

So we dropped them off on North Island and then made the ten minute hop to the Navy Hospital near Balboa Park. Ash and I hugged and kissed before they made me get in a wheel chair right there on the helipad – how humiliating! Next thing I remember is opening my eyes just as my beautiful wife was leaning down to kiss me.

"When are they going to take me in?" I asked.

"You want to go in again? You just got out!" she teased.

I looked down at my arm. Sure enough the bandage looked different.

"The doctor said to wear this sling for three days and take it easy, then come back to see him or any other Navy doctor in five days."

He gave me instructions on changing the bandage and some antibiotic cream to put on the wound and said, "I think you're going to live."

"Can I check out of here now?" I asked Ash.

"We've got some paperwork to fill out first. Can you sign with your left hand?"

"Sure, what time is it?"

"0 nine hundred," she replied.

"Let's get out of here. I want to get over to North Island and see what's going on. You fill out the paperwork and while I'm signing it, call a cab."

"No need. The Captain sent over a Navy car to pick us up – he's right outside."

"Well whadaya know, they remembered the poor wounded peon," I thought to myself.

When we got to the situation room, to her surprise, Ashleigh was on the access list. Her brother had asked the CIA Director, Robert Gilmore, to add her since she held the proper clearance and she had inadvertently become part of the program.

We entered quietly and what we saw was puzzling. Admiral Bennington, Captain Garcia, my brother-in-law Mark and my uncle Bo were all huddled around a 30 inch monitor and something was wrong.

Chapter Eighty Seven

NSA Multi-Force Situation Room
North Island, San Diego NAS
Sunday, March 23, 1986 0940 hrs PST

"Admiral, it's probably best that you make the call, but I'll handle the explanation – I feel like I've really screwed this thing up. I should have seen what was going down before we took action," said Mark Garrison looking like he'd just seen a ghost. Bo saw us coming in and motioned us back out to the ante-room.

"Bad news guys, Mark just figured out what's happening and they're going to reconvene the session with the President, the agencies and Chairman of the Joint Chiefs in the White House Situation Room. I'll try to explain quickly so we can get back in there for the hand wringing."

My first thought: "So things didn't go well with the extraction plant take downs?"

"Not at all, everything went perfect. All nine plants were taken with no problems, until we discovered that there was no trace of cocaine at any of the plants. The CEO and two front-end employees at each plant are acting completely innocent – they know nothing. Word from the Jamestown is that the ten new guards at the villa were just hired three days ago. They have no idea who Max Horte is or why the villa needed new guards. As you know our whistle-blower and his family are dead. The CEO, Freddy and packaging supervisor at the Chula Vista plant have been replaced and of course the replacements know nothing. The only hard evidence we have from Alverez is on that plant. It appears that all the plants were sanitized sometime last week.

"Now the rest of this is conjecture, but will probably become fact as we look deeper. Mark is fairly sure that what we're looking at is Horte's exit plan. Freddy wasn't killed for revenge – it was just a step in Horte's plan. He knew what Alverez had disclosed because his goon found the key to the safety deposit box, but it took six fingers from his wife and daughter before he gave it up. That was the exit plan trigger. He needed to put us on a wild goose chase so he'd have time to execute the sanitization steps – that's why you were kidnapped Ash -- to be sure we were focused on the villa. Not because he thought he could negotiate his way out of his public enemy number one status and continue business as usual – that never did make sense.

"Now, here we are with a twenty some odd year supply of coke spread throughout the U.S. and a shadow network ready to begin distribution. We know what's happened, but the players have vanished and our only witness is dead. We don't have any of Horte's comrades. Even the guys in the three bunkers and the look-alike were recently hired. We even destroyed his naphthalene plant for him. Right now we can't prove a thing and Horte and his real comrades are on a beach somewhere in South America sipping single malt Scotch.

"Let's head back in – we all need to hear this and absorb as much information as we can. The going's gonna be tough from here on out."

Ash and I stood there dumbfounded. We both felt a pang of guilt that Mark was blaming himself. There were a lot of people who knew as much as he did about this situation. No single person should shoulder the blame, especially Mark. He already felt responsible for the execution of Freddy and his family. Then, on top of that, he had the stress of worrying about his own family.

When we returned to the room the Admiral was just finishing his call to Admiral Sterett to reconvene the group with secure video where possible and secure voice if not. He hung up the phone and turned to Mark.

"Mark, I know you feel bad about this – so does everyone involved. We acted, and are still acting, as a team. Not one of us suspected the motives of Horte. Not you, not me, not the Chairman, not the President nor the FBI, NSA, CIA or your boss Jim Doddington. The team has been blindsided – not the first time, won't be the last. We can't waste time blaming ourselves and what-ifing the past. We've got fresh information and intel we need to act on and time is of the essence. Horte's not smarter than we are; he's just smarter than we thought he was. We'll get him and I predict it'll be soon. So make the explanation to the rest of the team, but I don't want to hear you blaming yourself – are you with me?" asked Admiral Bennington.

"Yeah, Admiral, I'm moving through the guilt phase pretty quick – I'm getting into the pissed-off stage!" said Mark.

"That's a much better state of mind, now let's use this little bit of time we have before the others rejoin us and review what we know," said Admiral Bennington, taking charge of the situation.

"We know that Horte had an exit plan for the first phase of his operation and we're damned sure he's moving to phase two right now. We'd be in much better shape if we knew where the drug cache is and who is in charge of implementing the distribution plan.

"We're looking for the location list right now but finding it among Horte's villa possessions is a long shot at best. So, some immediate things we need to think about are: What is the likely physical implementation of the list? Is Horte, himself planning to implement phase two? Is he handing that responsibility to a trusted stateside comrade? Where is Horte now? Will he ever return to the U.S.? Does he have a fourth identity? We know he has dual citizenship, Mexico and U.S. and that he hasn't used his U.S. passport in the last six years. What about his Mexican passport? We verified his Mexican citizenship – why does the CIA think it's fake? He has a Columbian passport with his coffee broker identity. Is it real?"

Ashleigh interrupted the Admiral, "excuse me Admiral, I have some information that might be important. When I was abducted they used a syringe in my neck, I was out in less than ten seconds. When I woke we were out over the Pacific – no land in sight. I had acquired a pair of large coveralls over my flight suit and we were in a late model Lear. They hadn't taken my watch and my hands were secured in front, so I figured we'd been in the air for at least two hours, maybe more. We should have already landed at Mazatlan but I couldn't even see land. We flew for another hour before we landed at a small industrial or agricultural airfield somewhere well south of Mexico – I'd guess Nicaragua or maybe El Salvador. As we approached the air strip they blindfolded me, landed, taxied to a hangar and closed the doors. The "Petty Officer" who had grabbed me left to get the customs agent. He spoke English to the pilot who appeared to be American. The pilot spoke with what I would classify as a north Texan accent. Although the "Petty Officer" spoke native Mexican Spanish his English sounded just like the Pilot's. No hint of a Spanish accent. The pilot butchered Spanish.

"I told the pilot, who I was pretty sure had no Idea who I was, that I suffered from vertigo and was getting sick from the blindfold and didn't want to mess up his airplane – the blindfold was off in five seconds. This guy treated me well, asked if he could get me something to drink or somehow make me more comfortable. I asked for some water and while he was getting it I had a chance to look around the hangar. It was about a hundred and twenty feet wide and I'd say eighty, maybe ninety feet deep. There were two other airplanes in the hangar that I could see. One was a De Havilland Twin Otter, tail number N4483Y. The other was a Grumman Ag Cat, standard yellow, in good shape but I couldn't see the tail number. When the "Petty Officer" returned with the customs guy they spoke only Spanish. I had given them no hint that I understood Spanish so I was privy to their entire conversation. The customs agent was obviously on Horte's payroll and was taking orders from the "Petty Officer" with no objections. I was a mental patient being taken to Mazatlan for treatment and that was the reason I was being constrained. As he finished that sentence he glanced into the door from his position where they were doing the paperwork on the wing of the airplane and noticed that my blindfold was off. I could see the anger in his expression but he didn't make a move to replace it – I guess he figured the damage was done.

"Somehow, I had acquired a new passport which I could see being stamped by the customs agent who obviously handled the immigration work also.

"The pilot had left momentarily and gone out the side door of the hangar. Soon after that he returned through the partially opened large hangar door on what looked like an old lawn tractor with a tow hitch attached. Although I could see through the six foot opening in the big door, I couldn't see much. I did see a row of small tied down aircraft and a water tank in the distance with the large letters NAGB painted on the side. The "Petty Officer" told the customs guy to wait outside, then entered the plane and reinstalled my blindfold. He left the plane and had a low volume conversation in English with the pilot who was attaching the plane to the lawnmower with the tow bar. The only part I heard was the pilot saying, "she said she was sick and going to puke all over the plane." So he was obviously being chewed out for removing my blindfold.

We took off and flew north for another hour and twenty minutes. I could hear enough of the pilot's conversation with the tower to discern that we were in fact landing at Mazatlan's airport. After we landed we taxied for a long time before we entered another hangar. This time my blindfold remained in place. After about twenty minutes, I could hear the hangar door open, a vehicle enter and the door close again. I was transferred to a van and driven for about one and a half hours, the last part of which was over some pretty bad roads, to the villa where I was taken to the second floor, relieved of my restraints and blindfold and locked in what I guessed was the guest suite."

When Ashleigh finished, she handed the Admiral a small microcassette from a recorder she purchased at the Base Exchange while I was in surgery, adding, "That airstrip south of Mexico could reveal some interesting information about Horte if we're careful,"

The Admiral looked carefully at the cassette in his hand, turned back to Ashleigh and said, "Yes Commander, I believe it could – good work."

"I'll get you another cassette this afternoon with my observations while held captive."

"Actually, if everyone's up to it, we had planned a mission debriefing right here. I've sent for some food and more coffee. When we get done with the conference we can take an hour or so and fill in any details we've missed. Our CIA friends are holding a similar de-briefing on the Jamestown and we're waiting for a sat-phone call from them with more news about their interrogations and the examination of the contents from the villa. After that we can get a little rest and then get back to it. Commander McKensie, are you doing ok?" the Admiral asked turning toward me.

"I'm doing great, I'm the only one who's had a nap."

Chapter Eighty Eight

NSA Multi-Force Situation Room
North Island, San Diego NAS
Sunday, March 23, 1986 1230 hrs PST

The conference call with the President, CIA, FBI, NSA, DEA and the CJCS was unpleasant, at best, but each member of the team left the meeting resolved that we would catch that son-of-a-bitch, find his drugs and take him and his organization down. We just had to figure out how to do that.

Captain Joe and Bo headed back to El Centro with the Sherpa pilot. Ashleigh and I bummed a ride with Admiral Bennington in his staff car back to Miramar where Ash's car and Bo's plane were parked. Mark had asked us to find his parents and let them know it was alright to go home. He had called their cell phone twice but no one answered.

My arm was feeling amazingly well. Getting the bullet out sure helped. The doc said to take it easy for a couple of weeks and then I could resume normal duties, but he didn't want me to lift any more than ten pounds with that arm. I didn't tell him that I jumped out of airplanes for a living.

We talked with the Admiral on the way to Miramar and we all agreed that what we needed now was more information. The President had tasked the agency directors to: "find Horte. There's not a spot on this earth where that dog can hide and we won't come get him. We have *got* to find those drugs and destroy them. This shadow network of theirs *will* be behind bars soon."

We had given the Admiral everything we knew during the de-briefings. Ash's testimony was critical in our effort to find Horte, but we all knew that we needed every bit of intel we had captured to be thoroughly understood and integrated into our future plans. I reminded the Admiral as I had reminded the team during the de-briefing with the president that we had captured one of Horte's goons at our condo almost two weeks ago and hadn't heard about his status from the CIA yet.

Joe told me not to show my ugly face until a week from Monday and that's exactly what I intended to do. Ash and I hadn't spent a week together since we'd gotten married.

Chapter Eighty Nine

McKensie Condo
La Jolla, California
Sunday, March 23, 1986 5:00 p.m. PST

"Hi Mom, where are you guys?" I heard Ashleigh say when she finally got an answer to her calls, "we're at our condo in La Jolla." Then after a while I heard her say, "Mark says it's ok to go back home now. . He will contact the agency to get you released from the protection program, then we can talk. . . Yes it's been quite an ordeal. . . We'll meet at mark's house next week and tell you all about it. . . No, I can't really say anything over the phone; we'll get you filled in when we see you. . . Oh, let's say weekend after next.... yes Mother, that would be April 5th – that ok? We'll see you then – love you both. . . Tell Dad hi – bye now.

"Ok, now I feel better – I'm going to shower," she said with a big grin on her face.

"Help me get this plastic taped over my bandage and I'll hop in with you."

We were both dead tired – but not tired enough to put this off! We really enjoyed these 'team showers,' and this reminded me that I needed to have a bigger hot water heater installed in our condo. This one was only good for about twenty minutes – we needed to double that. Maybe one of those tank-less heaters for the shower only. They never run out.

Chapter Ninety

Horte Villa
Southeast of Mazatlan, Mexico
Sunday, March 23, 1986 6:30 p.m. PST

CIA agents Marco Juares and Alberto Salvador were both granted U.S. citizenship by enlisting in the Navy. After serving a second tour as members of Seal Team Four they were hired (probably recruited) by the CIA to maintain a presence in Central America.

After hiking four miles up a winding path leading to what appeared to be an abandoned copper mine and then climbing the remaining two hundred yards up a forty five degree rock slide to the top of the mountain above the vertical cliff overlooking Horte's villa, assisting in the mission and then climbing back down and walking around the mountain to the villa, they had had only a little more than an hours rest since eight o'clock the night before. They were both weary to the bone. Their search of the villa, however, had been fruitful. At least they believed so.

After a methodical search of Horte's beautiful mountain home, they discovered a hidden access door to a small attic and access to another small narrow room behind a wine rack in the wine cellar. The attic contained only an assortment of spare tiles used in the construction of the villa and some tile cutting tools. The room behind the wine cellar, however, contained another safe. At the end of the narrow room they found a door that opened into a wooden braced escape tunnel. The safe weighed at least 150 pounds and was bolted to the floor from the inside. Using the tile cutting tools they were able to cut and chisel through the three inch concrete under the safe and remove the safe with a fifty pound chunk of floor attached. It was a struggle getting the safe up the stairs, out of the villa and into Horte's Suburban for the trip down the mountain.

They took the safe to a small rented storage locker on the outskirts of Mazatlan that they used as a weapons cache. They used some safe cracking tools and a drill to open the safe. It was empty. Another dead end. It seemed that Horte had left a trail of meaningless clues. This guy was smarter than any drug king they'd dealt with to date. They wondered where he was now.

Chapter Ninety One

Top Gun T-38 Falcon
22,000 feet above the Grand Canyon
Tuesday, March 25, 1986 4:23 p.m. CST

"Kansas City Center this is Military Flight Oscar Two Four Seven, Angels two two, enroute VFR from Miramar NAS to Columbia Regional, CBI, over."

"Oscar two four seven, squawk ident one one niner seven."

"Roger Center, squawking one one niner seven."

"Oscar two four seven, radar contact, welcome to Kansas City Center. You are cleared VFR at Angels two two to Columbia Regional. Be advised, Columbia Regional has no Approach Control, contact tower at 126.7, no current enroute traffic.

"Roger Center, cleared at 22,000 to Columbia Regional. Tower at 126.7. Thank you sir."

"Yes Ma'am, have a good flight."

"And good day to you," replied Ashleigh McKensie as she flipped her mike-mode button back to intercom.

"It would be damned difficult to join the mile-high club in a tandem trainer," she mumbled as she grinned into the only visual connection we had in the small T-38 Talon trainer; the small mirror attached to the upper left edge of her windshield."

"The good news is we're headed for a college town with no military quarters and we have reservations at the new Hilton. This is going to be like a paid vacation," I responded, matching her grin. Joe had put me on restricted duty for a week which technically meant I couldn't fly. I didn't care – I was married to the best damned pilot in the Navy!

Ashleigh missed six flights during her little hostage action down in Mexico but Commander Erickson, her boss, had doubled up his own schedule as well as one of the junior instructor's schedule to fill the void.

She got back to Miramar just in time for yesterday's graduation ceremony and then to take a PR tour to a state university with an ROTC air cadet training program. There she would make presentations to the Navy and Marine candidate pilots and give a one hour introduction to jet powered aircraft in her T-38 to the top 15% of the candidate class.

The University of Missouri, Columbia accepted sixty air cadets a semester for their government approved ROTC flight school, during which twenty candidates from each of the three participating services, Navy, Marines and Air Force, received thirty five hours of flight training each plus twenty hours of ground school.

This duty/privilege normally belonged to the Top Gun Chief Pilot, currently Commander Dirk Erickson. But when Ashleigh came aboard as the first female Top Gun Instructor, Commander Erickson, after already providing this inspirational opportunity to ROTC cadets around the country for two years, suggested to his boss, Base Commander Captain Baker, that the program might jump up a notch or two if this pretty little super-pilot took over the honors. So they rearranged the schedules so that Erickson would take the first three days of each new Top Gun class giving Ashleigh five days to do the tour.

After hearing about the action at Horte's villa, Dirk asked me if I would like to go along. I had met him and liked him a lot. He knew how to manage ego-manic pilots (not including Ash, of course) and delighted in letting Ashleigh put them in their place.

Ashleigh was, of course, only responsible for the Navy and Marine candidates, so she had six one hour flights and one, two hour presentation to do in three days. If the weather was forecast to be acceptable she would do four flights the first day, the other two the second morning, follow up with the presentation late in the afternoon of that same day and the rest of the time would be ours, a good bit of which would be spent in bed.

Her T-38 was painted just like the Blue Angel's A-4F Skyhawk. To say that these ROTC cadets were inspired to fly this airplane with this gorgeous Navy doll in the rear seat is a huge understatement.

Later this year Top Gun was scheduled to receive two FA-18A Hornets, one in Blue Angel décor (the Blue Angels were upgrading from the A-4 Skyhawk to the FA-18A Hornet). The other one would be Ashleigh's for use in advanced air combat training, disguised as a Mig-29, The Blue Angel look-alike would be used by her for her practice flights and for these PR trips.

It looked to me like the Navy/Marines should be able to cut their pilot recruiting staff in half. According to Dirk, the quality of the incoming cadets had been rising steadily since the program was installed and had taken a sharp rise when Ash began the PR flights. Everybody wanted to be in the top 15% and the waiting list to join was growing.

We had a great five days. Saturday, on the way back we stopped at Whiteman Air Force Base to refuel and get a look at a new swing-wing B1-B Bomber that happened to be there – impressive. We spent the whole week making love and talking about us – not a single mention of Horte, drugs, or secret crap.

Chapter Ninety Two

Pacific Ocean

Three Miles off the Coast of Nicaragua

Friday, March 28, 1986 11:27 a.m. PST

"Now comes real test. We see how boat works when coming surface," said Alexis Kovanov to his co-pilot/student Mario Dannelli. Alexis had never quite mastered the English language even though he had lived in the U.S. for almost fifteen years, working the last ten of those years as a master design engineer for the Electric Boat Division of General Dynamics in Middletown, Rhode Island.

As the sub settled into a two thirds submerged cruise after surfacing Alexi said smiling, "Not bad for first run. We go back now."

Mario had never even ridden in a submarine; now he was tasked with the job of learning everything there was to know about this particular submarine and then teaching a squad of eight others to pilot one just like this one.

Mario was a light weight wrestler in high school at South Central High in Lancaster California, where he was born to an Italian father and a Mexican mother. Although he was only five foot five, he was capable of taking on several attackers considerably larger than himself. He was also fluent in five languages; Italian, Spanish, English, Russian and German. When Mario grew tired of dealing with Alexis' broken English he spoke to him in perfect Russian.

Alexis, aware of his shortcomings in articulation, quipped to Mario several times; "They hire me because I'm damned good submarine designer – not talker!" Alexis was hired because of his superb knowledge and experience in submarine technology from his careers at General Dynamics recently and the Rubin Central Design Bureau of Naval Equipment in St. Petersburg, Russia prior to his defection to the USA.

The sub they were testing was small by comparison to most subs, at only forty five feet long and nine feet two inches in diameter, but it would serve its purpose well along with its three sisters, yet to be completed. It was designed to displace one hundred ten tons of sea water when two thirds submerged with its thirty ton ballast tanks empty. This design allowed the sub to be loaded with up to twenty tons of payload prior to submerging. It had ballast capacity to offset an additional twenty tons of weight. With a twenty ton payload the ballast system provided a buoyancy range of negative six tons to positive twenty two tons. This was more than adequate to allow it to cruise at a depth of fifty feet – the maximum maneuvering depth of its design.

Included in its net weight were seventeen tons of lithium ion batteries, the electric motors and the necessary seawater cooling system to keep the batteries, motors, and the crew of two, cool. The sub could reach twelve knots submerged and sixteen knots on the surface. However, the most efficient submerged cruising speed was eight knots at a depth of forty feet. The lower, more efficient speed was required to make the long trip from mid-Mexico to southern California, a three and a half day voyage.

The sub's three sister ships were complete except for the attachment of the diving planes and control surfaces, and the integration of the internal drive system and control electronics. These final steps were delayed until today's first functional test in case modifications were required to any of these systems.

Alexis was completely satisfied with the performance of the sub during the four hour plus initial test run. "Boat needs just minor tuning of drive and maneuvering software. All systems work good. We start final construction of three brother ships when get back." Russian ships are given masculine names – a custom Alexi refused to abandon. "You need learn fast. This your training boat. Three days training all you get. I must work on other boats."

Chapter Ninety Three

McKensie Condo

La Jolla, California

Sunday, March 30, 1986 4:23 p.m. PST

Ash and I decided to start attending church. I wasn't sure if this was an indication that we were both looking to settle down and have kids in the next few years, if it was because we'd both been brought up in church going families, or because we were both early risers and needed something to do on Sunday morning. But we were currently in a situation where we could add church back into our lives so we decided to do just that.

I thanked God every day for giving me Ashleigh. My faith, which had drifted away after several years of seven day a week commitments, returned like a steam roller when we set our wedding date. I began to realize that a creature like Ashleigh McKensie could not possibly be an accident of nature – she was made for me and I for her and we both were looking for a re-connection with our maker.

So we found a little Episcopal church just south of La Jolla but not too far from our condo and made our first visit this morning. We found the congregation congenial and we made a few new friends. The priest was fairly young, as priests go, and had been a Marine Chaplain in Vietnam. This, of course, elevated him several notches in our corporate impression of him – but, as we soon found out, he was also highly regarded by his parish and we had enjoyed his sermon immensely.

I cheated and ditched my sling one day earlier than ordered – but my arm was feeling much better, I just needed to be careful. The next day I returned to El Centro in Bo's Mooney. I had an appointment with the base doctor at El Centro NAS at 9:00 and got a release on my arm with instructions to keep using the antibiotic cream on the wound for another week – my first, and I hoped last, battle wound.

ANGELS THREE FIVE

I began working with Leroy and Bo on getting the HAHO system ready for production. There was a lot to be done but we had documented the system in detail and written precise specifications for all of the subsystems so the job basically boiled down to generating assembly drawings and procedures with the help of one of the TI Ridgecrest Manufacturing Engineers. About two thirds of all prototype subsystems were built by the TI folks in Ridgecrest – right across the street from China Lake, where I used to work. By the end of the week they began a production run of four more units to get the bugs out of the production process. The system far exceeded the original specs and came in about 10% under target price to the government. Everybody was happy. Things were looking up for our Special Ops covert ingress capabilities.

So life continued. Ash taking on and teaching the best of the best Navy pilots at Top Gun. Me, testing the integration of several new improvements in the HAHO system at El Centro. Ash and I still only saw each other on the week-ends and I was putting a lot of hours on Bo's Mooney, but hey, he got me into this. Something had to change . . .

Chapter Ninety Four

Advanced HAHO Development Complex

El Centro NAS, California

Monday, April 7, 1986 10:47 a.m. MDT

"Hey guys," I said as I entered the break room where Bo and Joe were discussing the state of the system, "if things go as well as they have this morning I'll be done testing these new systems by the end of the week – what then?"

Captain Garcia looked up at me as if he had something he wanted to tell me but couldn't, "The wheels are turning, but we know nothing," he said, avoiding my 'you've got to be kidding' look. "Bo and I were just discussing the mission, have a seat." I did.

Joe continued, "The Feds are digging. I'm sure this little problem is somewhere near the top of President Stevens' list – they'll figure it out. Meanwhile, it might be helpful to get ourselves as up to speed as we can, try to recap the mission and better understand the current situation. Let me start with an update I just got from the Admiral:

"The safe Marco and Alberto blasted out of Horte's wine cellar was empty and the other safe they took from the villa held fourteen hundred American dollars, plus change – nothing else. No lists, no plans, no formulas, no nothing – except one dominant set of finger prints that matched with prints on all of the items that had a high probability of being Horte's personal stuff. There were thirty seven separate print sets found on the premises, excluding our teams. All prints were run through every known data base in the free world. There were only six that didn't have matches. Horte's was one of the unmatched – so we think we've finally got his real prints. The feds are trying to figure out how he left unmatchable prints when he was in the U.S. recently. They're exploring the possibility that the last U.S. visit might have been by the look-alike, whom they still know nothing about. Most of the other prints were from minor thugs from south of the border. There were five sets that matched U.S. citizens with Hispanic names. These are all being investigated.

"The guy in the blue Toyota that you guys took down in La Jolla turned out to be a hired hit man. They've got hard evidence that he killed Freddy. He'll be tried and fried. But there's no link back to Horte.

"The eight coke extraction plants are back in operation, legally producing naphthalene by-products. The managers that Horte hired just days before our raid knew nothing about the illicit front-end operation. The 'slag' packagers just disappeared. The vacuum stills were all converted back to their original functionality. Horte is some sort of diabolical genius. When he discovered the extent of the information disclosed by Freddy Alverez he immediately began execution of his phase 1 exit strategy. And, he's covered his tracks pretty cleverly. This son-of-a-bitch is going to be hard to find and kill – but we'll do that before it's all over. Now we've got a twenty plus year supply of high grade coke hidden all over the country already being distributed. All we can do for now is continue the HAHO deployment program. When the spooks get the proper level of intel we'll go take him down.

"Meanwhile we're putting together a HAHO training squad under the 7th wing at Miramar. Sam, the Admiral wants you to lead that effort. Wrap up your duties here in two weeks and go move in with your beautiful wife. Bo and the guys can handle everything else here. This will be a temporary assignment, probably six months or so, to generate the training program and materials, then get all JSOC personnel familiar with the new system with a short advanced program for those expected to use the system near-term. Your first class will be a train the trainer class with four of our most experienced HAHO operatives; one from each of the services. These four will be your instructors."

Not really wanting to remind anyone of this little problem, I lowered my head and responded, "I missed my arctic land training because of this little drug bust / rescue mission. Now I'm going to miss the summer BUD/S front end conditioning segment, which starts the third week in June. How can I accept my promotion and status as a SEAL without completing the requirements?"

Joe looked at me sternly, "Sam, in the Navy we have priorities. Certainly, training is one of our highest. But right now you are uniquely qualified to do this job. I said the Admiral *wants* you to lead this training effort. I believe you need to take that as an order. In the eyes of the team, the Admiral, the JSOC Commander, the Chairman of the Joint Chiefs and the President of the United States you are a member of the advanced weapons development organization of SEAL Team VI. I would work real hard to *not* piss off that particular group of people if I were you. We'll get your training finished including the diving part and the final eight weeks of SEAL Qualification Training. First we've got to get you out of the critical path on this drug cartel problem. When you get to Hell Week you'll wish you'd never heard the words *Navy* or *SEAL*. Until this training is complete you will be a SEAL pending qualification per order of the President.

I was surprised, elated, scared, and happy as a duck in water all at the same time. I didn't know what to say, so I smiled and said nothing. Maybe this Navy gig isn't so bad after all . . .

Chapter Ninety Five

Advanced HAHO Training Center

Miramar NAS, California

Friday, September 12, 1986 1:05 p.m. PDT

Ash and I had had a great two months. Together every night in our own condo. Weekends to ourselves. Beautiful evenings at our old haunts in La Jolla and down in San Diego and most important we were once again close to our beach and our rock. In early June we camped out in our two man tent on *our beach* just below *our rock*.

Determined to enroll in the first eight week session of the BUD/S training, I was able to bring Hal Nicholson with me to Miramar to set up and conduct the first train-the-trainer Advanced HAHO course in early June. During the month of May Hal and I found four HAHO qualified SF Operators who jumped at the opportunity to join the program to head up training operations for their own units – one each from Delta Force, the 23rd Air Force Spec Ops, Marine Force Recon and, of course Hal opted for the SEAL position. I had intensified my daily PT routine on that day in April when I made the decision to do my best to make the BUD/S class in June. I had done well in the Panama Jungle but my SEAL buddies all told me that was nothing compared to BUD/S. There is a tough eight week BUD/S Prep course designed to see if candidates can even hack the real course – I had to meet these requirements on my own. We held a very successful first course in early June and I was able to join the BUD/S group at Coronado Island

Ash made two more of her ROTC PR trips in between Top Gun classes. I didn't go with her on these trips because I was too busy with my own training program(s). She had checked herself out in an F-18 Hornet at the base and was anxiously awaiting the arrival of the first three Hornets promised to the Top Gun school.

BUD/S damned near killed me. All of the physical activity took me to the edge of my physical endurance but the swimming almost did me in. Even as an experienced certified diver I had never had to swim like a SEAL. I found muscles in my legs I didn't even know I had. The only thing that kept me going at several points during Hell Week was the fear of facing Joe and Bo if I rang out. In BUD/S if you decide to quit, there's this bell right off the PT area that you can ring three times to get coffee, donuts and then sent back to your old unit – or somewhere else. I made it through and got back to Miramar two weeks ago. Didn't lose weight like I did in Panama – the food at BUD/S is great. I think I turned what little fat I had to muscle – mostly in my legs.

Today, I had dedicated the entire afternoon to testing a new high wind auto approach capability developed by Bo's guys down at El Centro. And today's weather forecast called for winds at twenty gusting to twenty five mph in the afternoon. I had just completed my third successful jump from ten thousand feet and the system was performing well within specification.

As I gathered my chute and turned to walk down the taxiway toward the jeep waiting for me, I noticed a hornet on a tight base-leg at the other end of the ten thousand foot runway. This pilot was obviously a hot shot planning to do a low pass because as he aligned himself with the runway, his gear was still up, his flaps were up and he was hot – maybe close to three hundred mph. For sure, he wasn't landing.

Then as he started a slow roll at about a hundred feet above the mid point of the runway and I caught the blue and yellow paint job – this wasn't a 'he' – this was my darling wife. She'd finally gotten her new toy. After the prettiest slow roll I'd ever seen she hit the afterburners and shot straight up right next to me at the end of the runway. I had already covered my ears with my hands as best I could. These hornets are the noisiest jets the Navy ever flew and when the burners light you'd better have ear protection if you're within a quarter mile.

She leveled out at about ten thousand feet, did a split-S down to about three thousand, entered a shallow dive into the traffic pattern and made a typical Navy approach and landing – all of which was somewhat above my ability. If I didn't love her so much I'd have given her hell for showing off. She left the active runway at the second exit and taxied down toward me.

ANGELS THREE FIVE

I wondered why she flew her old T-38 down to San Diego this morning and why she responded, "none of your business," to my query about it. She was definitely going to be hard to live with for the next few weeks. She pulled off the taxiway onto the run-up pad where my jeep was parked, killed the engines and climbed down from the cockpit using the built-in steps – not easy for a five foot four woman. I dropped my chute and started jogging toward her and she began running toward me – I think I'd seen this in slow motion in a movie somewhere. I felt a strange mixture of burning love and happiness for Ash along with a little envy – why couldn't I get a job like hers? Oh well, life as a SEAL wasn't going to be all that bad. Our long, wet embrace told me I needed to save some energy for tonight. At least it was Friday. . .

Chapter Ninety Six

Sheerwater Hotel Restaurant

Coronado Island, California

Friday, September 12, 1986 6:25 p.m. PDT

Mark had invited us to dinner at the Sheerwater on Coronado Island in San Diego with Bo and Joe who were flying into San Diego NAS in Bo's Mooney. We drove down there in light traffic so we were the first ones there and grabbed a seat at the bar, ordered some drinks and waited for the rest of the crew. After about five minutes Admiral George Bennington slipped into the empty seat next to Ash in civilian clothes.

"Admiral, what a surprise," quipped Ashleigh, and she *was* truly surprised.

"Commanders, good to see you. Where's Joe & Bo – we're civilians tonight, let's use first names," responded the Admiral.

I said, "They're not here yet, but we're still a little early. Should we get a table?"

"I've got one reserved on the corner of the courtyard. It should be a little quieter there."

"Mark didn't mention you were coming. Should we read something into that?" asked Ash.

"Yeah, probably. This is the dinner I promised you all when we departed North Island a little over four months ago so I'm buying. I asked Mark not to mention that I would be here. This will be mostly a social meal but I've got a little business to discuss also."

"Speaking of the devils, there they are," I said as Bo & Joe walked in and I flagged them over to the bar. "Let's move to the table, shall we?"

Mark joined us and we ordered. The seafood at this restaurant is fantastic so that's what we all had. The other four had wine, Bo and I had the Lowenbrau Oktoberfest beer, just received this morning according to the waiter. The meal was better than advertised. We talked mostly about Ash's new toy and her recruiting trips, the new improvements to the HAHO system, the Admiral's summer vacation in Italy, Bo's latest news on Jameson Air and Joe's new ranch up near Flagstaff.

As the waiter cleared the table and we ordered our third round of drinks the Admiral broke the silence, "Well, I guess it's time to talk about the situation at hand. Mark and I have been involved in the single most intensive manhunt this country has ever executed. And largely due to your astute observations and the detailed information reported during your little vacation south of the border, Ashleigh, we've located the son-of-a-bitch. I can't get into details in a public place like this but I can say we have detailed information on much of the entire operation, thanks to inter-agency cooperation like I've never seen before - probably due to the leader of our little team.

"Our leader has requested our presence at a three day planning session at corporate headquarters beginning at 0800, a week from Monday. Lodging has been arranged and we will be met in front of Hangar A, here at the NAS, by a corporate jet Sunday morning at 1000 hours for the trip. I wanted to give you as much advance notice as possible because I know you all have very busy schedules. Ashleigh, Captain Baker is aware of your pending three day absence and has already got you covered. Joe, if you can't work around it we'll just have to put a three day dent in your schedule. We will need eighteen full-up operational systems for three teams and two spares as well as an additional eighteen ground units with two spares. Is that doable?"

"Yes Sir!"

"Any questions?"

"Admiral, I mean George, what is my role in the mission?" asked Ash.

"Purely mission planning, Ashleigh. You'll be away from your job only three days. But I told Reggie (Captain Baker) that I reserved the right to call on you 24/7 for your help and advice in ongoing planning and execution of the mission – that ok with you?"

"Certainly, sir."

"Any other questions?"

There were none. The conversation reverted to other topics like football, beer versus wine, the weather and Ashleigh's students. . .

Chapter Ninety Seven

Langley Air Force Base

Langley, Virginia

Sunday, September 21, 1986 6:15 p.m. EDT

The CIA Gulfstream G-III touched down softly at Langley Field after an uneventful flight. Bill Conroy had provided us with a very nice on-board dinner; fillet mignon with lobster bisque, baked potato, Italian green beans, hot wheat rolls and a freshly tossed Caesar salad with a choice of red or white California wine.

A company limousine (SUV) was waiting by the hangar and took us quickly across the bridge to Hampton and dropped us at a quaint little hotel on the bay called Strawberry Banks. Very nice, but not fancy or modern. Since we'd just eaten on the plane, Bo, Ash and I headed for the bar. Mark, Joe and George found a small conference room where they could review their presentations for tomorrow morning.

The bar was featuring a new brand of beer; Samuel Adams Boston Lager, and that being two thirds of my name I had to try it. So did Ash and Bo. Pretty good. After three or four beers and some non-business conversation we decided to call it a night. I think Bo suspected why. Ash and I knew damned well why.

Back in our room, Ash got serious, "I'm thinking I don't like your job so much anymore. When this all started I was doing what I love, flying, and you were doing what you love, flying, jumping out of perfectly good airplanes and inventing things. Now you're in combat shooting people and blowing things up and getting shot at. That doesn't make me happy. We've talked about kids and a 'normal life' in our future. I've got two and a half years left in my tour and you've got a little less than three. Let's make a deal. When my time's up I'll retire, we'll buy a nice little house somewhere off-base wherever you're based and settle down. If you want to re-enlist you've got to promise me you'll get out of the combat business. You're too damned valuable to the Navy to be shot at – what the hell are they thinking? Anyway, those are my terms. What's your take on that?"

"You've got a deal. What else can I say? I'd mop floors for a living if it meant keeping you. Besides, I think this mission is going to wrap up this 'national security' problem once and for all and let me get back to what I'm best at. Believe me, babe, I don't like getting shot at either! We've definitely got technology on our side and it looks like we're going to hit them from multiple directions this time. We'll find out more about what's coming down tomorrow. Right now I feel like a team shower. What say you?"

"You've got a deal sailor," she grinned.

Sex in a shower between two people with a mismatch of about nine inches in height takes some human engineering and the right sized shower. We made it work again this time and the hot water held up. Life is good!

Chapter Ninety Eight

CIA Headquarters
Langley, Virginia
Monday, September 22, 1986 8:00 a.m. EDT

The team had just about doubled. Bob McFadden and his two senior analysts were present as well as the President's National Security Advisor, three additional Joint Chiefs and the U.S. Ambassador to Columbia.

"Ok gentlemen, let's get started," said Admiral George Bennington. "The President asked me to lead this task force and found a capable replacement for me until we get this task accomplished. The task involves bringing down the two largest drug cartels in the western hemisphere *and* locating and destroying the twenty three year supply of high grade cocaine hidden here in the U.S. First we need to bring everyone up to speed. You all know CIA Director Bill Conroy, DEA Director Jim Doddington, and FBI Director Bob Gilmore. These gentlemen with the able assistance of Adam Kivel, NSA Space Systems, will fill you in on what we've discovered over the last four and a half months. Then Captain Garcia, Commander Jameson and I will put forth a straw-man plan of action to accomplish our mission. We've added advisors to our team; these folks along with the President's National Security Advisor will assist us in handling the political needs and requirements of the mission. Questions?"

No questions.

Bennington nodded to Bill Conroy and he rose to speak: "First, I want to thank our team for the above and beyond the call of duty effort put forth to get us to this point, and our leader for keeping us focused and working together. We all know the difficulty we have in bringing the various agencies together to solve any problem. In this effort we have eliminated inter-agency politics and significantly improved the agency interfaces. Of course it helped that the President and CJCS Jerry Sterett told us they'd fire our butts if we didn't ditch the sandbox syndrome." A brief chuckle filled the room. "We were also able to work around many of the inter-agency interface problems, both technical and organizational. If we can continue in the future to work together as well as we have here, our national security, both domestic and international, will be enhanced tenfold in timeliness, accuracy and execution."

Summarizing the remainder of the morning: Conroy, and then Doddington and Gilmore went on to set the stage. Through the use of the many intelligence gathering capabilities, both technological and human, the team had located Horte and tied him directly to the Medellin Cartel in Columbia run by Pablo Escobar. Horte's primary operation was located near Leon, Nicaragua, close to the airfield where Commander Ashleigh McKensie was taken by the mysterious Petty Officer who kidnapped her at Miramar.

The beginning of this drug pipeline is near Medellin, Columbia at the freight terminal of a secondary airport - Tuscala Field. Escobar owns a fleet of aging but well maintained WW II C-47 cargo planes – the military version of the DC-3. He also owns a front transport company complete with fake books which hauls about six metric tons of cocaine up to Horte's airstrip northeast of Leon Nicaragua each day. The coke is packaged in thirty kilogram heavy plastic fertilizer bags, tightly sealed and designed to closely emulate other popular South/Central American commercial fertilizers containers. Two flights a day at random times are required to haul the dope.

At the other end, two one ton pallets of "fertilizer" are loaded onto a respectable looking three ton covered truck with 'Gonzalez Farm Supplies' stenciled in Spanish on the doors. Three of the trucks are then driven on two different routes at random times each day to a large warehouse about thirty five kilometers north of Puerto Vallarta, Mexico and about five kilometers from the coast. The trip requires two days. It appears the cartels are storing the coke in this warehouse which appears to have been recently built and at least ten thousand square feet in size. The intel folks are speculating that a new method of transport is being devised, while the flow in the U.S. is kept constant with the hidden supply, but so far have no idea what the new method is. The warehouse, in a remote and rather isolated area, is heavily, though discretely guarded. This makes ground reconnaissance difficult if not impossible. The CIA and NSA are reasonably certain that the bad guys are not aware of their detection and our people want to keep it that way; so all surveillance is limited to covert ground, aerial and satellite. They calculate that the warehouse will hold about six thousand tons of product and that it would take almost three years to fill at the rate of six tons per day. The warehouse is clearly intended to buffer the supply while their new delivery scheme is implemented.

The NSA was forced by world current events to return two of the six satellites to their original orbits so reconnaissance has been supplemented by SR-71 Blackbird flights over the area.

Since the mission last March careful attention has been given to the consumption rate and the street price inside the U. S. in eleven key areas of the country. Everything seems to be stable; indicating that the flow of cocaine into the hands of users had not been significantly affected. All of the warehouses checked use a standard storage method where only their own barcode labels identify each item and its location within the warehouse. Tracing the owner-to-warehouse location to the warehouse-to-internal-location link has thus far proven impossible. We have yet to find an invalid owner on the front end of the scheme. With tens of thousands of potential storage facilities to search, and the kegs well disguised by external heavy cardboard crates of different sizes, the manpower necessary to find all of the coke is astronomical. So once again it looks like we won't solve the location problem until we capture Horte and find the key to this perplexing scheme. We know the solution exists and we must be vigilant in our efforts in this take-down to the discovery and protection of that key.

Based on current knowledge, the team expects to find the new infiltration transport scheme soon. When they find it they need a base plan from which to operate.

The objectives were:

1) Take down the Columbian operation; nothing less than total destruction of the production, packaging, transport, and transportation facilities, including the fleet of aircraft.

2)   Destroy the transfer depot and the cartel related facilities on Horte's airfield in Nicaragua including any aircraft, trucks and other equipment present at the time of attack.
3)   Destroy the warehouse in Mexico and its contents. Disable and destroy the new transport scheme.*
4)   Capture Horte and the Petty Officer. Locate/capture his remaining network in the U.S. Then locate/destroy all stored cocaine.*

Rules of engagement: Identify and shoot to kill, all but Horte and the Petty Officer. When resistance abates, take prisoners as necessary.

* Pre mission priorities: Find new transport method! Find key to locations of hidden cocaine in U.S.!

The original mission objective was to capture Horte and the information necessary to locate the cocaine stored throughout the U.S. This objective was changed and the mission accelerated to extract Lt. Commander McKensie from Horte's villa. The extraction was successful but the objective was not met because the team didn't have complete intel. This mission will be designed to insure *complete* intel with respect to discovering the locations of the hidden cocaine.

Chapter Ninety Nine

CIA Headquarters
Langley, Virginia
Monday, September 22, 1986 11:00 a.m. EDT

"Captain Garcia, said the Admiral, "let's see what your team is recommending. First, I want to congratulate the participating teams – both SEAL Team Four and your new HAHO team – on a job well done last March; quick and clean with only one minor casualty. Good job!"

Joe Garcia took his position at the front of the room and said: "Thank you Admiral. I'd like to recognize a couple of guys here who not only worked their butts off to design, develop, implement and test the system that made the HAHO drop possible but also flew the mission. Commander Bo Jameson and Lt. Commander Sam McKensie – both members of NSWDG (Naval Special Warfare Development Group), or DEVGRU. I was truly amazed at the speed with which this program was implemented - almost six months ahead of schedule and under budget. It also exceeded spec. in almost every category. Also, I'd like to congratulate Master Chief Manny Hernandez and his SEAL Team Four for a flawless execution on the destruction of the coke processing plant near Mazatlan.

"After looking carefully at what we now know and what we still don't know, we've come up with a plan that can be successful in neutralizing the complete operation in a matter of hours. I'll call it a straw-man because it will change based on future intel. I'll give an overview with rationale and then Commander Jameson will fill in the details.

"The plan calls for land, sea and air special operations forces – SEALS, Delta Force and CIA. We own the night, so we'll attack at night.

"Target one will be the multiple facilities in Nicaragua – the hangar at the southwest end of the air strip where the C-47s are unloaded and refueled, the truck barn outside the air strip perimeter fence where the trucks are housed and maintained, any cartel aircraft -- including Horte's Lear Jet -- parked on the General Aviation ramp and Horte's ranch home and operations base located six kilometers southeast of the air strip.

"Target two will be the warehouse located north of Puerto Vallarta along with any trucks or other transport vehicles present. This target plan will, for now, only include the facilities we are aware of. Our in-country CIA operators are reconnoitering the site again tonight. So far no solid information, other than the size and structure of the warehouse and the fact that it is taking in over six tons of material each day and taking none that we know of out. If we find an existing outgoing transport capability, that also will be destroyed.

"The warehouse is heavily guarded during operating hours. Employees work in two shifts. Non-operating hours are from 2230hrs to 0700 hrs with somewhat fewer security personnel.

"Target three will be the production and packaging facilities located fourteen kilometers southeast of the Tuscala Airport near Medellin, Columbia, the hangar on the airport where Escobar's C-47s are housed and maintained and Escobar's hacienda and base of operations seven kilometers south of the airport.

"Target four will be the domestic ports of entry for the drugs. This location or locations, if any, are yet to be found.

"We'll have to rely on timely intel to locate and destroy any cocaine en-route during the attack. It's a two day drive from the air strip in Nicaragua to the warehouse in Mexico. The trucks overnight at a truck stop on the highway southwest of Mexico City where the two known routes cross. The aircraft and trucks operate only during daylight hours so we should be able to get them all on the ground at night."

"Are there any questions on the scope of the operation?"

I raised my hand and asked, "How good is our visibility on the warehouse in Mexico? Is there any possibility that they're already shipping coke out of it?"

The Admiral stood and said to me, "That's a timely question Sam. I just got word that the morning SR-71 run down the coast and back spotted a surfaced submarine off the northern coast of Nicaragua. It stayed on the surface for about fifteen minutes and then submerged. The sub was less than fifty feet long and about ten feet in diameter. I'm waiting on the pictures which will arrive soon. This could be our new transportation scheme.

"Why don't we take a slightly early break for lunch and I'll see what I can get over the net before we reconvene. It's eleven twenty now. Let's be back at twelve thirty and see what we've got."

"Gentlemen, I hope you had a pleasant lunch. I can now report to you that we've received some very important intel," said Admiral Bennington as he switched an image of a small submarine onto the rear projector video screen at the front of the room. "The analysts now have accurate measurements: It is forty five feet long, plus or minus six inches and nine feet in diameter, plus or minus 3 inches. This sub is a little larger than the SEAL Delivery sub we are designing as we speak. This means its payload should be between fourteen and twenty two tons. And here's some food for thought: The analysts and intel specialists are speculating that there is a tunnel from the warehouse to an underground loading terminal with a wet channel to let the sub enter submerged, similar to the one in the 007 James Bond movie. This raises the possibility that the warehouse might also be a repackaging plant to transfer the coke into its final containers and crates prior to entering the U.S. and that this scheme might have already been in operation for some time. We don't know where the other end of this trail is but it's likely to be as far south on our coast as possible. The further north, the higher the risk of detection and the longer the round trip. And it has to have a tie into the shipping system and one or more domestic distribution centers. I spoke briefly with Admiral Sterett and he will task the Coast Guard with locating it from the sea. I will get our team working on the location from the air and land.

"So, that being said; Commander Jameson I believe you're going to brief us on some recommended operations."

"Thank you Admiral. As Captain Garcia mentioned, we will attack at night. All operations will commence in unison at a time yet to be determined, but around 0120 hours. We will use this time as the execution time for purposes of this briefing. This will allow for adequate execution time including search, seizure, demolition and egress. We will use four teams. Since we have incomplete intel on target four, I will discuss only the first three. Team one will attack in Nicaragua, team two in Mexico and team three in Columbia.

"Team 1, will be a Delta Force ODA (Operational Detachment size

A, 12 man) for operations in Nicaragua. The team leader is yet to be chosen. They will do a daylight HALO jump from a CIA CAPV-727 (Covert Air Penetration Vehicle - A Boeing 727 disguised as a civilian airliner) at forty thousand feet into the east-west valley to the northeast of the airstrip in Nicaragua. Opening at one thousand feet AGL just past the northern mountain range of the valley puts them well below the line of sight from the vicinity of the air strip to the top of the twenty seven hundred foot southern mountain range. A kilometer traverse to a one thousand foot opening will put the team just eight hundred feet above the northern range as they approach the valley. This team will then proceed on foot to the crest of the southern range just north of the airstrip, dig in for an overnight stay and send three two man recon patrols with night gear to each of the objectives for eyes-on observation. The following day will provide rest for the patrols and detailed planning time for the other six. The team will split into three squads for the attack.

"Team two, for operations at the Warehouse in Mexico, will be a six man SEAL Team. We're recommending Master Chief Manny Hernandez' Team IV. Obviously, due to the recent intel the scope and strategy for this attack will change. I do have some issues for us all to ponder: How can we watch the subs covertly? The P3-MAD (P3 Orion, Magnetic Anomaly Detector) sub hunters are anything but covert. The Blackbird has no sub interdiction capability. Do any of our orbiters have that capability? Can we figure out how deep these subs can go from what we know about their size and ballast capacity? I say these subs because they need at least two, maybe three, but probably four to do the job. I'm sure I've just scratched the surface here, but we've got some real homework to do before we can crystallize a plan for Mexico.

"We have a plan for the warehouse destruction, but I recommend that we rethink that operation from scratch based on this very recent intel.

"Team three, for operations in Columbia, will be the HAHO joint force team we used at Horte's villa, expanded to sixteen members, led by me. We'll use an MC-130E Combat Talon at 35,000 feet. This team will jump as three squads:

"The Hacienda squad will consist of eight operators led by me to take Escobar and his team at his home/fortress while minimizing collateral damage to innocents. We have much of the property and logistics intel and have requested and expect the rest shortly. This operation will commence at 0119:30, just before the explosion at the airport.

"The Airport squad will consist of four operators who will land in a parking lot inside the airport's secured area, just behind Escobar's hangar. These operators will covertly cause simultaneous demolition of the entire hangar including contents, all cartel aircraft and vehicles present at or near the airport and any other equipment or personnel identified as being associated with the cartel but not previously identified by intel. This entire demolition operation will occur simultaneously at precisely 0120.

"The processing/packaging plant squad will consist of four operators. These four will have the longest jump, but likely the easiest job. Current intel says the plant is lightly guarded due to the fact that it is located in a remote area central to cartel operations. We'll need a Little Bird at the egress point before the explosion to pick up the squad and then cause detonation after lift-off. There is a cartel helipad less than a mile from the plant with a single night guard. The team will egress to the helipad and take out the guard just prior to the arrival of the Little Bird.

"All members of each of the three squads will be equipped with the Advanced HAHO units. After landing, the pressure suit subsystem will be disconnected, taken off, and stowed in a common team cache until egress. We want those suits and the rest of each system back – no bullet holes!" Another chuckle. *Please* take care of them!"

"Egress from each of the airports will be via aircraft pre-positioned at the opposite end of the airstrip. In Columbia a Little Bird will arrive at a pre-arranged time and in Nicaragua our CIA guys will 'steal' one of Escobar's C-47s to be flown out with the team and captives by Lt. Commander McKensie. Egress from Escobar's home site, the plant site in Columbia and the warehouse site in Mexico will be via Little Birds. Each of these sites will have the support of one or more in-country CIA Operators. Only the Columbians will know what's happening. I'm told they are very supportive and will assist in our egress operations. We will not, however inform them of the exact time and date until 8 hours prior, but even so, they will stand ready to assist."

"That's all I have at the present time. As we gain additional intel we'll add to and change this straw-man mission plan until we are all confident of mission success. Are there any questions?"

The Admiral responded as he signed a document and returned it to his aide who immediately left the room, "One question, and maybe an answer to something that's bothering us all. Your question Commander: How can we watch the subs covertly?

"I just signed a TS Compartmental NTK clearance authorization to disclose to this group, whose names along with rank and serial number are included in the authorization, the details of a highly sensitive capability integrated into the Blackbird's optical surveillance system less than six months ago.

The SR-71E has a variety of photographic capabilities, but the one I'm disclosing to you at this time gives this aircraft a whole new surveillance role: Near Real Time Sea Penetration (NERTSEP for those who need an acronym for everything). From eighty thousand feet the SR-71E digital optics computer can eliminate surface noise – that means waves and reflections at the surface of the sea - and 'see' to a depth, in the waters we're concerned with here, of more than twice our need in sunlit waters and should still work well in cloud covered waters. The processing delay varies from less than seven seconds to no more than twenty seconds in good conditions. The circular surface area that can be accurately viewed to those depths from eighty thousand feet is over seven hundred square miles – that's a forty five degree look-down angle. The Blackbird that spotted the surfaced sub was not equipped with this new technology, but we've got one on its way from Groom Lake as we speak. Within two, maybe three days we should have most of the intel we need to put this last piece into the mission planning puzzle.

"Gentlemen and Lady, I believe we've accomplished what we needed to today. Let's break a little early and plan to complete our discussions with requirements for logistics, details, and additional intelligence tomorrow. Based on what we decide tomorrow we will need to set a date for execution. Any further comments?" asked Admiral George Bennington.

There were none – meeting adjourned.

Chapter One Hundred

Strawberry Banks Hotel Bar

Hampton, Virginia

Monday, September 22, 1986 07:30 p.m. EDT

Joe, Bo Ash & I had a really good dinner at Al's Smokehouse, just a little way outside the base. Good barbeque for the D.C. area. I asked where Al was from and the lady said "Pflugerville, Texas." Small world.

So we headed back to the Strawberry Banks' cozy little bar. We agreed to each give our thoughts on the day's proceedings, have no more than two drinks and then hit the rack.

Joe led off in the conversation. "This is one helluva complex operation. Chances for screw-ups are pretty good. The good news is we've got state-of-the-art equipment. The bad news is we're missing one hell of a lot of intel – especially in the final leg from Mexico to California. Hell, we're not even sure it's California! The biggest shell shocker for me today was the submarine thing. If I were Horte or Escobar or whoever runs this thing, I would have my alternate plan either working or very close before I pulled the plug on my current gig. He probably didn't miss a lick. We've probably got twenty five or thirty years of coke stashed around the country by now. What's your take Bo?"

"I'm with you brother. We just stepped on the dragon's tail last time. When we were done with the last mission and I had some time to think about it, I concluded that we never encountered a single bad guy that belonged to Horte. We thought we had Horte and the "Petty Officer" but they both got away. Even the perp in the blue Toyota was a rent-a-thug. That means we were set up from the git-go. Why can we expect any better this time? I've got to see a lot more solid intel and some gut-warming evidence that he, they, or whoever, don't know we know what we do know and what we don't know. As it is, I'm worried – not about my butt, but about our potential success. And, maybe a little about my butt too. Sam?"

"You guys aren't exactly instilling confidence in me. Back when I was a contractor they told me I could quit any time – it was just like a job. That's not true any more since I swore my soul to the SEAL Credo with a new three year commitment. We've gotta make this thing work!"

Joe cut me off, "Relax Sam, we gave you the easiest job. All you have to do is blow up a hangar full of C-47s and a few other aircraft out on the line and a maintenance shed with a few trucks in it with the push of one button, scramble your team up to the other end of the runway and take off in an unknown airplane put there by someone you've never met and fly back home. Absolute piece of cake! It's gonna work Sam. We won't go 'til we're ready. All missions start off like this. We'll get the intel and we'll make the right decisions."

"I know how this Special Ops stuff works. We're given the task. We request the intel. We do the planning. We go when we're ready. And we get the job done. If we do all these things right we get to live for the next mission. And, we're trained to do it all right. We did pretty well on the first mission with incomplete intel. I'm just concerned that we might not have enough information and how we'll know when we do. Ash what are your thoughts after today?"

"Yeah, there's a lot we need to know that we don't and we've got a lot of work to do to get ready, but I'm impressed with the folks involved in this mission and I know, because it is so important to the country, that you guys will succeed. There are some things I think we should know that nobody seems to be concerned with: who is the "Petty Officer" and how does he fit into the global operation? What happened to the 'CEOs', the front end managers and the shipping clerks of the naphthalene companies? How long has Horte been working for or with Escobar – or vice versa? What is their real relationship? Who is gathering intel for the cartel personnel in the U.S. and who do they work for? How did Horte find out about Freddie? Maybe these are just small things and inconsequential to the big picture, but I believe knowing some of this information could lead us to the mystery of where the drugs are hidden in the U.S. I'm not sure we're ever going to find the list.

"It's obviously going to be a complex land, sea and air mission with some very new technology driving all three parts."

"You're right Ash, it is just that. Let's hope it works just as well this time. We'd better call it a night guys. We're not going to solve this problem yet – we've got a lot of work to do so let's get some sleep," Bo groaned as he pushed his chair back and stood to leave.

So we did just that. No sex tonight – am I getting old or just tired? Maybe both. . .

Chapter One Hundred One

Current Intel Secure Video Briefing
Tuesday, October 14, 1986 01:00 p.m. PDT

Admiral George Bennington occupied the video camera after each of the assault teams had gathered in their respective secure video conference facilities. Joining the group was President Brad Stevens, former Navy SEAL and Commander of JSOC before beginning his distinguished political career; along with Admiral Gerald Sterett, Chairman of the Joint Chiefs. They were monitoring the briefing from the secure briefing room in basement of the white house.

"Gentlemen, POTUS and CJCS are with us today. I just spent Friday through Sunday with the NSA, CIA and FBI intel folks. I'm going to try to fill in the blanks today on the stuff you probably haven't heard yet. You will receive the full thirty seven page report via your secure telex while we are in this meeting. The document and everything said here today is Top Secret, Eyes Only and needs to be secured in your dedicated containers after you've digested it all. "Let's start with Max Horte: After consolidating, (read that; eliminating the leaders of), the major Central American drug cartels, Max Horte and his brother, Xavier, established a cooperative relationship with Pablo Escobar. Most of the drugs funneled into the United States through its porous borders come from South America or are imported into South or Central America from other countries around the world. Horte and his cohorts seem to have solved the transportation problem. First, with the naphthalene scheme and now, without missing a beat, the submarine fleet. These two thugs need each other.

"Horte has essentially retired. His much younger half-brother Xavier, who is by the way the very same "Petty Officer" who kidnapped Lt. Commander McKensie and very likely the brains behind the whole operation, is in the process of taking over all operations in Central America. He still resides in Mexico about twenty kilometers from the warehouse north of Puerto Vallarta. But, he currently spends most of his time at Max's ranch in Nicaragua or at the warehouse near the sub base. Our in-country CIA folks have cultivated an inside stooge in Xavier's organization. They tell us he will be at the ranch with his wife or girl friend this weekend. They are in the final stages of transfer of power and working weekends in Nicaragua to complete the process. Max has accumulated well over a hundred million dollars, plans to trade his Lear Jet in on a new Gulf Stream II, upgrade his yacht to a ninety five foot custom job and fall into the good life for the rest of his days.

"We have confirmed that the warehouse in Mexico is connected to a well hidden subterranean submarine terminal just north of Puerto Vallarta via a 5.1 kilometer tunnel. The drugs are re-packaged in the warehouse and carted down the tunnel, probably by rail where they are packed aboard one of four submarines and transported to a facility in California built to be an underwater research company but in reality is the U.S. distribution terminal."

"Escobar is, and has been for some time, located in his 'hacienda' fortress near Medellin, Columbia. We have accumulated a significant amount of intel on this stronghold. It was designed to withstand a conventional attack or siege. Our plan for Mr. Escobar will come from directions, and with overwhelming forces, that he never dreamed were possible. Thanks to the escape of the Horte brothers, our in-country operators have discovered Escobar's escape routes and will have them plugged. All that being said, this will be our most dangerous assault in the overall plan. We are adding significant additional resources to the assault on his hacienda - our guys will be ready.

Chapter One Hundred Two

CIA CAPV-727, 40,000 feet
Over Northwestern Nicaragua
Friday, October 24, 1986 01:15 p.m. PDT

Captain Vincent Harlow readied his men as they approached their target in northwestern Nicaragua. Harlow was career Army, grew up in the Airborne Rangers, Green Beret and had led this Delta Force Team for two years now. This was their seventh classified mission, four of which were HALO ingress. This was his first mission with the new system and he was impressed. He and his team spent three weeks at Miramar NAS learning the system from me and my training cadre. Although his mission required a daylight jump, four of his ten training jumps had been at night. The entire team was enamored with the capabilities of the system and what that meant to future missions. The three weeks at Miramar went without a hitch. He had a good feeling about this mission, but he had lost two men on previous missions – one in a night jump. So he knew the danger of over-confidence. Murphy's Law was a global statute: 'If anything can happen it will happen.' The Special Forces translation: If anything can go wrong – it will, especially when you're flying on the edge of technology and human endurance. So as they approached the target he stood, pointed to the lead jumper and said "go test." The first man lowered his visor, secured the helmet to pressure suit seal/latch and initiated the test. Then at two second intervals he pointed to the next man, until all had initiated the built in self test feature of the system. This test checked out the SATCOM, all networks, GPSNAV, starlight and infrared vision systems, the visor display in all modes, the pressurization system and the auto-landing system including the shroud pullers. The test takes thirty seconds if the system has no problems. So, after initiating his own test (he was the last man out) Harlow pointed to the first man and got a thumbs up about three seconds later and in two second intervals down the line he got the go sign from every man. When the pilot called one minute to IP, Harlow said calmly over the net "Disconnect." Each man reached for the small connector at the chest-pack end of a charging cable and disconnected himself from the aircraft charging system. The system's primary computer and laser altimeter are built into the front of a bulletproof pull-over vest with six lithium ion batteries built into a bulletproof belt worn just below the vest. In battle mode the batteries will last eighty hours after a maximum glide HAHO jump from thirty five thousand feet.

The entire jump had been pre-programmed into each man's computer, so barring Murphy; the system would depend on the jumper to body-glide to a position south of the northern ridge of the valley and automatically deploy the chute at one thousand feet. The auto-landing system would then guide each jumper as close to the target as possible with only a thousand feet of altitude.

As it turned out, much to Harlow's surprise and dismay, the HALO practice of body-gliding close to each other, in a V formation to resemble a flock of geese, caused the system to land jumpers on top of each other right on the target. Murphy's Law in its finest form. There were no disabling injuries, but a few of the guys were limping a little and I suffered a broken finger. Can't make it through a single mission without becoming a casualty. Lesson learned: *don't program close formation HALO teams to land on the same spot*. Another entry for the training manual.

The hike across the valley was difficult only because the afternoon was hot and we were carrying our chutes and pressure suits along with our standard gear for this mission. Actually, we had stripped to our tee shirts and light-weight trousers and were carrying everything else on our packs. Although the parachute and HALO/HAHO system together only weighed thirty two pounds, that was in addition to the forty pounds of gear and forty pounds of MREs (Meals Ready to Eat) and water each man carried.

It was twilight as we dug-in to a small ravine just below the crest on the north side of the southern-most ridge. The area had the only trees in sight. The three man airport recon squad led by me and the three man recon squad headed for Horte's ranch led by Captain Harlow, ate, drank, found comfortable spots and got some sleep while the others scouted the ridge and set up a defensive perimeter.

When the airport recon squad returned the next morning we

confirmed most of the then-current intel: The hangar contained two C-47s, Horte's Lear Jet that Ashleigh and the "Petty Officer" flew into this same airport, a crop duster, a light twin and two Super Cubs. Another C-47 was chained to the tarmac outside. The team would watch these closely throughout the next day to adjust the demolition plan as necessary. The truck barn held two three ton 'fertilizer' trucks, one of which appeared to be under semi-major repair, the other probably just in for routine maintenance. Two others were parked outside.

The last recon squad (Horte's ranch) stumbled back into the camp just before daybreak. They confirmed that Horte's ranch house was guarded. Five guards, two dogs, an electric fence, a sophisticated alarm system with IR surveillance and a lighting system that could illuminate a small football stadium. This was going to be a tough nut to crack just from the shear volume of defenses. The decision had been made to use only darts here because they worked so well on the last job. They had known from prior intel about everything except the electric fence and the amount of lighting.

Our squad had already been debriefed and we were asleep. Vince Harlow and his men had about eighteen hours to sleep, plan two missions with the latest intel, repack each man with only the items necessary for his mission, develop current contingency plans, check on the latest satellite/Blackbird intel via SATCOM and make last minute changes accordingly. It was going to be a busy day.

Chapter One Hundred Three

Two Six Man RIBs (Rubber Inflatable Boat)
Six Miles Offshore NW of Puerto Vallarta, Mexico
Friday, October 24, 1986, 2200 hrs PDT

Master Chief Manny Hernandez was bringing half of his SEAL Team in by sea with full advanced re-breathing SCUBA systems (re-breathers leave no bubbles, so SEALs can work under occupied boats or structures without detection) and the battle version (no pressure suit) of the ASDS system for each man. The six man team had to use two RIBs due to the large amount of equipment they were bringing with them. Their task for this night was to reconnoiter the under water sub base at the end of a five kilometer tunnel leading to the warehouse used to store cocaine. The other half of his team would arrive via Advanced HAHO tomorrow evening. Their task; to destroy the 'warehouse', surrounding structures, vehicles and equipment at precisely 0120 hours the next morning. The intel on the warehouse was current and conclusive. It was not a 'warehouse' per se, but a repackaging facility to remove the coke from its fertilizer bags, weigh it precisely, place it into sealed pony kegs and pack from two to six of these kegs into a variety of heavy cardboard crates the shapes of which, while different, were engineered to stack tightly into the cargo hold of a small custom built submarine. The crates were labeled at this facility, transported by submarine to a terminal base in southern California and then trucked to a distribution center where they were shipped to warehouses throughout the U.S., waiting to be retrieved by local cartel agents as needed.

The sub base near Puerto Vallarta, Mexico was entirely invisible to conventional aerial surveillance. But the SR-71E was able to observe four different subs cruising at eight knots at a depth of thirty to forty feet leaving this base and completing a three and a half day trip to its sister base near Imperial Beach, California. Each sub would then recharge its batteries for twelve hours and return to the opposite terminal. Four subs each with a fifteen ton cargo capacity and an eight day round trip including charging time yields seven and a half tons a day – up from the six tons that was estimated last January. The terminal near Imperial Beach was actually built as an under water research facility by a well known non-profit conservation organization. The feds were currently trying to figure out how that happened.

A single eighteen wheel tractor trailer marked *SeaQuest Under Sea Labs* and bearing a fancy logo with the words *Saving Our Sea Life* made the trip every other day to the same distribution center used by Horte's original Chula Vista naphthalene plant with fifteen tons of coke to be distributed all over the U.S

But, practically nothing was known about the southern terminal. That's what Manny and his five fellow SEALs were doing tonight. After the recon tonight they would have tomorrow to plan the destruction of the terminal. Current intel says there will be one sub in each terminal re-charging their batteries and the southern sub being loaded Saturday night. The other two subs will be en-route with pretty good predictions on where they will be at 0120 hours Sunday morning. The Navy will have sub hunters lying quietly nearby each predicted location ready for the kill. The terminal at Imperial Beach will be taken by FBI and DEA agents.

The observed schedule for the subs was: A sub arrived at each terminal every other day at or before 6:00 p.m. and left the next morning at 6:00 a.m. sharp. At the southern terminal, loading began at 6:30 p.m. and was complete by 9:30. Eight employees who came to work at 3:30 p.m. on loading nights could be seen leaving the southern terminal shortly after 10:00 p.m. That gave the SEALs a little over three hours to complete their work Sunday morning, which included setting charges and finding and removing all data in the terminal.

Manny and his senior SEAL, Senior Chief Rob Curtis, entered the sub base from the open sea using the re-breathers. One of the subs arrived every other day between four and six p.m. Pacific Standard Time, depending on the sea conditions. Upon arrival there would be a load of cocaine waiting on the loading dock stacked exactly as it would be when placed in the sub's hold for its trip north. Tonight there was no sub at the terminal dock. Tomorrow night when they returned to set the charges a sub already loaded with cocaine would be moored at the loading dock.

The base was dimly lit and there appeared to be only one guard slumped at a desk on the far side of the loading dock – asleep! Definitely a situation better than he'd hoped for. Hernandez had with him a small canister of odorless 'sleeping gas'. He quietly pulled himself up onto the loading dock at its seaward end and sat there for a while to let the water drip off him and to quietly remove his flippers. He then, very quietly, approached the sleeping guard, re-inserted his re-breather mouthpiece and released a five second dose from the low pressure applicator. This was enough to guarantee an additional heavy sleep for four hours and give Manny and his sidekick much more time to recon the facility than he had planned. He breathed through his re-breather for five more minutes to let the residual gas dissipate completely while he rifled through the desk where the guard was sitting. The last thing he wanted to do right now was fall asleep.

Senior Chief Rob Curtis, was a Vietnam veteran with nearly as much seniority and experience as Manny. They were a matched pair, each knowing what he should do as well as what the other would do in any given situation. Rob began a complete survey of the periphery of the loading/charging dock area, including the rail system that led into the unlit tunnel that ran up to the repackaging plant five kilometers inland and some three hundred feet higher in elevation. Aiming his flashlight into the tunnel he noticed the grade as far as he could see was constant at what he guessed to be three to three and a half degrees. From this he deduced that the freight cars used gravity to move down to the dock and a light weight winch to pull the empty cars back up. He also found the ground level entrance to the sub terminal. He counted fifty seven steps to a platform below a horizontal hatch-like door that he suspected was very well camouflaged on the top side.

Meanwhile Manny found an interesting log book in a half sized file cabinet next to the desk to which he gained access by picking the lock. The book contained printouts of what looked like the owner id barcode labels for maybe a few thousand or so shipped items. Each sheet had exactly the same format. A format that matched a standard 8.5 X 11inch barcode label sheet; four columns of three quarter by two inch barcode labels with fourteen rows. These sheets had a ten character alpha code in column one followed by barcodes in the other three columns. The alpha codes were randomly repeated. Manny didn't want to waste time trying to figure it out here, so he called Rob over.

"Grab your document camera out of the waterproof pack and copy these two hundred or so pages while I finish searching this file cabinet – I think we're on to something here. We'll copy the two fifty gig hard drives too. I want everything that's on this computer. I'll start the transfer first. I think eight two pound C4 shaped charges all detonating at 0120 hours will take care of the sub, which will be loaded by then, and this terminal facility nicely. We'll come back tomorrow night to set the charges, what do you think?"

"Since we'll be there working under water why not bring an additional eight charges, four each on the seawalls parallel to the sub – we might get a cave in," Rob replied.

"Amen brother. Never let it be said that we didn't do our part. C4's cheap, considering all the fun we're gonna have!

"I'm thinking we may need to rethink our plan for tomorrow night. I don't think these labels were printed by this computer – for one thing, there's no printer down here. And, the logical place to print ID labels is where the merchandise is processed and packaged – the very same place we're planning to blow up tomorrow night. I'm going to call the boss & suggest some changes. The key to where all that coke is hidden might very well be in that building. Those pages you just copied are copies of the barcode labels used to identify packages in a warehouse. They're used by and linked to both the shipper and the storage facility. But there's not nearly enough here, probably less than a years worth. Maybe just the ones used since this 'warehouse' has been in operation.

"Let's get everything we can and get back to base so we can contact the Admiral."

Chapter One Hundred Four

Pablo Escobar's Hacienda Fortress
42 Kilometers Southwest of Medellin, Columbia
Saturday, October 25, 1986 01:15 a.m. PDT

Sancho Domingo and Earl Davidson, two in-country CIA agents were driving a perimeter road adjacent to Escobar's country hacienda looking for a power pole they had observed earlier in the week. This particular power pole was the only one of all the power poles in the vicinity of Escobar's hacienda that had an underground drop (a power connection running down conduit attached to the pole and entering the ground to provide underground service). And, it happened to be the closest pole to the main building of his country hacienda complex.

The complex consisted of the main building, a two story, ornate, split level, Castilian style building of approximately eighteen thousand square feet in size. The complex had two one hundred foot by one hundred foot internal courtyards with well tended French gardens and a and fountains with a forty foot tower at the center of each. Each tower was manned with two thirty caliber machine guns each of which covered one hundred eighty degrees giving each tower a three hundred and sixty degree field of fire. The roof near the outer walls sported dormers from which additional fire power could be brought to bear.

When they found the pole they proceeded two hundred feet further down the road, donned their night vision goggles, turned off their lights, turned left onto a small gravel road, drove another hundred yards and turned left again into an open field with fence-line trees between them and the power pole they were interested in. After making these two left turns they drove parallel to the main road for about two hundred feet, parked their SUV and hiked back to their pole of interest. Domingo watched carefully for approaching traffic while Davidson inspected the pole to determine how best to disable the power to Escobar's property.

ANGELS THREE FIVE

Their task was to disable the power feed on command from the leader of the attacking SEAL team as they landed on-site early the next morning. Davidson said quietly to Sancho, "the service is three phase – looks like two hundred amps, two-twenty volts. That checks with the intel photos showing an identical service running from a small building twenty yards behind the main house, obviously the emergency generator. If it weren't for the noise it'd make we could use C-4, but our plan says "as quietly as possible." I have a twelve pound ax, sharp as a razor, with a fiberglass handle. A good swing will cut that turkey clean in two. We'll get a flash and some sparks. Protective eye-ware and a small flashlight. No night vision, maybe sunglasses. I'll call in our ready status. Let's get some sleep."

Chapter One Hundred Five

MC-130E Combat Talon Cargo Plane at 33,000 feet
45 Miles Southwest of Medellin, Columbia
Saturday, October 25, 1986 0320 hrs PDT

Master Sergeant David Saunders, a decorated veteran of Vietnam and a HALO proficient Delta Force team leader, readied his squad for their first combat HAHO jump. He and his five men were tasked with delivering the heavy fire necessary to overcome Escobar's hacienda fortress. Saunders and his team had trained with our Advanced HAHO School at Miramar and had helped perfect the cargo version of the HAHO ALS (Automatic Landing System) in early September. The system behaved much like the manned ALS but it guides a cargo package with up to two tons of equipment to a safe-soft landing on a pre-programmed spot (the green X). The system used a much larger chute and more powerful shroud-pullers, but other than that it used the exact programmable GPS driven navigation system that the manned version did with appropriate small changes to the software.

Saunders and his team were programmed to land at 0400 Saturday morning in a field on the far side of a small ridge west of the hacienda and just out of range of Escobar's night vision sensors which were placed around the perimeter of his hundred acre complex. The jump proceeded without a hitch. All HAHO/ALS systems worked flawlessly. After landing, he and his men watched in awe through their helmet integrated night vision systems as the cargo package, weighing thirty six hundred pounds S-turned to bleed off altitude and then circled into the wind to a perfect landing on a spot near the area where they had landed. Twenty four hundred pounds of the cargo consisted of two John Deere XUVs with trailers which together would carry four of the team plus all the equipment to the ridge just west of the complex perimeter, on the far side of which they would set up their fire base. Saunders and his scout/sniper would reconnoiter the area on foot to be sure the current intel was fresh.

* * * *

A four man Delta Force squad, led by First Lieutenant Jose Madara, a second generation U.S. citizen whose family actually resided in Medellin, Columbia, and who was also the Delta Force liaison to the CIA operations in Columbia, will execute a thirty three thousand foot HAHO jump from a MC-130E Combat Talon cargo/transport plane Sunday morning at 0030 hours into a remote parking area for cargo vehicles inside the security perimeter of the Tuscala Airport. This team will plant explosives on Escobar's hangar, aircraft and land vehicles, timed to detonate at precisely 0120 hours. A CIA Little Bird helicopter based at the airport will depart with the team aboard at 0110 hours and transport the team to the USS Iwo Jima, stationed twenty miles northwest of the Columbian coast.

* * * *

The third squad is led by Major Troy Mills, a Delta Force liaison to JSOC responsible for deploying newly developed advanced weapon systems to all multi-service Special Forces units. Troy served in the Vietnam conflict as a Sergeant First Class sniper. In the mid seventies he finished his degree in mechanical engineering, completed OCS and was commissioned as a Delta Force First Lieutenant. His four man Delta Force squad will jump HAHO from the same MC-130E at 0035 hrs tasked with destroying the processing-packaging facility southwest of Escobar's hacienda. After eliminating any threats this team will set charges to detonate at 0120 hrs and egress via a troop transport manned by two operatives of the Columbian *Combat Search and Rescue* organization within the Columbian Air Force. They will be driven to the U.S. Embassy in Bogota where they will change into civilian clothes, take a limo to the airport and catch the 1030 American Airlines flight to Miami.

The fourth squad leader, Commander Bo Jameson, and his six man SEAL squad will jump HAHO from the same MC-130E and arrive tomorrow morning at 0140 hours just inside the eastern entrance to Escobar's complex after the gun towers and all power systems had been compromised. Their task is to achieve relative superiority, secure the complex, retrieve intelligence material and then destroy the complex. Upon completion of their respective missions Saunders' and Jameson's prisoners, (if any) and all non-expendable equipment will be picked up on site by a CH-53E Sea Stallion helicopter and transported to the Iwo Jima.

Chapter One Hundred Six

Operation One Shot Headquarters
San Diego NAS, San Diego California
Saturday, October 25, 1986 0800 hrs PDT

"Admiral, I've got Master Chief Hernandez on the secure line," yelled DEA Director Jim Doddington. "He wants a conference; you want it in here or in the situation room."

"Put it there, I'll be right in," replied Bennington.

"Hey Manny, we got your message and your data – very interesting. The analysts were up all night looking at it and they say it's good enough to find the last four months of shipments. We need the last eight years. What are your recommendations?"

"Well Admiral, we've got to go back in tonight to set the C-4 anyway. Rob and I could set the charges on the sub and seawall early, then run up the tunnel, take out the internal guards, grab all the hard drives and documents we need. Scoot back down the tunnel, meet up with one of my guys with an additional waterproof container, scramble back to our base before the big bang and upload some of the early data back to your analysts for conformation. They'll have all day to look at what we've got so far and tell us what to look for tonight -- so you can still change direction if necessary. If we're sure we have what we need we can remotely detonate the warehouse at 0120 right along with the terminal and sub. This would keep us from destroying the evidence I believe is in that building and save us from having to deploy the other half of my team to destroy the warehouse from the outside and maybe allow our guys to just vaporize Horte's place instead of doing the capture thing."

"We're going to need Horte anyway for many reasons, so we'll still have to take him alive. But if you can get all of the location information it could simplify that part of the operation considerably. Manny, you're over forty years old. Can you physically handle this with all the time constraints?"

"Admiral, I can still do fifteen miles in full gear in the time it'll take us to do this and get clear. Don't worry about me!"

"Did you sleep last night?"

"Like a baby – seven hours."

"This is Granada all over again. Go for it, Manny – Godspeed! I'll inform the rest of your team to stand down."

Chapter One Hundred Seven

USS Sadie Mae, US Navy Sub-Killer
25 Miles West of the Baja Peninsula, Mexico
Saturday, October 25, 1986, 0830 hrs PDT

The USS Sadie Mae, a highly modified WW II torpedo class sub chaser, was steaming slowly off the coast of Baja California toward its stationary point for the next twelve hours; fifteen miles off the coast, just north of Cabo San Lucas. The Sadie Mae could carry either two Sea King anti-submarine Helicopters or up to six AH-6 sub-chaser versions of the MH-6 Little Bird. Today she carried two AH-6s and one Sikorsky SH-3H Sea King. The SR-71 Blackbird surveillance intel indicated that two of the Cartel's four subs would pass each other at approximately 2345 hrs this evening in this area. The little birds were equipped with AQS-13 Dipping SONAR (SOund Navigation And Ranging) systems - a SONAR system whose active and passive sensors are contained in a module that is lowered into the sea from an aircraft. The AQS-13 is capable of providing accurate vectors (magnetic bearings) to the targets. Once the subs are located the Little Birds will continue to passively track the two subs with their dipping SONARs until 0115 hrs when the SONARs will be switched from passive to active, yielding very accurate range and bearing from each of the Little Birds to the sub it is tracking. Passive vectoring relies on noise (engine, propeller or crew) from the detected sub while active vectoring relies on the return of a sonic 'ping' generated by the SONAR. The sub only realizes it's being tracked when the SONAR goes active and by then it's too late to run. The location and track bearing acquired from the active mode SONARs will then be transmitted to the Sea King for final positioning of each torpedo launch to take out the two subs.

Chapter One Hundred Eight

SEAL Team Four, Operation One-Shot Base Camp
Six Miles North of Puerto Vallarta, Mexico
Saturday, October 25, 1986, 2130 hrs PDT

"We've got everything we need Manny; thirty two pounds of C-4, twenty pounds of thermite, ten flash-bang grenades, two silenced automatic rifles, thirty two darts, eight magazines of 7.62 mm ammo, four sleeping gas cartridges, five hundred fifty feet of primer cord, two remote detonator boxes, two hundred feet of antenna wire and our night vision gear packed in two waterproof containers. Anything else you can think of?" asked Senior Chief Petty Officer Rob Curtis.

"I think that's it," replied Master Chief Hernandez, "let's move out.

The SEALs were using two 'sea sleds'; torpedo shaped, battery powered and steerable underwater propulsion units, each designed to propel one two hundred fifty pound SEAL plus a one hundred pound torpedo shaped waterproof container, for three hours. They slipped into the surf about one and a half miles up the coast from the sub terminal for the thirty minute trip to the under sea entrance to the terminal. When they arrived they adjusted the ballast of their gear, anchored it securely to the sea floor just beneath the sub, opened the waterproof unit containing the explosives and proceeded to set the charges that would destroy the sub and the terminal at 0120 hrs the following morning.

After completing this task Manny Hernandez carefully and noiselessly maneuvered around the end of the sub, raised his silenced MP-5 assault rifle loaded with tranquilizer darts, put the scope's crosshairs on the upper right shoulder of the guard and pulled the trigger. The 'pffft' of the shot was hardly noticed by the guard until he looked down at the dart, puzzled at what had just happened. He reached for the dart with his left hand but before he could grasp it he fell face first onto his desk, spilling a partially full cup of coffee. The cup was plastic with no handle, resembling a glass, and it rolled off the desk clattering to the concrete floor. Manny was already scanning the terminal looking for anyone else. As he cleared the area and began to climb onto the seawall, the com unit on the guard's desk buzzed. He ran to the desk and picked up the unit, coughing as he spoke "hola" into the mouthpiece and then listened as the voice on the other end said in Spanish "Security Check," to which Manny responded, still coughing, "all is well."

The other voice asked, "you all right?"

Still coughing, Manny responded, "drinking coffee when you called – choked."

"Stay awake Juan – no more sleeping on the job, understand?"

Manny responded, "Yes, of course, don't worry about me."

Rob had emerged with the waterproof containers. He opened the one from which they had taken the explosives, dumped the water out and turned it upside down on the dock to let it dry out as much as possible. Then he opened the other container and removed four additional eight dart magazines, four 7.62 mm magazines and their night vision goggles.

"He's down for the count – let's hit the tunnel."

"After you," replied the Master Chief.

Chapter One Hundred Nine

Delta Force Teams North of Horte's Airfield
Northwest Nicaragua
Saturday, October 25, 1986, 2145 hrs PDT

    Captain Vince Harlow led Team A, seven of his total twelve man Delta Force team, in the assault on Horte's ranch. His recon team had done a thorough job the night before, locating the off-property electrical service entrance and confirming the location of the back-up generator as well as other important intel necessary for a successful mission. Now they were loaded with gear and heading south to their target four miles away. Since Horte's ranch had to be secured forty five minutes before the 0120 'big bang' so that Team A would have time to egress to the airport, the other team of four men, Team B - led by me, would leave camp a half hour later since our targets were only a little more than two miles away. But, our task of placing C-4 charges on the C-47s, the trucks and the buildings had to be complete before 0100. Harlow had changed the original plans to accommodate a recent accomplishment by one of the resident CIA operators. Disguised as a mechanic, he had managed to 'borrow' the keys to the C-47 tied down on the ramp between the hangar and the runway, including the keys to the locks on the tie down chains. He did this three nights ago, copied the keys day before yesterday, tested all the copies and returned the originals. He gave me the copies last night when we arrived on our recon mission. I had the key copies in my pocket. I was the only SEAL on Harlow's Delta Force team and the only officer other than Harlow. Hence I was the Team B leader. I was also the only pilot on the whole team, so I had to fly us out of there at 0116, four minutes before the big bang. I wanted some time to unlock the chains and then climb aboard the C-47 to re-familiarize myself with this bird. I had actually never flown a C-47 but I did have around twenty hours in the DC-3, the C-47's civilian sister. I had no idea if the cockpit layout of the two aircraft were anywhere near alike.

Team A had to secure Horte's entire ranch, set any necessary charges and retreat with prisoners all the way back to the airport by 0105. This would give us time to load them aboard, taxi out to the closest end of the runway and take off by 0116. This was a very tight schedule. Our lives depended on meeting it!

Chapter One Hundred Ten

FBI/DEA Operation One Shot Team

Coast of Southern California

Saturday, October 25, 1986 2315 Hrs PDT

DEA Director Jim Doddington and FBI Director Bob Gilmore were crammed into a hotel suite about three and a half miles from the "under water research facility" (northern sub terminal) near Imperial Beach California with four of their best operations leaders. They were observing the take-down of the cartel's northern sub base on monitors located around the room. They also had a secure video feed from the primary operations site at Langley.

The three assault teams were assembling at their respective initial positions around the complex. These buildings will not be destroyed and the sub preparing to leave at 0600 in the morning will be captured along with the recently unloaded cargo – seven and a half tons of pure cocaine. The building, including its contents will be secured by FBI and DEA agents until all illicit drugs and intel material had been removed to the appropriate government agency for analysis and disposal as necessary. The personnel involved in the U.S. end of the drug operation had been under surveillance for the past two weeks. The current location of each of the nine men was known and they will be apprehended at their respective residences by FBI teams at 0120 hrs The four on-site guards will also be apprehended at 0120 hrs by FBI agents.

Chapter One Hundred Eleven

Zero Dark Thirty

Various Locations

North, Central and South America

0030 Hrs PDT, Sunday, October 26, 1986

President Bradley Stevens pressed the Net Alert button on the command console in the CIA Covert Operations Center at the CIA headquarters at Langley, Virginia, where he, CIA Director Bill Conroy, CJCS Gerald Sterrett, the president's Chief of Staff Robert Sanders and his National Security Advisor Gary Bishop were gathered to observe the Operation. One Shot execution in real time. This signal caused the network control computer to wait for the next two second silent condition on the entire network before issuing a Net Alert and switching all network stations to the command console. Each mission operator was aware that there would be a net message from the president at 0030 hrs, so there was no traffic on the net and the alert was issued immediately.

"POTUS here, I'll be brief. As a team you are the most formidable Special Operations Force ever gathered on this planet to fight the forces of evil. Our country wishes you Godspeed and safety in your quest. Remember these things: On this mission our intel is as complete and fresh as is technically possible. You will receive real time updates as events occur. We own the night – make all your decisions to take advantage of that fact. To gain and hold relative superiority you must surprise the enemy and execute with haste. Very important here; we must find the information that will unlock our access to the tons of drugs stored throughout the Continental U.S, Hawaii, Alaska and Puerto Rico by the cartels. Those teams assaulting the cartel operations bases have the additional burden of recovering this valuable intel to accomplish this requirement, but I want to emphasize that all teams need to be vigilant to the recovery of this intel. It is a vital requirement of this operation.

Finally, I want to see every single agent and special operator involved in this mission back here in D.C. three weeks from yesterday for a victory party. Stevens out."

Escobar Hacienda 0035 Hours

Sancho Domingo and Earl Davidson had re-traced their route from the previous night and were approaching a culvert near the power pole where they would disable the electrical power service to Escobar's hacienda complex. They will sit out of sight until 0115 hrs and then cut the service cable which supplies power to the complex. The cable will be cut with a single blow by Davidson swinging a *Woodsman* twelve pound axe at precisely 0120 hrs.

At 0140 hrs Commander Bo Jameson and his team of five SEALs will approach Escobar's hacienda from the north, having executed a HAHO jump from twenty five thousand feet twenty miles southwest of Medellin, Columbia. The team will land in the courtyard at the northern end of Escobar's complex. They will be the primary assault team on the hacienda after a twenty minute shelling from Master Sergeant Saunders fire base located on the back side of the hill just west of the complex starting at 0120 hrs.

Southern Sub Terminal 0035 Hours

When Manny Hernandez and Rob Curtis reached the top end of the five kilometer tunnel they found a metal vertical rolling door, down and locked, preventing the use of the cable car. But there was a chain-link door providing access to the building where the cable car and rolling door controls were located secured by a lock complete with a key inserted. Obviously, security wasn't a high priority for the night shift. Standing in the shadows of the tunnel opening, the SEALs carefully watched the dimly lit open office area to the right of the packaging/loading stations where the workers converted bags of 'fertilizer' into sealed pony kegs of cocaine packed in cardboard crates.

After about five minutes they had only observed two guards sitting at desks containing video screens that received infrared video from external and internal cameras. They were surprised that no cameras were aimed down the tunnel they had just traversed – another lucky break, or just sloppy security. On the hand count of three they simultaneously fired their silenced MP-5s. These guys didn't get darts since they would be in the warehouse when it became a fireball at 0120. Pfft - pfft, not as quiet as they would have liked due to the dead silence of the huge warehouse. Both took head shots and fell forward on their desks. They waited. About three minutes later a third guard appeared, looked over the situation, raised a portable radio to alert someone, probably the guards outside, pfft – Manny shot him in the neck. The guard seemed to melt like a candle thrust into a pizza oven. Rob stood on a desk and unscrewed the single bulb that hung above the desk area. The warehouse had no windows so no one on the outside would notice the light being switched off. But if a security check was missed by the outside guards or if the guard Manny just shot had succeeded in contacting someone outside, the SEALs wanted it dark when they entered.

Rob Curtis extracted the thirty six pounds of C-4 and twelve timed igniters from his back pack and began rigging the warehouse for destruction at 0120 hrs while Manny retrieved the necessary data.

The three desks between the guards' desks each had a large file cabinet next to it. Hernandez worked quickly to find the records they were looking for using the infra-red light source attached to his infra-red goggles, neither of which could be seen in the dark by anyone not equipped with IR night vision. Each of the cabinet's bottom two drawers contained date-coded folders with copies of the shipping labels by month. They accounted for eight and a half years of shipments of six or more metric tons per day. The important part of the records were copies of the 'Warehouse ID' barcodes which would identify the warehouse the package was being shipped to and the corresponding Customer ID barcode labels which allows the warehouse manager to find the link to the location of the package in his warehouse. In the upper drawers of the center desk he found shipper and warehouse information to match the IDs thus saving the NSA and CIA analysts the trouble of decoding the IDs. Altogether they needed to extract about two hundred pounds of documents and six pounds of hard drives (each computer contained two), carry it five kilometers back down the tunnel and pack it all into three waterproof containers. The shear volume of material had Manny worried. The data was likely duplicated on the paper and the hard drives, but he couldn't be sure and he didn't know whether there was additional necessary information exclusive to either source – so it all had to go and they were pressed for time.

As Manny finished gathering all the intel he could find, Rob returned with a thumbs up signal indicating that the warehouse was ready to blow.

They had exactly forty five minutes to get everything down the tunnel, packed into three water-proof containers and transported via sea-sleds out of range of the hellfire that would destroy the terminal and warehouse at exactly 0120 hrs. He made the obvious decision to breach the tunnel gate that kept them from using the cable car to move the files, hard drives and themselves down the tunnel to the terminal. He was certain the car would be faster than the physical struggle on foot down the tunnel, and he was sure that he and Rob would be in much better shape to get the rest of the job done when they got there. A small shaped charge of C-4 easily defeated the lock and the gate was raised via a switch next to the gate. Senior Chief Curtis found the controls for the cargo cart's emergency brake. They decided to load the cart and sever the cable with a small C-4 charge and take their chances in an uncontrolled, but much quicker, decent down the tunnel.

"You got a hand on that brake!" Manny yelled as they approached what they felt was near the half-way point between the warehouse and the sub terminal.

"We're clockin' man. This fucker's flat-ass movin'," yelled Curtis as they flew down the shaft. "I'll slow us down a little to see how - or if, this brake's gonna stop us at the other end."

The brake worked but it was obvious that heat would be a problem at the other end. The brakes were purely mechanical and took all of Curtis' weight on the lever to slow the cart. After he had slowed it to about five miles per hour the brakes were smoking badly so he released them and they began building speed again.

"There's the light from the terminal," Hernandez yelled, "start braking!"

Manny was at the front of the cart. The brake lever and Rob were at the rear. As the cart approached the terminal opening and Curtis had slowed it to about five miles per hour, he realized that the cart was not going to stop before hitting the barrier at the end of the track.

Just as Curtis had yelled, "Brace yourself, we're gonna hit the wall," they heard the unmistakable roar of an AK-47. They were being sprayed with bullets as they faced a collision with a barrier that was clearly going to win the contest. Before Manny could duck behind the front of the cart he grabbed his chest and then his throat – he'd been hit. Then they careened into the barrier. Manny was thrown out of the cart, somersaulted over the barrier and landed flat on his back, unconscious.

Horte Ranch 0040

Captain Vince Harlow had his eight man squad surrounding Horte's ranch ready to launch its attack. The plan here was to dart the guards and dogs, capture Horte and his half-brother Xavier, do a quick search while setting charges and then retreat to the airport two miles north. All indications were that surprise would be to their advantage. The ranch had been under close and careful scrutiny for the past two weeks. Current human intelligence (CIA), satellite and SR-71 intel put Horte, Xavier and two women inside the ranch house along with two guards carrying AK-47s. Outside there were currently four armed guards and two dogs.

Harlow's team had been outfitted with the ground assault version of the Advanced HAHO system. So the night belonged to them as soon as they disabled the power to the ranch. This was accomplished fairly easily; the power service to the ranch ran directly to the diesel powered back-up generator where the power could be switched automatically from the normal utility power to the back-up generator when the power failed, which happened fairly often in Nicaragua. The system was usually able to make the switch in less than two minutes, depending on how long it took for the diesel generator to start and reach a stable operating status. Little thought had been given to security as both of the system's very visible power sources were easily disabled with a simple Rocket Powered Grenade (RPG) aimed at the generator's gas tank. The resulting explosion took out both the primary and secondary power sources and left the entire complex with just candles and flashlights for light.

After this was accomplished, Harlow and his men advanced on the ranch house and easily took out the two dogs and four guards with darts. The guards were handcuffed with plastic ties and left to fend for themselves when they would regain consciousness around 0400. Intel had determined that these men were hired guards with families and no real ties to the drug cartels. The two men inside, however, were Horte's personal bodyguards.

As two of the assault team were clearing the house from the rear entrance they were sprayed with an AK-47 before they could drop the bodyguard shooting at them. One operator took a round in the leg just above the knee; the other took one round in the chest which just missed his body armor and another round in the upper right arm.

Horte and his brother Xavier were taken without resistance. Both bodyguards suffered head shots. The two women were bound and left seated on an overstuffed couch in the dark living room.

By the time the team had done a thorough search of the ranch and secured all material deemed to be of possible use in locating the cocaine hidden in the U.S. or containing information about cartel operations anywhere in the world, it was 0140 hrs They had to transport two prisoners and two wounded operators, both of whom couldn't walk, over two miles of rough terrain back to the airport. . .

Northern Sub Terminal 0045 Hours

A Navy Sea King SH-3H anti-submarine helicopter rose from the runway on Coronado Island bound for the exit of the northern sub terminal near Imperial Beach, California armed with two MK6 anti-submarine torpedoes and a M134 GAU-17 door mounted 7.62 mm Gatling gun with ten thousand rounds of ammunition. The Sea King was flying a contingency mission. The plan was to capture the cartel's submarine and all the personnel present at the time – likely just guards at this time of the morning. But on the chance that the sub's crew was present and an attempt to launch the sub was made, the Sea King would stand ready to take it down. Also any personnel exiting the terminal to the sea by boat or otherwise would be taken out by the Gatling gun.

Tuscala Airport Parking lot 0045 Hours

Lieutenant Jose Madara and his Delta Force squad made an uneventful HAHO jump from the MC-130E Combat Talon to a cargo parking lot at the Tuscala Airport near Medellin Columbia. They quickly placed C-4 charges set to explode at 0120 hrs on three of Escobar's C-47s and five three ton trucks marked 'Garcia's Fertilizer'. These were the trucks that hauled the cocaine packaged in fertilizer bags from the processing plant to the Tuscala Airport. After darting a single guard, Madara and his team met no resistance and were finished and aboard a CIA Little Bird headed for the *Iwo Jima* by 0112 hrs

Escobar's Processing/Packaging Plant 0045 Hours

Major Troy Mills and his Delta Force squad arrived at the processing/ packaging plant south of Escobar's hacienda after a 30,000 foot HAHO jump from the MC-130E. After darting two guards and a dog they planted sixty pounds of C-4 explosives timed for 0120 on the building and two trucks, climbed aboard a Columbian Air Force troop transport waiting for them and headed for Bogota. They would get some sleep on their Delta flight to Miami in the morning.

USS Sadie Mae 0045 Hours

The Sadie Mae's AH-6 Little Bird helicopters had located the two cartel subs passing each other about four miles off the Mexican coast near the middle of the Baja Peninsula. The AH-6s were still tracking the two subs passively. The subs were now twelve nautical miles apart; the southbound sub empty and the northbound sub packed with cocaine.

The Sadie Mae's SH-3H Sea King had just lifted off her flight deck and was approaching the northbound sub for a 0115 hrs launch of a MK 46 SONAR guided torpedo after which the Sea King would turn south to overtake the southbound sub and launch a second MK 46 at it. The Little Birds would begin active sonar surveillance near each sub five minutes prior to each torpedo launch relaying the more accurate location to the Sea King for the kill.

Horte's Airport, 0050 Hours

We had to dart two guards and then got the charges set for 0120 hrs My team of three Army Delta Force sergeants and myself with my broken little finger taped tightly to the ring finger on my right hand, were aboard the C-47 and I was pleased to discover that the cockpit layout was virtually identical to the DC-3 I had flown for an aircraft parts company back in my pre-Navy days. We expected fourteen passengers; our twelve Special Forces Operators along with Maximillion Horte, his brother Xavier and all the equipment we brought in-country with us which we had previously lugged from our base camp, hidden in a nearby cache and just now loaded aboard the plane – a pretty light load for a C-47. Man, I was feeling pretty confident about this mission – if Harlow's turkeys just showed up on time. . .

Southern Sub Terminal 0050 Hours

Chief Petty Officer Tommy Gilbert was tasked with bringing the third waterproof container to the terminal and remain submerged until Manny and Rob appeared and then to assist in packing the containers and getting the hell out of Dodge.

Tommy heard the AK, looked at his watch; it was 0050 hours – they had Thirty minutes to get packed, submerged, out of the tunnel entrance and into the open ocean alive – otherwise. . .

As he quietly surfaced with his MP-5 in the ready position he saw the bad guy reloading his AK while approaching the unconscious Hernandez. One un-silenced head shot put him down. Was the shooter alone? Didn't matter. He didn't have time to waste. Manny was hit and they had to scramble or they'd all be hamburger.

"Where'd that prick come from – thought you guys got 'em all," Tommy groused.

"Talk later, Manny's got a serious hit and we've got to get him out of here. Help me get his fins, mask and breather on." Manny blinked his eyes and moaned.

"Manny, can you swim?"

"Think so – need to stop the bleeding a little."

"You were hit in the neck. Blood's dark, probably nicked the jugular – that's much better than the carotid – but you're still going to lose blood. Can you steer a sea-sled?"

"Think so – we'll see."

"When we get to the entrance we'll turn right immediately, sled north and surface as fast as we can. After the blow we'll get help – you good for that?"

"Think so – got to."

Horte's Airport, General Aviation ramp 0100 Hours

At 0100 my satellite phone rang as we were sitting in the C-47 discussing contingency plans. It was Vince Harlow informing me that they had taken casualties and their ETA would be delayed by approximately thirty five minutes to 0145. I told him that we would taxi to the far end of the runway at 0115 and leave the engines running, ready for take off. That would shorten their trip by a little over two hundred yards according to my map.

Operation One Shot Headquarters, 0105 Hours

"Admiral Bennington, Langley is on line and watching our video feeds. We've got the President, CIA Director, and CJCS," announced Jim Doddington, DEA Director.

"Okay, welcome gentlemen. We just got word that we've taken two casualties on Captain Harlow's team. We're awaiting details. You should have video on six feeds. Helmet video on Lt. Commander McKensie, helmet video on Commander Jameson, helmet video on Captain Harlow, helmet video on Sergeant Saunders, hand video on the Sea King pursuing the subs. We expect hand video from Master Chief Hernandez momentarily when they clear the sub terminal. It appears they are cutting it a little close, said the Admiral with more than a hint of concern in his voice.

Escobar Hacienda 0110 Hours

Master Sergeant David Saunders sent four of his team forward over the hill that concealed his fire base from Escobar's hacienda to deal with the two towers containing machine guns. Each pair was driving an all wheel drive XUV. Each XUV had a mounted wire guided TOW anti-tank missile launcher and two missiles.

Southern Sub Terminal, 0110 Hours

Senior Chief Rob Curtis and Chief Tommy Gilbert got Master Chief Manny Hernandez into his re-breather, mask and fins and the three watertight containers loaded with papers, hard drives and gear and then secured to the sea-sleds. They were submerged and on their way out of the sea entrance to the terminal. They had seven minutes to travel the remaining hundred yards to the end of the tunnel and make a hard right turn into the open sea to avoid the shock wave from the thirty two pounds of C-4 they had planted in the terminal just behind them. Gilbert led the way followed by Hernandez with Curtis bringing up the rear. Toward the middle of the tunnel Curtis could see that Manny was having problems . . .

SH-3H Sea King, 0115 Hours

The Sea King launched the MK 46 torpedo at exactly 0115 hrs from two thousand yards behind the coke laden north bound sub and made an immediate one hundred and eighty degree turn to overtake the south bound sub and sink it. As it approached the south bound sub one of the little birds reported a positive hit on the north bound sub – complete annihilation. At 0120 hrs after receiving the active sensor location of the south bound sub the Sea King launched the second MK 46 SONAR guided torpedo.

Southern Sub Terminal, 0119 Hours

As Chief Tommy Gilbert neared the end of the tunnel and prepared to execute the right turn Senior Chief Curtis noticed that Master Chief Hernandez was lagging behind a little and having trouble maintaining a straight course. In the beam of Curtis' helmet mounted light he could see Manny clear his mask, requiring him to remove one hand from the sea-sled. He was using his right hand to clear his mask which caused the sled to veer to the left – the wrong way. As he appeared to have succeeded in clearing the mask and made an adjustment in course to follow Tommy Gilbert, Curtis thought he saw a dark cloud dissipate in the water in the vicinity of Manny's head. Blood? Rob took his sled to full combat power, knowing that his battery could not sustain this level of drain for more than about three or four minutes and still have enough reserve to get him to shore. As he pulled up right behind Manny, Rob was shocked to see Manny clearing his mask again. This time he could clearly see that it was blood. Manny was using his left hand this time to avoid moving in the wrong direction. This time he removed his mask completely, looped it around his left hand between his thumb and forefinger and re-grasped the sled's steering handle. As Curtis pulled along side Hernandez he could see blood coming from his nose and the mouthpiece of his rebreather. This was definitely not good. He glanced at his watch; it was 0119 plus 15 seconds. Curtis immediately dropped his sled, water-tight container and all. This gear was rugged; he could find and retrieve it later. He grabbed Manny's steering handles over his hands, at the same time tilting them all the way forward to full combat power and began to edge toward the right side of the tunnel. As he passed Chief Gilbert he signaled full speed ahead and began the right turn. He knew they were short on time. . .

* * * *

T Equals Zero
Escobar Hacienda 0120 Hours.

Earl Davidson, former right tackle for Navy at Annapolis, former member of Navy SEAL Team Four and current in-country CIA Agent in Columbia took careful aim at the power conduit containing the three #2 copper cables supplying power to Pablo Escobar's hacienda complex. Davidson stood a little over six foot five and weighed a little less than three hundred pounds. His axe was a twelve pound Woodsman model with a fiberglass handle which he had sharpened to a razor's edge.

He swung with all his might at the conduit; maybe a little two hard. The axe severed the conduit and power cables, embedding itself deep into the pole. Both men had donned sunglasses prior to the swing, but neither was prepared for the light generated by the power cables welding themselves to the axe. After about two seconds of intense light and a shower of sparks the conduit above the axe began to glow bright red until they heard an explosion a few hundred yards away. The pole mounted transformer supplying this two hundred twenty volt three phase power distribution line had destroyed itself. They had expected to trip a circuit breaker somewhere, but evidently that's not what happens in Columbia. So much for a quiet job!

Davidson tried to remove the axe from the pole but all he got was the handle. The heat had melted the fiberglass and it broke off.

* * * *

After launching the second M 46 torpedo the Sea King made a slow and wide two hundred sixty degree turn toward the coast and headed back toward the Sadie Mae. This allowed them to confirm the destruction of the south bound sub. Just before flying back over the predicted position of the sub the night vision systems worn by the pilots allowed them to see the sea erupt into a fountain of water with a shock wave expanding rapidly around it. The second sub was gone.

* * * *

Two covered trucks loaded with bags of 'fertilizer' parked in back of a truck stop located next to a thirty room motel southeast of Mexico city mysteriously blew up at 0120 hrs The drivers were, unfortunately for them, asleep in the cabs. The drivers were receiving per diem pay for each trip which included funds for expenses. Sleeping in the trucks on the overnight trips added to their take home pay. They became collateral losses.

* * * *

Jim Doddington and Bob Gilmore observed the successful take-down of the northern sub terminal. No shots fired – no one injured. They quickly turned over the clean-up operation to their operations experts and boarded the FBI helicopter waiting in the hotel parking lot for the fifteen minute flight back to the mission ops center at the San Diego NAS.

* * * *

Three C-47s and five trucks were destroyed in the cargo area of the Tuscala Airport southeast of Medellin Columbia and a ninety thousand square foot processing building and two large fertilizer trucks were similarly annihilated several kilometers south of Escobar's hacienda.

* * * *

Manny Hernandez was struggling to stay conscious. He had begun to accumulate blood in his mouth and nose and Senior Chief Rob Curtis knew this was not good, especially because he was using a re-breather unit. A normal SCUBA system would allow him to purge the blood in his mouth through the mouthpiece, but with the re-breather he had to force the blood to exit through his nose. His mask had a one way valve just under the nose which could expel part of the blood, but not all of it, causing him to remove his mask. Rob had seen his problem, dropped his load and sled, grabbed Manny's sled, clamped his hands over Manny's and they were now at combat power doing close to eighteen knots, hanging on for dear life. They were just rounding the corner at the opening of the access tunnel and heading upward when the shock wave from the southern sub terminal explosion caught them. . .

* * * *

We were now at the opposite end of the runway a little over fifteen hundred yards away from the hangar and truck barn in take off position with the engines running trying to be invisible to the security folks who would arrive shortly after the big bang. Then the fireworks started. When the buildings blew up, part of the hangar roof, I think that's what it was, landed smack dab in the middle of the runway. The C47 seemed to be in fairly good shape and with a load of fourteen people, full tanks and about fifteen hundred pounds of gear we should be in the air well before we hit the debris. This was the primary subject of the prayer I was currently engaged in with my Lord and Maker.

Meanwhile we were sitting here very exposed with only light arms and a few grenades waiting for Harlow and his band of pirates and captives to show up. Twenty minutes was going to seem like an eternity while we sat here, lights out, as inconspicuous as possible.

* * * *

Saunders' XUV mounted TOW Missiles made direct hits on both north and south courtyard towers within the hacienda's surrounding walls, eliminating the primary firepower threat of Escobar's fortress. His men were, however, still armed to the teeth. Escobar had designed this cartel-operations/home/fortress to ward off the efforts of his business enemies; he probably didn't contemplate a well thought out attack by Delta Force and SEAL operatives.

The second missile in each XUV was quickly loaded into its respective launcher and fired at the parapets at the northwest and southwest corners of the fortress wall, taking out two additional heavy machine gun emplacements.

As the XUVs began their hasty retreat back over the hill a ma deuce

(Browning M-2, fifty caliber heavy machine gun) opened up on them from the central region of the wall in a spray and pray pattern. Unfortunately, for the gunners, they were using tracers. Saunders had an RPG (Rocket Propelled Grenade) team in ghillie suits spread out on the hill at the only three firing positions with natural cover. Two of these fired simultaneously at the source of the tracers punching a large hole in the center part of the wall, vaporizing the fifty cal, its operator and anyone else nearby.

Then Saunders let loose the artillery. Three, four minute GPS directed barrages separated by two, two minute observation pauses pretty well laid the hacienda to rest. But they knew from intel that there were underground facilities and there would be survivors ready to fight. As the third barrage completed Commander Bo Jameson reported his HAHO team's ETA of one minute.

Saunders thought, "It just doesn't get any better than that!"

* * * *

An airborne shockwave can yield a terribly destructive force, as was discovered during the atomic bomb testing in the late 1940s and early 1950s. A waterborne shockwave is much worse due to the relative densities of the two media. This particular shockwave was focused, due to the fact that it was forced to travel down a long tunnel. By the time the wave had gotten to the SEALs it had thankfully begun to expand into a characteristic curved wave-front. Rob and Manny were about twenty feet above and to the north of the mouth of the tunnel, but Chief Tommy Gilbert was ten feet behind them. All three were separated from their sleds, masks, fins, re-breathers and buoyancy compensators. Gilbert suffered multiple fractures in the bones of both feet and ankles as his fins were ripped away by the force. His eardrums were destroyed and his eyes were temporarily damaged with multiple hematomas. Although the last breath he had taken was forced from his lungs by the shockwave and his buoyancy compensator was ripped to shreds he managed to drift thirty feet to the surface without drowning.

Curtis grabbed Hernandez the instant he felt the sled's handlebars being pulled out of his hands. In spite of a ruptured right eardrum and the loss of most of his equipment he was able to quickly swim to the surface with Manny, who now appeared to be unconscious. Rob saw Tommy surface about fifteen feet away. He swam Manny the thirty or so feet to shore, dragged him above the surf-line and then returned for Tommy.

Gilbert was bleeding from both ears, his mouth and both eyes, yet he was semi-conscious. He gurgled, "How's Manny?"

"Not good," replied Curtis. "I think he's lost a lot of blood. Help me kick if you can."

"Can't hear you and can't feel my feet," gurgled Gilbert.

"No sweat, hang on, we'll be back in a minute," shouted Curtis, doubting that the other SEAL could hear him.

When they got to the shore Rob was relieved to see two of his remaining team had arrived and were there with Manny. Chief Petty Officer Neal Thomas looked up at Curtis as he dragged Gilbert out of the surf. He said quietly, holding Manny's head in his lap with tears forming in his eyes and blood on his face, "Manny's dead, I tried CPR – no good."

Master Chief Petty Officer, Manuel Hernandez, veteran hero of the Vietnam war, Operation Eagle Claw, the Grenada conflict and other classified operations, esteemed leader of SEAL Team Four, leader of numerous classified missions, holder of the Navy's Distinguished Service Medal and three Purple Hearts, loving husband, father of four beautiful children, respected brother to all Special Operations personnel, was dead. His best friend and second in command, Senior Chief Rob Curtis stood in disbelief as he mouthed a silent prayer for his friend , his brother. How would he face Carla?

* * * *

As we sat there on the approach to the runway, engines at idle, lights off, cargo door open and ladder ready to be dropped, I kept praying that Harlow and company would show up ahead of their last ETA. At the other end of the runway we could see security people, police, firefighters and civilians scurrying around trying to deal with the situation.

Two of my guys were sniper trained and carried silenced sniper rigged MP5s. I stationed them in the drainage ditches on either side of the runway about fifty yards down the runway in case we had visitors from the other end. They were wearing the battle version of the new HAHO system, so they had night vision and network communications we could all hear. At 0135 a vehicle began driving down the runway toward us. I watched for a few seconds then told the snipers: "be alert; if they drive past you, take them out. Be careful not to shoot each other." I'm sure they were thinking, "smart ass!"

I continued, "It's an old Willis (WW II Jeep) so the tires are solid – can't shoot them out. Catch the jeep, shoot the occupants, put the bodies in the ditch, continue driving slowly toward us to the end of the runway, then turn around and drive back to the first taxiway turnoff. Turn left; drive slowly about fifty yards and stop. Leave the lights on and engine running. High tail it back to your posts and maintain watch. If they have a radio and someone tries to call you just click the transmit button in reply. We're trying to buy a little time here. I'll let you know when our people show up."

Sure enough, the bad guys drove all the way up to the snipers, who shot them, jumped into the jeep and continued toward us. It was 0140 now and I got a call on the net from Harlow – he had us in sight. Three minutes and he'd be here – five more minutes for the guys carrying casualties. I told the snipers to park the jeep on the taxiway and double-time back to us to help get all these people and other assorted crap aboard.

At 0152 we had everything and everybody aboard and were rolling, balls to the wall down the runway, still no lights. At the other end of the runway we could see another, much larger vehicle, coming toward us. I jammed the throttles forward again. For some reason, this C-47 didn't seem to accelerate like the DC-3s I had flown. . .

* * * *

Commander Bo Jameson and his team of Delta Force troops aborted the HAHO ALS (Automatic Landing System) and landed manually in the chaos of Pablo Escobar's hacienda court yard. They had eliminated five more of Escobar's men on their way down with their silenced MP5s and disabled three. Bo estimated there were twenty more fighters left, plus or minus five. That seemed like a fair fight to him.

Bo's Special Forces team had several advantages. First, Master Sergeant David Saunders and his seasoned team were approaching the hacienda from the west and would soon enter through the holes they had blown in the western wall. Second, they all had the night vision advantage. And third, it appeared they had completely surprised Escobar's fortress. Most of the survivors at this point were in some form of sleeping attire.

Bo noticed an immediate problem. Two bad guys were setting up a tripod to mount a heavy machine gun in the southwest corner. He took cover behind the colonnade that separated the courtyards and as he took aim to take them down he warned the others to check the corners for gun teams. He also noticed a large spread in fighting skills among his adversaries. The temptation was to take out the novices first, but their training told them to do the opposite. If they take out the few experts, the others will fold. This was exactly the case tonight. Four remaining leaders were taken down and suddenly the firing stopped, hands started going up and the gun fight was over.

Unlike Mexico and Nicaragua, our CIA guys knew who to trust in the Columbian government. The Columbians knew this was going down tonight and were ready to take the survivors off to jail – with one exception; as part of the deal, Pablo Escobar, whether he survived or not, was to be extradited to the United States where he would be tried for multiple murders, trafficking, and conspiracy charges from years past. Under the table the Columbians were promised he would not live to see the new year. Unfortunately, for him, he didn't even make it through tonight's fire fight.

* * * *

"Come on you friggin' airplane, FLY!" We had traveled down almost a third of the runway and I barely had the tail off the ground. I had to make a very quick decision; fix the fucking plane or abort! I jammed the throttles forward again – they were still against the stops. Same with the prop controls; all the way forward – full power. Then I jammed the mixture controls forward; the damned levers advanced another two inches and the engines began to growl. The friggin drug assholes had put a detent in the mixture controls. Mixture controls adjust the fuel-air ratio to the engines. To get full takeoff power from the engines, the throttles, propeller pitch controls and mixture controls must all be fully forward. During my run-up I had pushed the mixture controls all the way forward (I thought). But I had just gotten them to a detent position in the adjustment range. Later I found that it actually wasn't a detent, it was a plate screwed on to the throttle pedestal that stopped the forward progress until you moved the lever to the right a quarter inch to get around it. The only reason the levers went forward the second time was the force I used and the fact that I was pushing forward and to the right. This was something installed by the cartel to keep the engines at optimum fuel-air mixture at the detent position while cruising at a predetermined altitude, reducing fuel costs and increasing the life of the engine. This would be illegal in the U.S. because some dumb-ass pilot – like me - that didn't know about the detents would try to take off with the fuel mixture at cruise setting instead of take-off.

Right now though, even with full power, I was still in deep-shit trouble. With half the available runway gone and the mangled and burning hangar roof on the runway just over two hundred yards in front of me we were only at sixty five knots. Add to that the idiot shooting at me with a truck mounted ma deuce.

Normal rotate speed is eighty four knots. You can yank a C-47 off the runway at about seventy eight knots but that will slow the initial rate of climb and the burning mess looming in front of me appeared to be at least twenty feet high.

Seventy knots, not looking good – a hundred yards to go. The shooter in the truck had already disappeared to the shoulder on our left. I was sure he had turned around and was shooting at us from the rear. At about thirty feet we hit eighty knots and I pulled hard on the wheel. We got airborne but the right landing gear caught the roof. It made a hell of a noise and shook the plane but we made it over still in the air. I lowered the nose and raised the gear to gain airspeed and then we gradually began to climb. I got a green light on the left landing gear but the right gear light remained red. . .

It was going to take us over six hours to get to San Diego partly because the C-47 is a damned slow airplane and partly because I chose to fly with the gear down and that cost us five knots in airspeed. I didn't want the landing gear hydraulics straining to get the gear stowed in the wheel well for the entire trip. I knew the gear was either gone (totally ripped off) or bent. I was hoping for the latter. When we got there we would make a low pass in front of the tower at San Diego NAS to see what our options were.

Chapter One Hundred Twelve

FBI/DEA Operation One Shot Command
San Diego Naval Air Station
Sunday, October 26, 1986 0225 hours PDT

Jim Doddington looked up as Admiral George Bennington entered the secure operations room, "Admiral, we've gotten reports from every team except Manny's."

"Keep trying to raise them. Run through the reports again - anything we don't know about?" queried the Admiral.

"The Columbia team was successful; twenty seven enemy dead, eleven wounded and eight captured. All but Escobar were turned over to the Columbian Government. His body is on its way to us along with our team via our C-130 transport at the Medellin airport. We had one casualty, a non-critical leg wound. The processing plant, five trucks and three C-47s were destroyed with no problems.

"The Nicaragua team searched the ranch facility, darted four guards and two dogs, killed two body guards, captured the Horte brothers and left two women crying in the dark. Some documents were found which when combined with the documents we expect to get from Hernandez' team will very likely enable us to unscramble the hidden coke mystery. Horte's hangar was destroyed with two C-47s and his Lear Jet inside. His truck barn was destroyed along with two trucks. A third C-47 was confiscated by our in-country CIA guy and Lt. Commander McKensie. It's on its way here with the team and the Horte brothers aboard. Commander McKensie reported a landing gear problem and he will probably have to execute an emergency landing when they get here. We had three casualties there; one with a critical chest wound, another with non-critical leg and arm wounds and McKensie broke a finger.

"Two trucks were destroyed, one loaded, one empty, along with the drivers sleeping inside, southeast of Mexico City.

"The north sub terminal is secure, including the just delivered seven and a half tons of coke. All associated personnel have been arrested and locked up.

"Two subs were sunk, one loaded, one empty, off the coast of Baja California, Mexico.

"No word yet on Master Chief Hernandez or his team. The Sadie Mae sent out a recon flight to check out the situation."

The Admiral turned to pick up the hotline and held up his hand to signal quiet to Doddington. "No Sir, not yet. Yes Sir, we'll query the Sadie Mae and get right back to you." The Admiral didn't 'sir' many people so Doddington knew who was on the line.

President Brad Stevens and Master Chief Manny Hernandez crossed paths a little more than eighteen years earlier at the Coronado Island BUD/S training facility. Then a Captain, Stevens with thirteen years as a Navy SEAL, commanded the Naval Special Warfare Command unit at Coronado Island, California. At the graduation ceremony for the ninety seventh Basic Underwater Demolition / SEAL (BUD/S) class, Stevens had decorated then Petty Officer Second Class Manuel Hernandez for achieving the third highest ever combined BUD/S training score in SEAL history. Stevens, himself, had achieved the ninth highest.

* * * *

"Admiral, we just got a report from Senior Chief Curtis at the south sub terminal. Master Chief Hernandez is dead. He took an unlucky hit in the neck from a bad guy and died on the way out. The team had to jettison their captured Intel to escape the blast. They just finished retrieving it – he says nothing was lost. The Senior Chief has a blown ear drum and some minor injuries. Chief Gilbert blew out both ear drums, has broken bones in his ankles and feet and broken blood vessels in both eyes. The recon Little Bird is retrieving the Intel, the Master Chief's body and part of the equipment. The other Little Bird is on its way with litters to retrieve the team and the rest of the equipment. Curtis says they're pretty sure the recovered Intel will solve the problem."

"That's a tough pill to swallow, Jim," replied Admiral George Bennington, "he was one of our best – wish I had talked him out of going. The President's gonna have my ass for this."

As President, Brad Stevens had personally awarded Hernandez with the Navy Distinguished Service Medal for his heroics in the Grenada conflict. While Stevens held a high regard for all SEALs, Manny Hernandez was at the top of that list – he was devastated when he got the news of Manny's death.

* * * *

"Romeo Alpha Two Niner, I see your right landing gear. It is not completely down. Do you have a green light?" asked the tower operator at San Diego NAS.

"Negative," I replied. "No surprise, I figured it was non-functional. Problem is I can't get it all the way up either. I'll make another pass with the gear up and see what you think."

So I did.

"Two Niner, looks like the rear strut is collapsed and the wheel is cocked to the right and totally outside the wheel-well. Also looks like the tire is shredded. How could that happen?"

"Very likely it is," I replied, "The hangar roof landed on the runway when we blew it up. I had just raised the gear-up lever when we hit it. What do you recommend? We've got enough gas for about thirty minutes."

"Two Niner, we recommend foaming the runway. If we don't, that wheel will likely cause a ground-loop on the grass and probably increase the possibility of injury and/or damage. It'll take us fifteen minutes to get it foamed. What say you?"

"Foam it is. I forgot to mention – eleven of the fourteen souls on board have no seats or restraints. I have one in the jump seat and six against the cockpit bulkhead, but I'll have five hanging on to the exposed fuselage stringers. I'll need lots of foam – I've got to keep this flying turkey headed straight down the runway when we belly in."

"Roger Two Niner, we'll lay your foam on runway two six –

straight into the wind, and have emergency vehicles standing by. Wind two six zero at ten knots, steady. Altimeter, two niner six four. You are cleared for emergency landing. All other traffic will be diverted from the area. I'll contact you when we are ready – good luck sir!"

I asked Captain Harlow who was sitting in the co-pilot's seat to go aft and get everyone placed for the wheels-up landing. Unfortunately, two of the six spots against the bulkhead would have to be given to the scumbag Horte brothers since they were bound, hands and feet. We decided to put the heaviest of the remaining six team members in the jump seat in the cockpit. This left five in the rather precarious situation of having to lie flat in the cargo deck, feet toward the front, and holding on to the exposed aluminum stringers (curved beams that formed the fuselage's shape). Two of the strongest lashed themselves together with the critically wounded operator between them and physically tied themselves to the aluminum stringers on the left side of the plane using their belts and cargo straps so that if the plane veered right as was expected the wounded man would be protected. If I screwed up this landing these guys would be in the most danger. The good news was that the wind was on our nose at ten knots – that meant we would hit the runway at sixty five knots instead of seventy five. I planned to land as close to the left edge of the runway as possible to help keep us on the foam as long as possible.

The key to a successful belly landing is approaching as slow as possible with full flaps and hitting the runway at the correct angle of attack. When you reach the proper speed (just above a stall) the nose must be gently lowered to the correct angle of attack. If you wait too long and the airplane stalls with the nose high, it will slam into the runway and break up with a high probability of significant injury/death to passengers and crew – especially when most occupants are not secured in seats.

So here I was, making my third emergency landing in my relatively short flying career – the first one with passengers. I had to get this right! I decided to make a long, slow approach using just enough power to stay on the gradual glide-path I had chosen. At about a half mile out I began to ease on the flaps which allowed me to slow the plane even more. As we came over the approach end of the runway I slowly cut the throttles, shut down both engines and feathered the props (turning the blades parallel to the wind which stops the rotation and reduces damage to the engines when the props hit the runway). I then eased the wheel back to bleed off the rest of the excess speed, and lowered the nose just prior to a stall to what I guessed was the correct angle of attack.

I wasn't ready for the noise. When we hit the runway it sounded like a tornado inside a garbage can. I held the wheel all the way back to keep the nose as high as possible and help reduce the damage to the props. We skidded for about a hundred yards before I lost steerage from the rudder as we slowed. I was holding full left rudder to keep the nose straight and as we slowed the plane started turning to the right due to the drag caused by the partially extended wheel and shredded right tire. We took out two runway lights on the way off the runway and proceeded to do a one eighty to the right as we came to a rather sudden stop in the grass.

Vince Harlow jumped out of his seat and rushed back to the cargo bay to assist anyone who might be injured. As it turned out only the Horte brothers were seriously injured. When the plane was slammed to the right after sliding off the runway the brothers were thrown across the cargo deck head first and slammed into the uncovered structure. Both were bleeding profusely and Max was unconscious. Too bad! The others who had their hands free suffered only from bruises and minor cuts. The wounded man lashed between the other two was not injured further.

The fire engines and other emergency vehicles were on us in a flash, spraying fire retardant foam and evacuating the plane as quickly as possible. I don't know what their hurry was – they knew we were out of gas. . .

Chapter One Hundred Thirteen

Arlington National Cemetery

Arlington, Virginia

Sunday, November 2, 1986 1500 hours EST

It wasn't a really cold day by Washington DC area standards but it was cloudy and there was a chill in the air. The horse drawn caisson containing the body of Master Chief Petty Officer Manuel K. Hernandez was followed by a somber group of family, friends and colleagues. The Pall Bearers were: Commander Bo Jameson, Captain Joe Garcia, Admiral George Bennington, Admiral Gerald Sterett, Manny's brother Hector and President Bradley Stevens. The funeral was a quiet affair as Manny would have wished. His wife, parents, brother, four children, a few aunts, uncles and close friends, the Pall Bearers and his SEAL team.

The Navy Chaplain conducted the service after the casket was removed from the caisson and placed on the lift above the grave. After the service a four piece ensemble from the Navy Band, a beautiful young Ensign and a handsome, not so young Lieutenant JG, from the Navy Choir at Annapolis played and sang the Navy Hymn. It was beautiful.

The Honor Guard, seven of Manny's team, led by Senior Chief Rob Curtis, removed the flag from the coffin, carefully folded it and Chief Curtis presented it to Manny's tearful wife, Carla. He then assembled the Honor Guard and executed a perfect three volley rifle salute.

The President approached Carla Hernandez and after saying a few words quietly, gave her a small box containing The Navy Cross. He told her how sorry they all were at the loss of Manny and that they would hold the appropriate ceremony in a few weeks. The Navy Cross is the highest honor the Navy can bestow on one of its heroes. Only the Congressional Medal of Honor is higher.

Then, in order of rank, as is SEAL tradition, the team passed by the mahogany casket and placed their SEAL pin on the casket with one hand

and drove it into the lid with the other. When the team had completed this honor it was continued by Commander Bo Jameson, Captain Joe Garcia, Admirals Bennington and Sterrett, and President Brad Stevens who was in his Admiral's uniform.

Just as this ceremony was complete the entire group of SEALs stood at attention and looked skyward as a vee formation of five Blue Angel F-18 Hornets roared toward the group. About a quarter mile away and not more than five hundred feet above the ground, the center plane in the left echelon gracefully entered a vertical climb and with full power disappeared into the clouds above. The remaining four Hornets held their positions in the "missing man" formation.

Standing next to me, Bo asked, "Where's Ash?"

"In the clouds," I replied.

Epilogue

Southwest of Guam, Pacific Ocean
Thursday June 6, 1989
1900 hrs Local Time

"Well, not too bad, I guess. Twelve landings, no bolos but I got one damned 4th hook," quipped my extremely talented and beautiful wife as we were reminiscing the last three days of F/A-18 carrier landings in the pilot's lounge of the USS *Carl Vinson*. A bolo is a wave-off from the landing officer because the approaching aircraft is not aligned properly with the ship for a safe landing.

I couldn't argue. I'd had eleven landings but boloed on my first attempt and I also had a fourth hook. The fourth landing cable is the last one. Hook it or you go around for another try. "Well, I never claimed to be a better pilot than you – but I am better at some things," I retorted, not wanting to be totally outdone by my smiling blue eyed spouse. "I think we did the right thing. Another three year hitch will let us get done all these things we always wanted to do, but never had the chance."

Right after the 'Drug bust of the century' Ash and I had decided to see if we could start a family without giving up the Navy – other people were doing it. But after two years of trying really hard – and we'd gotten real good at that - nothing happened. The doctors said nothing was wrong with either of us. But they also said that this is a common malady for career oriented couples. So we decided to do some things we wanted to do and maybe do the family thing later. Admiral Bennington got us billets on the USS *Carl Vinson* to replace two hornet squadron leaders who were rotating out at the end of November. So we had three months to learn the ropes involved in leading a squadron of ten to twelve F-18Cs and support aircraft. We were both slated to advance to Commander before the end of the year (even though she would get hers in September and mine didn't happen 'til December – so she would still out rank me). Life was good!

ANGELS THREE FIVE

Back on October 25th, 1986 it took Bob McFadden and his analysts only three and a half hours to connect the dots on all the information gathered by SEAL Team IV and generate a list of storage facilities across the U.S. containing the tons of illicit cocaine along with the owner ID bar codes which allowed the warehouse personnel to locate the drugs in the warehouse. This information was consolidated by the Department of State and classified orders were dispersed to DEA, FBI and National Guard units across the country. Two days later, expecting this operation to be successful, the President had asked the Chief Justice of the Supreme Court to hold an emergency session at 0800 hours the next morning to approve an unprecedented nation wide search and seizure warrant for the facilities listed in the warrant request. The warrant was issued and sent by secure data link to the execution teams across the country by 0830. Each execution team typically consisted of three agents; one FBI, one DEA and one National Guard sergeant in full combat gear with a loaded AR-16 assault rifle and side-arm. The latter was for effect only. The warrant included forceful entry if necessary. If the manager refused to cooperate, a second local law enforcement team would be called in to arrest the manager and close his facility until the seizure was complete. By 2300 hours the next day over eighteen thousand metric tons of cocaine had been confiscated and was en-route to a classified DEA location in western Iowa for supervised destruction. All storage facility personnel cooperated.

President Brad Stevens postponed the victory celebration he had promised to the mission operators and agents for a month. He changed the event to a celebration of the life and distinguished career of Master Chief Manny Hernandez. Carla Hernandez and her two sons and two daughters were present and the other team members and their spouses were invited for a weekend at Camp David during which the President presented Carla with Manny's Navy Cross and each member of Manny's SEAL Team spoke cheerfully of his Navy life experiences with the Master Chief. The last to speak was Brad Stevens.

In the first year after the bust, the street price of cocaine more than tripled, drug related crime doubled, prisons were overloaded and the southern border was secured. There was certainly a price to pay for driving the drug business out of the country, but it was well worth that price. The national government with full cooperation of the states doubled down on drug pushers as they depleted their remaining supplies. Seventeen more states implemented the death penalty for selling drugs to minors and seven of these increased their penalty for selling any amount of illegal drug to forty years minimum and possession of any amount to twenty years. The public got involved in helping the authorities locate and prosecute drug dealers. Things were finally headed in the right direction.

Ash and I were in hog heaven. We both wanted some career building time in a carrier squadron and while life as a married couple aboard a carrier was setting some sort of military precedent, the "new Navy" was accommodating us. The *Carl Vinson* had a visiting dignitary suite which Captain Joe Garcia assigned to us. It was small. There were two bunks that folded into the wall, one above the other – but we didn't care. The shower was adequate and a nuclear aircraft carrier never runs out of hot water. . .

Author's Notes

Jimmy Buffett, one of my favorite song writer/singers wrote and recorded a song entitled *It's a Semi-True Story*. In the lyrics he wrote: "It's a semi-true story, believe it or not, I made up a few things, and there's some I forgot . . ." What you just read is a semi-true story. Much of the military structure of the book is as correct as I, with the help of my research, could make it. There are, however, many areas where I have taken liberty as an author of fiction to alter reality as necessary to fit my story. The book is heavily focused on life as a Naval Aviator – I drove tanks in the Army - go figure.

Much of the technology used herein was available during the time frame of the book. In particular, the GPS technology and development status at the time, which included Differential GPS, could have led to the systems described in the story, but didn't. I was involved in two Phase One GPS User Equipment development programs and the development of the NAVSTAR GPS Satellite Simulator and DGPS at TI.

Sam McKensie's wife in the story is in many ways my wife in reality – the primary difference being, my wife was a career elementary school teacher, not the Navy's first female Top Gun Instructor. At five foot two she couldn't have reached the rudder pedals in a Hornet, so I made her five four. The blue eyes and killer smile, however, are genuine. We flew together many times but she had no desire to fly herself. In the book we were married on our favorite beach on Jost Van Dyke, British Virgin Islands. In reality we were married at the St. Louis County Courthouse. We have sailed together many of the world's finest sailing grounds. If we knew then what we know now, White Bay Beach on Jost Van Dyke is where we would have tied the knot. All characters are fictitious and any similarity to actual persons is purely coincidental.

I taught many University of Missouri ROTC candidates to fly at the Columbia Regional Airport, where I also taught ground school, non-ROTC students and flew charter flights. I logged many hours towing banners (aerial advertising) in the greater St. Louis area. Some of the incidents in the book regarding these facts are partially true but actually occurred in Missouri, not Kansas and in significantly better weather conditions.

Recently retired Admiral William H. McRaven, fellow Texan, Navy SEAL, distinguished former commander of the United States Special Operations Command and prior commander of the Joint Special Operations Command (JSOC), provided me with clarity and inspiration through his book *SPEC OPS, Case Studies in Special Operations Warfare, Theory and Practice,* 1995 Ballantine Books. I paraphrased his six principles of Special Operations Warfare and added a seventh: Intelligence. Although intelligence is not under the control of spec ops (and thus not one of his six principles), it is one of the most important elements of a successful operation, and often one of the least reliable – so I added it. I thank the Admiral for his knowledge and inspiration.

Acronyms

AAA	Anti Aircraft Artillery
AGL	Above Ground Level
AGM	Air to Ground Missile
AIM	Air to air Infrared seeking Missile
ALS	Automatic Landing System
ASCII	American Standard Code for Information Interchange
AP	Armor Piercing
ATF	Bureau of Alcohol Tobacco & Firearms
ATR	Airline Transport Rating
BN	Bombardier-Navigator
CAG	Comander Air Group
CAPV	Covert Air Penetration Vehicle
CAVU	Clear And Visibility Unlimited
CEO	Chief Executive Officer
CDT	Central Daylight Time
CIA	Central Intelligence Agency
CST	Central Standard Time
CJCS	Chairman, Joint Chiefs of Staff
CMAS	Constellation Management Analyzer System
CRRC	Combat Rubber Raiding Craft – see RIB
DEA	Drug Enforcement Administration
EDT	Eastern Daylight Time
EST	Eastern Standard Time
EWO	Electronic Warfare Officer
DEVGRU	Special Forces DEVelopment GRoUp
DGPS	Differential Global Positioning System
ETA	Estimated Time of Arrival
FAA	Federal Aviation Administration
FBI	Federal Bureau of Investigation
FBO	Fixed Base Operator
FDA	Food and Drug Administration
GMT	Greenwich Mean Time (also ZULU)
GPS	Global Positioning System
HAHO	High Altitude High Opening
HALO	High Altitude Low Opening
HARM	High speed Anti Radiation Missile
HUD	Heads Up Display
IFF	Identification, Friend or Foe
IFR	Instrument Flight Rules
IR	Infra Red
IYK	FAA Symbol for Inyokern airport
JFS	Jameson Flight Service
JSOC	Joint Special Operations Comand
MDT	Mountain Daylight Time

MRE	Meal Ready to Eat
MST	Mountain Standard Time
NAS	Naval Air Station
NATO	North Atlantic Treaty Organization
NDA	Non Disclosure Agreement
NFWS	Naval Fighter Weapons School (Top Gun)
NSA	National Security Agency
NSWDG	Naval Special Warfare Development Group (DEVGRU)
NTK	Need To Know
NVA	North Vietnamese Army
NWC	Naval Weapons Center
OCS	Officer Candidate School
ODA	Operational Detachment – size A (12 man)
OSHA	Occupational Safety & Health Admin
PDA	Personal Digital Assistant
PDT	Pacific Daylight Time
POL	POLar coordinates
POTUS	President of The United States
PR	Public Relations
PST	Pacific Standard Time
RIB	Rubber Inflatable Boat – see CRRC
ROTC	Reserve Officers Training Corps
SAM	Surface to Air Missile
SAMSO	Space and Missile Systems Organization
SATCOM	SATellite COMmunications network
SCUBA	Self Contained Under water Breathing Apparatus
SEAL	Navy SEa Air and Land Special Forces
SECDEF	SECtary of DEFense
SF	Special Forces
SONAR	SOund Navigation And Ranging
TS	Top Secret
USECDEF	Under SECretaty of DEFense
UTM	Universal Transverse Mercator
VFR	Visual Flight Rules
VOQ	Visiting Officers Quarters
XUV	John Deer all wheel drive Utility Vehicle
YPG	Yuma Proving Ground
ZULU	Greenwich Mean Time (also GMT)

Dawn's Early Light

Don Candy

DON CANDY

Dawn's Early Light

This novel is a work of fiction. Names, characters, places and incidents are either the product of the author's imagination or are used fictitiously. Any resemblance to actual events or locales or persons, living or dead is entirely coincidental.

No part of this material may be reproduced in any form without express written permission from the author and/or publisher.

No representation is expressed or implied, with regard to accuracy of the information contained in this work of fiction and no legal responsibility can be accepted for omissions and/or errors.

Copyright © 2018 by Donald W Candy
All Rights Reserved.
ISBN: 978-0-9964409-3-6

PROLOGUE

Three Hundred Miles Southwest of Taiwan
Tuesday, February 20, 1990 0520 hrs, Local Time

Commander Ashleigh McKensie glanced at her mach meter after nosing her F/A-18 Hornet into a shallow dive with her burners lit. She was only 2400 feet above the water, not much room to dive, but she had to run that missile out of fuel before it got to her. Two point zero on the mach meter – zero point two mach faster than her F/A-18C Hornet should do in low level flight but still a little slower than the Soviet missile on her tail.

"Commander that missile is a hundred yards behind you and slowly gaining – your last flares ignited behind it!" yelled Gator Two, McKensie's wingman. Her life had already begun flashing before her – there was nothing more she could do - other than eject and let that missile take her favorite Hornet into the deep blue. She heard Gator Two yell, "EJECT, EJECT, EJECT". She yanked the throttles and the stick back in an effort to slow down enough to eject. This caused the missile to swing wide and then overcorrect She looked over her shoulder and saw the heat seeking missile re-converging on her vertical track and then the exhaust expired – the missile was out of fuel – but it was too late. It was too close. Before she could accelerate the missile coasted into her starboard engine and exploded . . .

Three Hours Earlier

Night takeoff from an aircraft carrier has always been a hair-raising experience for all carrier pilots. On a Nimitz Class Carrier like the *USS Carl Vinson* in a fully loaded attack aircraft like the F/A-18C Hornet piloted tonight by Squadron Leader Ashleigh McKensie, the pucker factor, always present when operating from a carrier at night, was at least twice that of a normal training flight.

Commander McKensie was leading a flight of three Hornets on a face-off mission in response to the sinking of a Filipino fishing boat by a Chinese MiG-19 yesterday; fifteen miles off the coast of the Amphitrite Group of the Paracel Islands in the South China Sea. Almost every country bordering the South China Sea had at one time or another laid claim to these islands but China currently occupied them and had also recently laid claim through the United Nations to pretty much the entire South China Sea. The United States, a friend to most of the local countries involved, defended the international maritime law limiting the sovereign authority of any country to twelve miles off its shore and countered, once again, China's aggressive claims to international waters. Thus, this mission; to remind China that there was no international legal precedent or mechanism for claiming ownership of international waters. This was the third mission of a similar nature executed by *Carl Vinson* Hornets in the last month – the second for Squadron Leader Ashleigh McKensie.

"They need to make these damned helmets lighter," she thought to herself as her head was snapped backward against her headrest when the catapult shuttle was released and then again yanked forward 2.6 seconds later when the shuttle released the aircraft as it was just getting airborne doing a hundred fifty five knots. The flight formed up in a left echelon formation which they would hold loosely relying on exhaust light to maintain position until daybreak. No identifying lights on a combat mission. They had launched four hundred miles northeast of their target and were cruising at two hundred twenty five knots to preserve fuel while the *Carl Vinson* steamed toward them. The plan was to fly between two groups of tiny islands staying thirteen miles or more off shore. This would take them through a twenty eight mile wide channel between the Amphitrite Group and the Crescent Group of the Paracel Islands – something the Chinese didn't like very much. The crescent group lay to the southwest and the Amphitrite Group to the northeast. The entire Crescent Group and one Island in the Amphitrite Group were occupied by the Chinese but the Islands were claimed by four other South China Sea nations as well as China. In 1974 China tried to lay claim to (control of) the entire

DAWN'S EARLY LIGHT

South China Sea – an action soundly rejected by members of the UN including those bordering that body of water.

The moon, just a sliver tonight, hung a little off kilter about twenty degrees above the western horizon. The stars were brilliant at angels two zero – twenty thousand feet above the dark and peaceful sea below.

They expected a visit by two or more MiG-19s from an Air Base on Hainan Dao Island north of the Paracels. So far this latest set of face-off missions had resulted in close-in passes where opposing pilots made faces at each other and the MiGs tried to force the Hornets inside the twelve mile limit. Things might be a little more difficult if the chinks were flying a real airplane – the MiG-19 was no match for the Hornet.

As first light spread over the glassy sea from their rear left, Commander McKensie pressed the mike button on her stick, "Gator Flight this is Gator One, follow me down to angels six and close up to attack formation. Watch your GPS track carefully and let me know if anything looks wrong. We don't want to start a war out here because of a malfunction. Acknowledge. One out."

"Two."

"Three."

As the morning sunlight intensified to their rear left, the deep purple shadows in the eastern sky gave way to dark red, orange and pale yellow striations in the thin stratus cloud layers above them. Ashleigh couldn't avoid momentarily diverting her thoughts to probably the most beautiful sunrise she'd ever witnessed. *"Dawn's Early Light,"* she said aloud to herself as she wondered if the sunrise that inspired Francis Scott Key to pen our National Anthem could have been nearly as spectacular as the one before her eyes at this very moment.

"God made this beautiful planet, our home, among the billions of stars in the universe," she thought, "and humankind is intently focused on fucking it up.

"Father," she prayed aloud, "please let this world of ours last at least until I die of old age with lots of grandchildren. And Father, please keep watching my six while I hunt and kill the bad guys hear on Earth."

While flying their route along the northern edge of the archipelago things seemed peaceful. Ordinarily the Chinese would have intercepted them on the north side of the archipelago. Maybe they weren't going to waste the fuel today. Nothing north on the radar, but they could be hugging the waves below. Ashleigh began her wide turn south keeping the flight firmly glued to the pre-programmed GPS track. Still nothing. Then as she looked up from her Horizontal Situation Display (HSD) while rolling out onto a southeast course between the island groups she noticed what looked like a gunship about two thirds of the way down the channel and a few miles off to the south, probably inside the Chinese claimed territorial waters.

"Gator Flight, this is One, let's keep our eyes peeled. I don't like the looks of that gunship lying in wait down channel. Look's like he's not in what the Chinese consider international waters – this could be an ambush. Look for others boats or MiGs coming out low from one of the islands." Then she saw them . . . "MiGs, two of 'em eleven o'clock low – on the deck. Arm your flares. Let's stay calm; we don't want to be party to an incident here. You guys watch the MiGs – they might separate. I'll watch the boat."

"Flight, this is Three. The MiG to our port (left) is coming up, I'll take him".

"Roger Three, this is Two, I've got the starboard MiG".

"Flight, One. Arm your guns. Do NOT fire unless fired upon and target is clearly in international airspace. I'm going to move us to a parallel course three miles to the northeast." McKensie was doing everything she could to avoid an incident.

The F/A-18 sported a six barrel 20 mm Gatling cannon. Today they were each carrying four active radar guided air-to-air missiles; the Air Intercept Missile (AIM)-120, also known as the Advanced Medium Range Air-to-Air Missile (AMRAAM), two AIM-9 Sidewinder, infrared heat seeking, air-to-air missiles and two Air to Ground Missiles; the (AGM)-65D Maverick, air-to-ground (tank, ship, building, etc.) missiles, with imaging infrared seekers – an excellent choice of weapons for the threats they were now facing.

DAWN'S EARLY LIGHT

"OK guys they're still coming up to us – don't let them get behind you. This looks like a full blown ambush. I'm going to break off and make a run at the gunboat on the deck until I get to their airspace. We need to know what we're dealing with here. Sure glad we brought the Mavericks. Turn your cameras on."

Commander McKensie rolled over and headed straight for the water, rolled another one hundred eighty degrees on the way down and pulled out of the dive just a hundred feet above the surface headed straight for the gunboat. As she approached the twelve mile boundary, about a mile from the boat she realized that it had no guns - then she saw three figures emerging from the forward cabin and taking positions on the bow, each holding a shoulder mounted weapon. One of the figures fired a missile at her!

"OH SHIT!" she yelled to the flight. "HSSMs (Heat Seeking Shoulder-mounted Missiles) – three of 'em. I'm gettin' the hell out of Dodge!"

She had three choices; she could launch a Maverick or two which she had armed on the way down and take out the boat which could cause an international incident because the gunboat was definitely inside the twelve mile limit. Or, she could execute an Immelmann (half vertical loop followed by a half roll. A maneuver used to gain altitude and reverse direction – the reverse of the split S maneuver she used to get to her current position), light her burners on the way up and run like hell. Or she could do both. She had to jettison her missiles if she was going to run. So she fired both her Mavericks at the gunboat, hauled her Hornet vertical and lit her burners as she jettisoned her sidewinders and AMRAAMs. The F/A-18 could reach mach 1.8 from sub-sonic flight in about four and a half seconds in low level flight. She was pretty sure she could outrun any shoulder fired missile the Chinese had but she was praying these guys didn't have the Soviet made 9K38 ILGA missile. She recalled it could do mach two plus a little versus her maximum (unclassified) speed of mach 1.8.

It was in fact, exactly that type of Soviet missile that they had fired at her. As she rolled out of the Immelmann, approaching mach 1.5, Gator Three called, "One, you've got a missile on your tail and it's gaining on you. We've been fired on! Cuffs off?"

Ashleigh replied, "Yeah, you guys take out the assholes in the MiGs – I got the boat already. We're not even gonna leave an oil slick out here. I'm gonna fire counter measures - call the hit for me; quickly please!."

The problem she faced was the second and then more likely the third missile. She was going to fire two thermite flares to fake out the first missile. These flares would fire slightly upward, ignite and then and spiral back toward the flight path of the F-18. Each would produce a tremendous heat signature. The missile processor would then have two converging primary heat signatures to choose from. To be sure the counter measures worked she would throttle her engines back out of after-burner briefly to reduce her heat signature and jink to the left to keep her hot engine off the boresight of the missile. The missile shooters had to wait a second or two between launches to keep the missiles from shooting each other down. So when Gator Three called the explosion of the first missile in the flare's heat signature it would be difficult to predict what the second missile would do. The slight loss of speed caused by retracting the throttles momentarily would put the second missile in fairly close proximity recovering from being called off course by the flares and maneuvers intended for the first missile s well as its resulting explosion. She decided to fire two more flares immediately when Three called the first hit, and then wait for the hit-call on the second one to fire a third set of flares.

Gator Three called, "First missile killed!"

She fired the second set of flares.

A second later Gator Three called, "Second missile killed!"

She immediately fired the third set of flares. Ashleigh couldn't believe it; the second missile went for the flares. Maybe the third... But her elation didn't last long – just a split second. The third set of flares had ignited behind the missile, which now, having only one target, flew directly into her starboard engine exhaust. Simultaneously she heard "EJECT, EJECT, EJECT" from Gator Two. She had already pulled the handle. Just as the rockets in her ejection seat fired the missile blew up inside the engine. The explosion of the engine was horrific, sending her tumbling out of the cockpit head over heels in her ejection seat. She immediately

DAWN'S EARLY LIGHT

felt severe pain in her right thigh and buttock. The ejection seat flight system stabilized her in mid air and her chute was able to open normally.

As McKensie floated toward the ocean after her chute opened she heard on her helmet VHF; "Two this is Three, your MiG is headed for the Commander! You see him?"

"This is Two, copy that Three, I've got a Sidewinder right behind him – hold one. . . Splash one MiG."

"Three, this is Two - I'm gonna follow the commander down and check out what's left of the boat. Go get the other MiG, climb to angels ten and call for help."

"Roger Two, I've got an AMRAAM after him already, hold one. . .Splash that second MiG! I'm going up for help as soon as I send one of my Mavericks to the chink's boat. It's listing but not down yet."

"Three, this is Two I'm also sending one now – that'll leave us with one more each. Four Mavericks will take that boat and who ever's in it to the bottom pretty quick. We'll go bingo in about thirty minutes (bingo meant just enough fuel to return to the carrier with minimum reserve). I'll give you a sitrep on the Commander. Have 'em send a couple of Hornets out here to guard her 'til the chopper can get here."

"Did you get everything on camera?" asked Gator Three.

"Roger that brother, got it all with GPS position and time tags. We'll probably never hear from the chinks about this little party. How'd your video look?"

"Same as you – I got everything and all the tags.

"Three, here's your sitrep; alert and waving. Blood in the water! Tell 'em to hurry!"

As Commander Ashleigh McKensie bobbed in the South China Sea under a beautiful crystal clear sky to the east, she realized she was bleeding badly from the eight inch gash in her right thigh. The shrapnel from her exploding engine had penetrated her ejection seat and she had been fortunate the ejection system had not malfunctioned. Now she had to find and disperse her shark repellant before her successful ejection became all for naught.

Chapter One

Forty Two Thousand Feet Above the Yellow Sea Saturday, May 5, 1990, 0015 Hrs, Local Mission Time

"Okay Commander. We're at Angels Four Two, ten minutes out, the ramp is yours," barked the pilot of the CAPV-727.

Thank God for small favors - in this case a pretty large one. We were at Angels Four Two - 42,000 feet above sea level on a night as dark as they come. A new moon. All of our equipment and all of our training is focused on nighttime operations. The darker the better. My uncle Bo Jameson and I, now made brothers by the yet to be written Navy SEAL creed, and Master Chief Petty Officer Rob Curtis were ten minutes from our IP (mission Initial Position) on our most dangerous mission yet. We had a fifty two nautical mile traverse to our target, the last seven to ten miles of which would be through dense clouds. We were depending on a very complex *Airborne SEAL Delivery System* (ASDS); a computer/GPS controlled High Altitude High Opening (HAHO) parachute system that our SEAL team helped developed during the mid eighties. It allowed multiple teams of up to six Special Operators each to traverse up to sixty nautical miles from an aircraft at an altitude of up to forty five thousand feet to a specific target; each operator landing within two feet of a pre-programmed spot. It did this using a built in Automatic Landing System (ALS). In addition to the ALS and the hi-tech parachute, the system consisted of a pressure suit with oxygen, a chest-pack computer, battery belt, a helmet with an integrated GPS receiver, classified infra-red (IR) night vision, a GPS driven visor system that displayed the relative location of each member of the team as well as the image from the night vision system, an intra-team secure communication system and a separate satellite communication system allowing secure communications to friendly forces anywhere in the world. Upon landing, the parachute and pressure suit could be discarded leaving the rest of the system completely operational with eighty hours of remaining battery life. If everything worked correctly we would arrive at our target a little less than two hours from now.

On a dark night like this we had some real advantages. First of all, stealth. Our delivery systems are essentially silent from the ground, whether the CIA's covert 727 or practically any military transport capable of flying above twenty thousand feet and able to dump special operators safely at night. Our parachute system makes only a small noise when opening and at high altitude can not be heard from the ground. On a cloudy night parachutes are very difficult to see after penetrating the cloud layer even when looking for them. Secondly, most of the world's military and police forces use an ancient light amplification technology which uses ambient light to generate a fuzzy green image in which it is difficult to pick out a stationary human target over ten yards away. These night vision systems are useless in total darkness. Our highly classified infrared systems, on the other hand, work best on cool nights in total darkness. Our night vision technology isn't limited by most atmospheric conditions such as fog, smoke and clouds – even rain. We learned a while back that by staying ahead of our enemies in night vision technology we *own the night*. In any enemy engagement, we do *not* believe in a fair fight.

Bo, Master Chief Rob Curtis, and I were already sealed up in our pressurized high altitude flight suits and communicating with the pilot through the ASDS (Airborne SEAL Delivery System) team network. The pilot had just given us control of the ramp on the Covert Air Penetration Vehicle (CAPV-727), a well equipped, highly modified Boeing 727 Airliner built for the CIA which was capable of passing for a commercial airline passenger or cargo plane in all phases of operation. It could land as a commercial flight at Los Angeles International, or even Beijing China for that matter. As long as the paperwork was done properly no one would be the wiser. For those of you who missed the hay-day of the 727, it was the smaller three engine Boeing with stairs that retracted into the fuselage aft of the cabin.

We were members of a SEAL team called DEVGRU, the Naval Special Warfare DEVelopment GRoUp. From its inception in 1980 until 1987 this team was known as Seal Team Six. When formed there were only two other SEAL teams; one and two. Its founder, Richard Marcinko, wanted to keep the KGB guessing about SEAL Teams three, four and five, which, of course, didn't exist at that time.

We were the DEVGRU Black Angel Team (BAT), attached to the SEAL Black Assault Squadron. Our job was to introduce the latest technology into the development cycle of all Special Forces equipment, making it generations ahead of the current state-of-the-art. And then, to test those systems on combat missions before and during initial deployment to special ops units in all the services. So we were the development / test arm of DEVGRU located at El Centro NAF (Naval Air Facility, sort of like a junior Naval Air Station - NAS). The operational arm and headquarters of DEVGRU were located at Dam Neck Virginia. We joked that our primary job was trying to spend all the gold in Fort Knox. Bo joined the group as a three tour veteran A6 Intruder pilot in Vietnam with lots of post Vietnam HAHO/HALO experience. Rob was the previous temporary commander of SEAL Team Four. He and his team joined up with ours on several early missions using the new hi-tech equipment, after which he decided to move over to DEVGRU. I joined the team as a Lieutenant test pilot / engineer without the foggiest idea of what I was getting into. The BAT consisted of only twelve men, six SEAL operators and six very intelligent civilians.

Bo Jameson was pushing forty, about six two, lean, rugged, sandy hair, intense blue eyes. Didn't smile much. He was an accomplished pilot with over twelve thousand hours. Most of which was as a Navy pilot. He also had more than twenty one hundred HALO/HAHO jumps, possibly a record for all military forces. Bo owned an airport about thirty miles from downtown

DAWN'S EARLY LIGHT

Manhattan, Kansas – *Jameson Flight Service,* (JFS). I actually owned ten percent of JFS. Oh yeah, he's my uncle. More about that later.

Rob and I, each a little over six feet, could pass for brothers although he had nine years on me. We brought the humor and wise cracks to the team and we both kept short cropped brown hair and beards. Rob, A Master Chief Petty Officer with eighteen years experience in the Navy, eleven as a SEAL, came from a small farming community in central California. He had finished his degree in Language Arts at Cal State via Navy sponsored correspondence courses but decided he didn't want to do the officer thing. I bug him about that more often than I should. He's Fluent in English, Spanish, Arabic, Russian and Farsi. Smarter, more capable and much more experienced than most Navy Lieutenants I know.

I'm Sam McKensie; Aeronautical engineer, test pilot, hornet driver, Navy SEAL and the devoted husband to my wife Ashleigh, a former pursuit / instructor pilot flying disguised F-5Es and F/A-18 Hornets at the Navy's Fighter Weapons School known as 'Top Gun' at Miramar NAS, California.

Bo calmly asked, "ready?" over the ASDS network. Bo, Rob, Hal Nicholson and I were sealed in our pressure suits in the 'ready to pressurize' mode which the system automatically enters after passing all ready-to-fly self tests. After receiving a thumbs up from each of us he raised the safety shield and pressed the 'depressurize' button on the aircraft ramp control panel. As the ramp area of the aircraft depressurized our suits automatically pressurized keeping us at a comfortable ten thousand foot ambient pressure – no major ear popping. We were approaching a relatively small target on top of an eight story building so we timed our jumps at fifteen second intervals to allow the person in front to clear the area before the next person arrived.

Rob was first to go so he took his place at the top of the ramp as it lowered; waiting for the red blinking light on his right side to turn solid green. When it turned green, he walked down the 727's stairs and jumped. My turn. When my fifteen second timer flashed on my visor screen I jumped, then fifteen seconds later Bo jumped.

Then Lt. Commander Hal Nicholson, also a DEVGRU SEAL and BAT Team member, sprang into action. He was suited up but not jumping. His job was ramp management, which included the launch of a nine hundred pound cargo pack with all of our equipment in it twenty five seconds after Bo's exit. He pushed the button that collapsed the stairs on the 727 ramp, rolled the cargo pack to the top of the ramp, now actually a chute, attached the static-line ripcord to the ring provided on the left wall of the ramp area and waited for his timer to flash. When it did he pulled a lever on the left wall that opened a slot under the front wheels of the dolly supporting the cargo pack such that the surface of the dolly matched the slope of the cargo chute and the package slid gracefully down the chute into the dark void below.

Nicholson, who was wearing a full-up ASDS suit could immediately see the blue colored dot on his visor screen moving quickly rearward from the aircraft and he noted the three half second flashes of the blue dot that indicated a successful deployment. He announced over the net, "Good drop – Godspeed brothers."

The CAPV-727 maintained course, speed and altitude. After all, to the rest of the world it was a scheduled commercial aircraft on its way from Tokyo To Beijing. . .

As I swung gently beneath my chute my visor displayed a red dot (Rob) about three quarters of a mile ahead of my location (center screen), a green dot (Bo) about three quarters of a mile behind me and a blue dot (the cargo) a mile and a half behind Bo. So we were all out successfully and on our way. There was no moon but the starlight faintly illuminated the cloud deck, far below us at about fifteen thousand feet, providing a surreal, almost unimaginable feeling of being suspended in an alien environment. The feeling became more intense as time elapsed. The clouds looked like a bed of dimly lit fluffy cotton candy into which we would eventually be enveloped. I grew more familiar with this phenomenon with each mission and offset its weird effect by ignoring the fact that soon we would be landing in the bad guy's back yard without their knowledge and instead concentrating on thoughts that I seldom had time to ponder.

I had almost two hours and a lot to think about. First things first; the love of my life, my wife Ashleigh. When we met I was a test pilot at China Lake Navy Weapons Center near Ridgecrest California - in the Mohave Desert - testing High-speed Anti Radiation Missile (HARM) variants, mostly for foreign allied aircraft; British, German, NATO, etc. She was a basic jet instructor at San Diego NAS flying T-38s. For me it was love at first sight – a beautiful five foot four blue eyed blonde jet flight instructor – what else could a guy ask for? Less than a year later we were married on the beach at White Bay, Jost Van Dyke – the most beautiful beach in the British Virgin Islands.

Three months ago we finished our F/A-18 Hornet Squadron Commander tours aboard the USS *Carl Vinson* at the invitation of her Captain, Joe Garcia, the previous commander of the DEVGRU BAT – my Uncle Bo is the current commander. Ash and I had decided that we wanted to start a family. But things just didn't turn out that way while she was employed as a Top Gun pursuit pilot and I was still involved in ASDS production, deployment and training. So we decided to put off the family thing for a while and go be fighter pilots – and it had been fun. We could have done another tour, but while she was recovering from her little incident in the South China Sea we decided to take two weeks of the month's leave we'd accumulated to vacation in Tahiti and then take assignments back in the States. So we rented one of those little huts out over the water and had the first real vacation alone since sailing in the BVI on our honeymoon almost five years ago. We had two days left in paradise when I got a hand delivered message – no phone in our little hut – giving me a week to report to home base at El Centro NAF. At least we got to finish our vacation.

So I get back to my buddies at DEVGRU and we got all briefed up and trained for yet another trip down range to God knows where and she calls me day before yesterday from Miramar saying she just left the base doctor's office and she's pregnant! So at last I'm going to be a father – if I live through this mission *and* make it back to the real world.

DON CANDY

Sometimes, when I have time to think - like now - I wonder what the hell I'm doing here. I left college with a degree in Aeronautical Engineering, a lot of flight time and a high level understanding of complex systems to become a test pilot for the Navy. I didn't even really know what a SEAL was, nor did I know that my uncle *was* one. I went to work for DEVGRU before I knew that it was previously SEAL Team VI, the tip of the special forces spear which became responsible for helping develop and test early high-tech weapon systems like ASDS for the Navy and then pushing them through the development cycle with defense companies like Texas Instruments, Lockheed and Boeing or government oriented organizations like DARPA, JPL and Aerospace Corporation for deployment to all special forces organizations. I became the lead design/development/test person on the ASDS program and helped TI, the lead contractor on the program, get the system into production. ASDS became very successful during its first few missions and caused a lot of visibility at the top of the command chain. I was then told what DEVGRU really was and asked if I would like to become a permanent member at a top secret meeting in front of a group of government dignitaries which included the President. How could I say no? I was just a lowly Lieutenant at that time caught up in circumstance that presented me with an awesome opportunity. All I really wanted to do was fly and have fun. But I jumped into the fire. Since then I've endured extensive water, jungle and arctic training, all part of the grueling Navy SEAL BUD/S training – a six month plus B*asic* U*nderwater* D*emolition* / S*EAL* training program designed to wash out all but the mentally and physically toughest trainees (damned near did me in). Down range I've been shot at a lot and hit a few times, wasted a bunch of bad guys and blown up myriad stuff – I think I'm getting to like this life as a SEAL – and folks, that's scary!

My problem was that 'this life' was beginning to define my being – I'm becoming addicted to the rush and excitement of the mission work and the camaraderie and brotherhood of my team. Part of my problem was my upbringing; growing up in a relatively safe and comfortable environment on a farm in Kansas. Never really seeing or knowing evil. Never understanding that there existed in this world radical elements that hide behind women and children to do their evil deeds or drug lords who routinely slaughtered innocent people as well as their enemies just to make a buck. The satisfaction of bringing these assholes to their own brand of justice grew with each down range assignment, as did my dedication to my brothers and love of my country and family. The average person just can't relate to the things we see and do and the resulting personal pride and honor we feel in doing what we do when we do it well. But then there's the personal sacrifice we endure from the reduced family time and social isolation associated with belonging to one of the world's most clandestine organizations.

*****

In the starlight, the cloud tops far below, I was cold but not uncomfortable. I seemed suspended in a time-warp. It was eerily quiet. Nothing was moving except a shroud puller occasionally making a minor course correction at the command of the ASDS' Automatic Landing System (ALS) which was programmed to land me within an imaginary two foot circle on top of a building somewhere in no mans land.

This would be my fourth ASDS mission through heavy thick clouds. You'd think I'd have enough faith in a system that I helped design to be completely relaxed. Not so. A fifteen second delay between jumps put us a little over three quarters of a mile apart so I couldn't see Rob's IR locator on his helmet in the thick cloud. All I could see was the little colored locator dots from the GPS system. If my system failed I might have no way of knowing for sure which part failed and whether or not I was still heading for the target. On this mission if I missed the target it literally meant a sure and very unpleasant death. This always caused a mild state of uneasiness until I broke through the clouds and once again acquired visual reference to the jumper in front of me – but tonight the uneasiness was a little more that mild. I think I know a little too much about how complex this system really is, I know where the hell we're headed and I'm about to become a father. Rob doesn't have the detailed technical understanding of ASDS that I do –

that's why I always honor his standing request to go first.

Then just before I broke out of the clouds, the little green x, representing the two foot landing circle pre-programmed into the ASDS, came into view at the top of my visor. I could see the target, or at least its location, on my facemask display. The tension evaporated, replaced with a feeling of mild elation, only to be gradually replaced by the apprehension which had subconsciously nagged me from the minute I was first briefed on the location of this mission – three days ago.

At the target everything went well. Rob was clear when I landed and I was clear when Bo touched down. I Watched the cargo pack, clearly visible with my IR night vision, s-turn and then turn into the light wind for a soft landing. It never ceased to amaze me even though I designed and tested that part of the system and had watched it work many times. The large nine hundred pound cushioned canvas equipment canister made just a slight thump as it settled on the roof of the Ministry of National Defense of The People's Republic of (North) Korea (PRK) in the center of Pyongsong, twenty two miles north of Pyongyang, North Korea's capital city - deep in Indian Territory. Enemy territory - completely surrounded by bad guys. . .

Made in the USA
Columbia, SC
14 April 2019